HARSH
GODS

ALSO AVAILABLE FROM MICHELLE BELANGER
AND TITAN BOOKS

Conspiracy of Angels
The Resurrection Game (August 2017)

HARSH GODS

A NOVEL OF THE SHADOWSIDE

MICHELLE BELANGER

TITAN BOOKS

HARSH GODS
Print edition ISBN: 9781783299546
E-book edition ISBN: 9781783299553

Published by Titan Books
A division of Titan Publishing Group Ltd
144 Southwark Street, London SE1 0UP

First edition: August 2016

2 4 6 8 10 9 7 5 3 1

A CIP catalogue record for this title is available
from the British Library.

Printed and bound in the USA.

Did you enjoy this book? We love to hear from our readers.
Please email us at readerfeedback@titanemail.com
or write to us at Reader Feedback at the above address.

To receive advance information, news, competitions, and exclusive
offers online, please sign up for the Titan newsletter on our Web site:
www.titanbooks.com

In memory of Michael Wiggins (1965–2016).

You asked to see an early draft of this story,
but I thought you had more time.
We all did. Journey well, old friend.

1

Three more steps for the perfect kill shot. I checked the ammo on the crossbow to be sure I had the right poison applied to the tip. This had to be quick and neat. I was tired of getting clobbered by the city guard.

The chair squeaked as I hunched closer to the computer screen. A muscle cramped in my neck. I ignored it, shifting my wings. Two hours I'd been at this, and I still didn't have the damned achievement. Fighting the tension in my fingers, I advanced my character by slow inches.

Flawless victory would be worth the pain.

Across from my character's position, the target paced a restless circuit on a high balcony at the back of his manor house. The corrupt nobleman paused every six seconds to lean on the railing and peer at a hideously ornate fountain that squatted in the middle of his garden. Fat cherubs erupted like boils from the fountain's central spire, water cascading around their stunted wings. If I angled the shot just right, I'd be able to pass the crossbow bolt through a small space between a curtain of water and one ugly cherub's head.

That had to be the way to get this achievement—I couldn't see any other clear shots that allowed my character to remain hidden, and I'd skulked through every corner of this damned map.

I brought up the targeting reticle, holding down the mouse button till the icon went from gray to red. The nobleman took out a snuff box, dosing both nostrils, then rested a hand on the railing, just like he had every other time I'd fucked up this stage of the assignment. I had approximately three seconds before he started moving again. I took a breath, feeling a tremor in my pointer finger.

Someone pounded on the door to my apartment.

My mouse hand jerked. The crossbow bolt smashed into the head of the cherub, alerting the manor guards. Uniformed non-player characters dashed in from every corner, quickly swarming me. My computer screen filled with splashes of vivid red.

"Fuck me running," I snarled. Cursing the nobleman, the game designers, and whoever thought it was a good idea to come knocking at nearly eleven o'clock at night, I slammed my fist on the desk.

I almost had that shot!

The four terracotta demon jars sitting at the base of the computer tower jumped with the impact. Anakesiel's jar toppled right over, rolling dangerously close to the edge. The game forgotten, I snatched up the jar before it crashed to the floor. Breaking it shouldn't release the spirit, but I didn't want to chance it.

The person at the door knocked again, louder this time. Briefly, I debated relocating to the apartment's single bedroom, grabbing a paperback, and ignoring them till they got bored and went away. There weren't a whole lot of people I wanted to see who might come to my door at this hour of night, not even on a Friday.

The few who leapt to mind didn't actually qualify as people.

Whoever it was, they were stubborn. The knocking settled into a nerve-shattering pattern of dogged persistence.

"Hang on!" I said loudly. My voice came out all gravel and phlegm. The only talking I'd been doing over the past couple of weeks involved swearing at the computer and ringing up restaurants for deliveries.

Closing out of the computer game, I scooped up the rest of the demon jars from where they rested on my notes. Yanking open the bottom drawer of the desk, I stowed the four spirit-prisons inside. I slammed the drawer, feeling the neat regiment of wards lock into place.

My computer desk was hardly the most secure location for the stolen artifacts, but I'd warded it as best I could until I could come up with a more permanent solution. The demon jars—and the spirits trapped inside them—posed an awkward responsibility. I didn't like the idea of babysitting them indefinitely, but I couldn't trust them to anyone else.

Setting them free wasn't really an option, not with what I knew. Despite the names of the vessels, the spirits imprisoned in them weren't demons, but angels. That didn't mean they were nice guys though. They were family—and my family was fucking terrifying.

Scowling, I scrubbed at my face like I could wipe away all my concerns with that simple gesture. As if. A week's worth of stubble rasped beneath my palm. Normally clean-shaven, somewhere between the insomnia and the nightmares that galloped madly along after it, I'd stopped giving a damn. One sick day had turned into seven, and now I was burning vacation days fast.

The apartment looked like hell, too.

My unwanted visitor continued to knock.

"This had better be good," I grumbled. Murmuring the phrase that obscured all the important items on the desk, I pushed out of the computer chair and headed for the door.

There were wards there, too, and they glimmered faintly in the wan light of the living room lamp. They kept the door from being a point of open access over on the Shadowside. Without them, anything wandering that non-physical echo of the flesh-and-blood world could just saunter into my apartment however it pleased.

I'd used the trick often enough myself.

The floor creaked as I approached the door—at six foot three, I wasn't exactly light on my feet. The knocking slowed, and I paused with my hand above the doorknob. I had a lot of enemies in the world—certainly more enemies than friends. The door to my apartment had the standard fish-eye peephole, but I'd learned not to trust what could be seen.

So I closed my eyes.

Unclenching the imaginary fist I kept tightly wrapped, I let my psychic senses spill forth. Like a belling hound barely broken to the leash, my awareness surged into the hall, spreading to the apartment across the way, then rushing eagerly down the stairwell to the floor beneath. Dizzying and wild, the perceptions threatened to expand beyond my ability to contain them. I'd lost my finesse, and struggled to rein it all in.

"Focus," I breathed, and I did.

Disjointed impressions drifted in from beyond the door, most of them the dregs left in the wake of mortal lives—worn scraps of emotions, echoes of intent, the sense of ceaseless motion from one space to the next. The instant I recognized anything from a neighbor, I cast that information aside. What remained was a tenuous perception—nothing so clear as a picture. One person.

Slight in build. Human. Nervous. Rushed.

If not for the door, I could have reached out and touched her.

Female. That was another piece.

Young—not a child, though. A young adult. There was more information fluttering at the edges, and I probably could have picked it out, had I pushed, but I had more than enough.

With an effort that felt like sucking a hurricane into a knapsack, I reined my senses back in, shoving them to their regimented corner of my mind. My eyes snapped open, and my fingers still hovered above the handle to the door. A scant few seconds had ticked away.

Satisfied that my visitor offered no threat, I flipped the deadbolt and pulled open the door. The young woman outside blinked up at me with unusually dark eyes, peering through glasses with hipster-black frames. Her puffy winter coat was snow-bunny pink with faux fur trim that hoped some day to meet a real rabbit. Long, glossy black hair spilled out from under a knitted cap with a little pompom on the top. Despite the heavy coat and ridiculous hat, her arms were wrapped tightly across her midsection, as if she was struggling not to shiver.

When she saw me looming in the door, her cinnamon-colored skin went several shades lighter. The hair and whiskers probably made me look like a crazy man, but I hadn't expected that kind of reaction.

I must have looked worse than I felt.

"You're Professor Zachary Westland?" she asked. She didn't sound too sure about it. Leaning a shoulder against the doorframe, I slouched a little in the hope of putting her at ease. I was nearly a foot taller than her, and that height bothered some people.

An anxious little voice in the back of my head whispered that she'd noticed something else about me—my hidden nature. I told the little voice to shut the hell up.

"Just Zack," I answered. "I haven't taught at Case for nearly two years."

She chewed her lower lip and fussed with her car keys. She couldn't have been much more than twenty. Not old enough to be one of my graduate students, not young enough to be selling Girl Scout cookies—which was a shame. Some thin mints would have seriously improved my mood.

"What can I do for you?" I asked to break the silence. My voice still carried a jagged edge. I cleared my throat, trying to remember how to talk like a normal person. My words could channel a lot of power—literal magic—

and this girl didn't deserve to get hammered just because I'd been cooped up too long.

"Father Frank sent me," she replied, flashing a nervous smile.

She said it like I should know the name. I didn't. Then again, it might have been one of the things that had been taken from me. I didn't want to explain my mutilated memory, and I *really* didn't want to hear any well-intentioned platitudes from a complete stranger. Those would just drive me to slam the door in her face. So I played it off.

"What did Father Frank want, exactly?" I asked.

She brightened a little, saying, "He needs your help with a case. He told me to tell you that he understands you don't want to be bothered right now, but it's really important. And she lives close—I can take you there tonight." She held up the car keys like they were some kind of talisman.

I wracked my broken brain for any recollection about Father Frank, and whatever sort of "case" he typically managed—particularly at eleven o'clock on a Friday night. The best I dredged up was a brief flash of an older man, nearly as tall as me, and built like a welterweight boxer. It might have been a memory—or I might have pulled it out of the girl's head. That usually took physical contact, but catching a stray thought or two wasn't beyond the realm of possibility.

Then a larger concern began to gnaw at me. It was probably just residual paranoia from the nightmares, but it couldn't be ignored.

"If it's that important," I asked suspiciously, "why

didn't he come here to speak with me himself?"

Something in my look made her back up a step. Anxiety that verged upon fear wafted from her like a sour perfume. I was pretty sure she was responding to my physical appearance—lazy bachelor with a side of Unabomber—but out of reflex I pulled my wings tight against my back. She *probably* couldn't see them.

My wings weren't part of the physical world, and mortals gifted with enough sight to peer through to the Shadowside were few and far between. Nevertheless, I felt oddly naked in front of her, despite my jeans and rumpled T-shirt. Belatedly, I tried focusing on a cowl to tuck my inhuman nature more or less out of sight. I was terrible at the things, though, and half the time I forgot to keep one up.

No wonder so many of my nightmares revolved around having my nature exposed in front of a mob of angry mortals. It was my personal version of naked-in-front-of-the-class.

So I pictured the veil of energy settling over me, wings and all, and tried to radiate *just a normal guy*. It didn't seem to help, though, and my late-night visitor still couldn't meet my eyes.

"When you wouldn't respond to his texts or his calls, he was going to head up here," she mumbled in a subdued voice. "But then Halley started seizing again. So he sent me."

That broke my concentration, and the cowl shivered to pieces. Pompom Hat Girl didn't seem to notice. Whatever she might be, she wasn't psychic.

"Hold on," I said. "Seizing? What kind of case are we talking about?"

A look of confusion flickered across her dark features. "An exorcism, of course."

I stammered as thoughts whirled too fast for my mouth to keep up. A priest wanted *my* help with an exorcism. *Seriously?* That was a smothering level of irony, considering my many winged relations. Was this a regular thing or was the universe having extra fun with me?

How much did my inhuman nature tie into the request? He couldn't possibly know about me—could he?

I mentally tallied half a dozen scenarios, few of which I found desirable. Eventually, I managed to reply.

"Why don't you come inside and tell me the whole story?" I offered, hoping it didn't make me look like a creeper. "And start from the beginning."

"No." She shook her head, and the little pompom at the top of her hat bobbled. "I'm supposed to take you directly to the Davis house, or just head back there myself."

I started to object. She squared her stance and dragged her eyes to meet mine with a hard-won look of defiance. Her anxiety still quavered beneath the surface— something about me had really rattled her—but she held it back with a steely sense of purpose. Her throat hitched with a convulsive swallow, but when she spoke again, a little of that steel could be heard in her voice.

"I don't really know you," she said. "I just know that Father Frank trusts you. He needs your help." At those last four words, I felt an all-too-familiar compulsion tug in my chest.

Fuck.

Had I taken some vow in the distant past, to just

drop everything when someone asked for help? If so, I'd forgotten about it—along with nearly everything else—but clearly, forgetting didn't let me wiggle around the consequences.

I sighed. "Let me grab my leather."

2

I snagged my biker jacket from where it had fallen behind the couch, then went in search of my cellphone. I'd thrown that somewhere and had done my best to forget about it. Funny thing, me and memory. There was so much I fought to remember, and just as much I struggled to forget.

While I dug around for the phone, the girl lingered awkwardly in the doorway. She hugged herself in her puffy pink coat, though I couldn't imagine how she was still cold. The super kept the apartment building somewhere next to boiling in the winter—most of the residents were retirees, except for me.

Her obsidian-chip eyes flickered behind her glasses, taking in the whole of my apartment—the packed bookshelves that lined the living room, the framed pages of illuminated manuscripts hung on the walls, the milk-carton-sized TARDIS perched next to the computer tower not far from an old-school Han Solo posed with his blaster.

Han always *shoots first.*

The books and art and toys were lovingly maintained, everything orderly and in its place—but then there were the stacks of empty take-out cartons scattered across the coffee table. A pile of dirty laundry had made it as far as the easy chair and had sprawled, forgotten, ever since. Half-empty coffee mugs stood like stranded soldiers atop the counters, the side tables, and the mantle over the gas fireplace.

"I know it's a mess," I muttered.

"I didn't say that," she responded guiltily, looking away from the sink full of dirty dishes.

"Word of advice?" I offered as I finally spied the smartphone half under a pile of notes on the *Book of Enoch*. I checked the charge—it was in the red—and pocketed it anyway. Striding over to my visitor, I said, "Don't play poker."

She pouted, then used her middle finger to shove her glasses up her thin, straight nose. On anyone else, it would have been a none-too-veiled response to my smartass comment. With her, it seemed both habitual and oblivious.

While she hovered at the threshold, I buckled the biker jacket like I was girding for war. A vintage piece from the post-punk '80s, it had been through a lot with me, especially one cold November night on the dark waters of Lake Erie.

My friend Lil paid a professional leather cleaner a small fortune to restore it—a "kindness" she gleefully dangled over my head whenever she could. I'd had my own guy go over it back in January to make a few strategic changes, including a whole new lining with a custom inner holster for my new favorite gun. The thick, black leather with its many zippers and buckles settled across my shoulders with a reassuring weight. I felt comfortable in the hardy second skin. The subtle lines of the SIG against my ribs certainly didn't hurt.

"All right," I intoned. "Take me to your leader."

She stared blankly at me. I was kind of used to that. One thing I'd retained was a near-encyclopedic knowledge of pop culture. I found the references amusing, but had long ago stopped expecting anyone else to follow along.

"Never mind," I said. "Let's go."

Nodding, the girl turned and headed down the stairs. Pushing through the vestibule door, she fought with the outer one, straining against the wind. It was practically like an airlock, and an icy blast from off the lake swept into the glassed-in space. March had come in like a lion, and was still mauling the city with chilly tooth and claw.

Once outside, she winced as the relentless fingers of the wind plucked at the edges of her coat. Quickly, she zipped it all the way to the top before tugging her hat down to cover her ears.

My body registered the temperature in a distant manner. She stared for a moment, then led me to her car—an anonymous white compact. I climbed in and ended up sitting with my knees up my nose. As she put the keys in the ignition, she stole a sidelong glance in my direction. She pursed her lips, but didn't say anything.

A colorful, laminated rectangle dangled from her rearview mirror, decorated with a little brown tassel. I sent it spinning as I struggled to adjust the seat. Then I caught it between my first two fingers, stilling its wild orbit and muttering an apology.

Looking closer, I expected to see a picture of Saint Christopher. Instead, the image of a woman in a head-scarf gleamed in bright, almost cartoon-like colors. She rode a white horse through what looked like a Mughal horde, casually lopping off an opponent's head with her gleaming scimitar.

"That's Mai Bhag Kaur," Pompom Hat Girl explained. "She's a warrior-saint."

"I've heard of her," I replied. "She's Sikh, right?"

My reluctant chauffeur gave me another sideways stare.

"Yes. Not many people know that."

I snorted. "Don't let the leather jacket fool you. I'm not some knuckle-dragger. I taught at Case, remember?"

She did that nervous thing with her glasses, then turned her full attention to her crowded ring of keys. Singling one out, she inserted it into the ignition. I tapped the icon of Mai Bhag Kaur, sending it spinning again.

"I didn't think Sikhs believed in anything like Christian possession," I said casually. "How'd you end up doing exorcisms with Father Frank?"

"I don't do exorcisms," she said curtly. "He teaches me judo and mixed martial arts. In exchange, I give him some of my time. Tonight, that involves driving."

It was my turn to stare. "Trying to live up to your warrior-saint?" I asked.

She grabbed the icon, stilling it. Her throat worked as she swallowed.

"I don't like being afraid."

So I shut the hell up. She put the car in gear and headed toward Mayfield Road. Instead of making small talk, I scoured my cellphone for any calls or texts I might have missed, especially from this mysterious Father Frank who taught judo to Sikh girls and did exorcisms on weekends.

My sibling Remy had sent about a dozen texts over the past two weeks, all of which I'd chosen to ignore. Most of them only said, "*Call me*," anyway. There were a couple of calls from work—likewise ignored.

Nothing about an exorcism.

"When did you say this guy was calling me?" I asked. If I hadn't gotten such a wholly guileless vibe from her, I would have been plotting ways to get out of the vehicle—there were a lot of reasons to doubt her story. Given the life I led, it was a good policy to assume everyone was out to get me. Most of the time, they were.

"Last night. Most of today," she answered. "Maybe fifteen minutes before I showed up. It kept going straight to voicemail, but he said sometimes, you get real busy and turn it off."

I powered down the smartphone then brought everything online again—which was about the extent of my knowledge of how to screw with the thing. Give me a search engine and I could perform miracles—hand me the hardware that ran the search engine, and I felt like a Neanderthal working a Wii.

The screen reloaded at what felt like a geologic pace. I checked for texts again.

"Nope," I said. "Nothing."

As I put the phone away, the scar on that hand gave a twinge. I massaged it automatically. It had been giving me trouble for a couple of months now, always itchy on the wrong side of my skin.

"I made the last three calls myself," the girl said. "I heard your voice on the message. You have a very distinctive voice."

"I don't know what you're calling, but it can't be my cellphone."

"It's your voice," she insisted, pulling up to a light.

"I'm telling you, I've had this phone since November, and nothing about exorcisms has come through—"

I cut myself off, twitching with the force of revelation. Pompom Hat Girl caught the motion from the corner of her eye, turning her attention from the road long enough to spear me with a quizzical glance. Churning anxiety spiked through my gut, and I didn't know how much of it made it to my face.

Someone behind us honked as she idled too long, and the car rabbited forward as she gave it too much gas. I barely noticed—my thoughts spun back to a night of pitiless skies, cold, seething waters, and the nightmare shrill of cacodaimons rising from Erie's muddy depths.

I'd lost so much on that lake.

"Do you have a work phone?" she asked tentatively. I made a monosyllabic sound that wasn't really a response. Our little compact glided past the high stone wall of Lake View Cemetery, and I found myself drowning in memories.

I'd had a cellphone before that awful night—used it to call the apartment with panicked messages for Lailah. Beautiful Lailah. Dead even in my dreams.

22

I shoved the thoughts away before they could gut me. I'd spent weeks now fighting not to think of her, video games filling the hole where my memories should be, because whiskey didn't do shit.

The phone was probably somewhere at the bottom of Lake Erie, buried in the silt and the dark along with the Eye of Nefer-Ka. All I had left of that horror was my Swiss-cheese brain and the scar on my hand.

Sensitive on some level to what I was feeling, my driver sat rigidly behind her steering wheel, eyes resolutely fixed on the road. It made me wonder if some of my emotions were spilling out. The laminated image of her warrior-saint rocked lazily with the motion of the tiny car as we descended into Little Italy.

"When you get a chance, I need that number," I said.

Maybe there were more voicemails. Maybe one of them was Lailah, and I could finally hear her voice again outside of nightmares. But if my old cellphone lay at the bottom of the lake, how was it even taking calls? It shouldn't even be in service—I hadn't paid any bills on it since November.

It made no sense.

"You want the number to your own cellphone?"

"Humor me."

She frowned, and again, I caught the sour whiff of anxiety, verging upon fear.

"Is my head on backwards or something?" I asked, damping down irritation. "You keep staring at me like I belong in a sideshow. I know I haven't cut my hair or shaved in a while, but seriously—I can't look *that* bad."

Pompom Hat Girl hunched her shoulders and focused

on the road. There wasn't much cause for that level of concentration—traffic was light, and it was too cold out for snow. Old drifts piled up against the sides of the cars parked along the curb, but the street itself was clear.

"You look like someone I met a long time ago."

"Pretty sure I've never seen you before," I responded.

She stopped at a crosswalk to let a trio of tattered pedestrians pass. Their clothes were insufficient for the weather, and they hunched miserably against the wind.

"If you were him, I would never have let you into my car," she said. Some of the night's chill had crept into her voice. The stumbling group of homeless finished their slow procession across the road, and she nearly spun the wheels when she accelerated.

Curiosity welled up in me—and I did my best to beat it to death with a mental stick. If I focused too hard on her while she was immersed in those emotions, there was a decent chance I'd pick up on some of what she was feeling. It didn't take a psychic to guess it involved some kind of trauma.

I had enough of my own shit to deal with.

Clenching the imaginary fist in my mind while the nails of my left hand bit into my tingling scar, I got so focused on shielding myself from the echoes of her trauma that I failed to notice when she stopped the car in front of a row of houses along East 124th.

"Someone took my parking spot," she said, and she pouted.

Her annoyance broke the cycle. I relaxed my hold on the shields a bit. Closing my mind off like that might keep me sane, but it also made me feel claustrophobic and—if I was being honest—a little scatterbrained. I hadn't worked out a good middle ground.

"It's that house," she said, pointing to an old Craftsman painted a fading shade of slate. "You get out. I'll go park."

"It's late, and it's dark," I observed. "Sure you don't want me to walk you back from wherever you end up parking this thing?"

"I can take care of myself."

The whetted edge to her words reminded me momentarily of Lil, my dead girlfriend's gray-eyed sister. She regarded me with Lil's same intractable glare, so I shut my mouth and got out of the car. She started pulling away as soon as I closed the door—another echo of Lil.

At least she wasn't as terrifying a driver.

I stood for a moment on the icy stretch of street in front of the tired-looking house. A very practical—and legitimately suspicious—portion of my brain kept warning me that this could be a trap, but that little voice was sounding increasingly irrational. I didn't think the girl could lie convincingly if she wanted to, and the house she indicated seemed excruciatingly normal.

An electric-blue tricycle with shiny Mylar ribbons on the handlebars sat half-buried in a drift of snow near the front steps. Lights in pastel Easter colors were strung across the porch while the front door sported a wreath of colorful straw and plastic eggs. Little clings of rabbits, eggs, and crosses were visible in the windows stretching all the way along the porch. Even the welcome mat had a seasonal theme—though if the weather kept up, Peter Cottontail was going to freeze his ass off when he came to deliver his chocolate eggs.

"Yep," I told myself, just before pressing the doorbell. "Only thing you have to worry about here is being kitsched to death."

3

The doorbell didn't seem to work, so I tried knocking. Immediately, I heard footsteps from the other side of the door, then a woman's voice, muffled.

"Sanjeet—I told you," she called cheerfully. "You don't have to knock any more." The door swung open, as she continued, "You've been over enough you can just walk—"

The woman stopped short once she caught sight of me. Her mouth remained slightly agape. Comfortably curvy, she looked to be on the near side of forty. Her dark-blonde hair had even darker roots, and her hazel eyes were shadowed by bruised circles of fatigue.

"You're not Sanjeet," she said.

"Nope," I responded.

"Well, it's late and we don't want any." She started closing the door in my face.

"Late? You people sent for me," I responded. "I'm here to see Father Frank."

She caught the door at the last instant, keeping it

open a crack, peering through the narrow slice of space.

"Where's Sanjeet?" she asked.

I hooked a thumb in the direction of the street. "Pompom Hat Girl is out parking her car." Yep. I said that with my out-loud voice. Hermit life didn't help much with my social filters.

The woman silently mouthed the nickname, brows creasing in a frown. She was saved from offering comment when a strident boy's falsetto erupted from deep within the home.

"Mooooom!"

The sound Dopplered as the child pelted from one unseen point to the next. I could just make out the rapid slap of tiny bare feet across what sounded like hardwood floors. The mother turned to respond, still keeping her body wedged against the opening of the door.

Snow crunched on the steps behind me and Pompom Hat Girl—Sanjeet—bounced onto the porch.

"Hi, Mrs. Davis," she chirped. "This is the guy."

Mrs. Davis didn't budge from the nearly closed door. She didn't outright say that she thought I was a crazed serial killer, but her look was eloquent enough. I rubbed my scruffy chin, not quite apologetic.

"I wasn't exactly expecting company," I said.

From her wintry expression, it was a good thing I didn't mind the chill. Eyes on Sanjeet, Mrs. Davis stepped away from the door, pulling it open as she went.

A skinny little boy with a mocha complexion and brown eyes full of mischief rushed up behind her. He body-slammed her leg, throwing his arms around her thigh in something close to a flying tackle. She rocked with the impact like a ship weathering a storm.

"Tyson!" she cried, reaching down to tousle his hair. "One of these days you're going to knock me right over. Didn't I tell you to get ready for bed?"

"I'll take him, Mrs. Davis," Sanjeet said, skirting past me and into the house. She grabbed for the little boy but he clung like a burr, his huge brown eyes fixed upon me. I stared back, wiggling my fingers in what I hoped was a non-threatening gesture. Tyson buried his face in his mother's thigh, giggling.

At least the kid liked me.

Mrs. Davis helped pluck his fingers from her slacks, muttering gratefully. Once they'd pried him loose, Sanjeet scooped the boy up, holding him in the air and rubbing her nose in his belly till he squealed with delight. He had her hat off in an instant, and streamers of her long black hair floated after it like she was attached to a Van de Graaff generator. He peered over her shoulder at me, then shoved the hat against his mouth, stifling his grin.

Mrs. Davis watched the boy, a weary smile tugging at her lips. Then she turned back to me.

"Father Frank is in the room with Halley," she said, stepping further into the living room. "He hasn't left her side since her last… episode." Her voice hitched on the final word.

"OK," I said, still having no idea what to expect. "Which way?"

She pointed to a hallway leading away from the main room, then hovered near the couch, her eyes still wary. I closed the door behind me, tapping snow from my boots onto the mat.

The sound echoed through the quiet home. Moving past the entryway, I navigated around a spill of toys almost certainly left behind by little Tyson. Framed inspirational sayings decorated the living room walls, along with one tongue-in-cheek prayer that stated, "Bless this mess." Despite the humorous plaque, the place was tidy enough, with simple furnishings that looked well-used but hardly shabby.

"I'm Tammy, by the way," Mrs. Davis blurted suddenly, extending a hand.

I shoved both of mine immediately into my pockets. I'd forgotten to grab my gloves, and skin-to-skin contact often made it impossible to block out emotional impressions. Once in a while, that was useful, but mostly it was a pain in the ass.

I nodded a brusque greeting. "Call me Zack."

Her hand lingered in the air between us for a few moments, her expression flickering through uncertainty, disapproval, and finally, resignation. With a little sigh, she dropped it back to her side.

"Father Frank says you work at Case Western?" she ventured.

"Used to," I replied. "On sabbatical." A family photo angled on the mantel above the fireplace. A balding man with deeply hued skin and piercing eyes sat beside a glowing Tammy, who dandled an infant Tyson on her lap. A thin girl with a tangle of dark hair slouched beside them, maybe twelve or thirteen. The girl's face was almost impossible to see. Shoulders hunched, she hung her head, looking away from the camera. Everyone else—Tyson included—wore happy family grins.

"Is that Holly?" I asked.

"Halley," the mother corrected. "Like the comet, not the actress. My husband works for NASA. He likes astronomy names."

"He around?"

She shook her head. "His father died a few weeks ago. There's a bunch of property on the East Coast. He's handling that while I watch the kids." She reached for my sleeve. "You can help her, right?"

I shrugged off her clinging touch.

"I'll go talk with the padre and see what's up. No guarantees. I've got no idea what I'm dealing with."

"Of course," Tammy stammered. Tyson's tintinnabulating laughter echoed suddenly from upstairs, followed by an answering giggle from Sanjeet. Mrs. Davis turned in the direction of the sound.

I seized the opening to make my escape down the hallway. Soft light spilled from a partly open door at the end. The air got heavier the closer I got to that door. Not oppressive, exactly. Just... *thick*. Curiosity got the better of me, and I relaxed my shields a little, peering across to the Shadowside. A filmy echo of the home shimmered there, agitated by pulses of power that moved like ripples along the surface of a lake. I wasn't certain what to make of the disturbance, but it was clear the epicenter lay beyond that doorway.

I nudged it open with my elbow. A single lamp burned in the room beyond, the glow of its bulb soft and muted. The lamp—Tinker Bell green with glittery plastic fairies dangling from its shade—rested on a nightstand amid a small regiment of prescription bottles.

Nearby, a frail girl lay on a steel-framed hospital bed that looked three sizes too big for her. Dark hair spilled over her pillows, framing a narrow oval of a face. Her thick lashes fluttered restlessly against waxen cheeks, and her hands plucked at the edges of her blanket, one of them clutching the pink and green beads of a garishly colored rosary.

The bed angled toward a big picture window, curtained now to keep out the late winter chill. Beside the window sat an old wooden rocker. Perched on this was a solid man wearing the black clothes and white collar of a Catholic priest. He had proud, patrician features surmounted by a shock of gunmetal gray hair. His precise age was uncertain—he could have been anywhere between fifty-five and seventy. Although his skin was lined and weathered, his eyes remained bright and startlingly intense.

I recognized him immediately from the flash I'd had earlier—though he'd been a bit younger in the image in my head. The instant he saw me, he stood with a smooth grace that reminded me more of a panther than a priest. He seemed to know at least some of my quirks, because he didn't bother extending his hand in greeting. Instead, he cracked a smile that chased decades from his features.

"Zachary," he said. He had a big voice, but he did his best to soften it, out of deference to the slumbering girl.

I nodded. "Father Frank."

His poker face was better than Sanjeet's, but I still caught uncertainty flickering around the edges.

"It's been a while," he said carefully.

Nodding again, I tried to work out how to respond.

It would have helped if I'd had some idea how I knew him—and how well he knew me. There were lots of things I preferred not to share about my life, if I didn't have to. All of it, really.

I teased my sight open a little more, trying to get a solid sense of the man. To all appearances, he was mortal. Theoretically, he could have been hiding himself behind his own variation of a cowl, but usually there were tip-offs for that. Cowled like that, a person came across as *too* normal, or gave off no impressions whatsoever. I felt a strong compulsion to like him, but figured that had more to do with his easy charisma. The man practically radiated affable competence.

"Thanks for coming out on short notice, Zack," he said, breaking the awkward silence. "The way you were ignoring my calls, I figured you had to be in the middle of something. I know the demands on your time."

I shrugged. The subtle pressure in the room teased my neck hairs to attention. Glancing in Halley's direction, I tried to tell if the agitation was coming from her, or if it belonged to something that was *attracted* to her. The presence was vague enough that it could have been either.

The girl stirred, as if sensing my attention, muttering fitfully in her sleep.

"Exorcism, hunh?" I ventured, still not certain how much credence to put into that, despite the Roman collar.

For a long moment, Father Frank searched my face. I could feel the weight of his scrutiny as surely as I felt the odd pressure bearing down upon the room. His eyes were the color of old copper pennies—a brown so burnished and rich it lost you in its depths. I met his gaze without blinking. He parted his thin slash of a mouth to say something, but then seemed to change his mind. He shook his head once—a swift twitch of his narrow jaw—and gave a pensive noise.

"I'll give you the high points," he said.

I nodded.

He looked as if he expected me to say more. When I didn't, he continued with the terse, efficient tone of a soldier reporting to a commanding officer.

"Her grandfather, Joe Davis, passed a few weeks ago. After the funeral, she started talking about this voice. Tammy thought it might be Joe reaching out to Halley from beyond the grave. The girl had been his favorite of the grandchildren."

I glanced to the pill bottles clustered on the nightstand, trying to read the labels.

"Halley hear voices a lot?"

"With her talents? Yes," Father Frank responded. He held his shoulders a little stiffly. "She has a lot of problems, Zack—severe autism, seizure disorders—but I know legitimate abilities when I see them. I've been around you long enough."

My eyes snapped to his.

"Yeah?" I asked.

His brow knitted and I got the feeling he was trying to read me right back. Again, the weight of his attention plucked at me.

"You all right, Zack?"

"Tell me about the girl," I responded. "She heard this voice. Mom thought it was the grandfather. What made you think it wasn't?"

While I spoke, I paced the length of room on the near side of the bed, skimming the contents of the bookshelves. They were packed—every full-color Disney book imaginable, but also Narnia, Potter, Tolkien. Shakespeare on the shelf below that, along with Octavia Butler, George MacDonald, and a full run of Andrew Lang's fairy books. Whatever else she was, the kid was a reader, and a precocious one.

"She got progressively more agitated," the old priest replied. "Started calling it Whisper Man. Said it was asking her to do things, though she wouldn't explain what. She's not always good at communicating."

I nodded, picking up a Tupperware container full of beads from the nightstand. There were similar containers stacked all over the shelves, each meticulously sorted by shape, color, and size. A quart-sized freezer bag stuffed with plastic crosses and coils of waxed cord lay on a desk on the other side of the bed.

"She makes rosaries for the parish," Father Frank explained, gesturing to the little tub of beads in my hand. A weary smile tugged at one half of his mouth. "She obsesses on making things or taking them apart—common for kids like her who fall on the spectrum. The rosaries help give that a direction. She's very proud of them."

I nodded, returning the plastic container to its carefully allotted space. The girl murmured in her sleep, her fingers worrying the beads twined round her hand. That rippling tension contracted again within the air. I still couldn't tell what was causing it—there weren't any obvious spirits or other entities lingering on the Shadowside.

Father Frank watched me intently.

"What was it asking her to do?"

He sighed. "It might be easier to show you." He crossed the room in a few quick steps, withdrawing a stack of papers from a shelf of the nightstand. They were covered in symbols. "The first time, she wrote all over the walls before anyone knew what was happening. Like with the rosaries, we helped her steer it toward something less destructive."

He shuffled through the papers, holding them out so I could see. Some were scribbled in magic marker, a few in crayon, others in what appeared to be finger paint.

"Can you read them?" he asked.

I took the papers, sorting slowly through the stack. The symbols crowding each page looked like a legitimate language—but it was gibberish to me.

"No," I said, a little shocked by the admission. I had a knack for languages, kind of a superpower, really.

"No?" he responded, and his eyes widened. "But Zack, you read practically *everything*."

I studied him over the papers. "Is that why I'm here? Because I taught ancient languages at Case?"

"Taught them?" Father Frank scoffed. "You learned Sumerian first-hand. I thought if anyone could make sense of these symbols, it would be you. Are you telling me they're nonsense?"

I stared at him, too gobsmacked to respond. He misinterpreted my shock for a look of alarm.

"What's wrong?" he asked.

"How do you know that about me?" Fear stropped a wicked edge on my voice. This was the nightmare that

36

plagued me every time I dropped into sleep—exposure, then judgment. My nature revealed for everyone to see.

Father Frank shushed me, then grabbed my arm with a familiarity more shocking than his statement about Sumer. Hand firm on my elbow, he steered me to the farthest corner of the room, well away from the sleeping Halley. Fear glinted in the burnished depths of his eyes. Not fear of me—

Fear *for* me.

"Zaquiel, what's the matter with you?" He kept his voice low, but quiet as he was, those first three syllables resounded to my core. This man knew my name. My True Name—a name older than the body I wore around me, older than the priest who uttered it, older even than the city in which we both stood.

He knew *me*.

Questions jostled through my thoughts—too many to frame coherently. How long had he known me? When had I revealed myself to him? Did this man know anything about the events leading up to my attack on the lake?

I didn't get a chance to ask any of them.

Behind us, Halley jolted upright in bed. She scrambled backward in a panic, kicking furiously at her blankets. Little mewling sounds erupted from her throat.

"Shit," the priest cursed.

He reached to calm her. She clawed wildly at him.

"Is this a seizure?" I asked, moving to assist.

The air in the little room grew thick enough to choke on, and the pall of strange power roiled around the girl like a sentient cloud. Frail as she was, desperation rendered her incredibly strong. She shook off both of us, drawing her knees up and trying to press herself into the tiniest space possible. Her thin shoulders smacked against the wall and still she pushed backward, digging her heels into the mattress. All her hair fell across her features like a dark, tangled veil. She crushed her palms against her ears, whipping her head back and forth while crying out.

"*Nonononononononono!*"

"Halley," the padre said. He tried for her hands again, but she twisted away, nimble as a cat. She shook her head so violently, she was in danger of hurting herself. "Halley, *please—*" he begged.

She muttered with the singsong rhythm of a nursery rhyme, repeating the same pattern of words breathlessly over and over. From the way she clutched the rosary, I thought it was a prayer.

Then I caught the words.

"*Hands to take and eyes to see. A mouth to speak.*"

She said it again, rocking in time till the whole bed shook beneath her.

"What the hell is that?" I breathed. The girl kept rocking, growing louder with each repetition.

"Hands to take and eyes to see. A mouth to speak."

"It's trying for her again," Father Frank whispered, as if stating it any louder would invite it to become more real. Halley clutched her rosary to her lips, murmuring in a rush against the beads.

"Hands to take and eyes to see. A mouth to speak— he comes for me. He comes for me!"

"Oh, that's not creepy," I breathed.

With each cycle of her words, the presence—whatever it was—bore down harder upon the space. The pressure made my ears ring.

"Can you see it?" Father Frank asked as he wrestled with her. "Tell me you see something so we know what to fight."

I let my sight spill wide till the Shadowside aspect of the room hung thicker in my vision than any of its physical objects. Father Frank and the girl grayed out in the wake of the suffocating power.

"I can feel what it's doing, but I can't see anything behind it," I said. "Just power. Ripples of power."

"Leave me alone!" Halley wailed, then started up with the rhyme again. With hooked fingers, she tore at her ears, yanking away long drifts of hair in the process. I moved to grab one wrist while the padre struggled with the other. The instant I made skin-to-skin contact, Halley's head whipped around. Her eyes pinholed till there was hardly any pupil left.

She darted at me, saying in a rush, "He can see you. He can see you, even without his eye!"

I staggered back, the scar on my palm blazing. *The Eye of Nefer-Ka?* She couldn't mean that. How could she even know about that?

The padre dragged her away from me, raising his voice to a stentorian bellow.

"Halley. Listen to me. Make the wall in your head. You're a strong girl. Make the wall and drive him out!"

Halley flailed in the old priest's grip, then suddenly calmed.

"Brick by brick by brick by brick," she breathed in

a rapid patter. She nodded her head in time with each word, but without the frenzied rhythm that had driven the creeptastic rhyme before. The overbearing sense of pressure dwindled by stages in the room.

From elsewhere in the house came a thunderous crash—followed swiftly by the piercing wail of a terrified little boy.

"Fuck me running," I swore. "You stay with her. I'll check on Tyson and the rest."

4

Tingling power rushed to my fingers as I charged down the hall and into the living room. I held it back—no sense in starting the fireworks till I knew what I was up against. Still, my hands itched with the memory of twin blades forged of pure light, and the power was there, if I wanted it.

The front door stood wide open, a cold wind blowing in from outside. I felt a pang of guilt—I didn't remember locking it behind me, and as far as I knew, I'd been the last person inside. Snowy footprints—already melting—were visible across the hardwood. They moved past the fireplace, toward the kitchen, then backtracked to the staircase.

There was another crash, and something heavy struck the floor above me with enough force to rattle the pictures on the walls. I ran up the steep flight of stairs, taking them two—and sometimes three—at a time. I hesitated a moment at the top, not sure which room was which, but I didn't have to wait long.

The door at the end burst open and a grizzled man in greasy sweatpants came stumbling backward into the hall. Sanjeet stood backlit in the doorway, her stance wide and her hair flying. Her glasses were askew and she had a purpling bruise on her jaw, but she had clearly landed more blows than she had taken.

The intruder recovered from her kick and tried grappling her. She broke the hold with the ease of someone trained to do it, then dropped and twisted to slam him bodily into the wall. Little bits of plaster cascaded from a hole left behind by his elbow.

"Don't you touch that little boy!" she cried fiercely, all her timidity forgotten in the heat of the conflict.

Tyson wailed in the background and I could hear Tammy speaking rapidly in an effort to soothe him. The old guy—he looked like a vagrant who had wandered in from the street—groaned, but shook it off.

"Hands to take," he babbled. "Eyes to see!"

Nope, not a random home invasion.

The guy made another grab for Sanjeet, and without hesitation, she kicked him solidly in the nuts. When that blow doubled him over, she brought both fists down on the back of his neck. He dropped to all fours, wheezing. That should have knocked the fight right out of him, but instantly he scrambled to pick himself back up.

"Who the fuck is this guy?" I demanded.

"Look out!" Sanjeet shouted. Her eyes flicked to something just behind me.

Power danced across my hands and the world around me slowed. Dimly, I was aware that I was the one moving fast—faster than I should have in front of Sanjeet and the others—but that inhuman speed allowed me to dodge the rusty tire iron that came whistling toward my head. I turned to face a shabbily dressed woman with picking scars all over her face. Her pupils were blown and I wasn't sure she had enough brains left to be aware of what she was doing.

Instinctively, I peered through the Shadowside to see what was pulling her strings. I expected to confront the leering grin of a cacodaimon—they liked to ride addicts and the brain-fucked—but there was nothing around her except that weird pressure distorting the air. I still couldn't see what was making it.

"Won't—*stop*!" she shrieked, and she took another swing.

The woman held the tire iron like it was a baseball bat, bringing it in a wide arc from just over her shoulder. I was already half in a crouch from ducking the first attempt, so I simply dropped lower and let her swing over me, moving too fast for the scar-faced woman to compensate. As her arms crossed her body, I thrust hard with the base of my palm, connecting above her elbow. The joint popped. She kept her grip on the tire iron— barely—and the combined momentum of blow and swing sent her spinning.

Lady Scarface stood only a couple of feet from the top of the stairs, so I did the most logical thing in the moment—kicked hard at the central mass of her body. She flew backwards with a startled yelp, uselessly cartwheeling her arms. The tire iron clattered down the stairs alongside her. With a miserable groan, she struck bottom, splayed like a heap of dirty rags.

One down.

The old guy, who was still babbling about hands and eyes and other wild things, twisted away from Sanjeet and crashed into me. He twined his arms around my midsection, clinging with a strength I hardly expected. With his filthy sneakers scrabbling for purchase on the runner of hallway carpet, he started driving me back in the direction I'd sent the lady.

Sanjeet rushed forward and tried to drag him off of me. Trained as she was, she lacked the bodyweight to effectively wrestle from that position.

Running on adrenaline and instinct, I didn't really think about how I responded. I shouted my power and wrapped my fingers round the guy's head. Blue-white fire that only I could see blazed from my hands, leaping from me to the deranged hobo.

He jerked like I'd hit him with a Taser. I pried his face backward with my thumbs planted at the outside corners of his eyes. I was just about to blind him and snap his neck when a tiny voice of reason shrilled in my mind.

Sanjeet was watching.

Tammy was somewhere close by. So was little Tyson. Killing the guy with my bare hands in front of so many witnesses—

That would be bad.

I wasn't exceptionally concerned about committing murder—just the part about getting caught. That snapped me out of the battle lust, leaving a sick feeling to slither in my gut. I flexed with the gathered power, sending concussions of it *into* his head. I didn't consciously understand the technique, just knew in the moment that it would fuck him up, but not in any way that would be fatal.

The frenzied man's eyes rolled wildly and he dropped to the floor like a sack of filthy laundry.

Breathless, Sanjeet leaned on the wall beside me.

"What kind of hold was that?" she asked.

I didn't answer. In the final moment of contact, I'd felt something, and now I stared at the intruder's prone form, my eyes focused on the space beyond his body. I caught sight of it again—a little tendril, smoke-like, questing around his head. It was the most I'd seen of whatever plagued the people in this house. The wispy tendril stretched like a tether in the space behind him, but I still couldn't make out what it was attached to.

Marshaling my focus, I softly murmured the syllables of my name. The thing jerked away suddenly, like a cuttlefish startled beneath a rock. Before it slipped away completely, a rapid series of impressions flashed behind my eyes.

Not the main force. These were a distraction.

I bellowed for Father Frank, practically leaping down the stairs. Sanjeet stared after me in shock.

"It's fine. I can handle this," she called down the stairs. She almost sounded like she believed it.

When I hit the bottom, Lady Scarface was waiting. She'd dragged herself to her hands and knees. She snatched at me, fingers hooking into the leg of my jeans. I kicked her in the jaw. I didn't do it full-force—given my steel-toe size thirteens, that probably would have killed her. She collapsed again anyway.

Fine by me.

I sprinted toward Halley's room, my engineer boots thundering against the hardwood. I nearly wiped out on a little plastic lawn mower left in the middle of the floor, but caught myself, splaying my hand against one wall for balance. My wings spread wide reflexively—not that they could exactly help with my balance on this side of reality, but my brain seemed wired to expect that they would.

Still teetering a little, I pelted down the hallway and crashed headlong into the door. When I tried the knob, it was locked. That wasn't a good sign. I yelled for Father Frank, smacking my hand against the door.

No answer.

The Davis house was old, and this seemed like one of the original doors. The thing was solid. I kicked at it, aiming for the region around the knob. My bloodsucking sibling Remy could probably have yanked the door off its hinges with a single, elegant flourish, but things didn't work that way for me. I was a lot stronger than your average mortal, but I was no Superman.

I had to bash the heavy rubber heel of my boot against the door three times before the thing finally splintered. I still strained as I shouldered it open—Halley's hospital bed had been shoved against the other side. The thing weighed a ton.

"Mazetti! Report!" I barked. The words leapt from my mouth before I could question them. For a minute, I felt like I'd been possessed by the ghost of a former self. Memories surged at the edge of consciousness—a jungle. Wet. Stiflingly hot. An urgent sense of purpose jangling like the clarion of an alarm.

The old priest groaned a semi-coherent response from

somewhere on the floor. In an instant, the memories scattered. I was myself again—and a little empty for it.

Father Frank levered himself up.

"Where's Halley?" he muttered. He spat blood. His lower lip was split and a deeper cut purpled above one eye. The room lay in shambles, shattered glass from the big front window crackling underfoot. The rocking chair was in pieces, and it looked like the old priest had been using part of it as a makeshift club. There was blood and some stray bits of hair matted on one splintered edge. A little splash of crimson painted the nearest curtain.

I didn't think it was Father Frank's.

Creakily, he pulled himself to his feet, one hand going to his side. Wincing, he sucked a shallow breath. There was a pipe on the floor behind him, and I really hoped he hadn't been hit in the ribs with that. Old bones were fragile, and they didn't mend easily. I bent to help him, but he waved me away.

"Don't worry about me. Where's the girl?"

Pillows and covers had been torn from the bed, creating deceptively person-shaped lumps on the floor. One of those lumps twitched when I neared it. It moaned with a phlegmy male voice—definitely not Halley. Mismatched Army boots poked out from beneath the blanket. I toed the crumpled form, worried he was playing possum, but the guy just cringed beneath the blanket and groaned again. Down for the count.

I continued searching.

A soft mewling came from a brightly painted toy cabinet on the other side of the room. Covered in flowers and dancing, winged ladies, it matched the fairy theme of the night lamp. It was a little bigger than an old steamer trunk, and its slanted lid lifted half an inch as I approached. I could just make out a single dark eye peering through the crack.

"Halley?" I asked, ducking down so I was closer to her level.

She whimpered in response. The lid snapped shut.

"The kid's safe?" Father Frank slurred. He pressed the back of his hand against his swollen lip and scowled when it came away bloody. "There were three of them—strong. Two… went out that way," he added, nodding toward the broken window. "They must have scattered."

I crouched down in front of the toy chest and very carefully started lifting the lid. The girl inside scuttled backward, pressing herself against one corner with such force, the whole thing jumped. She yanked back on the lid—it must have had some kind of handhold on the inside.

"Come on, Halley," I said soothingly, intoning each word with as much gentle sincerity as I could muster. "You're safe now. You can come out."

I pulled on the lid a little more insistently. She tugged it back down in response. After the third time, she giggled. It turned into a game, like peek-a-boo and tug-of-war combined. Each time I took a turn, she let me lift the lid a little higher. Eventually, I had the toy chest all the way open. Halley lay half on her side, knees tucked up to her chin with her Disney Princess nightshirt pulled down around them. For a girl of her age, she was so tiny. She held herself more like a toddler than a teen.

As she looked up at me, her lips parted in wonder. One word escaped them.

"Wings."

5

I had no idea how to respond. I wanted to play it off, but there was no mistaking what held her attention. Forcing an uneasy smile, I reached out to comfort her with a pat on the head. Halley ducked her chin, neatly avoiding the contact. She peered sideways through her lashes, a thick veil of hair draping one eye.

"Pretty," she murmured, reaching a hand toward my shoulder.

Instinctively, I jerked my wing away. Bad enough she could see them. I didn't want to find out if she could touch them, too. That went against all the rules as I understood them. I flexed, so both wings stretched well beyond her reach.

Halley's eyes tracked the movement.

An inhuman voice deep in my psyche screamed for me to kill the girl—kill her now. She was a danger. She could expose me.

I silenced it the most effective way I knew—humor.

"You start thinking I'm a fairy, kid," I said wryly,

"and we're going to have issues."

Her gaze flicked forward and, briefly, she met my eyes. She held contact for less time than it took for all the air to rush out of my lungs, yet in that short span, dozens of impressions spilled into my mind—images of everyday objects, flashes of carefully formed letters, snippets of songs. All of it was a jumble, as if she'd dumped out the contents of a drawer, only that drawer happened to be her head. One thought resonated with pristine, near-paralyzing lucidity.

Angel. I would never tell on you.

I blinked dumbly, trying to find my voice. Halley tore her eyes away, then abruptly clambered out of the toy chest. She straightened up less than a foot from me, tugging down her nightshirt. Fragments of her mental chaos still whirled in my mind, everything scattering like smoke when I sought to make sense of it. Only the clarity of her promise remained, echoing like a vast bell struck once, then fading into silence.

Without further acknowledging my presence, Halley stepped nimbly around me and padded barefoot toward her bed. It wasn't in its usual position, so she grew agitated, pacing restlessly alongside it. I was afraid she would cut her feet, but she somehow managed to dodge every piece of broken glass scattered across the floor. After making little huffing noises of displeasure, she settled onto the bed anyway, pulling up her knees and hugging them to her chest.

"Told you she was special," Father Frank said. The old priest bent with his hands resting on his thighs, still winded from his fight with the attackers. The cut above his eye bled sluggishly, and he grimaced when a fat drop landed on his lashes. "Stupid blood-thinners," he complained, dashing it away. There was a *ping* and he pulled his phone out of a pocket. I thought maybe he was calling the police, but instead he wiped his hand on his slacks and rapidly tapped a text. Then he glanced, saw my questioning look, and answered my question before it made it to my lips.

"It's Sanjeet. She texted to let me know they're all right upstairs. Tammy's talking to the police."

"She's texting from a floor away?" It came out meaner than intended—fear always brought out my inner asshole.

"Come on, Zack," he replied. "I'm nearly seventy, and you're still the old-fashioned one?" The priest laughed, the sound nervous and tight. His wry expression collapsed into a scowl of pain, and his free hand gripped his ribs.

"You going to be all right?" I moved to offer help, but he waved me away.

"I'll live. You keep an eye on Halley." The girl rocked quietly in the middle of her bed, regarding us from under the veil of her hair.

I didn't like the gray stamp of pain on the priest's patrician features, but I liked the idea of getting close to Halley even less. I stepped around the unconscious attacker sprawled across the floor, and went to the window. A cold wind gusted through the broken panes of glass.

"Street's empty," I observed.

"I banged them up good," Father Frank responded. "They won't get very far." He sucked the cut on his lip.

MICHELLE BELANGER

"Leave them for the police."

I could already hear the sirens, rising and falling on the chill night air. Distant, but getting closer. With a grimace I stepped back from the window. I didn't like cops. I'd been a fugitive myself, not that long ago, and while Bobby Park had helped sort that out, the whole thing had left a bad taste in my mouth.

I poked the blanket-wrapped lump on the floor.

"Any idea who these guys are?"

"You're usually the one with all the answers." Father Frank held himself up with the wall at his back, trying to pretend that he could stand without the support.

I grunted a comment that wasn't, then yanked on the edge of the cover. A middle-aged man tumbled out, half his face covered in blood from an ugly head wound. Given his clothes and the questionable state of his hygiene, it was a fair bet he was homeless, too.

"That's a lot of blood," I muttered.

"Head wound," the padre responded.

"Who the hell sends an army of deranged hobos?"

"Weak minds are easier to control," Father Frank ventured. "You taught me that." He pushed himself off the wall, moving like an old clockwork whose pieces didn't all fit together. Bending to grab one of Halley's scattered pillows, he yanked off the pillowcase. Wadding this up, he knelt creakily beside the dazed vagrant, then applied pressure to the man's wound.

"Seriously, padre—you should look after yourself," I warned. "Broken ribs are no joke."

"I've had broken ribs. These are just bruised. Besides, this guy might talk," he said with a practicality at odds

54

with his vocation. He held the makeshift bandage in place with one hand, feeling for a pulse at the guy's throat with the other. Grunting his satisfaction, he swept his free hand along the fallen vagrant's torso, checking for injuries but also deftly searching for concealed weapons in the folds of his dirty clothes.

"They teach you that in the seminary?" I quipped.

"You know they didn't," Father Frank said, and he laughed. He lifted his eyes to mine and we stared for a moment, each struggling to recognize something in the face of the other. "Or maybe you don't."

I stepped back awkwardly.

"You dropped off the radar there for the better half of a year, Zack. You planning to tell me what's up?" He didn't look at me as he said it, but bent back to the wounded intruder. One-handed, he loosened the man's stained and ratty pea coat.

"About that..." I muttered, not even certain where I could begin.

Beneath the pea coat, the man wore a shirt of quilted flannel with half its buttons missing. The inside of the flannel was caked with blood, gobs of it clotting in grizzled chest hair. Father Frank picked the cloth away.

"Um, Zaquiel?"

Those syllables alone would've gotten my attention, but I saw it, too—gaping red symbols scored the man's chest, deeply carved into his mottled skin.

"Shit," I breathed, dropping to one knee to study them closer.

"Shit is right," the padre said. "Those are three of the symbols Halley's been writing."

"What the hell is going on?"

"Whisper Man wants in my head," Halley piped up. It was so easy to forget she perched in the room, silently taking in everything. She hugged her knees against her chest, the rosary dangling from one skinny wrist. "I don't want him, but I can't always keep him away."

Before either of us could respond, a heavy footfall hit the porch. I leapt to interpose myself between the others and whatever new threat might come through the broken window. The curtain shifted, knocking glass from the panes in a tinkling cascade. Spirit-fire danced round my fingers as I readied for another fight.

Whoever was out there stopped, then gave two loud raps on the window frame to announce their presence. More glass shivered musically to the floor.

"Police," a rumbling baritone announced.

Shit.

I clamped down on my cowl so hard it felt like I was standing inside a vacuum.

6

The curtain twitched aside, revealing a broad-shouldered man easily as tall as me. His ginger hair was cropped in a high-and-tight, and his smattering of freckles lent a boyish quality to a face that otherwise looked carved from a solid block of granite.

He held a pistol at the ready while his partner, a ponytailed woman nearly as tall as he was, held the curtain aside with one hand and covered him with the other. She tensed her jaw when she saw the gore-soaked man on the floor. The male officer hesitated at the shattered window, gold-green eyes flicking rapidly around the dimly lit room. He settled briefly on me, brows ticking up with recognition.

I didn't like that one bit.

"We got a call from Tammy Davis," the officer said.

Halley whimpered on the bed, averting her face from the new intruders. She pressed both her hands against her ears and started to hum.

"Tammy's upstairs," Father Frank said. Slowly, he

drew his hands away from the blood-smeared vagrant, but he stayed crouched there. "She, Sanjeet, and the little boy are fine, but you'll need ambulances for the others. The people who broke in didn't expect a fight."

The ponytailed officer activated a walkie clipped to her vest at shoulder height, conveying the request for backup. She canted her head as it crackled a response. The big guy stepped carefully through the picture window, glass crunching underfoot. He shifted to one side to give his partner room enough to follow, then stood with his back to the wall, holding his gun downward.

He didn't put it away.

"All right, everyone, I'm Officer Roarke. This is my partner, Officer Potts." He said it without taking his eyes off of us. "What I'm going to need you to do is put your hands where I can see them. Everyone. No sudden moves."

Halley's tuneless humming underscored the words. Roarke stared at her, the tectonic plates of his heavy visage shifting quizzically.

Potts gestured sharply to me. "You—get up against the wall."

"He's on our side," Father Frank objected, and I held my hands out to show I was harmless.

"Is it the beard or the biker jacket?" I quipped.

Potts just glowered, so I shut the hell up and did as I was told. It was about as easy to do as rolling an oil tanker up Murray Hill. I wondered idly how often my smart mouth had gotten me killed over the years.

"Why's it so dark in here?" Roarke asked. Not waiting for an answer, he threaded his way past Potts, reaching for the switch beside Halley's door. He glanced expectantly at an overhead fan with a light fixture. Flipping the switch, he scowled when it did nothing.

"They don't keep bulbs in the ceiling fan," Father Frank explained. "And you really should move slow— Halley's already upset."

The girl hunched on the bed, resolutely focused on her own inner world. Roarke clearly didn't know what to make of her.

"Uh, sure," he said, then he focused on the priest. "How many people are in the house?"

"Six—more if you count the ones who broke in," Frank replied.

"There's three of those, at least that I saw," I offered. "The one in here and two by the stairs."

"Against the wall," Potts repeated, her voice rising sharply. She kept her eyes on me as she sidled toward the priest. She gently nudged him. "Father," she said, "I'll look after that man till the EMTs arrive. You need to step away, all right?"

He didn't get the angry cop glare. I chewed my cheeks to hide a frown.

With reluctance, Father Frank handed off the pillowcase bandage and hauled himself to his feet. He got about halfway up before the torsion at his waist made him gasp and clutch his ribs. Potts's hand shot out to steady him. He scowled, but he didn't reject her help. Once he straightened, he politely removed her hand from his elbow.

"How many of you are hurt?" Officer Roarke asked.

"I've had worse," Father Frank declared. Officer Potts regarded the old priest skeptically, then bent to the man on the floor. Her eyes went wide when she saw the gaping symbols cut into his skin.

"What's all over his chest?"

"We were wondering the same thing ourselves," said Father Frank.

"They all seemed strung out on something," I ventured. I didn't make eye contact with either of the cops. I wondered if either of them knew Bobby, and if mentioning him would get them to calm the hell down.

Potts pulled a pair of gloves from a pocket. After slipping them on, she started checking the unconscious man's vitals. The instant the officer touched her fingers to the vagrant's neck, the volume of Halley's humming spiked. The girl coiled into herself, covering her head with her arms.

"What the hell's wrong with her?" Roarke choked.

"Too loud. Too loud!" she cried.

"She's autistic," Father Frank answered tersely. "She doesn't know you, and she just had her home invaded. As far as she's concerned, you're invaders, too."

"But we're police. We're here to help," Roarke said.

I glanced toward the girl. That pulse of power was back, thrumming heavily upon the air. I didn't see any of the tendrils, but that didn't mean nothing was there. I shook my head a little, hoping the padre caught my intent.

"Let me go to her," Father Frank offered. "She knows me. Familiar things help calm her."

Officer Roarke made a halting gesture. "I'm sorry, but you need to stay right where you are. All of you." Holstering his gun, he approached Halley.

"Hey, little lady," he said, pitching his voice higher in

that way some people do when talking to small children or cute pets. He extended his hand in what he clearly meant as a harmless gesture. All I could think of was that old black-and-white *Frankenstein* movie, where Karloff's monster tries making friends with a little girl—and she ends up face-down in the water a few frames later. Roarke wasn't *that* scary, but he still could've palmed Halley's entire face with his broad, calloused mitt.

The girl didn't even notice him. She tightened into a little ball of skinny arms and knobby knees.

"Too loud!" she said over and over again.

"She ever get violent?" the cop asked. He paused with his hand hovering just above her shoulder.

"No," Father Frank answered, "but I wouldn't recommend touching—"

The officer's hand had already connected. The moment it did, Halley jerked into a sitting position like her spine was set on a hinge. Roarke stumbled backward, yanking his hand away like she'd burned him. Halley turned and pinned him with her gaze.

"It's blood. It's all blood," she declared in a voice that was hardly her own. "How can you kiss him when that's all you can taste?"

Roarke struggled for a response, but all that came out was a tiny squeak.

"Jesus, what's wrong with this kid?" Potts whispered.

At the mention of blood, my focus lasered onto Roarke. Blood held a special significance for one branch of my extended family—the Nephilim. They were the next best things to vampires, and I had a litany of reasons to distrust them. Roarke didn't look like a member of that tribe, but that didn't rule out a connection. The Nephilim could twist mortals into blood-slaves, supernatural servitors they called anchors.

Whatever was going on with him, Halley's words had struck a nerve. The hulking officer blanched so pale his freckles stood out like cornflakes in cream.

"Lydia?" he finally managed, voice cracking. He didn't tear his eyes from the girl. "When's that backup set to arrive?"

"Ten minutes, tops," his partner responded. She had paled, too, though she didn't look quite as rattled as Roarke.

"I think I'm scaring the kid," he said.

There was no question who was pants-shitting scared in the room, but I saw no use in pointing it out.

"I'm gonna go find the lady who called this in," he said. "You got this. Right, Lyds?" He backed away from the bed as he spoke, till his broad shoulders connected with the door frame behind him. Halley squatted like a statue in the middle of her bed, eyes gone glassy as she stared a hole through his forehead.

Roarke was out of the room before his partner could reply. Lydia glared at the empty space where he had stood.

"Yeah, sure," she muttered. "Leave me with the freakshow."

As soon as Roarke was gone, Halley's rigid posture melted away and she slumped with exhaustion.

I racked my brain for signs that might identify a Nephilim blood-slave. Anchors tended to be knuckle-dragging no-necks, and Roarke was bulky enough to fit the bill. Before I could give it any more thought, though,

Halley started freaking out again.

"No. No! Make him go away!" she wailed, head buried in her hands. Another wave of that power pressed down upon the room.

"He's gone, honey," Potts offered. She gestured vaguely to where her mountain of a partner had just stood, but Halley continued to whimper. With a look of annoyance, Potts bent back to the unconscious vagrant. She adjusted the wad of bloody cloth on his head.

The man's eyes snapped open. His hand shot out and he seized Officer Potts by the wrist.

"What the hell?" she gasped.

His grip tightened, and he used the startled woman's arm to drag himself into a sitting position. Spittle flew from his mouth.

"Hands to take!" he shouted. "Eyes to see!"

With an incoherent shrill of disgust, Potts torqued her wrist to break his hold. He clung with a ferocity born of madness.

Halley started screaming.

The vagrant's head whipped around so sharply all the vertebrae in his neck crackled.

"A mouth to speak!" he lisped wetly through gaps in his teeth. Potts yanked again to break his grip, but his fingers were locked like a vise. Father Frank darted forward to help the officer.

"Back off," Potts snarled. "I've got this." She dropped the bloody rag to free up a hand, reaching across her body to seize her pepper spray. Without breaking eye contact, she hissed, "Last chance, buster."

The possessed vagrant roared in her face.

She averted her eyes and maced him, point-blank.

Halley coughed on a backwash of fumes. With a peculiar casting gesture, she hurled a hand toward the intruder.

"My room," she shouted. "*Get out!*"

A shimmering bolt of power that only I could see launched from her fingers at the possessed man. It wasn't bright, like the power I could throw around, and it didn't look exceptionally cohesive, but it was enough. It struck the guy in the chest, splashing across the mutilated symbols like some kind of napalm-filled water balloon. The vagrant dropped Lydia's wrist and began to seize. The heels of his mismatched Army boots beat an irregular rhythm on the floorboards.

Father Frank turned to me, looking for answers.

All I could offer was an ineffectual shrug. I didn't understand as much as I once had, but everything about Halley bent the rules as I currently knew them. My senses told me she was mortal. Mortals didn't hurl bolts of energy like they'd just graduated from Hogwarts. Psychic mortals, sure—that could happen, and it gave me the heebie-jeebies when it did. But striking a spirit from the Shadowside? That was a power unique to my tribe, the Anakim.

Even the Nephilim couldn't do that.

"Lyds!" Roarke bellowed. "You OK, Lyds?" Wild-eyed, he burst back into the room.

Halley loosed a little sigh and fell back against the mattress. Her spine bowed once, then she lay terribly still. The vagrant continued to jig against the floor, blood-flecked foam forming at the edges of his mouth as he bit down on his tongue.

"Jesus!" Potts cried. "Help me with this guy, Jimmy. Shit got real weird."

"The girl—?" Roarke asked, though it wasn't clear if he was asking after her well-being or about her role in the weirdness. Given the mindfuck that had driven him from the room, I suspected it was the latter.

"I'll watch her," Father Frank said, moving to her bedside whether or not the officers agreed.

I stayed put against the wall in case Potts was feeling generous with the pepper spray. Scattered at my feet lay the crumpled papers scribbled from top to bottom with Halley's mysterious script. A set of three symbols identical to those carved in the vagrant's chest recurred with ominous regularity.

If only I could read them.

7

An ambulance arrived, then more police. They split us up—Father Frank insisted on staying with Halley. I didn't get a chance to see if they let him, though. I got hustled into the kitchen.

Then it was a whole lot of hurry up and wait.

More sirens, more ambulances, and EMTs dragging various bits of equipment through the tidy little house. I leaned just out of sight but not out of earshot. While they strapped Lady Scarface to a backboard, one of the officers—not Roarke or Potts, but some new guy—tried asking her questions. The woman couldn't even give her own name. She babbled in broken sentences that sounded like word salad.

An hour went by.

Then another.

Finally, Roarke came to interview me. Of course I would get Roarke—half a dozen Cleveland cops scurrying around the Davis home, and I got the one who might have ties to my least favorite tribe. The big guy glanced over his shoulder at the bustle in the living room, then gestured for me to take a seat at the kitchen table. It was tucked in a little breakfast nook, completely out of sight from the rest.

I hesitated.

The burly officer flattened his lips into a look, then waved impatiently toward the table again.

I still didn't move.

They had to interview witnesses separately—that was standard procedure, *blah, blah, blah*—but I still didn't like the idea of being alone with this lumbering gorilla who looked like he bench-pressed Hondas in his spare time. Was I being a paranoid dick about it? Sure. I was a fan of staying alive. Most of the Nephilim were fans of the opposite, especially when it pertained to guys like me.

"Quit wasting my time, Westland," he said.

That made me dig in even harder. I'd been cooling my heels for close to two and a half hours, and none of the officers had asked for my name. I hadn't offered it, either, just sat and waited like a good little drone. Now I flashed back to the moment he'd come in through the window. That little lift of his ginger brows.

"You know me from somewhere?" I demanded, and yeah, I sounded suspicious—because I was. He gave me a look again. This one as much as said, "*Why the hell are you even asking?*"

Eventually he grumbled, "Fine. You want to play it like that, but they're all busy out there. No one can hear us."

Right, I mused. *Because that totally fills me with confidence.*

Roarke tried herding me back toward the table by advancing one ponderous step at a time. I didn't appreciate the idea of having the Big Blue Ox all up in my personal space, and there was no direction to go but backward, stopping when my legs met with the edge of the kitchen table. Even so I refused to sit down. Instead, I stood there with my fists stuffed into the pockets of my leather jacket, defiantly meeting his eyes while I held tight to my cowl.

Roarke practically ground his teeth.

"Look, Westland. It doesn't take a genius to see this isn't an ordinary crime scene. What am I covering up?"

I squinted, as if seeing him better could lend clarity to his words.

"Is that a trick question?" I asked.

He made an unhappy sound, and it came out like the kind of snort I'd expect from an angry bull just before it charged.

"You're not as funny as you think you are, and I don't have time for it tonight. Give me the 411, and stop screwing around."

"Yeah," I said, chewing the inside of my lip. "Thing is, there's nothing to cover up. Some guys broke in. They acted crazy and threatened the kids, and we beat the snot out of them. Self-defense. End of story."

Roarke ground his teeth again, a prominent vein at his temple throbbing. I took subtle pleasure in knowing that I wasn't good for his blood pressure—though I managed not to grin too much about it.

On some level I was probably being unreasonable. Not everyone I ran into was tangled up in the messy web of betrayal that tied me back to my extended family. Maybe Roarke was just an overgrown teddy bear, misunderstood because of his size. Maybe Halley's babble about blood had no connection whatsoever to the Nephilim.

Maybe I was a tap-dancing Dalek.

Yeah, right.

"Fuck this," the big man spat. "When he said you'd changed, I thought he meant you stopped being an asshole. You don't want my help, Westland, fine by me. I've only ever done you favors because of—"

He halted mid-rant at the sound of movement near the doorway. His partner, Lydia, stood there. The tense body language between Roarke and me wasn't lost on her.

"You 'bout done in here, Jimmy?" she asked. Her glacial eyes shifted between the two of us.

"Getting there, Lyds," Roarke replied. He stepped away from me, rubbing the back of his neck. He looked like a big kid who'd gotten caught doing something embarrassing.

Blood and favors. That seriously screamed Nephilim, and only one of those had any reason to be nice to me—my sibling, Remy. He had some connections with the local police—he'd used them to help cover up the incident on the lake. Was Roarke on my side? I almost felt bad for being an ass.

Almost.

"Am I being charged with anything?" I asked.

Officer Potts canted her head.

"I don't know. You feeling guilty?"

"Well, I did kind of rough up the one I sent down the stairs," I admitted. "But she came at me with a tire iron, so I'm inclined to say she deserved it."

Neither of them answered. The kitchen clock ticked audibly while we held an unofficial staring contest. Lydia broke the silence first.

"You didn't see any of the others that broke through the window in the girl's room, did you?" she asked. "Your priest friend said there were more."

I ran my fingers through unkempt hair, leaning a little against the table. I still wasn't going to tell them everything that was going on—hell, I hadn't worked out all the details myself. But I figured I'd throw them a bone.

"When I got to Halley's room, the others were gone. There was the guy on the floor, and the padre was down. I had the choice to chase after them, or help the priest and the girl. I opted to help. But, yeah. I think there were more."

Lydia gave Roarke a look as if to say, "*See? That's how it's done.*" He glared back at her from under his beetling eyebrows, then shouldered past her without so much as a word.

If Roarke actually *was* a friend, he had every reason to be pissed off. I made a mental note to talk to Remy so I could sort that out later. No sense in making enemies out of the cops—though it might have been a bit late for that.

Officer Potts asked me a few more questions, like what had brought me to the Davis house in the first place. I half-lied and said I'd come to help Father Frank look after Halley. The padre and I were old friends, I explained glibly, and we'd done work together before.

As far as I'd been able to gather, that was actually true—though it was a good thing Potts didn't ask *when* it had happened, or how long we'd been working together. I didn't have a clue.

She ran my ID and pulled up my conceal-carry permit. She asked about my firearm. I handed the SIG over for her to inspect.

"You had this the whole time, and never took it out?" she asked—though she wasn't asking in her interrogator voice. She seemed genuinely puzzled.

I shrugged. "Never hit a point where I felt the gun was going to solve any of our problems. Why escalate?" Besides, the fireworks I could work with my hands beat a gun any day with nasties like Whisper Man—but she didn't need to know that.

Potts looked at me as if she was suddenly seeing a very different person under the mess of whiskers and wild hair. She handed my ID and gun back to me, then walked away.

I was free to go.

8

Once Officer Potts was done with me, I ventured into the living room. Most of the chaos had cleared.

Upstairs, Tammy sang a lullaby to soothe little Tyson. Her sweet, clear voice echoed hauntingly through the house. The last of the EMTs came down the hall from Halley's room carrying a mammoth kit of first-aid supplies. He slipped out the front door to a vehicle parked at the curb. Roarke lingered near the bottom of the stairs, taking pictures and entering notes into a tablet. He gave me the stink-eye when I emerged from the no man's land of the kitchen.

I briefly considered talking to him, but decided it was in my best interest to avoid Officer McMountain for the time being, so I headed down the hall to check on Halley and the padre. When I got to her room, Halley's bed was empty. The curtain was down and someone had tacked a section of plywood and plastic across the broken picture window to keep the cold out.

Father Frank stood off to one side putting his

undershirt back on. His ribs were taped up, half-obscuring an old military tattoo that stretched between his shoulder blades. The faded blue lines were going soft at the edges, but it was still possible to read the words *Semper Fidelis* emblazoned on a scroll above the head of an eagle rampant. The eagle seemed to rise from the topmost layer of medical tape, the tip of one outstretched wing nearly obliterated by a pale, puckered scar—almost certainly from an old bullet wound.

Curiouser and curiouser... Belatedly, I rapped my knuckles on the wooden door frame to announce my presence.

"I heard ya about a minute ago," Father Frank said without turning around. "You're not exactly subtle with those clunky boots you wear."

"Sorry," I muttered—though whether I was apologizing for the intrusion or the "clunky" boots even I wasn't sure. I started to withdraw from the room, but Father Frank continued talking with the ease of someone used to dressing around other people—which made me wonder how long he'd been a priest and not a Marine. No one got a tattoo like that just for show. I lingered on the threshold to listen, my back half-turned to give the man his privacy. He might not have cared, but I did.

"Halley's in one of those ambulances, headed to University Hospital. They insisted on taking her in for observation," he said. "I've got to go and be with her—there's no doctor who will know what to do if this thing gets its claws in her again."

He settled his plain black cleric's shirt upon his shoulders and began buttoning it from the bottom up.

He focused on the simple task, his long fingers working with a dexterity that defied his years.

"I barely avoided an ambulance ride myself," he mused. "They wanted me in for X-rays, but I know the difference between bruised ribs and broken ribs—I've broken enough bones over the years."

I chuckled at this. "Anyone tell you you're a stubborn old coot?"

He grinned, the expression unearthing the remains of a much younger man. "All the time, but I learned from the best—and look who's callin' me old." His smile faltered. "Look, Sanjeet will be down with the car keys any minute now to drive me to the hospital, so we don't have long. You planning to tell me what's wrong with you?"

I hesitated, wondering where I could even start. Amnesia was the official story—memory loss due to oxygen privation. It was plausible, considering I'd all but drowned in Lake Erie's chill waters—not once, but twice.

The truth was uglier than that. My memory hadn't failed me—it had been assaulted in a willful excision of information. That made it sound surgical, but my attacker had used something more akin to a chainsaw than a scalpel to cut the pieces of me out. Dorimiel's assault had left me with a head so full of holes it made a sieve look seaworthy.

I sighed through my nose, then stepped more fully into the room, pulling closed what was left of the door. I leaned my shoulders against the wall, ignoring the way my wings ghosted through the physical structures of the house. Father Frank watched me the whole while, his keen, expressive eyes fixed upon my face.

"Come on, Zack," he urged. "I haven't seen you look this rough since they burned Xuan's village on the Mekong."

Memories—tenuous as shadows—stirred at his words. They carried echoes of emotions. Fury. Loss. A wrenching sense of guilt. And that name—Xuan. I knew it belonged to a woman. Probably not a lover, but someone I'd sworn to protect.

That was where the recollections stopped. If I tried to grasp any of it head-on, the whole thing would be lost. I could remember *around* the holes—usually stuff that wasn't essential, like the sound of fish leaping in the water. The way the air hung hot and damp and reeking of green. I knew where the Mekong could be found—a detached kind of textbook knowledge about Vietnam ran like ticker-tape beneath the kinesthetic memories of the place—but whatever meaningful kernel these recollections were wrapped around remained hollow at the core, devoured by the hungry worm I knew as Dorimiel.

All the most important ones I carried were like that. Lifetimes' worth of experience—all gone. My past prior to the moment I dragged myself out of the lake was a jigsaw with the middle punched out, and no reference picture left on the box.

"Zack?" Father Frank urged.

"There was... an incident," I began. "It jacked up my memory."

"Jacked up?" he asked.

I shook my head. "Gone," I said. "It's all gone. I might as well have met you for the first time tonight."

I turned away as I said it, but not before I caught the stricken look that crushed the dignity from his face. "For what it's worth, you make a damned impressive first impression," I offered.

He didn't seem to hear. Wobbling on legs suddenly bereft of their strength, the priest dropped heavily onto the edge of Halley's bed. All the air whooshed from his lungs, making him grab at his taped-up ribs.

"How do you forget?" he muttered in a gravelly voice. "You don't forget. You remember. That's what you are."

"I wish," I answered. Restlessly, I rubbed at the scar on my hand.

"You were attacked." It wasn't a question.

I nodded.

Something fiercely protective chased the pain from his face. When he spoke, his voice was all gunpowder and steel.

"Who do we need to hunt down?"

"We?" I replied. "There's no we. It's over and done. Nothing you can do."

From the way he flinched at those words, I couldn't have wounded him more if I'd knifed him in the gut. He made a fist and stared at it, lying there uselessly in his lap. A muscle ticked in his jaw.

"Don't tell me that."

I wondered again what kind of priest the padre was—and if his parish knew anything about his extra-curricular activities with the likes of me.

"You lied that night at the church," he said through gritted teeth. "I knew something was up the minute you left your weapons. I asked, and you said it was nothing. Nothing!" All the fight leapt back to his eyes, only now I bore the full brunt of it. I fumbled for some meaningful response, staggered by his revelation.

"Did you think you couldn't trust me?" he said. "After everything we've been through?"

My thoughts roiled with questions—when did this happen? What weapons was he talking about? Was it a normal thing for me to leave stuff at his church? I was desperate for any answers, but his stricken look of betrayal stoppered my throat.

Before I could collect myself, the door behind me creaked and Sanjeet poked her head into the room. She wore her puffy pink coat and held that silly pompom hat of hers in one hand. A bruise the color of eggplant covered one side of her jaw. Like I had before her, she rapped belatedly on the frame.

"You're not interrupting," Father Frank said. I stood with my mouth open, still struggling to marshal my words. Sanjeet looked skeptically between us but didn't contradict.

"You ready?" She held her keys up.

It took all I had not to chase her from the room and press Father Frank for answers. Now was not the time, though—Halley took priority. I busied myself by gathering the various samples of writing that had been scattered all over the floor during the fight. The police had left them alone—probably had no idea what to make of them.

"Yeah. He's ready," I said, neatening the stack, then turning back to Father Frank. "You go look after Halley. She needs you."

Righteous fire still kindled in his eyes, but at the mention of Halley he settled somewhat. He slid from the side of the heavy metal-framed bed and joined Sanjeet at the door.

"I'll call you from the hospital," he said. "Keep me in the loop this time."

I couldn't meet the accusation in his eyes, so I focused my attention on the papers.

"And Zack," he added, a quirk of his lips softening the sting of his words. "Answer your damned phone for once."

They headed down the hall while I puzzled over the three recurring symbols. The answers to Whisper Man were right in front of me, scribbled in fingerpaint and crayon—I just had to figure out how to read them.

I got so fixated on the problem, I forgot to even mention—they were calling the wrong cell.

9

As I finished jotting down some notes on Halley's papers, I realized the other thing that had slipped my mind while I'd pondered the issue of unreadable words.

Sanjeet had the car.

I stepped quietly from Halley's room, listening to the unexpected stillness of the Davis household. After all the fighting and chaos, the silence hung like a weight upon the air. The living room was empty, more toys than I remembered scattered across the floor. A mop and pail leaned in one corner where Tammy had apparently tried to clean up all the slush and dirt tracked into the house by the emergency workers. From the look of it, she'd given up.

Tammy and Tyson were upstairs, probably asleep. I closed my eyes, unfurled my senses, and could just barely feel them over the residual echoes of the fight.

A nagging thought wormed its way into my head. I couldn't shake a guilty suspicion that the situation with Whisper Man had escalated because I'd come into their lives. Trouble seemed to follow behind me as surely as my wings.

Folding Halley's papers, I tucked them into the front of my leather jacket. Then I tightened the buckle at the bottom and quietly slipped out the front door, pausing on the porch to make sure the door latched behind me. Not that locks made much difference when the bad guys just knocked out the windows when they wanted to get in.

I hesitated, wondering whether or not it was safe for Tammy and little Tyson to be left alone in the home. I might be good at attracting danger, but I also did a bang-up job of kicking its teeth in when it threatened people in my care. The Davises were on that list now— at least until this business got resolved.

The sound of a car door drew my attention to the street. A tall, slender black man in a knee-length coat of heavy gray wool slipped into a sedan parked across from the home. He gripped two steaming cups of diner coffee in his hands, and made a point of not looking in my direction. The door shut quietly behind him. He and his companion were barely visible through the glare of the streetlight on the windshield.

The guy passed a cup of coffee over to the woman behind the wheel. She took it gratefully, wrapping gloved fingers around it for warmth. It didn't take a psychic to see they were cops.

The police were taking the break-in seriously, and I wondered what they knew that I didn't. This kind of response wasn't typical for a first-time home invasion. Maybe the officers expected the remaining vagrants to return to the house. Personally, I figured they were long gone.

Whatever the case, as I stepped off the front porch and cut across the yard, I didn't envy the officers their chilly vigil. The temperature had dropped in the middle of the night, falling somewhere between arctic and the cold of deep space. The snow on the ground was frozen so thoroughly that it squeaked under my boots. As I walked, bitter gusts picked up wicked shards from the surrounding drifts, flinging them against my face. Only the whiskers saved me from the brunt of it.

The night had stilled to that point where the streets were so empty, the city felt abandoned. No one was out in this sub-arctic chill. The windows of all the houses along the street were dark, their residents dreaming safe until morning.

I stuffed my fists into the pockets of my leather jacket and headed toward Mayfield Road. The white-and-red sign for Mama Santa's spilled plastic light across the pavement behind me as I turned east, heading up and out of Cleveland's Little Italy. To my left, the first few sections of wall marked the southernmost boundary of Lake View Cemetery. I hugged the weathered concrete, keeping an eye out for patches of black ice.

The eight-foot barrier of concrete gave way to staggered sections of overgrown masonry. Runnels of ice glittered amidst the patterned segments of quarried stone that dated back to the origins of the massive boneyard. The wall rose higher and higher the further I went on the steepening sidewalk, until it towered fifteen feet or more above my head. Clinging runners of ivy and denuded branches of trees dangled from on high, seeming to spill from a wild garden hidden behind the stone barrier.

A single car climbed the hill toward Coventry, engine purring. It caught me in its headlights and slowed momentarily. I kept my head down, though it was unlikely the driver had any real interest in me. Whoever they were, they were probably just startled to see a scarecrow figure all in black wandering the streets at this hour.

The vehicle ghosted past and I continued the chilly mile-and-a-half trek back to my apartment. My breath plumed against the night and I fell into the rhythm of walking, my thoughts clamoring with all the things I'd witnessed since Sanjeet had brought me to the Davis household. Whisper Man. Halley's uncomfortably keen perceptions. Whatever the hell kind of history I had with Father Frank. The language scrawled on page after page, all of it unreadable.

The quandary of the channeled symbols gnawed at me, because it was something I thought I should be able to solve. Even with my amnesia, I'd yet to encounter a language that didn't strike *some* echo of comprehension deep within my mind. Halley's sigils held a certain passing familiarity, but it was one I frustratingly couldn't place. They reminded me a little of Hittite, enough for me to be certain they were a language—but if I'd encountered anything like these symbols before, it was never to read them. That was a new experience for me.

More unsettling than the language was the enigma of Whisper Man.

I'd watched cacodaimons riding around in both the living and the dead, so possession was nothing new to me, but cacodaimons were a one-person deal. It took them a lot of effort to go joyriding around in someone else's skin, and you could see them doing it. Or at least I could. I could also reach across to their side of things and smack them for the audacity.

Whisper Man was an entirely new quantity. From everything I'd seen with Halley and the hobo army, whatever he was, he could control multiple people while remaining all but invisible, even to my psychic perceptions. Just that one little tendril, and as soon as I'd noticed it, it had disappeared.

I had no idea what I was dealing with, and that didn't sit well.

The lofty wall of the cemetery on my left began shrinking to meet the sidewalk again. About thirty feet ahead, it gave way once more to an eight-foot fence of lichened concrete. In the distance, the traffic light across from the Mayfield entrance blinked lazily in the frigid night.

I didn't notice the people until they were right on top of me—literally. There was scrabbling from high above, and then a tattered figure jumped down from the cemetery wall. She hit the sidewalk and rolled to her feet directly in my path. She was followed by a man who dropped with his full weight onto my back. He draped himself over my shoulders, wrapping his arms around my throat. I stumbled beneath the sudden burden, but managed not to fall.

"What the *fuck*?" I gasped. Power leapt to my fingers and I reached up to twist the guy off of me. The angle was wrong, and he clung with a strength that nearly matched my own—a strength that wasn't properly human.

"Choke him, kill him, make him bleed!" the woman sang in a ragged voice. She circled warily and the amber glow of the blinking traffic light caught the glint of a blade in her hand. Long, slender, and serrated on one side, it looked like a fishing knife—meant for scales, but it would cut flesh just as well.

"Get off me!" I snarled.

Straining to keep the man from locking his arms round my throat, I seized both of his wrists. With a sharp pivot, I smashed him into the wall. His shoulder hit the stones with bone-jarring force. It did nothing to slacken his grip.

"Hands to take. Eyes to see!" He spat the words wetly against my ear.

More of Whisper Man's crazed vagrants. Great. These were probably the ones who'd gotten away. I wondered if they'd doubled back, and how long they had been following me. Stupid of me not to check.

"Hold him! Hold him!" she cried. "He can't know. He can't see. Not this one. Master says he sings the names!"

While I struggled with her companion, the woman darted forward. She held the blade low, and if I didn't get out of its way I was going to be singing soprano for a very long time. I could move fast when I wanted—a brief, inhuman burst of speed. It wasn't something I could sustain for long, but it was damned useful in fights like this.

With a hundred and sixty pounds of dead weight hanging from my neck, however, even my speed couldn't save me from her knife. I sidestepped, nearly losing my footing as I hit a patch of ice. It kept the knife-wielding woman from making a castrato out of me, but her blade still nicked me high up in the hollow of one thigh. It was such a swift cut that I only processed it as a brief flash of stinging heat. I teetered under the lumbering burden of the male attacker, controlling the motion in the next instant so his own ballast carried him thuddingly into the wall.

His head smacked into stone. The fingers of his left hand spasmed, and I used the opening to slip my own hand between his arm and my throat. He was skinny as a refugee, tendons and muscles cording over the knobby ends of his bones. Blue-white power leapt between us as I closed my hand round his wrist and jerked hard on his forearm. All the strength fled his fingers, and I tore his hand away.

Following through, I ducked forward, dragging him by that arm till I flipped him from my back. He landed on the sidewalk at the Fish-Knife Lady's feet, the back of his skull hitting the concrete with an ugly crack.

I staggered backward, my left leg buckling suddenly beneath me.

Something wasn't right. I didn't feel pain, exactly, just a rushing sense of heat. It felt like water gushing down my skin.

Except it wasn't water.

It was blood. Lots and lots of blood. My heart thudded in my head, and answering spurts of crimson gouted from my thigh—a little spray at first, but thicker with each pulse.

Fuck.

She'd nicked the artery. The pressure tore it further with each heave of my racing heart. In a panic I clamped my hand over it, pressing down as hard as I could. The femoral artery—that was a big one. That was bad. That was really bad.

I was going to bleed out.

The street was empty. The nearest house was more than a hundred yards away. I could scream, but no one would hear me. At this hour, no one was awake. Running wasn't an option. I'd never make it.

With every course considered, then rejected, more life flooded through my hand.

I was immortal, but this body could die. Untethered, my soul would drift on the Shadowside. With my memory loss, I had no idea if I could navigate the process of rebirth that allowed me to survive. So much had been torn from me—maybe I would dwindle to a scrap, and lose myself entirely.

The thought left me terrified.

Fish-Knife Lady lunged again. Desperate to survive, I lashed out with my left hand faster than even I could track. I bellowed the syllables of my Name, even as black spots started chewing the edges of my vision.

How long does it take to bleed out from the femoral? I knew it was quick. Seizing her wrist, I twisted and felt the bones splinter even as I heard the snap. The knife sailed from her useless fingers. Squealing, she tried a haymaker with her remaining hand, wildly swinging for my face. I brought my forearm up in a block, then crunched my elbow into her nose. The palm of my left hand remained jammed against my leg. Blood spurted through my fingers. Gleaming arcs of it spattered the snow along the curb, a startling crimson against street-stained white.

I won't die here. Not before I remember myself.

The words thundered over the stuttering pulse in my head. The world smeared hazy around the edges. Headlights starred in my vision. A car—turning onto Mayfield from Coventry Road. A few blocks away. I was close enough to the traffic light, maybe they would see.

No. Not close enough. Not enough time.

The guy on the sidewalk was getting up. Fish-Knife Lady's broken arm dangled useless at her side, but she wasn't out of the fight. I'd smashed her nose and it looked like a potato. She squinted around it with bleary eyes, blood making a grisly mask of the bottom of her face. It bubbled on her lips as she whispered—messages from whatever was controlling her, singsong rhythms of madness and pain.

She dove for me again and I welcomed her. My left hand shot out—I knew that was dumb, but there it was anyway, wrapped around her throat till her eyes bulged. I needed that hand to stop the bleeding. What was I thinking? I was dying here. I was going to fucking die.

Still I held her, elbow locked, lifting her up till her feet danced against the air. I dug in my fingers till I could feel the pulse in her neck. It thudded hard and wild against my palm. My own heartbeat leapt in answer, rapid and thready. It trembled down the length of the scar.

Thud.
Light burning around my fingers.
Thud.
A wash of brilliance spilling across her flesh.
Thud.
Heat like a bonfire. A swift, burning river of it, racing along my arm, down through my belly, settling in my leg.

She jigged and twitched as I held her, bloodshot eyes rolling back in her head. Scrabbling with her good hand, her fingers plucked ineffectually at my own.

I didn't drop her until she stopped moving. By then the blood had staunched along my thigh.

10

What the hell was that?

I stumbled away from the dead woman, choking on the bitter taste of blood.

Memories exploded like flashbulbs behind my eyes. None of them were my own. I didn't want to hold on to them, couldn't stand their feel as they seethed within my mind. A life of loss, addiction, maddened whispers that never let her rest—the flood of foreign data drowned all but the panicked thunder of my heart.

Then another impulse leapt from the torture of her memories to mine. My skull felt too small to contain its booming words.

I WILL REBUILD MYSELF, ANAKIM, AND ALL WILL BOW AGAIN.

A hail of violent perceptions drove me to my knees—chains, smoke, the shattering of stone. On its heels, a strangling sense of panic. The sensations washed through me with no context or order. Spewing desperate curses, I pressed my hands against my ears as if that was

91

going to help block things piped directly into my brain.

At my outburst, the guy bolted, stumbling over his dead companion in his haste to get away. The intruding presence withdrew as well, departing as swiftly as it came.

Tires squealed. The headlights, distant before, veered in my direction. A car lurched onto the curb. Spotted— I'd been spotted. This registered only dimly as I fought to bring order back to my brain. The pale corpse lay five feet from me, eyes fixed and staring.

I looked away.

I'd sucked the life out of her mortal shell. Drained her to heal my own wound. The certainty left me staggered and nauseous. I hadn't bitten her, but I could still taste her blood.

I thought only Nephilim did that.

"Zack? Zack?"

A hand on my shoulder. I shoved it away.

"Mother's Tears, Zaquiel. Talk to me. That's arterial spray."

I looked up, blinking stupidly. Gradually, she came into focus—warm bronze skin, red hair spilling forward, eyes like twin hurricanes.

"Lil?" I gasped incredulously.

"How much of this is your blood?" she demanded, tugging at me. "Can you stand?"

"I killed her," I said.

"I can see that," she replied. "No point in you just laying down and dying, too. Where were you hit?"

"Femoral," I managed. My mouth was dry. All my muscles felt like water now that the adrenaline was wearing away. "She had a knife. Sharp little fucker."

Lil's gray eyes flicked to both my legs. Her full, red lips pressed into a hard line.

"Seems like the blood's stopped," she said. "What did you do?"

"I fucked up, Lil. I really fucked up this time."

"Well, if you're not bleeding out, you can walk," she insisted. "Let's go." She seized both my wrists, trying to pull me bodily to my feet. I yanked my left hand away from her grasp.

"Don't touch me," I said in a panicked rush. "I don't want to do it to you, too." Drunkenly, I lurched away. Lil's eyes narrowed, flickering over me again.

"You can have a breakdown later, flyboy," she cautioned. "You don't kill people in the middle of the street and just wait for the cops to come."

"I fucking *ate* her," I shouted.

Implacable, Lil stopped trying to grab my wrists and instead seized the front of my leather jacket. I shoved her away with a snarl. She backed off, but didn't look happy about it. Positioning herself between me and the spill of light coming from the streetlamp across the road, she waited, one boot tapping out an impatient rhythm on the bloodstained sidewalk.

Warily, she glanced from me to the road. Aside from her car, however, Mayfield remained empty. The whole city felt like it was holding its breath.

She was right, though. We needed to disappear. That much made it through my hobbled brain.

Steadying myself with the cemetery wall at my back, I stood in stages. Nausea halted me about halfway up. Gray waves pulsed through my vision. Blood loss—no way to know how much, but my pants were soaked and freezing to my skin. The sidewalk looked like the set of a slasher flick.

Feeling around, I found the tear in my jeans. The skin beneath was smooth and whole. I turned my head and spat into the snow. It came out threaded with crimson. Had I bitten her? No—no, just wrapped my hand around her throat. Seized her pulse with something harsher than teeth.

"Fuck," I breathed. I swallowed hard, fighting not to vomit.

Lil sighed with exasperation. Waiting wasn't her style. The wind dragged chill fingers through her wealth of red hair, whipping long strands in every direction.

"I really hope you start making sense soon," she grumbled. "By the way—the shaggy hipster look? Not the thing for you."

"Screw you," I shot back.

She snorted. "Last I checked, you were too chickenshit for that."

I glared, but didn't argue. Lil eyed me a moment longer, then turned on her heel and headed back to her car. She produced a silk handkerchief from somewhere on her person and scooped up the bloody knife as she walked past the corpse. "Your DNA on file?" she called over her shoulder.

"Don't know," I yelled back. "You know I can't remember."

"These are things you should look into, Anakim." She pushed a button on her key fob and the engine of her Sebring growled to life before she even had the door open. When I was certain my legs would hold me, I took a step in her direction. That meant walking right past the woman whose life I'd snuffed.

I faltered.

"Lil?" I asked.

"What?" Radiating impatience, she pivoted on her heel to fix stormy gray eyes on me.

"How'd you know?"

"About the DNA?"

I shook my head and regretted it—the world swung crazily long after the motion stopped. My stomach hitched, and it was an even bet whether it was tied to the vertigo or to the sight of the dead woman discarded in an ungainly heap outside the cemetery gates. Closing my eyes, I willed the dizziness away, then forced myself to stare at her ghastly pale face. She was dead, but she had a name. *Patty Wolford.* The knowledge clung to the back of my thoughts. I'd taken that along with her life.

It was a power that belonged to the Nephilim.

I clenched my fingers over the scar on my palm. With a terrible certainty, I knew exactly how that power had been passed down to me.

"How'd you know to show up, I mean." My voice rang hollow in my ears. "You always seem to find me."

"A little bird told me." Lil gave me a look that rivaled the Mona Lisa.

"Lailah." It wasn't a question, and Lil didn't offer any confirmation. She was stubbornly close-lipped about herself and her sisters. Lil was the Lady of Beasts. Her sister Lailah was the Lady of Shades. Neither of them were strictly human beings.

Since her death, I'd only seen Lailah once. It was barely a vision, conjured by an old Streghoneri in a psychomanteum. She'd appeared first as a woman, then as a spectral, soot-colored owl. The image had haunted my dreams.

"She's watching me?" It came out desperate. I shut my mouth and stepped over the corpse, fighting not to stumble as another wave of vertigo spun my internal gyroscope.

"You better hurry it up," Lil warned, "unless it's your goal to end up in the prison system." She said nothing further about her sister. I let it drop.

Once I got to the car, Lil slipped behind the wheel and opened my door from the inside—a kindness which told me I looked way worse than I felt. She stowed the little knife, tidily wrapped in her handkerchief, in the armrest between the seats, and I dropped into the bucket seat, immediately banging my knees on the underside of the dashboard. The passenger side was set all the way forward.

"Who did you have in here last?" I growled as I fumbled for the lever. "Tyrion Lannister?"

Lil pulled her door shut and hit the locks.

"Who?"

"*Game of Thrones?*" I prompted. She gave me a blank look as she put the car into gear. "Never mind," I mumbled. Lil never watched TV—I wasn't certain she even owned one.

"Geek babble," she said. "I guess that means you're feeling better." Then she shot me a look out of the corner of her eye. "Try not to get blood on the seat. It's a bitch to get out of the leather."

Gunning the motor, she backed the car off the curb, then hit the brakes so abruptly, I nearly kissed the windshield. An instant later, the car lurched forward, slamming my shoulders back against the headrest.

"Holy fuck, Lil." I flailed for the seatbelt.

"Wimp," she shot back.

She peeled away from the cemetery, tires squealing, and took the turn onto Coventry at approximately warp speed. Lil's driving tied my stomach in knots on a good day. In my current state, she was going to have to worry about more than blood on the seats.

"You going to tell me what happened back there?"

I hunched forward as if I could physically hold myself together.

"What are you even doing in Cleveland?" I asked. "It's a six hour drive from Joliet."

"So that's a 'no,'" she replied.

Given the time, the traffic light at Euclid Heights had switched to a blinking red. Lil didn't bother to slow, just banked sharply right and headed toward my apartment building. She swung the car into a parking space in a maneuver so swift it made the world spin. Once the engine was off, she stared at me, pecking the steering wheel with her fingernails. For once, they weren't painted red.

"Are those shamrocks?" I asked, blinking stupidly.

Lil extended her hands like a model in a Palmolive commercial. "One of the girls did them for me. I'm not sure about the rhinestones, though."

"Now I know I'm delirious," I mumbled. My brain—which was already limping along thanks to shock and blood loss—felt as if it had just encountered the conversational equivalent of rumble strips.

"It's for St. Patrick's Day," Lil explained. She slid open her sable driving coat to reveal an emerald green blazer over a black, plunging V-neck. Sweeping green palazzo pants completed the outfit. "I had my burlesque troupe perform at Remy's Lusty Leprechaun event, over at Club Heaven."

I just gaped at her. Lil hated the Nephilim even more than I did, so for her to do anything at Club Heaven aside from tearing the place up was hard to swallow. Of course, both of us made exceptions for my sibling Remy. As Nephilim went, he was tolerable—even likable. Lil "tolerated" him well enough that she'd married him, once upon a time—somewhere back in the thirties, though it had ended messily.

"Lusty Leprechaun?" I managed. "You dance in a *burlesque* troupe?"

She arched an eyebrow. "Think of me as multi-talented—good at dancing *and* killing things."

I settled my head against my hands.

"Remy needed dancers, and I hadn't danced with the girls in a while," she continued blithely. "I might hate Sal, but I have to admit, he's always been good at making money for his performers."

"*She*," I corrected automatically.

Lil rolled her eyes, but didn't bother to amend the pronoun.

Saliriel was the head of the Nephilim in Cleveland, ruling under the title of "decimus." Sal was the actual owner of Club Heaven and, somewhere along the line, had decided that life would be better as a woman. I had plenty of reasons to dislike Sal, but I saw no point in being an ass about her life choices—at least, not the ones that didn't involve her being an incredibly manipulative sociopath.

Lil didn't share my magnanimity, and made no pretense at steering the conversation away from the topic. Her storm-gray eyes flickered over the mess on my jeans.

"I'm still waiting to hear what fire I pulled your skinny ass out of this time."

"How about I get out of these pants first?" I picked at the blood clotting in a seam.

Lil made a decidedly salacious sound at the back of her throat. "Killing makes me frisky, too," she purred.

"Stuff it, Lil," I said. "I'm just tired of smelling blood." Clicking my seatbelt off, I got out of the car. Standing up made my vision tunnel.

"You going to make it all the way up to your apartment?" she asked. All the teasing flirtation was gone, replaced with an expression that almost passed for genuine concern.

Gripping the rag-top, I nodded. I found it oddly comforting that not everything had miraculously fixed itself. That meant I was still somewhere close to human.

11

I dragged myself up the two flights of stairs without falling over. *Yay me.* Sagging against my front door, I fumbled for my keys. Lil hovered near my elbow, gray eyes fixed on my—no doubt—ashen features.

I pushed the door open and lurched inside. Lil stepped after me, pausing at the threshold.

"Aren't you going to invite me in?" she asked, looking at me sweetly. I'd have made a vampire joke at her expense, but just then it was a little close to home. She wasn't the one tossing around the powers of the Nephilim. Instead, I waved vaguely.

"Come in," I muttered. Dropping my keys on the side table, I went straight for my little kitchenette. I needed liquids desperately, and had to have some orange juice or something.

I didn't remember the last time I'd gone out for groceries, and it showed. While I dug around in my decidedly empty fridge, Lil paced a tight circle in my living room. Her stormy gaze settled on all the empty take-out cartons and abandoned coffee mugs. She pursed her lips, then whistled her disapproval. The only thing that separated my kitchen from the rest of the living space was a little half-wall set up as a kind of breakfast bar. I glared over it.

"Don't start," I grumbled.

Striding smartly over to the breakfast bar, she eased her hip onto one of two stools sitting there.

"You always were a champion sulker, when you put your mind to it," she said. "So how long have you been depressed? Your place didn't look this bad a month ago."

I dragged a half-empty bottle of orange juice from the furthest reaches of the fridge. The fluid inside swirled thickly, and it was a week past the expiration date. I lifted the cap to check it anyway, reeling back in disgust. With a string of unhappy expletives, I chucked it into the wastebasket, where it balanced precariously on top of all the other trash.

"I'm not depressed," I objected, turning to the coffee maker. Coffee was good. Coffee was something I knew I still had. "Just got a lot on my mind."

"So next you'll tell me you're perfectly fine after that fight." Lil made a skeptical noise, tapping her nails against the counter. "Weren't you getting out of those pants?"

"Hunh?" I looked up from where I was struggling— and failing—to separate a single coffee filter from all the rest.

"Pants, Zack. You're still walking around in your bloody pants. Are you going to tell me what has you so rattled—or did they knock you stupid with a blow to the head?"

Still holding the coffee filters, I looked down. "Pants. Right." Moving past her, I headed back to the apartment's single bedroom. She plucked the coffee filters from my hands, then trailed after me, halting at the beginning of the hall.

"You drop dead back there and I'm going to do horrible things to your corpse," she threatened.

I slammed the door. Moving unsteadily, I shucked off my jeans. The process seemed more awkward than it ought to be. The blood had soaked through everything. I had to lose the boxer-briefs, too. I was halfway through this process when I remembered I was still wearing my leather jacket. With my boxers tangled around my ankles, I fumbled with the jacket, everything below dangling in the wind. When I finally unzipped the leather to shrug it off, Halley's collection of scribbled papers drifted to the floor.

I stared at the rows and rows of channeled symbols. The repeating three leapt out at me, and suddenly they seemed familiar in a way they hadn't before. A name whispered at the edges of memory.

Terhuziel.

I hadn't known that name before.

I dropped to my bed with a muttered curse. Whisper Man had been riding shotgun in Fish-Knife Lady's head, and I'd plucked out his name when I'd taken everything else from her. Life, knowledge, memories, all swallowed with just a touch. That wasn't something I should be able to do—not as one of the Anakim. Those were Nephilim powers. Abilities I'd briefly borrowed that bleak night last November, courtesy of the Eye of Nefer-Ka.

The Eye was the icon of the Nephilim primus, a dauntingly old artifact created to share his skills with those chosen as heralds. All the tribal heads had an icon, and the items had caused such chaos among my extended family, the primae had sworn never to use them after the Blood Wars. As part of a grand pact, every icon had been hidden away—buried and lost to the passage of time. That was until Dorimiel, the asshole who'd swallowed my memories, had turned up the Eye while he was banging around Egypt with Napoleon.

"Zack?" Lil called. "Everything OK in there?"

I didn't answer. In point of fact, I couldn't answer. Saliriel had oathed me, preventing me from speaking about the Eye of Nefer-Ka. Sal had played me in a bid to get the icon for herself. What she *didn't* know was that Dorimiel had acquired not one, but *two* of the ancient objects—the Nephilim Eye and the Anakim Stylus, belonging to my tribe. I'd managed to divest Dorimiel of both.

I'd tapped into the Eye's powers to use them on him. It was the only way to free Lil's sister, or any of the others he'd bound away in demon jars. In order to use it, however, there had to be blood. The scar on my palm was a reminder that I'd willingly paid the price.

Then the Eye had gone to the bottom of Lake Erie. I'd hoped like hell that losing the icon would sever the tie.

No such luck.

"Zack…"

Flexing the fingers of my left hand, I tilted my palm to the bedroom light. The pale scar tracing across the middle of my palm didn't look any different. It was just a scar, healed to a thin, textured line.

No pretending now. The bond was still there. I wondered what else that might mean for me.

Lil rapped her knuckles and called through the door.

"You don't give me an answer this instant, I'm going to come in and drag one out of you."

"Hold on." Moping on my bed, naked from the waist down, wasn't how I wanted Lil to walk in on me. I scrambled for something to replace my jeans. Almost all my clothes were in the dirty pile heaped up on the chair in the living room. My Millennium Falcon pajama pants were near at hand, though, so I grabbed those. I went to slip into them—only to discover I still had my boxer-briefs tangled around my feet.

Impatiently, I kicked out of the underwear, then slid the pajamas up to my waist.

"I'm not dead," I called irritably.

"Prove it," Lil said, throwing wide the door.

If I had greeted her by smacking her between the eyes with a rubber mallet, she couldn't have looked more stunned. She blinked rapidly for several seconds, her brain clearly stripping gears.

"What the *hell* are you wearing?" she choked.

"T-shirt," I replied. "Pajama pants."

"There is a raccoon on your T-shirt. Riding a tree."

"You don't watch movies much, do you?" I asked.

"None of the movies I watch involve raccoons in jumpsuits riding trees," she snorted. "You look like an idiot."

"Laugh it up," I said sourly. Then I caught a familiar and fortifying scent wafting from the kitchen. "You made coffee?"

"Considering you were too dazed to even figure out how the filters worked, it seemed like the safest choice for us both," she answered.

I pushed past her, bee-lining for the kitchen. Coffee sounded like the best thing on the planet in that moment.

12

" You have your damned coffee now," Lil said, leaning on the counter across from me. "So tell me what the hell happened outside of Lake View that ended with you covered in that much blood."

She tilted her cleavage in a maneuver I knew was calculated. Her V-neck plunged so deep I could see the edges of something black and lacy. A tantalizing scent of spice and vanilla began overpowering the coffee. I stalwartly directed my attention elsewhere.

"A couple of Whisper Man's lackeys jumped me," I answered.

She shifted, and the view grew even more distracting. I angled away from her on the stool, riveting my eyes on my calendar. David Tennant's Doctor peered back at me, wielding his trusty sonic screwdriver. The month was still set to February—and we were halfway through March already. Maybe Lil had a point about the depression.

"Someone new is trying to kill you?" she inquired archly. "You have such a talent for making friends."

She tired of the game of taunting me with her cleavage. Rolling her shoulders a little, she began to pace while cradling her own mug.

"I'm not sure he's a someone so much as a some*thing*," I replied.

"Do tell," she encouraged.

Warmth prickled my hands where they gripped the mug of coffee, reminding me how cold I felt all over—not a familiar sensation for me. Plunking my elbows onto the counter, I pressed the mug against my forehead, willing the heat to chase the spins away. My eyes fluttered shut for just a moment.

"Some time this year, Anakim," Lil prodded.

With effort, I focused again on the woman standing on the other side of the counter. My lids felt gritty.

"There's this girl named after a comet," I explained, "and she's writing all this weird crap in a language I can't read. Kind of looks like Hittite, but not quite."

"You can't read it?" Her tone was incredulous.

"I said that already," I snapped. I almost lost my train of thought, but it came back to me with effort. "Her mom thought her dead grandfather was talking in her head, but it's definitely not her grandfather.

"Why do you want to know this stuff anyway?" I asked.

"I don't need a reason," she replied. "Just keep talking."

So I recounted the highlights concerning Whisper Man, Halley, and the crazed hobo army. It took me a while—my thoughts felt sluggish even with the jolt of caffeine. Lil paced and interjected periodically, steering me toward clarity. She poured herself a refill, then paused to lean against my fridge.

"A possession," she mused. "So that's what dragged you outside after nearly a month."

"I knew it!" I cried. "You've been watching me."

She took a careful sip, expression inscrutable through the steam.

"It hasn't been a whole month, has it?" I objected.

"Not that you would know from your calendar," she responded dryly.

I resisted the urge to get up and change it just to shut her up. I think she noticed, because she smirked. With me, Lil delighted in every awkward moment she could inspire. The fact that I couldn't remember *why* she teased me seemed to amuse her even more.

"You've told me all about the fight at the house, and the strange things this mortal girl can do, but you keep dancing around one troublesome hole." She fixed me with her hurricane gaze, and I was struck for a moment how much her face was shaped like Lailah's. "There was a *lot* of blood out there, Zaquiel. I didn't see any open wounds on the dead woman. So if all that blood was yours, how are you still walking around? You're immortal, not indestructible."

I opened my mouth—and ran headlong into my oath. The answer involved the Eye, so I couldn't say shit about it. I made a frustrated noise and glared at the dregs in my cup.

My sluggish thoughts stumbled around the barrier with little success. Fortunately, Lil knew about both the Eye and the binding, so it took her only a few moments to figure out what was halting me.

She wasn't happy about it.

"The Eye again?" she demanded. "I *told* you not to use it, Zaquiel. Those icons were buried for a reason."

I shrugged, unable to answer. "Plus side, still breathing," I muttered. I could manage that much at least.

The only living person with whom I could discuss it was Saliriel, and I'd crawl over a mile of rusty, tetanus-laced cheese graters before I approached her to talk about what had happened on that sidewalk outside of Lake View.

"That's what you meant when you said you ate her," Lil hissed. "Mother's Tears, Zack. You have no idea what that thing is doing to you."

I rolled a shoulder as dismissively as possible, but I'd been thinking much the same thing. The prospect was terrifying. I tolerated Remy, but I wanted nothing to do with the Nephilim. The way they were tied to their blood unnerved me on a profoundly visceral level. As one of the Anakim, I was technically vampiric—all the scintillating power I could throw around was fueled by people—but I took what I needed in little sips and dregs out of the air. It was all ethereal, tied to emotion. It was nothing like Remy's tribe.

They had fangs for fuck's sake.

"You have to sever your tie with the thing," Lil said. She started pacing again. The heels of her expensive leather boots clicked with metronomic precision.

"Wish I'd thought of that," I managed curtly. It was a struggle even to get that much out.

If I really wanted to be rid of my ties to the thing, I'd

have to find someone else I trusted to pay the price. No candidates sprang to mind. It was moot, anyhow, since the damned Eye was at the bottom of Lake Erie.

"You have a real talent for fucking yourself over," Lil said, and she hissed a string of colorful expletives in a long-dead tongue.

"Tell me something I don't know." I plunked my empty coffee mug down much harder than intended and pushed away from the counter. The stool nearly toppled when the back legs connected with the little hump separating the tile from the carpet. Snarling my own string of curses, I kicked the stool the rest of the way over, then stomped over to the sofa. I flopped down across the cushions as muscles in my shoulders, neck, and back complained about what a rotten day they'd had.

"Temper, temper," Lil chided.

"Giving me shit about it isn't going to change anything," I replied. "Maybe you could try being helpful for once?"

"I'm very helpful." Lil settled into the easy chair across from me, tucking her legs under herself as she sat. "I picked you up before the cops could find your sorry ass, didn't I? Even made you coffee," she pointed out. "You think I make everyone coffee?"

I grunted my response. The couch was distractingly comfortable. I heard her blow across her mug, then take a careful sip. It took me too long to work out that I had closed my eyes. Fluttering them open, I squinted blearily.

"When's the last time you slept, Zaquiel?" she inquired.

She sounded suddenly closer, as if she had teleported out of the chair. I looked up to see her standing over me. My brain told me that was a bad thing, but my body made it clear it was too tired to give a shit. The body won the vote. I rolled over and answered with my face buried in the upholstery. Even I wasn't certain what I said.

"You're so lucky I actually like you," she whispered.

The implicit threat of mischief chased me down into my dreams.

13

Lailah waited for me. She was dark and beautiful and entirely solid. In every dream prior to this, she had been nothing more substantial than a shade. Black hair swirled in the sighing gusts of wind, spreading across her shoulders like a cloak of ebon silk. She wore a simple shift dyed a Tyrian hue. It clung to every curve, leaving arms and shoulders bare. Her warm skin glowed with a vibrancy that almost made me forget that she was dead.

Almost.

No feathers this time, but the owl was present in the shape of her eyes—huge and black and inscrutable.

"Are you really here?" I wondered.

She reached out to touch me and I backed away, afraid that contact might shiver her presence in the dream. The ground slid treacherously beneath my foot. I whirled only to find that I was backed against a precipice. Waters boiled at the bottom, black as tar. With sick fascination, I stared into their churning depths.

Scarlet eyes and razor-blade teeth glinted in the dark. Cacodaimons. They weren't *in* the water. They *were* the water, writhing like a sea of slick, black flesh.

"Just a nightmare, then," I whispered mournfully.

The Eye of Nefer-Ka—set in a huge, gold amulet styled as an Eye of Horus—weighed heavily against my hand. I could feel the bite of the artifact where the ancient stone drew blood from the gash on my palm. The wound throbbed in time to my heart, and an answering glow of ugly crimson pulsed deep within the gem. A rush of whispers surged within my mind—nothing English, but I comprehended well enough. Promises of knowledge, memory, power. And all I had to do was feed the icon.

"Don't look down there." Lailah reached up to turn my face away. Words floated on her breath like distant music. "Not yet. Be here with me."

I could feel the influence of the Eye twining through my veins. It burned like the venom of a particularly vile snake. I thought of the woman—driven by Whisper Man—whose life I'd stolen to cheat death, and felt the hunger to kill again. With an inarticulate shout, I hurled the icon from my hand and pitched it into the abyss. The antique gold with its inlays of lapis and jet turned end over end before finally sinking into the living mass of cacodaimons that writhed at the bottom. The sanguine light pulsing from the Eye winked out in the darkness.

"Zaquiel, please," Lailah pleaded. "I know you're afraid, but don't waste this."

The answering pulse still throbbed through the wound in my palm. I shook my hand, scattering fat drops of crimson in a gleaming arc. The thrumming weight of connection clung to my fingers, my wrist, gnawing the bones of my arm. Desperately, I squeezed the edges of the cut, trying to force the poison back out. More blood welled up, and I saw images in its depths— an endless march of screaming faces. I blinked away the swirling phantasmagoria, stumbling nearer to the edge of the cliff.

Lailah reached out, and started shaking me.

The lip of stone crumbled. I nearly lost my footing, pebbles raining on the beasts below. I spread my wings to catch myself. She dragged me from the edge.

"Don't go after it yet," she said, gently leading me away from the vicious drop. Her voice was velvet strung upon the air.

"I wasn't going to keep it," I choked, not sure if I was trying to convince her or myself. The rapid rhythm of my heart lent a tremor to my voice. I swallowed hard against it. As she watched me, I swore I could see whole galaxies swirling in the depths of her black eyes.

Softly, she murmured, "You may not have a choice."

A steely rush of rebellion routed my fear. "I always have a choice," I snapped, more heated than I'd intended. The sadness in her features deepened, slim black brows drawing together.

"Do you?" she asked.

The anger boiled over, dozens of retorts bursting from my throat. I was better than that. I wasn't a monster. I didn't need that kind of bargain—excuse after excuse. The words shook the air with power, stirring her hair, though she did not flinch. She listened while I ranted, then finally, moving with a languid grace as if she were underwater, she laid a finger against my lips.

"Sssh, Zaquiel."

I wanted to believe in the soothing, sensual presence behind that touch. Wanted so badly to reconnect.

"I barely remember you," I murmured against her flesh. It was both apology and excuse.

"I remember you," she affirmed.

My mind still struggled with her presence in this space. The cacodaimons, the windswept plain—all of it was a dream, and the woman standing before me could be nothing more than a bitter tease conjured by my tortured subconscious.

"You can't be here. You can't be real," I insisted, seeking ways to poke holes in what I was seeing. "The Eye. Sal's oathed me—I can speak to no one. Yet here I am, speaking with you."

"You cannot speak with any *living* being," she reminded me. "Every oath has a loophole. You can speak about it with me."

"Loopholes," I scoffed bitterly. "That's something Sal would say."

Her voice caressed like silk as she whispered to me. "This is really me. I'm here with you in this moment, Zaquiel. I am the Lady of Shades. Do you think death can stop me?" She reached up and trailed cool fingers along my cheek. I seized her hand, brushing it lightly with my lips. She tasted of spice and sweetness.

"This is just a nightmare," I protested. "I'll wake to find you gone."

"So don't wake up yet, *majnun*," she encouraged.

She closed the distance between us. In the feel of

her body pressed against mine, all doubts melted. My awareness narrowed to the heat of her flesh. I took her face in my hands and kissed her. Entire worlds were born and blinked from existence in the mystery of that embrace. Wrapping my wings around us, I held her close. I lifted her. She locked her thighs around my waist, and we danced, closer.

Precious, stolen moments in the space between dreaming and death.

14

Waking, I found my neck angled painfully against the arm of the couch. My thoughts staggered, sleep-thick, through the vestiges of dream. I stretched my legs—only to have the movement arrested by the arm at the other end. I wasn't exactly sized to fit the thing.

"I thought you'd never wake up."

I jerked toward the voice in the kitchen, choking. "Lailah?"

Lil scoffed. "Just for that, no coffee for you."

I dropped back against the cushions with a groan. Sexing up my dead girlfriend in dreams? I'd *definitely* spent too much time alone.

"With the noise you were making, I thought you were having a nightmare," Lil observed. I could hear the clink of a spoon rhythmically swirling against ceramic. Had she done my dishes? We'd used up the last of the clean mugs the night before. I peeled back an eyelid to see.

If Lil was being domestic, it had to be a trap.

The Lady of Beasts moved through my kitchen like

119

she owned the place. She raised her cup and took a sip.

"When I checked on you, I realized it was an entirely different thing," she said bemusedly, and she clucked her tongue, lips curling in an ironic grin. Her eyes were fixed on me. I followed the direction of her gaze—and immediately grabbed one of the pillows from the couch. I dropped it over my lap.

"For fuck's sake, Lil," I cried. "Privacy? Decency? Are they even in your vocabulary?"

"Zaquiel," she cooed. "You act like I've never seen your little soldier before." Her grin widened as she craned her neck, pretending to peer beyond the barrier of the pillow. "Well, not-so-little soldier," she amended. She took a long, luxurious swallow of her coffee, gray eyes dancing with salacious delight.

I launched the pillow at her head. Her hand snapped up. She caught it. She didn't even spill the contents of her mug.

"Do you ever quit?" I demanded through gritted teeth.

"No," she said, and laughed. She returned fire with the pillow and bounced it off my chest. I choked back a series of unpleasant words that leapt to my throat. Angling my hips self-consciously, I swung my legs around and sat up on the couch. The fabric of the pajama pants was really thin.

Fuck my life.

"Don't stand up too fast," she warned. "You might get dizzy. Not enough blood to go around."

I snarled at her.

"Why, Zaquiel, I was referring to the blood loss from

last night." She fluttered one hand against her cleavage like some blushing Southern Belle.

"It's too early for this shit," I grumbled, dragging my fingers through the tangle of my hair. Half of it was sticking up at right angles to the rest, thanks to the way I'd been lying.

"It's nearly one in the afternoon," she replied. "You slept *hard*."

I smacked my hand into my forehead with a groan. "Come on, Lil. Really?"

She grinned, showing all her white teeth.

"I need a fucking shower."

"Cold?" she suggested with a smirk.

"Shut. Up," I snapped, stomping past her to the bathroom. Her maddeningly sexy laugh followed me down the hall. Lil could be such a brat… and I think I'd kind of missed it.

Shoving that thought aside to pick apart later, I got the water going. Cranking the heat as high as I could stand it, I peeled off my T-shirt and pajama pants and dropped everything on the floor in a heap. Little flakes of dried blood drifted onto the tiles.

Yuck.

Steam billowed from the shower, helping to clear my head. I pushed the curtain aside and stepped into the needling spray. One thing I could say about my apartment building, we never hurt for good water pressure.

I lathered up and scrubbed away the dirt and gore. There was a scar above my femoral—white, already fading. I tried to pretend that didn't bother me. Not that inhuman healing was a bad thing—it was the cost

MICHELLE BELANGER

at which I'd accomplished it. Taking a life just to keep myself going? That was a habit I wanted to avoid.

Replays of the fight flickered behind my eyes in wretched, gruesome color—the expression locked upon the woman's features, the way her skin had blanched as I drained away her life. My brain wasn't a fan of sparing me in flashbacks. I had a near-photographic memory—one more reason the amnesia was such a kick in the teeth.

I tried focusing on the feel of the water as it sluiced over sore muscles. That helped a little. I bent at the knees so I could tilt my face up to the spray. Some day I would get an apartment with a shower tall enough for me. Some day.

Turning, I wiped water away from my nose. The growth of beard bristled against my palm and I grimaced. *Fuck it.* I grabbed my razor, tired of people staring at me like I was an escapee from a mental hospital anyway. I made two passes over my chin. By the third stroke, the disposable made it clear that it wasn't up to the task. I tossed it back into the shower caddy.

Once I finished with the shower, I dragged my old electric razor out from under the sink. I had to take a spare towel and wipe at the mirror to see what I was doing. Even so, the glass steamed up again almost immediately. I buzzed away the worst of the whiskers, grabbed the shaving cream, and bicced the rest. Then I examined my handiwork in the streaking mirror.

Aside from a couple of nicks on my jaw, I almost looked human again. Well, like a human-shaped person, at least. My hair was still a haystack, but I'd deal with that when I had time for a barber. Whisper Man came first.

Wrapping a towel around my waist, I grabbed my pile of clothes and slipped down the hall. I hoped there was something clean back in the bedroom—though given how little motivation I'd had lately, there was no guarantee.

Digging around in the "kind-of-clean" and "mostly-clean piles," I found one black T-shirt with a Ravenclaw logo, and a reasonably fresh pair of jeans. Socks and boxers required some serious excavation, but I found a few pairs tucked away in the furthest reaches of my dresser.

I really needed to get off my ass and clean this shit.

"Zack!"

Lil's tone was particularly strident.

"What?"

She marched to the head of the hall and stood there, gray eyes flashing.

"What the hell do you think you're doing?"

I blinked stupidly at her. "Getting dressed?"

She brandished something at me. It was about the size and shape of a No. 2 pencil.

Shit!

"A *pen* cup?" Her voice cracked with emotion. "You're keeping this in a *pen* cup? Have you taken leave of what little sense you have left?" The crisp afternoon light angling through the kitchen window caught the carved and yellowed bone of the Stylus— the icon of the Anakim primus.

"Oh, that," I said, trying for nonplussed. "Where the fuck else can I keep it?"

She threw her hands up in aggravation. "A bank vault?

123

A lead-lined case, at least? Mother's Tears, Zaquiel, I'd have never handed it back to you if I thought you'd be this careless. Do you know the kind of trouble this thing can cause?"

"Could we discuss this once I have pants on?" I slammed the bedroom door and locked it before she could argue—because Lil always argued. It was one of her superpowers, right along with the ability to ooze sexy pheromones. I hastily finished throwing on the clean clothes I'd managed to acquire, stepped out into the hall—and stopped dead.

Lil was standing so close to my bedroom door, I almost crashed into her. She looked up at me, one hand on her hip and the Stylus pointed accusingly.

"I swear you need a babysitter," she huffed.

I plucked the icon from her outstretched hand. She didn't resist, and she certainly could have. Striding past her, I headed toward my computer desk. Lil trotted after me, working to keep up with my long legs.

Moving the cup back to its carefully chosen place on my desk, with a certain gravitas I slipped the Stylus among the bristling collection of pens, take-out chopsticks, and mechanical pencils. Then I turned to face her wrath.

"How long did it take you to see it?"

Her brows stitched. "I noticed it just now."

"Don't you think you should have sensed it the minute you walked through the door?" I persisted. I was actually proud of this work—it was the best fix I'd come up with, given the few tools and memories I had left.

"You warded it," she said, realization dawning. Lil's

eyes narrowed, flicking across the lines of my desk. "The pen cup. The whole desk." What she didn't bother pointing out was the fact that she typically picked up on wards the instant she encountered them.

I'd managed something so subtle, even she hadn't noticed it without me pointing it out. I counted that a smashing success.

"I haven't just been sitting around and fucking off," I told her. I gestured to the laden shelves around my living room. "I've got notes and theories scribbled in the margins of practically every book here. I've been reading. Learning what I can."

"Funny," Lil said. "From the sticky notes on your computer, it looks more like you've been playing something called *Assassin's Creed*."

"Got to do something to amuse myself," I responded defensively.

"Normal people go out and have sex," she quipped.

I glared at her. She glared back. We stood and had a glare-off as the seconds ticked by. To my surprise, Lil broke first. She loosed a sigh of exasperation.

"You're missing my point, flyboy," she persisted. "It needs to be locked away."

"Where, exactly?" I demanded. "I can't think of any place safe enough. I get a bank vault, and then what? I die. Who gets their hands on it after that? It's not like I can leave it to myself. I don't know where I'll turn up next, or even *if* I will." I caught my breath as that last part came rushing out. It wasn't something I'd admitted out loud till just then.

Fear.

The attack outside of Lake View had really driven the point home. I was afraid of dying—of getting lost once this body was dead. Immortality didn't count for shit if I couldn't remember how it worked, and I wasn't certain that I did any more.

Lil blinked up at me, and my face must have held some intimation of my troubled thoughts. Her own expression shifted through so many different emotions, it was difficult to parse. Finally, she huffed a sigh, pushing a thick lock of red hair back from her eyes.

"I see your point, Zaquiel," she conceded, "but power attracts power. You've got two icons in this city now, and they both tie back to you. You need a better strategy than a warded pen cup." She started saying something else, but then the phone rang. We both comically over-reacted to the unexpected noise from my kitchen.

"I bet that's the padre," I said, willing myself to relax. Then I remembered that he didn't have the number for the new landline. The voice on the other end was still familiar. It was Bobby Park of the Cleveland PD.

"Zack?" he said. "You answered." He sounded startled. "I was going to leave a message."

"I can hang up and let you call back," I offered, half-serious.

Bobby laughed, though it seemed more from nerves than appreciation for my rapier wit.

"Nah. This is fine. I called to ask a favor. You free later tonight?"

Despite the fact that I hadn't talked with him in at least three months, he spoke with the easy familiarity of an old friend. I knew we'd been acquainted before

Dorimiel ate my brain, but I'd never asked how, and he'd never offered. That might have been a bad call on my part.

I didn't want another surprise like Father Frank.

"That depends," I said. I paced with the handset as Lil curiously examined the wards traced lightly along the edges of my desk. "What do you need?"

There was a pause on the other end, and I could readily imagine the trim little officer rubbing the back of his head where his black hair was buzzed short. It was a nervous gesture, and I'd seen it often enough.

"Case came in last night, and your name came up," he started. "This guy was all cut up—"

"I didn't do it," I said a little too quickly.

"Hunh?"

"You're talking about the Davis thing, right? That guy came like that," I said. "You can ask Potts and Roarke."

Lil gave me a querulous look from the sidelines. I gestured for her to mind her own business.

Bobby laughed, more awkward, less nervous.

"Jeez, Zack. Jumpy much?"

"Sorry. Kind of had a rough night."

"*Kind of?*" Lil mouthed with an exaggerated expression. I scowled, then put my back to her. I curled my wings around myself, knowing she could see them— though I doubted she'd take the hint.

"Hey, don't sweat it," Bobby said reassuringly. "I was putting off calling anyway. If this is a bad time—"

"It's not going to get any better," I said, running my thumb over a spot where I'd nicked my jaw.

Lil snorted behind me. I ignored her.

"So what do you need from me?" I asked as Bobby fumbled for a response.

He sighed, the handset making it sound like a windstorm. "The guy at the Davis house, he had these weird letters carved in his chest. You saw them, right?"

"Yeah," I said, not certain I liked where this was going.

Park hesitated, like he expected me to say more. When I didn't, he said, "I was wondering if you could read them, is all. They look an awful lot like something from another case that has me and my partner stumped."

"Hmph," I muttered. I left it at that.

"Could you come in, take a look at the photos? Off the record, of course," he added. "It'll be like old times."

Old times?

That was interesting. From messages I'd left myself last November, I knew I had a history with Park. While he was working on the *Scylla* investigation, he'd hinted that he sometimes did me favors. With the amnesia, I hadn't known what to expect from that, and frankly, I hadn't trusted the implication. When I hadn't pursued it, he'd let the matter drop. That, too, might have been a mistake.

"Sure. All right," I agreed. "When?"

Lil hissed sharply to get my attention. With mounting irritation, I waved her away, still trying to pretend my conversation with Bobby was some variation of private.

"In an hour?" he ventured. "Or—you know— whenever you can make it. I'll be here most of the night."

I glanced at the clock. Close to two thirty. I'd promised Father Frank that I'd try to translate Halley's papers.

"Got a couple of things I need to tie up here, but I'll swing around," I responded.

Suddenly Lil reached up behind me and grabbed one of my wings. She dug her fingers in, right at the joint. Jerking, I almost yelped into the phone. I didn't even know she could do that. Turning as best as I could, I shot her a warning glare. She stood, holding the stack of Halley's scribbled pages in one hand, the other locked firmly on the joint.

"Let go," I hissed.

"I didn't catch that last bit," Bobby said.

"Couple hours, Bobby," I answered quickly. "You still at the station on Chester?" I tugged my wing, but Lil held firm. It was the weirdest sensation. I fought down an unreasonable swell of panic.

"That's the one."

"Good," I said in a rush. "See you then. Gotta go." I hung up before he could ask anything further, reached around, and swatted at Lil's hand.

"Is this the language?" she demanded.

"What the hell, Lil?" I cried. "Let go of me."

"This is Luwian," she said, shaking the pages in my face.

My wing was starting to cramp where she dragged on it. I tried to flex and pull away, but she had me in some kind of joint lock. If she didn't let go soon, I was going to retaliate, and I didn't fully trust myself to pull my punches.

"Lil, seriously—you need to let go right the fuck now."

"I think you're dealing with one of the Rephaim," she insisted.

Instantly I forgot about the wing.

15

"Rephaim?" I said, almost choking. "What makes you say that?"

She'd finally let go, and I struggled with an urge to massage a muscle group that had no real substance in the flesh-and-blood world. I settled for twitching the invisible appendage in her face instead. From the way Lil wrinkled her nose, it was payback enough.

"These are Luwian hieroglyphs," she explained, ignoring my continued antics as she spread the topmost paper out on the kitchen counter. She plunked down her coffee mug to anchor a curling corner. "This bit is a name," she said, tapping a nail over an iteration of the symbols that had caught my attention the night before. "Tarhunda."

"Terhuziel," I corrected automatically.

"No," she responded in a tone she might reserve for a thick-headed toddler. "*Tarhunda*. The Luwians didn't have that suffix your people are so hung up about."

"I look at those three symbols, and I see Terhuziel."

"I thought you couldn't read it," she replied.

131

Things got awkward then. Explaining that I'd sucked the knowledge out of the head of a dead homeless woman infringed upon my vow to keep the Eye a secret. I struggled for a moment, then gave up with a silent *fuck it*. The names were so close, it probably didn't matter anyway.

"Why, can *you* read it?" I managed.

Lil piqued a brow, but for once she let it slide. "You boys weren't the only ones knocking around back then, you know. You just act like you were." There was no real heat to it. "When you were babbling last night, you said the language reminded you of Hittite. I wanted to take a peek."

"I wasn't babbling," I objected—though I didn't even remember bringing up the Hittites.

"You were totally babbling. In shock, and then you passed out cold. You're lucky I didn't do something embarrassing to you while you slept." She shot me a look that was full of mischief, adding dramatically, "Or did I?"

I drew myself up to my full six foot three and gave her my most formidable glare. It fizzled without even a whimper.

"You're thirty-something and wearing a *Harry Potter* T-shirt, Zack," she said dryly. "I fail to be impressed."

"Do not meddle in the affairs of wizards," I responded, waggling my fingers in a gesture of make-believe summoning. Lil sighed and shook her head.

"Spare me the road trip through your geekdom." Still, it got a chuckle. Bolstered by that, I grabbed a clean mug from the drying rack and poured myself some coffee.

"What about these Luwians? I'm an expert on the

ancient cultures in that part of the world, and the name's not ringing any bells."

The coffee let me know that I was three steps short of starving. I rummaged around in my empty fridge, searching for anything not covered in mold that might pass for breakfast. I had to settle for one of the protein bars left in the pantry.

"You actually eat those things?"

Using my teeth to tear open the wrapper, I ignored her and bent back to the paper.

"I've got holes in my memory you could drive an oil tanker through," I admitted, "but not usually when it comes to raw data. What makes you say Luwian?"

Lil tried to drag her eyes away from the sight of the protein bar, a curl of disgust reaching one nostril.

"Just trust me. I know these symbols. They're from one of the ethnic cultures the mountain-fortress people gobbled up." She straightened, rolling her neck until the vertebrae cracked. From the look of thinly suppressed fury on her features, there was more to the story, but she didn't elaborate. Typical Lil.

"All right," I acknowledged. "So we have a name tied to a culture. That gives me a general idea of how to Google-whack this guy. Maybe he has some mythic weaknesses. What's the rest of it say?"

"The usual chest-beating deity stuff," she responded. Adopting a mockingly bombastic tone, she read, "'I am the Conqueror, mighty and glorious. Tarhunda is my name.'"

Terhuziel, my brain corrected, but I managed to keep it to myself. Lil shot me a look like she knew better. Flipping rapidly through the other pages, she continued, almost bored, "'My breath is the breath of the storm. I rule over land and sky. All bow before my power.' Blah, blah, blah. You get the picture." She tossed the stack casually onto the counter beside the first one.

Her recitation, mocking as it was, unearthed a full-body flashback to the voice outside of Lake View. Rattled, I covered it by making a show of very carefully balancing the wrapper of the energy bar on the mound of garbage in my trash.

"So this is an ancient god speaking through an autistic girl?" I quipped, still fighting to shake off the memory. "Wait till I break that to the padre."

Lil smacked me lightly on the arm. "No, Einstein. He only *thinks* he's a god. That's why I'm saying Rephaim. The Idol-Riders were all about setting themselves up as central figures of worship. Storm gods were a favorite, because once they settled into a domain, they could influence the weather."

"Terael doesn't do that," I objected.

"Probably doesn't have enough power. It's not like people make sacrifices to him in the art museum." She thought about it for a moment. "At least, I hope not," she amended.

"Not typically," I responded, leaving out the matter of three slain doves. "But if you're right, we've got a real problem."

"You mean beyond having a rogue Rephaim trying to establish himself somewhere in the city?"

"Your Tarhunda reads as Terhuziel to me. That's four syllables," I said, holding up four digits for emphasis. "That's a decimus."

"Bleeding Mother," Lil swore. She smacked the paper as if that could somehow transmit her aggravation to the owner of the name—and for all I knew, it might. Names were power, and among the tribes of my people, they embodied our identities, our abilities, and our ranks. Each syllable was a component of our magic, and the more syllables in a Name, the more power that sibling had at his disposal—by increasing orders of magnitude.

In the books crammed upon my shelves, I'd spilled a lot of ink theorizing about how all of this figured into our natures and our skills, as well as the source we tied back to as a group—because, apparently, we'd lost touch and couldn't agree on what precisely that origin was. Shut away over the past month, I'd had plenty of time to reacquaint myself with those writings.

The highest rank in each tribe was the primus. As the title implied, each group had only one. The Names of the primae held a total of five syllables, a base of three appended with a suffix spelled variously –iel, or –ael. No matter how it was spelled, that suffix was a word of power in and of itself, simultaneously expressing what we were and what we'd come from. Regardless of tribe, all the brethren shared that suffix and its otherworldly implications.

For every primus, there were ten who held the rank of decimus. The name of each decimus was four syllables in length—two for the base, plus the two-syllable suffix. At the bottom of the ladder were grunts like me. Three-syllable Names—we didn't get any fancy titles.

If a primus was king of the tribe, a decimus was a lord, except, as far as power went, it was more like warlord, chief, and master-wizard all rolled into one. Dorimiel had been a decimus of the Nephilim, and when I'd faced him last fall, he'd easily wiped the floor with me. Some of that had been the Eye, but even without the ancient icon, the guy had been no slouch. If not for Lil's timely intervention, he'd have gobbled me up—mind, body, and soul.

If we had another decimus in town, things could get ugly, fast.

"I need to pay a visit to Terael," I said.

"Ugh." Lil made no effort to suppress a shudder of revulsion. She harbored such a creeping distaste for the Rephaim, she wouldn't set foot near his domain inside the Cleveland Museum of Art.

"Once you get to know him, he's not that bad," I insisted.

"Sure," she responded, voice ringing with skepticism. "If crazed, omniscient entities whispering inside your head is your thing, then he's great."

"Omniscient is kind of a stretch." Although hearing her put it that way made me wonder why I hadn't connected Whisper Man with the Rephaim, and much sooner. That voice in my head had thundered with the same suffocating intensity that Terael sometimes possessed—though ratcheted up to a power of ten.

Terael wielded near-total influence over the security and electrical systems of the art museum, not to mention having the ability to manipulate the thoughts and dreams of its mortal staff. He'd made the entire security detail sleep through a gunfight, for Pete's sake. All that, and he considered his powers "diminished."

"I really don't know how you work with that thing in the same building," Lil grumbled.

"He's family," I objected, then I glanced up at the clock. Almost four. *Shit*—I'd agreed to meet with Bobby, and I still had to check in with Father Frank. I needed to clone myself or something. At least I had news about the language.

Harried, I started searching around for my leather jacket. Lil hooked a thumb toward the hall.

"Bedroom."

"Oh, right." I kind of remembered taking it off back there. Walking back, I grabbed the jacket, checking the SIG as I returned to the kitchen. The in-pocket holster was set for a left-hand draw, and while it wasn't perfect for quick access, it was still the best bet for concealment, given what I typically wore.

Lil eyed me as I cinched the buckle at my waist.

"You had your gun on you last night, and managed to get stabbed anyway?" she inquired archly. "You've really let yourself go."

I shot her a sour look. "They got the jump on me—literally. I had my hands full... and I got careless," I admitted. "Didn't even think I might have people following me. Won't make that mistake twice."

Lil clucked her tongue. "You better pay closer attention today, flyboy, because I'm not going to be there to save your ass."

"Who said you were coming with me, anyhow?" I asked, although I'd kind of assumed she would, given Lil's typical intractability. But she ignored my question.

"At five thirty, I'm meeting up with the Windy City

Vixens. I already ditched them for the tour through the Rock Hall to make sure you didn't wake up dead. I'm at least catching dinner with them before they head back home."

Again my mind boggled at the thought of Lil in a dance troupe. I could picture her dancing, sure, and burlesque fit her like a slinky velvet glove, but performing with other people? That bit refused to parse.

"Are these normal ladies you dance with?" I asked, searching for my keys in the pockets. Lil pointed to the stand beside the front door. I moved to grab them, adding, "You know, like mortals?"

She set her mug in the sink and started collecting her own stuff—car keys, blazer, the clutch purse that always seemed brimming with limitless useful items. She paused in front of one of my larger framed pieces—a folio page from a medieval book of hymns—and inspected her reflection in the glass. Ran her fingers through her wealth of dark red curls. Dabbed at the edge of her lipstick.

"You might hide yourself away with computer games and books, Zaquiel, but I prefer to have a life among people." Her tone, for once, lacked the usual acerbic bite. "What's the purpose of immortality if we don't stop to actually *live*?"

I opened my mouth for a witty retort, but had nothing. She zipped up her boots and took her sable driving coat from a hanger in my closet. It was like she'd moved into the place while I slept. Settling the coat on her shoulders, she lifted her wild locks of hair so they cascaded down her back like a scarlet capelet. I had the feeling I was missing something—something terribly pertinent—and if I stared at her just right, comprehension would gel like one of those Magic Eye pictures emerging from visual static.

For the life of me, though, all I could think of was the way I'd watched Lil stab a corpse repeatedly in the head with an ice pick so it couldn't become host to a cacodaimon while we both crouched in the murky halls of a retired Navy gunboat. Lil was efficient and brutal and terrifying—and she was being civil to me. There had to be sorcery afoot.

"You know, you didn't have to stay and look after me," I ventured.

With a deceptively prim gesture, she tucked her little white clutch purse in the crook of an elbow, then shot me a smile that reminded me of a stalking cat.

"Somebody has to. See you around, flyboy."

She let herself out.

16

With Lil's parting words still banging uneasily around in my brain, I headed down to the parking area behind my apartment. I'd meet up with Bobby first, since the station was right near the art museum. Then I'd check in with Terael. If another Rephaim really was present in the city, my statue-bound sibling would sense it—I hoped.

Terael was fond of pointing out that his perceptions only extended as far as the museum walls, but it was worth a shot. He'd at least have some advice for how to deal with this new presence if, indeed, Whisper Man turned out to be one of the Rephaim. I didn't know a whole lot about that tribe beyond what I'd observed with Terael. Specifically, I had no idea how to hurt them.

It was tough enough dealing with Nephilim, who healed so fast that bullets were mostly a nuisance. The Rephaim were disembodied intelligences anchored to stone. "Killing" one didn't exactly seem like it would be an option. Not that any of us ever stayed dead for very long.

Maybe I could *reason* with Whisper Man.

Yeah, right. I'd have better luck inviting a Sith Lord over for tea.

Once I had something solid, I'd swing by the hospital and check in with Father Frank. He needed an update on what was going on. He and Sanjeet had probably tried calling me about eighty times already. Hopefully they'd had a less eventful night than I'd had.

If there was any way to protect Halley from Whisper Man's influence, I'd do it—even if all I could manage was scribing wards around her hospital bed. The poor girl had enough trouble without one of my bat-shit crazy siblings clawing around inside her head.

Outside, dirty drifts of snow piled to either side of the asphalt lot. A low building with flat, corrugated roofing squatted near the back. It held four covered spaces for cars. One of them housed my motorcycle and the new car. I hadn't quite gotten used to thinking of the car as mine. My old one—a lumbering Buick older than most college students—had been stolen the same time everything else in my life went to shit. The Buick never turned back up. For all I knew, it was at the bottom of the lake, too.

As a kind of consolation prize for her Machiavellian tendencies, my sibling Saliriel had bought me a bright, shiny Dodge Hellcat with more bells and whistles than a locomotive museum.

I hated it.

It was a gorgeous vehicle, no denying it, black and sleek with a profile reminiscent of the classic muscle cars from decades past. Some fragment of myself still lingering in my brain clung to a fondness for that type of automobile, and it was a safe bet Saliriel knew more about the previous me than I did. That must have influenced her choice of vehicular bribery.

When the Hellcat had showed up outside of my apartment building, along with keys, title, and a nicely penned note, I'd almost sent it right back to her. I still considered doing that. Sure, Sal's machinations had cost me, but the Dodge didn't match the part of my soul she'd extracted through her oath. To me the car was just another debt, and it was accruing interest with each passing minute.

Still, the insurance money from the stolen Buick would've barely covered a down payment, and I'd lost a lot of hours at work. So I drove the Dodge for the time being. Even I wasn't crazy enough to ride the motorcycle through a Cleveland winter.

It hadn't moved in close to a month, so I sat and let it warm up, sorting through the music I'd tossed on the passenger seat. The Hellcat came with some kind of fancy satellite radio hookup which I'd never bothered to learn. I still owned CDs. Hell, I'd found cassettes and eight tracks in my apartment, and from the range of titles, my musical tastes ran toward the eclectic.

Mahler. Sinatra. Tool. None of them appealed. I fished around in the divider between the seats, pulling out a battered iPod. I loosed its Gordian tangle of wires, plugging in the important bits. Choosing a playlist at random, I hit shuffle. As Billy Idol's familiar rebel yell started blasting through the speakers, I pulled onto the street.

The quickest route to the station was down Mayfield,

but that took me past Lake View. So I turned down Euclid Heights instead, and followed it all the way to Carnegie. The amnesia had robbed me of a lot of things, but my knowledge of the city's many back streets remained intact. As long as I didn't think too hard about it, I knew exactly where to go. It only got confusing when my knowledge of different time periods overlapped.

I pulled up to a corner with a traffic light. As the car idled, I glanced to my right, expecting to see a smoke shop. The garish colors of a McDonald's greeted me instead. A sharp sweep of nostalgia welled up, stealing my breath. I couldn't say why the place had been important, but I could practically see it still sitting there on the corner, shimmering through the fast food joint like a double-exposure on film.

I had a feeling that if I peered across to the Shadowside, the smoke shop would still be there, brimming with echoes of long-gone patrons. The patchwork of emotions this conjured was nuanced and complex. Intimations of meaning drifted on the very edge of thought.

The car behind me honked in irritation. The light was green. It had probably been green for a while. I sped up a little too quickly, feeling haunted by my own ghost.

Cutting down Stokes, I headed toward the big, rambling church that looked like it had a massive oilcan bolted to the top. It was a fixture in this part of town. The copper roofs—including the unfortunate oilcan-shaped spire—had weathered to a verdant green in the city's industrial rain, creating an unmistakable profile against the steely gray of the evening's gathering clouds.

The station on Chester Avenue was a broad brick

affair sprawling on a corner lot. I pulled around the building, finding visitor parking across from a row of squad cars. While Mick Jagger wailed about all his colors turning black, I eased the Hellcat into a space at the back corner of the lot. Killing the engine, I pulled out my SIG, double-checked the safety, then tucked the gun in the glove compartment. If I needed my pistol in the police department, something would've gone horribly, horribly wrong.

The Stones cut off abruptly as I opened the door. I thumbed a button on the fancy remote key fob, and the vehicle chirped twice. Arming the security system while the car sat in the parking lot of a police station seemed excessive. I did it anyway.

My cowl settled tight across my wings as I walked up the front steps, locking all my mental defenses into place. I'd spent enough time filling out paperwork at this station and I really didn't want to pick up on any of the emotional echoes that lingered inside its walls. Between the daily frustration of the officers and the ugly stew of anxiety, depravity, and guilt left behind by the worst of their offenders, I was happier feeling a little suffocated.

Bobby waited for me in the lobby. A compact figure with a slim, wiry build, he had a tightly wound intensity that practically vibrated on a molecular level. If it had been possible to harness the Korean-American officer's brimming energy, the cops might have leased him to Detroit to help power the failing grid. The instant Bobby caught sight of me, he flashed a cheery smile of such brilliant wattage that I felt like a total dick for ignoring him this long.

"Hey," I said, dipping my chin in an understated greeting.

Bobby swept over to me. I kept my hands stuffed in the pockets of my jacket. Like Father Frank, Bobby didn't bother trying for a handshake. The little officer—he couldn't have stood more than five foot four with his shoes on—rocked on his heels, pushing a sweep of gelled bangs back from his eyes. He held his arms out and did a half-turn, as if modeling.

"Notice anything?" he asked, a smile crinkling the edges of his eyes.

He wore a neatly pressed gray wool suit paired with a pale-yellow shirt that might have been silk. His blue tie had angled yellow stripes that were actually Minions marching across it, if you looked close enough. The suit looked tailored, and the cut of his wide-legged pants screamed more "club kid" than "gumshoe."

"You're out of uniform?" I asked.

"No more uniform!" he crowed. "You're looking at Detective-Investigator Bobby Park." He swept the edge of his suit jacket back with a flourish and flashed the badge he wore clipped at his belt.

"Oh, hey," I responded. "Congratulations."

He beamed. "They even put me with my old partner, David Garrett. Can't wait to re-introduce you two." He dialed back the smile, and asked, "How've you been? Growing your hair out again?"

I dashed a hand self-consciously through the unruly tangle. "Nah. Just lazy." Then I glanced around. "What did you need me to take a look at?"

"Pretty nasty case." Shadows like scudding clouds

darkened his buoyant expression. "But first, let's make you official." He held out a visitor tag.

I took it, frowning at my biker jacket. There was no good place to clip it and I didn't want to hurt the leather. I settled on clipping it to the end of one of the upper zippers. The laminated tag dangled precariously, but it held.

"I thought this was off the books?" I said warily.

Vigorously, Bobby nodded. "Just making sure nobody gives you grief. I'll try to keep things quick." He started walking, short legs pumping as he led me past the front desk. "I really appreciate you doing this for me, Zack. I didn't want to bug you—I really didn't—but this case, it's got so many things that make no sense."

I followed mutely behind, wondering whether or not the most puzzling aspects of the case might connect it back to Whisper Man, and how much I'd be able to explain to Bobby if they did. My sprightly police escort chattered as we threaded back through drop-ceiling halls, fluorescents buzzing overhead.

"I mean, people kill people all the time, but not like this," he said. "There's things you can't unsee, you know?" I nodded to show my sympathy, although with him rushing along ahead of me, he probably didn't notice.

"It's so much worse because of the kids," he continued. "Poor Garrett. He hasn't been right since the investigation began—his little girl is the youngest daughter's age. He even started smoking again." This time he did glance back, boyish features eloquent with concern. "You know how hard it was for him to quit."

"Actually, I don't," I reminded him gently. I even managed not to look bitter about it, but Bobby halted so suddenly that I almost tumbled over him. He gushed apologies, repeating "sorry" with such fevered rapidity, it sounded like he was going for some kind of record.

I held up a hand.

"It's fine," I assured him. "Shit happens."

"Yeah, but of all people, I should really know better," he said. "I worked the case. I know what those people did to you. I am *so* sorry, Zack."

"Seriously, let it go, Bobby," I insisted. I fought to keep the irritation from my face. I wasn't angry at Bobby—just worn out. Sorry couldn't fix my troubles. "Let's get back to this thing, OK? Your partner started smoking. How long've you guys been working this without a break?"

Bobby did that nervous fidget, rubbing his palm across the back of his head.

"Sorry," he faltered, then laughed miserably at himself. "I mean—sorry I keep saying sorry—"

"The case, Bobby. How long?"

"Right. Three weeks?" he ventured. He unclipped the work phone from his belt, tapped in his passcode, then scrolled through his notes to double check. "Uh, four this Tuesday. I know that's not a lot in the grand scheme of things, but it's a long time to live with some of these images. The little girls in that house, Zack—"

The next few words got stuck in his throat and I slammed down hard on my shields in a pre-emptive defense. I wanted to hear Park's opinions on the murder, not share the emotional toll it was so obviously taking on him. Maybe that was cold, but I had enough of my own trauma to wrestle with.

Bobby never managed to complete the sentence. With effort, he drove the haunted look from his eyes.

"We still haven't found the father."

"The language you called me about—was it carved into the bodies?" I asked carefully.

After a hitching swallow, Bobby resumed walking. I wondered briefly what had driven him to become an officer—especially in homicide. He was so bright and shiny—that level of idealistic dedication rarely survived the brutal attrition of the job. Not to knock Bobby, but he didn't seem like he had the grit.

"Some of it," he answered, "but there was a lot more on the walls." He led me down a narrow hall lined with cramped little offices, most of them closed up tight. "I won't make you look at the autopsy photos, unless you think you need to. I'm hoping the pics from the walls will be enough." He hesitated as he took a turn at the end of the hall, then adopted a more muted tone. "There's a delicate aspect to the case. It's why pinning down the language is so important."

I listened.

"The father did work for Doctors Without Borders. Based on where he just came back from, we need to know if there's a terrorism angle." He sighed, fussing with his tie. "I mean, the symbols don't look like Arabic at all, but you know how jumpy folks are these days. The higher-ups see bad shit and even the slimmest connection to the Middle East, and they make all kinds of assumptions—whether they're fair or not."

"Where was the father last?" I asked.

Bobby stopped outside the entryway to a large, open

room filled with a regiment of desks. Several of them were occupied. The low and constant rhythm of typing, combined with intermittent phone chatter, drifted into the hall.

"Syria," Bobby replied.

I indulged in a little mental geography, guesstimating how close modern-day Syria was to the old Hittite stomping grounds across the Anatolian highlands. Pretty damned close—to the point that they shared borders. One more thing that might link this case to Whisper Man, if Lil was right about the Luwian tie-in.

"For the record, I don't think it's terrorists," Bobby scoffed. "The brass thinks that's the answer to everything these days." He stood in the hall, shifting from foot to foot, as if his tightly wound dynamism required that he keep some body part in motion at all times.

"I sense a 'but'," I prompted.

"Yeah," he sighed. "The thing we can't figure, aside from the symbols, is the Special Forces guy, Lawrence Booker. Last anyone knew, he was in Afghanistan—nearly three years ago. They'd listed him MIA. Now he turns up dead at our crime scene. Whatever he was into before he disappeared, the Feds aren't sharing." He fixed earnest black eyes on me and whispered, "I really wish I could get you to the location, Zack. We could use your special insight on this one."

Special insight.

Maybe he was talking about academic expertise.

Suuure. Because my life was all about the simple answers.

"You mean reading the glyphs in person?" I ventured.

Bobby gave me a "don't joke around" look. I stared at him blankly, wondering if I had a good poker face.

Apparently, I did.

"I'm sorry," he sputtered. "You don't remember."

"I don't remember a lot of things."

His brows stitched. "I didn't think that was something you could lose. I mean, I knew the lake thing was bad but—oh, hell. I feel like an asshole for even bringing it up."

"Bringing what up?" I said. "Be specific."

"You used to be able to read a room like—well, like no one else I've ever met. You said you were psychic."

"Psychic," I repeated.

He misread my relief.

"There isn't a better word for it, right?" With a short, nervous laugh, he added, "This probably sounds hokey, especially if you don't remember."

"Maybe we can talk the psychic angle later," I offered. "Pictures for now, OK?"

He nodded fervently. "Yeah. OK, come on," he said, heading into the bullpen. "Let me re-introduce you to my partner, Garrett."

17

Bobby threaded his way among the desks, making his way to a bald man sitting with his wide shoulders hunched over the keyboard. Despite the temperature outside, the guy was down to his shirtsleeves, cuffs rolled up to reveal forearms layered with corded muscle and fading tattoos.

Most of the tats were tribal, though one looked like the lines of a prayer. The dark hair that forested his tanned and weathered skin made it difficult make out the words.

Tapping furiously with the fingers of one hand, he kept the other poised above his mouse in an oddly anticipatory gesture that made it look as if he intended to smack the device in some bizarre game of whack-a-mole. His attention was focused on the monitor, where multiple windows of text and images filled the screen, information flowing at an impressive speed.

"Garrett?" Bobby padded up to him on the thin carpet.

The burly officer didn't respond. Then I noticed the earbuds trailing down to an iPod clipped to his belt. I could just hear the faint buzz of music over the chatter from the handful of other workers scattered throughout the room. Whatever he was listening to, it was loud.

Bobby turned to me. "He's been so fixated on this case." Then with a cautious, companionable pathos, he reached out and touched his partner lightly on the shoulder.

The big man twitched violently, nearly sending mouse, keyboard, and monitor onto the floor with the spastic sweep of one arm. In a swift series of motions, he yanked the earbuds away, closed the windows on the computer, then whirled to face us in the swivel chair. He was on his feet almost too fast for me to follow—and I was used to tracking things at vampire-speed.

Bobby staggered back, understandably startled. Garrett regarded him with a wild look, hands half-fisted at his sides. Veins corded on his neck and the earbuds bounced against his thigh, spilling forth—no shit—*Flight of the Valkyries*. With the bald head, muscles, and tribal tattoos, he reminded me of a paunchy Drax the Destroyer.

"Oh, it's you," the big man said in a curiously flat tone—which didn't exactly help with the Drax comparison. He relaxed only slightly.

"Garrett, you remember Zack Westland." Bobby flashed his partner an easy smile. "He agreed to take a look at those symbols."

Garrett turned wary brown eyes on me, the corners of his mouth dragging with disapproval. I felt his attention—felt it like electricity dancing across my skin. All the hairs on the back of my neck tried climbing to higher ground. Out of reflex, I clung to my cowl.

"This man?" Garrett demanded of Bobby in an uninflected monotone. "Your 'expert' is this man?"

Bobby glanced between his partner and me, a look of confusion flickering across his features. His hand strayed to the back of his head and he squirmed nervously. The room had fallen so silent, I could hear the subtle whisking of hair against the skin of his palm.

The other officers working in the bullpen stared openly. Garrett never took his suffocating eyes off me. Wagner continued to pump out with tinny fidelity.

"I will not work with this one," Garrett said gruffly. Without further comment, he sat down, turned his back to us, and popped in the blaring earbuds.

Bobby boggled at the back of his bald head for a moment, then shot me a look of awkward apology. "This case is wrecking him," he said in whispered tones. "He's been like this for weeks."

The man's inattention felt like a literal wall. It rose like the battlements of some brooding fortress, adding a strained quality to the silence. Everything felt smaller by comparison. I debated the wisdom of dropping my cowl just so I could get a good look at Garrett from a different perspective. Something felt... *off* about the man. Even without calling on my preternatural senses, I realized that he was hardly as big as he'd initially appeared.

Not to say he was scrawny by any means, but his shoulders weren't much wider than my own. While he had muscle, it was softened by a layer of comfortable padding, no doubt added by his years behind a desk. He was a warrior, but one who'd passed his prime. When he'd stood and faced us, the presence he'd projected was that of a much bigger, much deadlier man.

What was that all about?

"You are still here," Garrett said flatly. He didn't turn around.

A duo of uniformed officers wandered into the room. They slouched near the copy machine as if they had something to do, watching us with expressions of guarded curiosity. We were becoming a regular attraction.

"Are you sure you want to blow Zack off like this?" Bobby ventured. He sounded peeved and made little effort to hide it from his face. "We haven't had any luck on our own."

No response.

"Come on, Garrett. I know it's been a while," he continued, "but Zack's a stand-up guy. You've worked with him before."

"*No.*"

The word reverberated with quiet thunder. Bobby rocked like it was a slap. Everyone who'd been gawking at our exchange strove suddenly to find something else to do. The quiet chatter of keyboards and the shuffle of paperwork once more swelled throughout the room.

"We'll talk about this later," Bobby promised. A spark of fury smoldered in his dark eyes. Motioning to me, he said, "Come on. I'll walk you back out. Sorry for wasting your time."

I turned mutely and followed the newly minted detective. Bobby moved swiftly, aggravation distilled in every gesture. A watchful tension spread in our wake as we exited the room. In the resulting hush, I could hear the rasp and whisper of Park's fashionable, wide-legged pants.

As I stepped from the bullpen into the hall, I felt eyes needling me in the back. I knew pretty much everyone in that room was staring, but this felt different, weightier. I hazarded one final look in Garrett's direction. The bald officer sat rigidly in his swivel chair, lucent eyes fixed on me with stifling intensity. There was no mistaking the warning in his gaze.

When the hell did I piss in his coffee?

Bobby was already halfway down the hall. I met Garrett's naked glare for a moment, then ducked after my friend.

18

"I am *so* sorry about that," Bobby said. He retraced our path through the winding back halls.

"Your partner always that friendly?" I asked.

"No," Bobby insisted. With a frustrated noise, he said, "I wish you remembered. Garrett's a big goofball, always joking."

"Could've fooled me," I muttered.

"Zack, it's not funny," Bobby objected.

I tried to put my inner smartass in a choke hold, reminding myself that silence was golden—or at least less likely to get me punched in the mouth.

"If you saw half the photos from this case, you'd understand," Bobby explained. He took a sharp right at one of the intersections, and I haltingly followed. If we were heading back to the front lobby, I was certain we should've gone the other direction.

We continued our trek in silence. The overhead lights lent a sallow cast to the beige walls, and a scent like sweat and nachos hung thickly on the air. A heavy brown fire door loomed at the end of the hall. Bobby used a swipe card and motioned me through. We emerged on the ass-end of the building with absolutely no one around.

The drop ceiling back here was full of warped and stained tiles, as if all the clean ones had been scavenged and switched out over the years. One bank of fluorescents was burned out while another flickered spastically at random intervals. Even when it wasn't flickering, it filled the tiny hall with an angry, insect drone.

An exit sign hung helpfully above another heavy door set into the outside wall. Painted the same ugly brown, it had a small rectangle of wired glass revealing concrete steps leading down to the back lot. The black polyp of a security camera distended from the ceiling within easy sight of the back door. Bobby angled us away from its leering eye. He unclipped the police-issue phone at his belt, swiftly tapped his passcode, then opened an album of photos and held it out to me.

"I don't have everything," he said. "I can't text any of them to you. But you can look at the pictures I took when we showed up. Make it quick."

Suddenly the trek into the lonely back hallway made sense. Wordlessly, I took the device. The protective case around the phone made it thick and clunky. It weighed a ton. There was some kind of film across the screen to reduce glare—and all it succeeded in doing back here was pick up reflections of the seizure-inducing fluorescents. I shielded it with one hand so I could see.

The first image was a mailbox with a house number on the side, mostly in focus. It was 5693. I scrolled past that. The next image was a house—a beautiful Tudor with ivy trailing up the sides, evergreen hedges, all of it dusted with snow. It looked like the opening shot of some sentimental holiday special.

I slid my finger over the touchscreen, advancing to the next photo. A close-up on a tactical blade. Blood beaded around it on the hardwood.

"Is that a Ka-Bar?" I asked.

"Not the only weapon present on the scene," Bobby murmured.

I scrolled to the next image—an interior wall, painted a color that had probably been marketed under some frou-frou title like Crème Brulée. My eyes were drawn to an asymmetrical knick-knack shelf hung near the far side of the photo. Carved from a single piece of dense, dark wood, it looked expensive and handmade, and didn't hold the standard suburban kitsch. I spotted a small clay cup that could have belonged to half a dozen ancient cultures. Next to that was a woven fiber doll with a white bone mask. It looked East African. Another statue of what appeared to be an authentic Egyptian *ushabti* was cut off by the edge of the photo.

"What's all this?" I asked, indicating the shelf and its contents.

"Souvenirs," Bobby replied. "Dr. Kramer collected things from all the countries where he volunteered—Iraq, Somalia, Sudan. We're not sure all of them are legal."

"I think you're right about that." I squinted at the crackled sky-blue faience of the *ushabti* figure. "These are the kind of things that cross my desk at the museum."

Bobby nodded, shifting impatiently while he waited for me to examine the real focus of the photo. The shelf and its curious contents were a secondary issue—the camera hadn't even been aimed at them. I directed my attention to the central portion of the wall where a series of brown and rust-colored smears arced across its dark yellow surface.

Blood. I was certain of it.

I enlarged the image, focusing on whatever had been painted onto the wall. I could make out perhaps two lines of what might have been script. All the shapes streaked unevenly.

"That's not the best photo," Bobby said, hovering at my elbow. "Skip forward a couple. We hit it with a black light."

The next couple of pictures just showed different angles, mostly. My finger hovered above one that gave a better view of the strangely stocked shelf. There was a large display case visible in the background. It, too, seemed crammed with artifacts from a broad range of ancient cultures. Dr. Kramer had been a busy and well-traveled man. I was about to ask whether or not he'd brought anything back from his stint in Syria—like, say, a Rephaim-inhabited statue—but then I advanced to the black light photo.

The question died forgotten in my throat.

Bobby caught my expression. "You recognize them."

The black light cast everything in ghostly shades of pallid blue. The vivid yellow of the interior wall washed out entirely. Against its now dull greenish expanse, brightly painted letters luminesced. Two lines, executed in broad, bold strokes. There was no mistaking the shapes. I still couldn't read the ancient Luwian—but I recognized immediately the three signs that made up the name Terhuziel.

"Fuck me running." It was out of my mouth before I could stop myself. "Whose blood?" I felt breathless.

Bobby hesitated. I glanced up from the photo to see an agonized expression twisting his face. He wasn't holding back on my account. He could barely bring himself to say it. Finally, he managed to choke it out.

"Youngest daughter. Kaylee. She was four."

I winced, thinking unpleasantly of Terael's often winsome nostalgia for blood-sacrifice. If Terhuziel was Rephaim, someone had been feeding him.

"Look, Bobby," I began, but cut off as the phone vibrated unexpectedly in my hand. I nearly dropped it. It was a text message.

Garrett. Two words.

Check in.

"Uh," I stammered, shoving the phone in Bobby's direction. "That's for you."

Park glanced at the screen and muttered a curse.

"I've got to go," he said. "Anything you can share on that language?"

"It's not terrorists," I replied.

"Figured," he answered darkly.

The phone buzzed with another incoming text. I could just make it out through the glare.

Don't trust him

Bobby frowned at the terse missive.

"You sure your partner used to like me?" I ventured.

Bobby tapped a quick response into the phone, then swept the edge of his suit jacket aside so he could clip the device back to his belt. I could see the lines of his shoulder holster. His movements were a little too abrupt.

"I don't know what's wrong with him," Park replied, glancing furtively at the dark bubble of the security camera. He could no longer hold still.

I opened my mouth, then bit back my words, wondering how much I'd trusted Bobby before I'd gotten the *tabula rasa* treatment. Cops made me nervous for reasons my stubborn memory refused to disclose, but Bobby had always acted like a friend—and maybe more than a friend. An ally.

"Look. You and your partner need to be careful with this," I offered. I kept my eyes locked on Bobby, gauging his reactions. His features grew sallow as he studied the look on my face.

"We stepped into something bad, didn't we?"

"I'm not sure how much I'll be able to tell you," I hedged. "It's not exactly police report material." He barked a bitter laugh. It rang hollow in the stifling air of the tiny back hall.

"When is it ever with you?"

His phone started buzzing again. Repeatedly. This wasn't a text message—it was a call. He stepped swiftly toward the door that had led us here.

"Now I *have* to go," he said, grabbing his phone.

I nodded, heading for the outer door. I paused with it half open, wind gusting into the building. I'd stopped noticing how rank it was back here till the harshly barren scent of winter blasted in. Bobby swiped his key card at the other door.

"Zack," he called as I stood upon the threshold.

"Yeah?"

"You be careful, too."

Then he was through the door, phone held to one ear. From his many agitated gestures, it wasn't a pleasant call.

19

I yanked off the visitor pass still clipped to the tongue of my zipper as I walked back to the Hellcat. Tossing the laminated tag onto the passenger seat, I keyed the ignition.

"Paint it Black" picked up where it had left off, startlingly loud. Jagger wailed frenetically as the song wound down. I reached into the glove compartment and retrieved my SIG, slipping it back into its holster in the inner pocket of my jacket. The Stones faded into Tunstall's "Black Horse and the Cherry Tree." Drumming along with the irresistible rhythms of her throaty vocals, I sorted through everything Bobby had revealed to me—the murdered family, the missing doctor, the highly trained soldier who'd likely disappeared during some black ops in Afghanistan. His connection had to be the doctor, but what the hell had he been doing in that house?

The black-light photo burned against the substance of my mind, its words inscrutable save for that all-too-familiar name.

I needed to meet with Terael.

Music blasting, I backed out of the visitor parking, threading my way past rows of off-duty cruisers and employee vehicles. It was dusk, and the leaden cloud cover that had settled over the city hastened the dying of the light. The street in front of the station was a choked river of headlights, the cars bumper to bumper in what I initially mistook for rush-hour traffic. But it was six thirty on a Saturday. Traffic shouldn't have been this thick—at least, not going in that direction. Maybe there was some event at one of the museums. It wasn't like I'd been keeping track of that sort of thing.

Whatever the cause, I sat impatiently as I waited for an opening so I could pull onto Chester. While the car idled, a prickly feeling settled in the middle of my back, right between my wings.

Someone was watching me. I could feel it as surely as if they had walked up beside me and huffed in my ear. I craned my neck.

Garrett stood on the steps in front of the station. He had a cigarette in one hand and his phone in the other. He was still in his shirtsleeves, the cuffs rolled halfway up his tattooed forearms. Puffing a plume of curling smoke, he fixed his eyes on me. I could feel their baleful weight like corpse fingers dragging along my spine.

He was thirty feet away, maybe more, and the windows of my vehicle were darkly tinted. There was no way he could see me—yet, the instant my eyes fixed on his in the rearview mirror, his broad, flat mouth curled into a mirthless grin. It was more a baring of teeth, one predator's warning to another.

What the fuck is this guy's problem?

Still gritting that mockery of a smile, he flicked the cigarette away. Fishing in his pocket, he brought out a curious object—a white, flat disk of ceramic or stone. About the size of a coaster, he juggled the item across the tops of his knuckles with a dexterity I found unlikely in a man of his size. Once, then twice, it made the flipping transit from his index finger to his pinky and then back again.

With a little flourish, he tucked the disk back into his pocket.

Something about the object—and Garrett's casual handling of it—made my guts twist uncomfortably.

At the first break in traffic, I gunned the motor, whipping the car onto the street and the hell away from Bobby's weird partner. He continued to track me, though, long after I pulled away. To add ironic commentary, Nick Cave and the Bad Seeds queued up from the iPod, singing of an ominous stranger and his red right hand.

I stabbed the mute button, having had about enough stereomancy for the night.

After the slowest half-mile ever, I caught the left onto East Boulevard and got the hell away from whatever was backing up Chester and Euclid. Trees lined the scenic parkway that wound past the lagoon, white holiday lights—long past the season—still gleaming in their naked branches. The tangle of traffic receded in my mirrors, transitioning to something that seemed far removed from the frenetic drive of the city. Funny the difference only a couple hundred feet could make in this corner of town.

Wade Park stretched to my left while the iconic lines of Severance Hall rose against the darkening clouds to the east. It was close to seven already, and museum hours ended at five on Saturdays. I found parking on the street and searched the glove box for my spare magnetic key card and employee ID.

Fuck me. I didn't have either on me.

Probably better to avoid my co-workers on this trip, anyway. I had alternate methods for getting into the building. I pulled my cellphone out of my pocket and stashed it in the glove box. My personal back door to the museum would turn it into a useless paperweight.

Thumbing the button on my key fob, I locked the car and armed the security system. Then I stuffed my hands into the pockets of my jacket and started walking toward the sculpture gardens. One of the most treasured pieces of CMA's collection—a casting of Rodin's famous *Thinker*—brooded front and center along the approach leading to the original 1914 entrance. Cleveland's version of the statue was unique, one foot obliterated by a pipe bomb in the '70s. The explosion—an act of anarchic violence credited to a group called "the Weathermen"—had forever changed the profile of the massive bronze figure.

It had also stamped a Crossing right outside my workplace.

Crossings were soft spots in the metaphysical barrier separating the Shadowside from the world of flesh. Stepping from one side to the other was the unique purview of my tribe, and it gave us a significant edge when dealing with spirits—which, as far as I had gathered, was one of our main functions.

Whatever strange alchemy of timing, location, and human emotion combined to blossom into a Crossing, I could sense the supernatural doorways once they were present. Typically, a Crossing was brought about by something traumatic, and echoes of the event lingered like a stain on the psychic landscape, locked in an endless loop. Murders and other violent assaults were the most consistent causes, but—as with Rodin's *Thinker* here—not all were tied directly to mortal pain.

Every day ten thousand scenes of human conflict played out across the space of any city—murder, rape, and untold instances of cruel predation. If an extremity of human suffering was the sole cause of a Crossing, then the world would be riddled with holes.

It wasn't.

That was probably a good thing.

I took a breath and flexed. The air thickened like the skin atop boiled milk, then, with a single step, I tore through. The breath exited my lungs in a rush and my cowl shredded around me—business as usual. Maintaining my cowl on the skinside was annoying enough. On the Shadowside, it was nearly impossible.

The landscape went monochromatic, smothered by silence. The wind, the traffic, all the noises of the city—they were just gone, as if a cosmic hand had hit mute. To my left, the *Thinker* exploded and became whole again in an endless cycle bleached of color and sound. Similarly, the nearby museum shuffled through snapshots of its imprinted history, layers of time and human perception locked into the rippling fabric of the Shadowside.

I shook off the last clinging tatters of the cowl, stretching my wings to their full expanse. They weren't flesh and blood, exactly, although they acted as if they were. They had distinct structure and musculature, and on this side of reality these were visible in outlines of gleaming bluish light. More than twice my height from tip to tip, they were a solid weight upon my back—though, fortunately, not as heavy as their size might suggest. Ghosting through my clothes, they were nevertheless real and perfectly functional.

Rolling my shoulders and neck, I took a running leap. With a single, massive downstroke, I took to the air.

Living flight. The Shadowside could be a grim and desolate place, but all its horrors were rendered tolerable in light of this one exhilarating treasure. If the atmosphere of this gray and haunted space weren't so metaphysically taxing, I likely would spend most of my time here, soaring through its sunless sky.

My jaunts, however, were curtailed by necessity. An entropic effect leached power from everything that crossed over, and that included me. The longer I lingered, the more the sere atmosphere of the place ground me down, and if I pushed myself too long—like a swimmer trapped underwater without a breathing tank—I could die. The physical bits of me, at any rate, and I wasn't keen on finding out what happened to the rest once those withered away.

I wheeled above the spectral echoes of a stand of ancient trees that clustered near the new entrance to the museum. Subtle currents moved through the air high above the patchwork echo of the building, and I let them do most of the work for me. Good thing, too, because the crushing psychic pressure wore me down quickly. My endurance had seriously taken a hit.

Some of it was likely from the blood loss the night before, but the rest—well, I hadn't exactly been taking care of myself the past few weeks. Quickly winded, I dropped to the faded ribbon of pavement outside the main entrance. I folded my wings against my back and started swiftly toward my basement office.

That was a personal sanctuary my sibling Terael had carved out for me, and there I could safely cross back into the flesh-and-blood world, free from the many watchful eyes of the museum's security system.

The instant I passed through the doors, however, my disembodied sibling greeted me. It felt like the mental equivalent of being tackled by a Saint Bernard with separation anxiety.

Have his soldiers harried you? Terael asked. *So long you were absent. I feared you had abandoned me.*

His voice, eerie and atonal, rang urgently through my head—so loud that stars exploded in my vision. Images, emotions, and a spider web of lateral associations clung to his every word. The emotions were the worst, because an underlying note of naked panic shivered through everything. My heart sped with sympathetic adrenaline.

"Whose soldiers, Terael?" I said aloud. "I wouldn't—"

He cut me off before I could match all the words to my completed thought. Anger, fear, and relief resounded in swift progression through my head.

You will help me then, my brother, he said, *as I so often have helped you?* The agitated emotions of the resident Rephaim lent an added weight to the already suffocating air of the Shadowside.

I staggered forward, seeking to tear free of the currents swirling through the lobby. Decades' worth of visitors had stamped a ghostly imprint of traffic both in and out of the main doors. I had to fight not to get caught in the undertow. A gleaming monolith of chrome and Lucite offered an island of calm amid the ceaseless motion. The main donation box. To Terael, this was the equivalent of an altar where worshippers left him sacrifice—though he tended to pout that it was no longer blood, but coin.

Pausing there, I clung for a moment to the structure— it had substance on both sides, looming even bigger on the Shadowside than in the mortal world. My vision started to tunnel—perhaps a consequence of Terael's thundering intensity, or of getting my ass handed to me the night before. I couldn't rightly tell.

The Rephaim hovered impatiently along the edges of my awareness. Waves of urgent anxiety continued bleeding off of him—nothing organized enough to interpret, but still stultifying.

"I got the memo," I said. "Something's wrong out there. Give me a minute to get to my office, then we can talk."

Relief and a surge of gratitude—both good emotions, but they didn't much help my pounding head.

He sent a herald within these walls, demanding that I serve or fall.

Insult mingled with his fear. I rushed through the museum's halls with his colossal presence bearing down on me. My thoughts grew scattered as the effort to remain on the Shadowside eroded my already dwindling reserves.

"Who did?" I asked as I pelted along. "Who are we talking about, Terael?" I was afraid I already knew the answer. Finally, I reached the stairs that led to the basement—the elevator wasn't exactly an option.

Our brother Terhuziel, the Thunderer of the Northern Hills. Has he yet to send his soldiers to threaten you with harm?

The blood sang in my ears.

"You know about Terhuziel?" I croaked.

Impatience and accusation slapped against me.

His emissary threatened me within these very walls! I waited and I waited, but you did not come.

There it was.

All this time, the problem had been building, and I wallowed at home, locked away. If I'd dragged my ass out of my self-pitying funk, managed to make it to work for even one day, I could have nipped this in the bud.

I must beg for your protection, he continued, *diminished as I am. We will face his threat together and drive him from our land, will we not?*

"Fuck me running," I hissed.

Zaquiel?

The Name rang like plaintive music upon the air.

"I am *such* an idiot," I snarled. Then I raced the rest of the way to my office to slam out of the Shadowside.

20

I emerged in a small, windowless room tucked away in a neglected corner of the museum's basement. The walls were cinderblock, painted a dull, flat white. They were bare except for a corkboard I'd managed to stick in place with about twenty strips of double-sided tape.

Metal shelving ran the length of the back wall, providing just enough room for me to get in and out of the swivel chair parked at my desk. The desk itself took up most of the room, and I often wondered how the staffers had gotten the metal hulk through the solitary door.

Wadded up take-out wrappers still filled the little wire-mesh trash can, adding a slightly rancid scent to the air. Nearly a month of vacation and no one had touched the space—not even the janitors. Terael was maybe a little too enthusiastic about keeping this room a private sanctuary for me.

"Tell me about Terhuziel," I said, leaning against the wall by the door. My head spun from the rushed re-entry. "Do you know why he's here? What does he want?"

He seeks to conquer as always he has done, Terael responded bleakly.

"I need details, Terael."

Maneuvering by touch past the desk, I dropped into the swivel chair, then felt around for my little gooseneck lamp, flipping it on so I could see. The overheads could stay off for now. Terael had his space so well protected, I probably could have flipped on every bank of fluorescents up and down the hall without eliciting the least bit of curiosity from security, but there was no point in pushing my luck.

"How do I stop him?" I asked. "*Can* I stop him? You guys have weaknesses, right?"

Terael dithered in the space, likely debating how much he should share. I ground my teeth, waiting. The clock on my desk read seven twenty-three. How late would the hospital stay open?

"Terael, I don't have time for a debate. There's this girl, Halley. He's been after her for weeks. Last night he sent his goons to abduct her right out of her house. I need—"

He didn't even let me finish. His presence closed on me like a fist, seeking to pluck an image of Halley straight from my brain.

Girl? Untouched? Pure? Show me. Stinging with emotion, the words were whip-cracks in my mind. I slammed up all my shields.

"Hey—back off," I snapped. "We've got rules about you digging around in my head without permission."

It would be faster. It was almost a whine.

Despite the protestation, though, he retreated far

enough to respect my boundaries, fretting the air like a storm front. Waves of anxiety pulsed from him, palpable even through my shields. An answering throb started up in my temples. Terael could be a literal pain when he got in a mood. Small wonder Lil avoided the museum.

I miss the days when you allowed me speech directly, my brother. Formless, my thoughts do not wed easily to so human a mind. Let me be made manifest within you.

The words dragged the air, so dense with layers of meaning they would take me weeks to unpack. Terael clearly expected me to get it all in one go. Wheedling, he pawed my shields like a toddler begging for sweets—except this was a toddler whose presence blanketed the room.

"Take it down a notch, Terael. I already took a beating once this week," I said, digging for the Advil I kept in my desk. Three pills left. I swallowed them dry.

And I stood threatened in the sanctum of my temple, he shot back. The wounded fury radiating from his words elicited a wince. *We both seek to rebuff him, do we not? Give me space so I may see this girl and the soldiers sent to claim her.*

"I don't know what you're asking," I replied. "You're already a voice inside my head."

I am more than just a voice, as well you know, my brother.

"No. I don't," I snapped. "My brain doesn't work right any more, and I'm sick of telling people that."

The Rephaim churned the air with impatience.

"I'm not being willfully dense, Terael." Aggravation made me nearly yell it.

Bounded by the architecture of your mind, my thoughts will be… easier, he said. *To bear. To understand.*

That would be nice for a change. I kept the thought to myself.

"You're going to have to spell it out, Terael—and be specific."

Will you allow me this?

"Allow you what?" I snapped.

To be specific.

Something in his tone rang oddly. It set my hackles up—and I was already pretty close to high alert. Picking at the blotter on my desk, I glanced again at the clock. Seven thirty. *Fuck.* "Will it make this conversation go any faster?"

Much.

"Fine, then," I relented. "Get on with it."

In answer, he flooded my head with pictures. Rooms and halls built from memories. How to pace the perimeter, walls to set the boundaries. Brick and stone and steel, crafted all from thought. The entire layout unfolded in an instant. It was a blueprint for a mental construct, what Giordano Bruno had called a "Theater of Memory."

This.

I dug a palm against my temple. Images still swam behind my eyes as the data unspooled. "Ow!"

You said I could.

"I did," I admitted, feeling like an idiot. "How the hell will that help Halley?"

When you send your thoughts to me, you show me what you think, yet not always what you have seen. I started to object, but he bulled right over me. *You have said it yourself. Your mind is hobbled and you no longer understand things as once you did, my brother. Yet details linger unrecognized within your halls of memory. If I can see as you have seen, I may help you comprehend.*

I chewed my cheeks, debating an answer. He framed a pretty argument, but I still felt leery. Letting him that deep into my mind—how was I supposed to keep any secrets? There were things I loathed to share, like what happened outside of Lake View.

My reservations were clear enough. He was keen to put my mind at ease, which only made me warier.

The boundaries are yours to set. This is not a new thing, brother.

"First you've mentioned it since I came back," I grumbled. Suspicion clung thickly to the words.

I had no need before. This helps us both, he insisted.

Pushing back in the swivel chair, I cracked my neck to relieve the tension that clawed at the base of my skull. The vertebrae crackled like bubble-wrap.

"If I agree to do this, I'm not swearing to anything, right?" I ventured. "I've had it up to here with oaths."

You and I stood in armies opposed more often than we stood as allies in the distant past. Yet no oaths were sworn to grant you access to my temple. If I can welcome to my halls a zealot judge who smashed the idols of my brethren together with the war-crazed Gibburim, then you can deign to lease me space within your mind so we may more clearly speak.

That was an interesting chunk of information. In my notes, the Gibburim bore the sobriquet of "Violent

Ones," but beyond that, I knew next to nothing about the tribe. I filed a mental note to ask Terael about them later. For now, the clock was ticking.

"This is a one-time deal," I cautioned. "I'll make this space in my head like you showed, but don't assume you can waltz in like you own the place whenever the mood strikes."

I accept your terms, Zaquiel.

As he intoned my Name, spectral sounds of wind and distant music tinkled through the little office. Not quite spectral—the breeze stirred my hair, blowing long strands back from my forehead.

Dammit. That sure as hell felt like an oath. At least I'd set terms that wouldn't fuck me—I hoped.

Too late to change it now, I thought.

I await you, Terael pronounced. He didn't even try to sound patient.

So I began with the girl's room. I'd show him that little corner of the world inside my head, and if nothing heinous occurred, we'd go from there.

Taking a deep breath, I slowly released it. Closing my eyes, I started running through mnemonic exercises to bring up all the details with photographic clarity. I had clear recall of individual elements, but putting them together in a mental construct, that was going to be tricky.

I felt worn pretty thin.

But when did that ever stop me?

Laying my head on the desk, I pulled all of my focus inward. As Terael had shown me, I set a perimeter and erected the walls. Once I'd started the process, I settled into it with a practiced familiarity.

Terael had been truthful on at least one point—I'd done this before.

The space took shape around me, each detail coming easier than the last. I added the worn carpet, the picture window with its patterned drapes, the ceiling fan that hung unused over the center of the room. Then I pictured Halley—wild hair, Disney Princess nightshirt and all. I placed the girl on the hospital bed, the Tinker Bell lamp on the table, Father Frank's broken rocking chair in the corner. On the floor, the groaning vagrant. Billowing curtain. Broken glass. I left out Roarke and his partner.

I put myself in the room so I could inspect all the elements. Bending to the wounded homeless man, I peeled back the blood-caked fabric of his shirt. I called up the three Luwian characters, imagining how they looked scored into his flesh with slashes of gleaming crimson. One was kind of a double-u. The next might have been the head of a bull. Before I fully shaped the Name, I felt a hand settle on my shoulder.

"Leave that part out."

Terael stood behind me.

21

He had golden hair and golden eyes—and even golden skin. Not shiny metallic gold, but the warm, golden brown of the tiger eye gemstone, with deeper browns as undertones. That struck me as odd, because I had seen his statue on display in the museum. It wasn't cast from gold or even carved from a gem, but shaped from dark and worn basalt.

It looked nothing like the slender youth standing before me.

He moved like flesh and he breathed like flesh but everything about him shimmered with the reticulated striations of the gemstone. Tall and long-limbed like all my brethren, he was slimmer than most. His flesh and features held an adolescent softness—boyhood not yet tempered to man. His thick, shimmering hair fell softly to his shoulders, darker by a shade than his warm and glinting skin. The aureate gleam of his extravagant curls matched the color of the two broad wings that spread behind him, rustling faintly with a sound like sand scouring against marble.

He wore not a stitch of clothing, standing naked and utterly unabashed by this fact. If he'd worn eyeliner and a little jewelry, he could have walked straight from Oscar Wilde's private stable of rent boys. I turned my gaze away, too stunned by the whole of his appearance to be able to formulate any kind of intelligent response.

"Even this, you do not remember," he murmured sadly. He had a lilting tenor, reinforcing his aura of sumptuous youth. "Oh, my poor, wounded brother. How fragile is the flesh."

His pity chaffed at me, but the shock of seeing him like a flesh-and-blood being overruled the emotion. I'd known Terael only as a disembodied voice strangely singing in my mind. He'd kept me company through long hours at the art museum—and, frankly, sometimes he'd gotten on my nerves with his constant, semi-lucid prattle. This new form jarred my awareness. My head twitched where it rested against my desk in the seemingly distant confines of my office.

"You're, uh—you're standing here," I stammered, opting to leave out the part about him being buck-ass naked and apparently happy to be alive. I didn't think he'd take well to a lecture on propriety. "How can you be standing here in front of me?"

Terael's lips curled into a consoling smile. "I am here. And in my idol, and in your office, sibling. And elsewhere. In the drifting dreams of my faithful, who guard the treasures of my temple."

"You do realize you're one of the treasures they're guarding, right?" I asked.

"As it should be." His smile broadened, exposing perfect, golden teeth.

I boggled at him, rubbing the hard angle of my jaw. "I always wonder if my life can get any weirder, and then I see shit like this."

Terael pressed a finger lightly to my lips and laughed. "That you did not mean to share. You are out of practice in this art."

His skin felt like living flesh, yet it lay against my mouth with the cool, unyielding weight of polished quartz. I recoiled from the touch. With a languorous grace, Terael stepped back into his own bubble of personal space. I scrubbed the back of my hand across my lips. If my reaction offended him, he made no sign.

"The walls and baffles of your mind must be firm," he cautioned. "Discipline is required to rein in stray thoughts."

I swallowed hard as I met the twin jewels of his eyes. "I've been working pretty hard on those walls and baffles. You might just have to live with a stray thought or two. It's always a little noisy in here."

"I have at least grown fond of your peculiar remarks," he answered. His bemused expression sloughed away, leaving his face an anxious, gilded mask. "Now let us see the extent of the trouble that has come knocking at my door."

He bent to the figure of the fallen man I'd conjured in the mental space.

"Terhu—" I began, but Terael cut me off sharply.

"Do not speak that Name in a space like this, Zaquiel," he warned. "We both risk much if you call him here, and I will not countenance such a danger." The sharp edge of his tone spurred my defiance.

"Is that a threat for him or me?"

"I will threaten any who side with that one, and stand in opposition until I have no strength left," he swore. The corona of his hair blew back in a sudden swell of power. I met the fire in his eyes without blinking. I'd won staring contests against Saliriel, and she was a decimus of the Nephilim.

"I'm not the enemy," I reminded him.

In an instant, all of his threatened fury dissolved, and I was reminded that Terael always seemed a little off in the head. Although he was tied to stone, his moods ran swift as mercury.

"Then do not speak his Name," he insisted. "My tribe works through idols and images. A Name whispered upon the lips of the faithful is a potent idol in its way."

"I'm not even part of his fan club," I objected. "I just want to know how to protect that girl."

On the bed, my recollected image of Halley lingered like a hologram stuck on pause. Terael nodded obliquely in her direction—at least acknowledging her—but he didn't budge from the man at our feet.

"I must see the extent of his fighting strength before I examine the lamb who might treble it."

"Lamb?" I demanded. Given my siblings' Biblical predilections, that didn't sound good for Halley. "You better not be talking sacrifice."

With dream-like languor, he trailed a finger along the vagrant's stubbled jaw. "In days long past, blood ran sweetly on the altar. Sacrifice sustains all members of my tribe." In his lilting tenor, the words rang like music, ugly though they were. I couldn't tell if he meant them as explanation or excuse.

Neither option made me happy.

"*No*," I snapped. The walls around us bowed with the force of my negation.

Mouth flattening in a moue of reproach, Terael glared from beneath a nest of golden lashes. The depth of hunger glittering in his inhuman eyes stunned me into silence.

"If the Thunderer sought sacrifice of the human girl, she already would be dead," he pronounced. "You yourself said his agents came not to kill, but to steal her from her home." Restless fingers stroked the face of the homeless man as Terael's expression grew distant. "A greater destiny is fated for the ones we choose as lamb."

"And by 'greater,' you mean worse," I said. "What's worse than sacrifice, Terael?"

He refused to respond. Unspoken on the air hung all the details he withheld, taunting at the edge of perception. My hands curled into fists, both here and in the office, as I struggled to rein in my temper.

"I'm here for answers, Terael," I snarled. "You better start to deliver."

Wherever his thoughts had strayed, it wasn't pretty. An aching mixture of loss, regret, and anguish scudded like clouds across his youthful features. The weight of those emotions added years I couldn't begin to count. When next he spoke, his voice seemed to resonate from two places at once—here, and the distant past.

"This is what you missed, my brother, seen but not perceived with waking eyes." He sounded inexpressibly weary. With a sweep of one dusty wing, he gestured over the prone man. A tapestry of smoky lines coalesced upon the air, each trailing from the minion. They rose to a point above him, like a puppet's many strings.

"I saw *one* of those," I sputtered. "Only one. On a different man, upstairs."

"Some part of you observed, and knew," he said. "And that is why we stand here now, for my delivery of answers." He cast the words like daggers. "I can pull your hidden knowledge where it can be seen."

Still gobsmacked that I'd missed that much, I thrilled with the brittle beginnings of hope. Maybe I hadn't recognized all those tendrils when I'd seen them in the first go-round, but the perceptions were there, locked in my subconscious. This projection was proof.

Dorimiel hadn't crippled me permanently.

That was *huge*. But if Terael had any sense of this revelation's impact, he didn't show it. He remained fixated on Whisper Man's wounded lackey.

"This one you show me is damaged, yes?" he mused. "A weakened mind. Fewer walls."

"Yeah." With difficulty, I pulled myself back to the moment. "My guess is he's homeless," I offered. "Might be mentally ill—a whole lot of people fall through the cracks. Not enough money for treatment." The pea coat and Army boots made me wonder now if he was a vet. No way to know for sure. "An easy target for possession."

"Not possession. Choosing," he corrected. "In ancient days, we called them god-touched. Minds like this are always first to hear our call." My gilt-skinned sibling cupped his hand against the seamed and dirty face. There was a tender, pitying intimacy to the gesture.

Something in me railed against it.

Focus, I urged myself—and was unreasonably thrilled when the thought remained private.

Terael's voice wove singsong rhythms on the air. "Through dreams, then waking visions, they hear our voices when they pass within our sphere," he said. "Those our whispers reach eventually let us in. Mortals crave our guidance, and the broken ones crave it most."

"Halley's not broken," I objected. "She's got challenges, sure. But she's worlds away from guys like this. How's this asshole getting to her?"

Terael frowned at my interruption. "The weak-minded are ours to call first, but that does not preclude others," he responded. "A god must build his flock in stages."

"Pretty harsh god if he asks them to carve his name in their skin," I grumbled.

"It is a sign of their devotion," Terael replied. "The token ties him to their flesh, thus to achieve communion." A jealous note of longing rang through the Rephaim's words. I fought to suppress a shudder. "They become his hands and eyes in the mortal world. Through it, he speaks to them beyond the limits of his temple. Rides them, if he must, though mortal minds are often crushed beneath the full weight of our presence."

"Hands to take and eyes to see," I muttered. "That creepy rhyme."

Hearing this, it made grim sense.

"We gift the worthy with a share of strength," Terael continued. "To bear the token is the first step to becoming anchor."

That was a word I knew, but in a different context.

"I thought anchors were Nephilim blood-slaves," I said, unable to hide my revulsion. "A nasty quirk of Remy's tribe."

Terael gave a little shake of his head. "All the tribes make anchors of the mortals, Zaquiel," he answered. "Just as mortal lives sustain us, each in our way."

A newfound level of disgust rose as I digested this information. None of these people had held the slightest chance—Terhuziel had swooped in when their lives were at their absolute worst, whispering promises of belonging and support. Of course they reached back—who wouldn't, in a moment of desperation?

From the ragged aspect of his hobo army, there was desperation to go around.

Once he got his hooks in them, he robbed them of their free will and bound them to his power. No wonder they shambled around like mindless zombies. He'd stripped them of everything human just so he could joyride in their skulls.

"I won't let him do that to Halley," I vowed.

Something akin to pity touched Terael's gemstone face. "For the Thunderer to reach the girl-child beyond the limits of his domain, she already bears his token."

"No," I said. "Not a chance. Halley doesn't have his name carved in her skin. Believe me, someone would have noticed."

Gently, as if explaining the death of a pet to a three-year-old, he said, "A token need not be carved into the flesh, my brother. The form it takes is determined by the devoted." He sketched a reverent gesture above the figure of the homeless man. "As much offering as talisman, it is a thing carefully crafted and carried always on the person. The Name is its power, along with the devoted's intent."

"Then we're fucked," I said. "She's been writing that name over and over again for weeks. In crayons, in paint—on her walls."

"Still you do not understand, my brother," he murmured.

I scowled at the man on display at our feet. The blood on his ruined chest pooled around the negative space where Terhuziel's Name should have been scored into his skin. The shock of the mutilation rose in memory. Several of the cuts had held puckered edges, like he'd gouged himself back open once they'd started to heal.

If Whisper Man broke her will, would Halley be consumed by the same destructive devotion to her newfound "god?" Just imagining it sickened me.

As the dark thoughts filled me, the flesh of the projected man's chest began to warp and bubble. Terael recoiled as echoes of Terhuziel's Name erupted from the skin.

"Drive his Name from your mind," he cautioned.

I struggled to suppress my awareness of those potent syllables, but it was like that game where someone tells you not to think about elephants. Suddenly, everything reminds you of the circus. The walls of the projection wavered and tiny details shivered in and out of existence as my concentration flagged. The three sigils of Terhuziel's Luwian Name pressed against their canvas of skin, struggling to burst through.

"*Voldemort*," I hissed, to drag my mind away. Terael's gilded brow creased. The word was meaningless to him, but it did the trick. Terhuziel's Name faded, covered over with a Death Eater symbol.

"You have the strangest mental talismans," he mused.

"It's not the tools, it's the result, right?"

Shifting my head against the desk in the office, I resettled the projection. With a vague sense of detachment, I noted that my hair clung damp with sweat. Holding an entire room vividly in my head took serious effort.

"I don't know how much longer I can keep this up," I said, "so you need to hurry. Take a look at Halley and show me what I missed."

Instantly, Terael bristled. "Do not frame it as an order, sibling. Much diminished I may be, but still I reign as god within my temple." Maybe it was proximity, maybe just the effort of imagining the shared mental space—whatever the reason, his anger ignited my own like a flash-fire.

"Fuck your tribe's god-complex, Terael," I snarled. "This guy is melon-balling people's brains and sending them out to wreak havoc in the world. A whole family is dead already. A little four-year-old girl—"

"That which is most precious makes the sweetest gift of all."

He said it as a taunt, and we both knew it. The rapturous expression that suffused his features made me want to vomit. It was a stark reminder that although Terael and I were siblings in a technical sense, we were worlds apart because of our tribes.

"You wish it was you out there, gathering mind-fucked followers to cut people up and bleed," I accused.

"Do not dare," he cautioned. "Those days are long

behind me." But his look remained wistful.

Suddenly, it didn't seem worth the headache to hold him here with me. He'd shown me that I already knew the answers—it was just a matter of figuring out how to get to them. The way he used the word "lamb," like it was some unique and precious status, made me want to shake an explanation from his gilded lips, but even that reaction suggested some part of me recognized the term.

While I fumed, Terael had finally turned his full attention to the girl.

"There is something special about this mortal child." His voice wavered with uncertainty and he held his hand poised, not quite touching her hair.

"You have no fucking clue," I said. Halley seemed innocuous enough, skinny limbs drawn close to her body as she rocked with her chin pressed against her knees. All her hair spilled forward, obscuring most of her face. The Rephaim regarded her as if expecting her to bite.

Terael shot me a doleful look and gingerly touched the top of her head. The instant he made contact, a glimmer of nebulous power leapt to life around her. Lavender flames licked up and down her skin.

With a startled yelp, he snatched his hand away.

"A trick, all this—a trick," he wailed. "Such a child cannot exist. My brother, what have you brought to me?"

Swift and galvanizing, the feel of her tumbling mind returned as a full-body memory. I had watched her hurl a bolt of impossible power to drive Whisper Man from the vagrant sprawled on the floor.

And I recalled my instinctive reaction.

Kill her, kill her now.

Chasing the heels of that thought, a deep, subsonic boom resounded through the space, as if a giant hand sought to pound to pieces a massive, distant door. The whole projection trembled.

Terael's wings stiffened as he froze.

That basso note resounded again, louder and somehow closer. Halley surged forward and hissed. Sharply, he recoiled.

"Shut it down," he snapped.

On the bed, Halley flowed to her feet in a single, sinuous motion as if every inch of her body held a joint. She wore an expression I had never seen on her face—hard and cold and… wicked.

"Shut down the projection," Terael shouted.

"What's happening? Am I doing that?"

He seized the front of my shirt, shaking me till my teeth rattled.

"Break the image, Zaquiel. Break it now!"

Motion blurred. Halley's limbs moved with the swift fluidity of a spider. Quick as a blink, the girl clambered from the hospital bed and skittered up the wall. She crab-walked across the ceiling, then clung to the blades of the overhead fan, her head twisting the wrong way around as she glared down.

"*I WILL REBUILD MYSELF, ANAKIM!*" she shrieked, and the voice pouring from her throat was the same that had invaded my thoughts outside of the cemetery.

Terael spread his wings in defiance.

"Few of our punishments were just, but some fell for a reason, Thunderer." Power whirled about him with the sound of a dust devil, and golden sparks danced upon the air.

"*YOU WILL FALL BEFORE ME, GILDED ONE!*"

"Just an image," I muttered in a rush. "Just an image in my head."

"Not *just* an image, as well you know," Terael snarled. "Cast him out!"

"I don't even know how I brought him here!" I cried.

"*Liar.*"

Terael's gilded features grew colder than any stone. Above us, Not-Halley's head turned as if on a swivel. With distended jaws, she swallowed a blade of the ceiling fan in a single, gigantic gulp. The light fixture swung crazily, awakening shadows in every corner of the imagined room. Chewing messily, she stretched forward to gobble pieces of the plaster. Wherever she bit, blackness gaped.

"Seriously, Terael—I have no fucking clue what's going on," I hissed.

"*FEED ME. FEED ME ALL YOUR POWER.*"

The Rephaim wearing Halley's skin leapt to the far wall, nightmare-quick and bending in all the wrong directions. She—*it*, for I could no longer think of it as Halley—clung to the curtains over the picture window. They billowed in a sudden gale. The bitter, freezing wind shrieked against the walls of my projection.

The Halley-Thing continued eating. Fragmented bits of the ceiling and walls rained upon the rug. Pain crackled sharp as lightning through my skull.

"A trap." Terael cringed away from me. "He's tied to you. You carried him in and trapped me here." He wore a look of utter betrayal. "How deftly you drew me in with your protestations of ignorance, all the while hiding him in the scarred corners of your mind. We were allies, my sibling, even friends," he quailed.

"This projection-thing was your idea," I reminded him.

"*Then cast him out!*"

Terael's command trebled the pain in my head. My vision blurred, then split, till I felt stretched intolerably between the physical space of the office and the imagined room. My nose started running. I had a bad feeling it was blood.

The golden Rephaim swept his wings like a windstorm, till motes of gleaming dust whirled through every corner of the room. Not-Halley shouted incoherent defiance. Wherever the motes settled, an ugly cluster of three symbols lay exposed.

Terhuziel's Name.

"No," I gasped.

The letters throbbed on every surface, gaining strength as the Halley-Thing chewed.

"Lie to me some more, my sibling. Deny again your pact." Terael's normally lilting notes dropped to something subsonic, each word gritty with threat.

Too late I made the connection.

Fish-Knife Lady. I hadn't just taken his Name from her memories. I'd swallowed his connection to her whole. Now it snagged me like a fishhook, and I twisted on the line.

"Fuck me running," I breathed.

Not-Halley gobbled another swath of plaster.

The edges of my vision frayed.

"*BOW AND SERVE ME AS YOUR MASTER,*" the Halley-Thing bellowed. "*I WILL BE WHOLE AGAIN!*"

Then I roared in fierce negation. Wind surged within the room. Blue-white power limned my fingers. Thrusting out with both my hands, I attacked the nearest instance of Terhuziel's festering Name. The symbols hissed and shriveled. Not-Halley choked in wordless rage.

Battle lust consumed me. My hands shone with brilliant light. I danced and slashed and shouted, twin daggers glinting as I cut him from my mind.

22

I slammed back to full awareness of the office. I sprawled in a heap on the floor, and had nearly brought the whole bookshelf down on top of myself. The office chair tilted crazily a few feet away, its wheeled base still spinning.

Terael buzzed like a nest of angry hornets from every corner of the room.

Liar! Traitor! he shouted. *You must kill her. Seek her out and kill her now. No other proof will I accept. You have conspired to bring me down.*

"No one's killing the girl," I croaked, painfully aware that I'd had the same impulse myself. I swiped at my running nose. The back of my hand came away covered in blood. *Great.*

You shall keep her for yourself, then? Or do you save her for our maddened sibling, to become sacrifice and vessel for his return?

I wouldn't have dignified that with an answer, even if I'd understood everything he intended. Shakily, I dragged myself up along the edge of the desk. Someone had stolen my muscles and replaced them all with jelly—useless, quivering jelly. The empty ache of soul-hunger gnawed fiercely beneath my ribs. It hitched with every stunted breath. I'd burned a lot of power kicking Terhuziel out of my head—power I didn't have in reserve.

You must have known, he insisted. *How could you not have known? The memory of her touch—such an instant, bright connection. Power leaping mind to mind. You knew and yet you lied. A fool am I to trust you so.*

Terael's every thought spiderwebbed through accusations and increasingly paranoid delusions. My skull hammered, and I had no strength to fend him off.

When did he turn you to his cause? So long you stayed away—I should have known when you did not come once he had encroached upon my Domain. A pact you made to carry him in the scarred spaces of your mind. Deny it! he railed. *I saw the proof of pact, stamped clearly once he no longer deigned to hide. Why betrayal now, my sibling—and for such a one as the Thunderer?*

"Stop it," I gasped. I could barely give breath to the words. Threads of light gnawed my vision.

The girl must die, he persisted. *The Elder Blood. We cannot stand before that force. He claims her strength and we must fall. All will burn, as once before.* The Gatling gun fire of his thought-speak left me dizzy.

"Terael, *dammit.* Stop already," I pleaded. "I didn't know he was in there. I was attacked last night. He—"

I ran headlong into the binding oath.

Walls I didn't even know I had slammed shut around the details of the fight. Terael took it for more proof of my betrayal, too panicked now to even match his thoughts to words. He roiled messily along the edges of our mental contact, his boundaries crumbling as fear robbed him of some essential level of control. I swayed before an assault of memories—all of them the Rephaim's, punishingly swift and jagged.

Backdrops of mountains, deserts, green and rolling hills—all perceived from a weird three-hundred-and-sixty-degree view that wove through every stick and stone. Temples—a stupefaction of architectural styles. They flickered by with such speed that all their profiles blended into one.

Domain.

My word or his, I couldn't tell.

Then, people. Priests and priestesses—some of whom appeared neither male nor female, but some sacred mingling of the two. An endless march of faces. Painted skin in every shade.

Those-Who-Serve.

I knew them as he knew them. Not merely as anchors. Precious assets. Heart and life-blood of the temple. Voices roared in a cacophony of forgotten languages, songs of supplication, ringing chants of praise. Sistrums, drums, and ankle bells struck fervent, rolling rhythms. All danced in *ekstasis* as they screamed the Name.

Then one—*the* One. The lamb slaughtered so other life could be renewed. A maiden. Pure. Unpledged. Child of the gods, filled to bursting with sacred power for the rebirth of the temple lord.

Always the most precious must be given up to serve.

All of this in an eyeblink, with nuances so complex

that they would take me weeks to sort out. Crushed beneath the weight of revelation, I fought to regain some sense of self—of where his mind ended and mine began. Still Terael's thoughts unspooled, rife with anxiety and bitter reproof.

You have led him to this. A pure one with strength enough to carry him even from the edge of his doom. He will heal and spread domain throughout this city. War will come again.

"No!" I cried in fierce denial. That I even spoke a word at all felt like a triumph. I barely had a sense of my own lips. But it didn't break his suffocating contact. More scenes tumbled through my head, blood-drenched and thick with the acrid bite of smoke. Terhuziel's ambition. Conflicts, proclamations, and the jealous call to war. The mouthpiece of the god—high priest and holy warrior—at the head of sweeping armies, eyes aglow as his very will tore lightning from the sky.

Conquest, Terael intoned. Then, with a note of soul-sick horror that made the breath stop in my throat, he added, *Reprisal.*

A sea of shattered statues, gemstone eyes gouged from blinded sockets. Arms and heads and hands severed in the wake of war. The mortal dead discarded, cut down in defense of their gods. Soot-stained figures working a vast and belching forge. Golden idols melted down and screaming as they died. Stone images smashed to pieces with massive, iron mauls. Some of the broken, twisted, yet alive—imprisoned by gleaming disks of power pressed against their brows.

I lay in Hinome Valley throughout that awful time.

Still I hear the sounds of the shattered—and the dreadful silence of those confined. His thoughts pummeled accusingly, fixating on images of a seal, fashioned from clay or carved from stone. Coiling runes covered its surface, locking in some spell.

A disk like that—I'd seen one recently, casually flipped across the knuckles of David Garrett. Before I could speak, however, the force of Terael's ire yanked me under like a riptide.

I will not endure it again, he insisted. *Not ever again. Kill the girl.*

He thrashed as if he was drowning—we both were—only the sea was the entangled boundary of our two minds. I tried to drag him out, deposit him on his own shore, but again and again, he pulled me under with him. Madness chewed around the edges—of thoughts, of self, of everything.

Then something rose up inside of me. Impassable. Unyielding. I thought perhaps it was the oath again, it had something of its flavor, but this ran deeper, spiraling down to some internal past which I could not perceive. Clinging to it like the last shred of solid ground in all of existence, I made it my axis.

Together, we used the point of reference to rebuild the walls where I ended and Terael began.

The final aftershocks of mental collision rocked me, raw and bleak and bitter.

A lone woman, escaping. A darkened grotto with a hidden shrine. The woman pressing a blade to her chest as she knelt at the foot of a statue. Blood and power flooding forth until she collapsed, an emptied husk. A swirl of golden motes and the sound of dusty wings. Her body reeking as he rebuilt himself from the substance of her death, healing within the new stone skin.

I knew that face of dark basalt.

Terael's idol in the museum.

"She killed herself for you." I wasn't even certain that I said the words out loud.

As our mothers always must.

His aching note of sorrow lingered long after he sealed the floodgates of his mind.

23

"For the last damned time, I didn't betray you. As thoroughly as you got yourself lost on the wrong side of my skull, how could you not see that?"

Terael pretended not to hear me. He did the Rephaim equivalent of pacing around the room, which meant he ended up brooding like a storm front. The last thing I wanted from him was the silent treatment. That shit wasn't going to help me or Halley—I still had a ton of questions, not the least of which involved how I was supposed to go toe-to-toe with a storm god.

Still the mental quiet was a welcome respite.

I leaned with my shoulders propped against the desk, giving up on being anywhere but on the floor until the room stopped spinning. My head pounded like an army of maniacal gnomes had launched a tunneling mission through my frontal lobe. They gave fuck all about the Advil I'd taken.

Scavenging a wad of napkins from a drawer, I used them to wipe some of the blood from the lower half of my face. As far as I could tell, my nose had stopped bleeding, though I could still taste copper at the back of my throat. It was a familiar tang, and I tried not to think about it.

Mostly I succeeded.

As soon as it seemed like I could stand, I levered myself to my feet. I didn't have the luxury of time— and neither did Halley. With every death, Terhuziel grew stronger. Stronger was bad. If I understood all I'd gleaned from Terael—both the details he'd volunteered and the stuff that had spilled wildly between us—the girl had a bigger problem than mere possession.

And I thought the Nephilim had a creepy way of cheating death.

For the moment, Terhuziel was able to reach her through whispers, but didn't have enough strength to claim her outright. Crippled by his punishment in the wars of the distant past, he was still recovering. If I could locate his base of operations before he built any more power, there was still a chance I could save the girl.

That brought me back to Bobby's murder investigation. How close was that to Halley's home in Little Italy? Both houses were in the Third District, covered by the Chester Station, but that didn't exactly narrow down a location—the Third District ran from the east bank of the Cuyahoga all the way to Shaker Heights. I needed more information on that house.

The Rephaim fed on sacrifice—the more precious, the better. The father of that four-year-old girl was still missing. I hated myself for thinking it, but if the souvenir-collecting physician hadn't died protecting his family, there was a high chance he had been the one to kill them.

A whole family. That was some precious blood to spill upon the altar.

I checked the time, debating how much I could spare for an Internet search.

Seven forty-two.

Barely ten minutes had passed since I'd let Terael into my brainspace. It had felt like hours. One of the benefits— if you could call it that—to working at the speed of thought.

A bright, fat drop of blood splashed onto my desk blotter. I dabbed my nose—and then reached for another wad of napkins.

"Fuck."

The nasal sound robbed the word of its usual punch.

Still holding the napkins to my face with one hand, I righted my office chair. The swivel mechanism gave an alarming shriek as I dropped heavily into it. I wheeled closer to the desk and stabbed the power button to boot up my computer.

"Let's say Ter-hoo-ha started off at this doc's house," I said, as if Terael was standing there. "The guy collects artifacts, and he just got back from Syria. He must have checked in with the black market before he crossed the border." The more I thought about it, the more convinced I became that the dad was the killer. "The cops have been all over the place for the past couple of weeks, so he can't have stuck around, but that's still ground zero for the first serious sacrifices. From there, I should be able to get a good feel for Terhuziel on the

209

Shadowside, maybe track him to his new domain."

My resident Rephaim made no response. I couldn't even tell if he was listening.

"I'm pretty sure Bobby meant for me to see that house number," I mused out loud. "If I can narrow down the neighborhood where the murders happened, I bet I can find the street that goes with it."

That got a reaction. Above me, Terael contracted upon himself, lingering as the barest tremor in the air.

"You all right?" I asked.

No.

A soul-sick feeling of misery spilled through the windowless office. I made a weak attempt at reinforcing my mental barriers. I really couldn't handle a repeat of earlier.

"Still think I'm a traitor?" I asked cautiously.

No, he said again, though he didn't seem as certain.

"Well, that's at least a start."

I Google-whacked Cleveland, murders, four-year-old-girl, and Doctors Without Borders. Set the date range for anything appearing over the past month. As it turned out, the murders were all over the news. I clicked the top link.

With her death, the Blood Wars truly begin again.

Terael meant Halley, but it was little Kaylee's face that flickered to life in the ghostly light of my computer screen. Her last name was Kramer.

"I'm not killing Halley," I said reflexively. My mouth was dry and the taste of blood clung thickly to my tongue. "I'll cut Terhuziel out of her head the same way I cut him out of mine. Then I'll hunt the bastard down. No more sacrifices."

You speak as if there is a choice, but that choice was forfeit long ago.

I ignored him, finding new resolve to wall away my mind.

Kaylee Kramer was a beautiful child of African descent, her dark, curly hair caught up in two puffy pigtails at the top of her head. She had bright hazel eyes and skin the color of polished teak. The easy smile she wore in the photo—a smile the world would never see again—gutted me. According to the article, she had two older sisters, Alana and Leah.

Paydirt. The father's name was Alan. I did a White Pages search for Dr. Alan Kramer. Terael fretted around the edges of my thoughts, tentative but questing.

Even should you drive off the Thunderer of the Northern Hills, war will come and seek us. Elder Blood is too precious. It has driven us mad before.

"You keep saying things like you expect me to recognize them. I don't."

He didn't bother to elaborate.

Gritting my teeth, I focused on the screen. There were seven Alan Kramers in the Greater Cleveland area. Only one had a street address that matched the numbers I remembered from Bobby's photo. Whitethorn Road in Cleveland Heights. I grabbed a sticky note and jotted it down.

You are not ignorant of the Blood Wars, my brother. His rising note of accusation made me worry.

"I don't recall specifics," I snapped.

Blood Wars, the Rephaim said again. *Wars of Blood. All the precious children of the tribes slaughtered, in order to rob us of their power.*

That got my attention.

"I thought we called them Blood Wars because the Nephilim were involved. They're vampires—"

No.

He threw the word like a slap at my face.

Wars among immortals can have no end, my sibling, but our children and our families—once stolen, such precious treasures could never be regained.

"Elder Blood," I murmured. In retrospect it seemed obvious—and my anger rose in proportion to my obliviousness. I glowered at the air above my desk. "Let me get this straight. You want me to kill an innocent girl, because that's what we've always done—killed one another's children." Anger climbed toward fury. "How fucked in the head are you?"

Terael recoiled, and for an instant it felt like he took all the oxygen with him. Blood thundered in my ears.

"You don't solve death with death," I bellowed. "And we sure as hell won't fix the past by repeating it."

It is a game of numbers, Zaquiel. He was so damned matter-of-fact. *One girl dies, or many. Her life is fated to disaster. Death would be kind for such a one as she.*

"Don't you even start," I threatened. "The kid has challenges. That's no reason to take her life from her."

If you do not, then another will. She bears too much danger in her birthright.

"How can you even be certain? I met her mother— the woman's as normal as khaki pants and cardigan sweaters. What if the girl's just a psychic? A garden-variety mortal with a spooky way of seeing my wings—"

You saw it in her. You saw, and you yourself considered the solution.

He was right—and I raged against it.

"That's not a fucking answer!" I was out of the chair and pacing, shouting into the air. "We deal with Terhuziel. He's the problem. I cut him out of her head, I smash the token—assuming I even find one—then I track him down to his domain. We fight. I kick his ass. End of problem."

It almost sounded easy.

We are immortal. That cannot be the end. If he knows, others will come.

As I drew breath to voice my objection, a subtle itching crossed my palm. My next few words snagged in my throat—halted either by the oath or my own gut-twisting shock at the thoughts that itch inspired.

The Eye of Nefer-Ka could fix everything.

All I had to do was get my hands on Terhuziel. With my tie to the Nephilim icon, I could scoop the memories of Halley straight out of whatever served as his brain.

No.

I curled my hand into a fist, clenching my fingers until the nails bit deep into the tingling scar. Terhuziel was insane, a blood-thirsty monster, and he had already cut a swath of destruction through my city. Halley had suffered. I could probably add little Kaylee and her sisters to that list, and who knew how many others. Could that much death justify doing to Terhuziel what had been done to me?

Dorimiel had felt justified.

I knew all too well what he'd been thinking—I'd spent

MICHELLE BELANGER

time inside of his head. The shadow-touched Nephilim had believed himself righteous—heroically wreaking vengeance upon the zealous Anakim. Before that, we'd killed everyone in his temple—*everyone*. Guards, servants, even the children. That was one memory he'd made certain to leave to me. It didn't matter if they fought us, didn't matter if they were too young to know better. They were his, and they were tainted.

So they died, and we felt just in killing them.

So incredibly, brutally *just*.

Justice lay in the minds of those who dispensed it. That was why Anakesiel and his lieutenants were still sitting in their jars, even though I knew how to release them. I couldn't bring myself to loose more monsters on the world.

One of those monsters was the head of my tribe.

No, I told myself again. *Some powers come with too high a price.* For a moment, the pulse inside the scar rose to a thunder that shook my whole world. Then, abruptly, it subsided.

Oblivious to my internal struggle, Terael continued his argument.

Our brother knows, and even if you best him he will return. Others will come. I have had too much of war, Zaquiel. I do not wish to see this city fall. Not for the price of one mortal child.

Still rattled, I played the asshole card.

"You're not going to win this argument, Terael. You're stuck in here. I can leave." The Rephaim chewed the air, but I didn't give him a chance to frame a response. "I'll figure out some way to fix this, and I'll

214

do it without killing the girl."

With that, I popped through the Shadowside, despite how wrecked I felt, and marched from the museum.

To my amazement, he let me.

24

Full dark had settled on the city. The cars along Euclid Avenue traced a river of light through the gloom. I walked toward where I'd parked on East Boulevard, reminding myself each step of the way why it was a bad idea to consider using the Nephilim icon.

There was no denying the lure of the icon. It offered such an easy fix to everything. The fact that it tugged at me was unnerving, though, and that was putting it lightly.

Scenarios whirled through my brain—backtracking through one of his followers, grabbing Terhuziel long enough to steal his powers. But would my shields be enough to protect me, once I set foot in his domain? The threat of another mental assault unnerved me almost as much as the siren's song of the Eye.

If not the Eye, there was always the Stylus. What about a binding? It wasn't like Anakesiel could object from his snug little jar.

"The damned things were buried for a reason," I reminded myself as I drew close to the Hellcat. I didn't realize I'd said it with my out-loud voice, though.

"I take it things didn't go well at the museum?"

That jolted me out of my reverie, and I jumped. Lil lounged against the driver's side of the Hellcat, her long spill of russet hair wild in the wind. She smiled, showing all her teeth.

"What, you didn't see me?"

Numbly, I shook my head.

She'd changed her clothes, and was sporting khaki cargo pants with a rust-colored V-neck that clung to her lavish curves. She'd traded the sable coat for a brown leather jacket with a sophisticated military cut, wearing it open despite the cold—the better to show off the way the shirt beneath hugged her chest. The jacket had a decidedly steampunk look, though it was a safe bet Lil didn't even know what that was.

Motioning her away from the door, I pulled out my key fob and thumbed the button. Nothing happened. I scowled at the little piece of black plastic, turning it over in my hand.

"How'd you even know this was my car?" I asked.

She rolled her shoulder languidly. "Smells like you."

"I have a smell?" I jammed my finger against the button to unlock the doors—again to no effect.

She nodded. "Leather. Cedar. Rose pepper. Something warm I can taste at the back of my throat." She trailed the tip of her tongue along the edge of her teeth for emphasis.

"I'm sorry I asked." I gave up on the key fob, and decided to unlock the car the old-fashioned way.

Lil threw her head back and laughed maddeningly as she canted her hips to the right, almost but not quite covering the lock with her butt. Eyes bright with mischief, she watched me fumble with the key.

"The way you blush amuses me," she said. "You never would have blushed before."

"Glad to be of service," I said. "Your amusement gives my life purpose." Finally she danced nimbly out of the way, and watched me from the empty street. She pointed at the fob.

"Those things have batteries, you know. You probably killed it on one of your Shadowside jaunts."

"Is there a reason you're taunting me?" I asked archly. Though, honestly, it was a welcome distraction from the welter of my thoughts. I got the car open and slid into the driver's seat. Lil darted forward and caught the edge of my door. I tugged to shut it, but her grip was immovable. She leaned down till her eyes were even with my own.

"Why don't you ask me what I've been up to?" she suggested.

"Probably because you're going to tell me anyway." I didn't blink as I met her gray-eyed gaze.

She frowned. "So cranky. You really need to get laid."

"Not up for discussion," I responded. "Are you going to get in the car, or do I find out how long you can hang on while I drive away?"

She wrinkled her nose at me. "Cranky," she repeated.

I keyed the ignition as she sauntered around the front of the vehicle, rolling her hips elaborately as she walked. Once the car started up, my iPod spat out the opening riffs of Tool's "Schism." I silently cursed whatever cruel mechanism of the universe had gifted my stereo with a sense of irony, then reached across to unlock Lil's door, stopping short of actually opening it for her.

She slid inside, pulling a sheaf of papers from her little white clutch purse. They seemed longer than the purse was tall, yet they came out unwrinkled. I pondered the Gallifreyan physics of her trusty handbag, then glanced over the pages.

They were printouts of articles from a variety of animal-rights websites, with a couple of news blogs peppered throughout the bunch. The news blogs didn't seem especially deserving of the name—they were mostly conspiracy theory nuts and fundamentalist rags.

"To prove that we're dealing with one of the Rephaim, I started looking for evidence of sacrifices," she said. "Sure enough, there's been a rash of animal mutilations. These are the most relevant stories. There were others."

"How is something called 'The End Times Blog' a reliable news source?" I inquired.

"Since they include pictures of mutilated animals, a makeshift altar, and a very real ancient Name," she hissed, snatching the paper from me. Folding it down, she stabbed her nail at a grainy photo near the bottom.

In my defense, it was a tiny picture. I had to squint to see the characters.

"Terhuziel," I grunted. "Are those cats?"

Her first response was an unintelligible sound of strangled rage.

"An old woman, living alone," she growled. "A dozen cats, maybe more. She skinned some. Burned the rest alive. A week before, they were her babies. The authorities put her in a home. Blamed dementia. She killed herself once she realized what she'd done."

As the words poured out of her, the scent of ozone crackled from Lil's hair. She gripped the leather clutch purse as if it had done her some wrong. The inside of the Hellcat suddenly felt too tiny to contain her.

"I'm sorry," I said softly.

"Then you're not a complete idiot," she snapped.

"Only most of the time?" I ventured.

It was a weak try, calculated to lighten her mood, but Lil didn't cave. She turned her face away and stared out the window. Her breath steamed the glass in slow, controlled bursts. If she'd been anyone else, I'd have assumed she was fighting back tears.

Lillee Gibson was the most cold-blooded killer I could imagine when it came to mortals. I'd never seen her moved by a death—at least not with grief. Not even with rage. This was an entirely new side of her. That it involved animals shouldn't have surprised me—she was, after all, the Lady of Beasts.

"The mutilations started back in February," she said, her voice still rough. "The first one I could credibly tie to all this was on the twentieth. I plotted them on a map. It's the page at the very bottom." The wounded anger slowly bled from her voice, until she mostly sounded tired. "Too many people overlook the suffering of animals. A mortal turns up dead, and the authorities are all over it—even if the person deserved it. Skin half a dozen cats alive, and some people fucking cheer."

"Lil," I said, reaching my hand out. She slapped it away without even looking.

After puffing a breath, she continued. "They started in a pretty concentrated area, then spread out as the weeks progressed. The activity's centered on a five-block radius in Cleveland Heights."

I switched to the map. "Nice neighborhood. Not the sort of place you'd expect that kind of thing." I squinted at the tiny lettering on the printout. "Is one of those streets called Whitethorn?"

She didn't bother to check. "Yeah. Whitethorn's near the middle."

"We've got ground zero, then." I fished in my pocket and handed over the sticky note with Dr. Alan Kramer's address. Lil took it, frowning—but at least it no longer felt like she was going to summon a hurricane inside of my car.

"What happened at this address?" she asked.

"They didn't stop at animals," I said.

Lil yanked the pages from my hand and shoved them back into her purse. They disappeared like she had dropped them down a well. When I didn't put the car into gear right away, she slapped the steering wheel.

"What are you waiting for?" she demanded. "We need to search that house!" She raised her hand for a second strike, and I deflected it, irritably shoving the arm back to her side of the car.

"It's on my list," I said, "but I have to stop at the hospital first. After that, I've got to track down Bobby's partner."

She loosed a snarl of impatience. "Why?"

Images of spirit-locks and ancient wars danced behind my eyes, courtesy of Terael's memories.

"Because reasons," I said, taking a page from her own book.

Lil's snarl of impatience developed to a full-fledged growl. I half expected to catch sight of her spectral lioness in the rearview mirror, looming and ready to pounce, but the sound had come from Lil's human-shaped throat. Still, there was nothing human about it.

The interior of the car started to feel more like the confines of a cage, and I was on the wrong side with the wild animal.

"Lil, he's not in that house any more," I insisted. "It's a crime scene, and the police have been in and out of it for weeks. At best, he'll have left some kind of imprint on the Shadowside. Something that might help me track where he's at now. If it's there, it'll wait a couple hours. I'm at least stopping at the hospital. Halley is our priority," I said flatly.

She pursed her lips, but didn't try talking me out of it. Slowly, the inhuman sound of displeasure abated. It felt like I was sitting next to a person again, as opposed to something... mythic. Lacking a steering wheel of her own to abuse, she ratcheted her nails against the dash. They were still painted with shamrocks, emerald glitter catching the light from the street.

"What's so special about the girl?" she asked finally.

I almost told her, and then thought better of it. Lil wouldn't share my compunctions about killing Halley. She'd side with Terael on the matter.

"She's got strong psychic abilities," I hedged. "He's using her to put himself back together again. I need to sever whatever ties he's already planted in her head."

"So he's one of the Shattered," she murmured. "That's the first bit of good news all day." After rolling that around in her head for a moment, she added, "Let's go."

"Just like that?" I asked.

She glared at me. "Yeah, just like that. Would you like me to argue?"

"No." I put the car in gear. "Just used to you making my life difficult, is all."

She barked a bitter laugh. "You have a decimus of the Rephaim trying set himself up as a new godling in your town. Right now, your life is difficult enough. Drive."

25

For close to nine o'clock on a Saturday night, the lot outside of University Hospital was packed. Half the city must have decided to get sick at the same time. I circled a few times while Lil churned toward the boiling point beside me.

After my second pass down one of the lanes, she seized the wheel, nearly jerking my car into the back of an Escalade. I crushed the brake pedal against the floor, slapping her away.

"What the hell, Lil?" I demanded.

"We're wasting time," she snarled through gritted teeth. "Park the fucking car."

I made a rude gesture at the lot in general, saying, "I don't know if you've noticed, but there's not a lot of parking out here."

She stabbed a shamrock-decked finger in the direction of a looming concrete structure to the far right of the lot.

"Parking garage. Use it."

I grumbled, checking my pockets, then pulling out my wallet.

"What?" she scoffed, adding mockingly, "Is that too far for you to walk? I could break your ankle, if you'd rather someone wheel you in."

"I walk more than I drive in this city," I shot back, glowering at her. "Doesn't matter—I don't have any cash on me."

"It's a modern facility, Zaquiel," she said in a patronizing tone. "They take this magical thing called plastic."

Swinging the car in the direction of the parking garage, I grumbled, "I almost forgot what a pain in the ass you can be."

"Just park this beast and let's get on with it. If I'd been driving, we could have been in and out by now," she said, folding her arms over her chest. "Do you even know what room she's in?"

"Nope," I answered, rolling up to the booth. There wasn't a rate posted, which meant I probably didn't want to know. I snagged a ticket and urged the Hellcat gently over the speed bump.

"You got a last name for this girl at least?" she huffed.

"Halley Davis," I replied. "She's special needs."

The first level of the parking garage was packed. I nosed past rows of sedans and compacts, all stained with salt from the winter roads.

"Shouldn't be too hard to find," Lil said.

I took the nearly forty-five degree turn up to the next level, almost ending up nose-to-nose with a Camry on its way down. Once it was past, Lil gestured sharply to what looked like an open space to the right. She lunged for the steering wheel again. I hunched forward, bodily blocking her with my shoulders.

"Motorcycle," I snarled.

She craned her neck as I crawled closer to the space, huffing when she spotted the ass-end of the Yamaha.

"Who the hell rides a motorcycle in this weather?"

"Whatever idiot parked there. Next question?"

"There—that spot. *Right there*," she said, pointing. She didn't attempt to take control this time. Small victories. I canted my head, studying the narrow slice of parking between a Scion and a badly angled Jeep Cherokee.

"Not sure the Hellcat will fit in there," I muttered.

"Oh, I can make it fit," Lil replied ominously.

I barely managed to bite back a *"That's what she said."* Lil moved to grab the wheel again, and I snapped my teeth at her to warn her away.

She laughed.

"Don't make promises you can't keep, flyboy."

Right. Forgot who I was dealing with.

"If you promise not to grab the wheel out of my hands, I'll try parking there."

"Zaquiel, I'm hurt," she cooed. "You act like I'm out to make trouble for you."

"You're still breathing, so yeah," I fired back. "Hell, I'm pretty sure I'd have to watch my ass, even if you were dead."

She actually chuckled. "Park already," she said. "The bad guys are doing bad guy things while we argue, and no one's there to stop them."

That almost sounded reasonable. I shot her a genuinely incredulous look, then decided it was smarter not to question it. Lil had probably taught the Trojans the meaning of a sucker-punch.

Banking the wheel sharply, I nosed the Hellcat into the narrow and off-center space. With the way the asshole in the Jeep had parked, it was a tight fit, but I made it work. Lil was halfway out before I cut the motor. She walked briskly toward the stairwell, the heels of her boots echoing hollowly through the cavernous levels of dingy concrete. She glanced at me over her shoulder as I jogged to catch up.

"It's after nine o'clock, flyboy," she said. "Visiting hours are over. You give any thought to how you're going to get to this girl?"

"Ask at an information desk?" I ventured.

"Amateur," she barked. "They're closed."

"I guess you'll show me how it's done, then," I answered, managing to keep most of the sarcasm out of my voice.

"Watch and learn," she taunted. She shrugged out of her leather and shoved it at me. "Hold this." Next, she dug a scrunchie out of her purse and pulled her wild locks back from her face. She added a second, twisting her hair into a loose knot at the nape of her neck.

Pressing the heel of one hand against her brightly colored lips, she patted away the lipstick till they were almost their natural color. She never stopped walking, but continued at a brisk pace all the way to the main building. She rubbed the excess lipstick off on her palms, then swept the backs of her fingers across her cheekbones, toning down her blush.

She dug again into the handbag, and it disgorged a

pair of tortoise-rimmed reading glasses. With a smug little flourish, she slipped these onto her nose.

Mutely bearing witness to the swift stages of this transformation, I tucked the jacket under one arm and followed gamely along. Sometimes it was worth letting Lil take charge just to see what she was going to do next.

26

Steal someone's lab coat.

That was what she did next. Then Lil strode straight to an empty information desk and slipped behind it like she belonged. From there, she nabbed a clipboard and a pen. She glanced through stacks of notes around the computer, moving them around with the tip of the pen, very conscious not to leave fingerprints. From the looks of things, she found what she was seeking, and did it in under a minute flat.

She ducked back out from behind the desk and headed for the elevators, motioning for me to follow. If I got too close, she quickened her pace, moving with the same brisk urgency as Alice's time-conscious white rabbit.

"You do this a lot?" I called.

"Keep your voice down," she snapped.

We reached the elevators and she pressed the "UP" button—again, using not her finger, but the tip of the pen. She waited, humming softly to herself.

"Is that Dixie Chicks?" I asked incredulously.

She kept humming.

The elevator chimed and the doors opened. It was empty. Lil hustled me inside, then stood about an arm's length from me, facing slightly away. She waited for the doors to slide shut before she said anything. Her voice was low and I had to strain to hear.

"Act like you don't know me. Hang back at least ten paces. And whenever you see signs on the walls, stare at them and look lost. That part shouldn't be hard for you," she added witheringly.

"It's a hospital, Lil. We're not breaking into Fort Knox. Why do you have to act like everything's a spy movie?" I hissed. "And why the hell didn't you tell me these things before we got inside?"

"I like to see how quick you are on your feet," she answered. "As it turns out, not quick enough." She stepped close to elbow me, then followed through with the motion as if her sole intention had been to reach toward the glowing bank of buttons. She pressed one with the tip of the pen. "Just do like I ask for once. You're armed. I'm armed. It's after visiting hours. I'd like to get in and out quickly, rather than have to tangle with security."

I huffed my irritation and shoved my fists into the pockets of my jacket.

"Fine. Whatever. I hate these places anyway."

"So do I," she answered hollowly. That was unexpected. I shifted in the elevator, tightening the cowl across my wings.

"It can't be all the death," I ventured. "I've seen you slice a man's throat down to the bone, and smile about it."

"He wasn't a man," she shot back. With an uncharacteristically prim gesture, she adjusted the glasses on her nose. "And death's one thing. Suffering—needless suffering—is something else entirely."

We fell silent as the elevator paused at the next floor. The doors slid open to the sound of a muted chime. No one waited outside. Lil stabbed impatiently at the "Close Doors" button.

"Torture," I said, once the elevator started moving again. "You're no stranger to torture."

"The suffering here is pointless," she responded tightly. "Why buy a few extra days if they're spent attached to machines in a chemical delirium? Sometimes death's a kindness. The world's forgotten that truth."

Letting my head drop back against the shiny wall of the elevator, I grunted a non-answer. My reflection stared back ghost-like from the mirrored ceiling. Lines of weariness traced the pale skin around my eyes—evidence of my recent exertions at the art museum.

At least I'd cleared all the blood from around my nose.

Soul-hunger gnawed deep under my ribs, and I knew I'd have to deal with it soon—or else I'd be no use to Halley or anyone else. The hospital was the last place I wanted to take care of it, however. There were plenty of people to draw upon, but I wanted no part of what they carried with them.

Lil was right about the suffering—it was bad enough tasting what bled through my shields.

"You going to argue with me, Zack?" she prodded.

"Nothing to argue." I sighed. "A hospital is a big

fucking Crossing, and this place is packed with over a hundred years' worth of experiences families wish they could forget." Tightening my cowl, I fought to marshal my shredded shields. Just talking about it caused the aura of the place to claw at the edges of my awareness. "For every loss, there's a dozen more successes. I know that. They're trying to save people. But all I pick up on are the failures."

Lil looked like she was going to respond—and for once, with something supportive—but the elevator chime dinged and the doors opened. A cheery sign in cartoon colors greeted us. Rainbow Babies and Children— University Hospital's answer to a pediatric ward.

"This is our stop," Lil muttered.

She strode from the elevator. In an instant she was a rushed and slightly scattered attending nurse. The transformation was subtle and settled over her like a deftly tailored coat. I stared long enough that the elevator started to close on me.

Catching the doors with an elbow, I realized suddenly why she'd been using the pen. It wasn't just an effort not to leave fingerprints. She didn't dare touch anything with her bare hands—not in such a psychically-charged location.

Lil headed right for the nurses' station, and I followed several steps behind, stopping to dither over some signs, taking the opportunity to slap a few more layers on my mental protection as I did so. The children's ward roiled with a suffocating miasma of brittle hopes and protracted misery. It made my teeth itch like I was gnawing aluminum foil.

She approached the nurse seated at the station, hugging the clipboard bashfully to her chest. When she spoke, she softened her voice, pitching it higher until I barely recognized it.

"Does the Davenport girl have any of her family still here?" Lil chirped. She glanced down at her clipboard, amending, "Davis. Sorry. Been a long shift." She held it up helpfully, showing only the back of it. "I forgot to get them to sign one of the release forms. Just caught it on my way out for the night."

The nurse at the station—a mocha-skinned woman with peppered hair buzzed close to her scalp—tapped a few commands into her computer. She wore reading glasses on a chain at her neck, and she squinted through these at whatever popped onto the screen. Lil rose to her tiptoes, peering inquisitively over the high counter.

"Looks like she still has a support person here," the nurse answered. "Not sure he's authorized to sign, though. You'll have to check."

Lil offered the woman a smile that managed to look weary, apologetic, and grateful all at once.

"Thank you. She in the same room?"

The other woman pointed vaguely. "Yep. End of the second hall. On the left." She peered over her glasses in my direction, a frown settling across her brow. "Who's that guy? He came up with you."

"Oh," Lil said with a little giggle. I had never heard her giggle. It was an intensely creepy sound. "Date night. He was walking me to the car when I remembered about the paperwork."

I angled my back toward them and tried thinking

harmless thoughts. My shoulder blades prickled under the older woman's scrutiny. She made a thoughtful sound in her throat. I tensed, expecting her to call security.

She sniffed. "Nice butt, for a white guy. Kinda skinny, though."

I felt all the blood rush to my ears.

"He has a motorcycle," Lil whispered. She held the air of someone sharing an enticingly dirty secret.

"Honey, if he's riding it in this weather, you kick his white-boy ass to the curb right now." The nurse laughed richly. "Ain't nobody got time for that kind of crazy."

Lil practically tittered with amusement. I struggled not to twitch at the uncanny sound.

"No, but he promised to take me riding once the weather breaks." After the two had shared another few laughs at my expense, the attending nurse made a shooing motion.

"Go on and get your paperwork signed," she encouraged. "And take your fella with you. I don't want to have to keep track of him."

"OK," the Lady of Beasts chirped. She turned and gestured to me. I was already halfway to the nurses' station. We strode together down the hall, Lil taking the lead. I had the distinct impression the nurse behind us was undressing me with her eyes. I walked a little faster.

"Date night?" I inquired archly.

"It worked, didn't it?" Lil responded.

"I do not have a white-boy ass," I muttered.

Lil snorted. "Have you looked in a mirror?" She grabbed me and gave a little squeeze.

The nurse at the station tried to be quiet about it, but

I could hear her snickering all the way down the hall. The instant we turned the corner at the end, I seized Lil by the wrist. Normally, physical contact blew a person right into my mind, but Lil had defenses to rival the firewall at the Pentagon. The most I got were tattered echoes of the façade she'd been projecting.

"Don't touch me," I snarled.

Lil strained against my grip, but I bore down with more-than-human strength. Her storm-gray eyes locked on mine, and we faced off in rigid silence.

"Seriously, Lil," I said. "That crossed a line."

Nearby, a door whispered open.

"You two done playing grab-ass in the hallway?"

We both jumped like guilty teenagers. Father Frank stood a few doors away, a tall cup of take-out coffee clasped in one hand. His knuckles were scabbed over from the fight the night before, and the wound above his eyebrow spread stains of grape and green beneath his weathered skin. His eyes were weary but alert, and they shifted watchfully between me and the Lady of Beasts.

Lil yanked her wrist from my slackened grip while I fumbled for a response.

"Uh, padre," I managed. "This is Lil."

He nodded curtly in her direction. "We've met."

Awkward volumes unfolded in the sudden tension across her shoulders. The padre never took his eyes off of her—and not because he was admiring the view.

"I'll wait out in the hall," she offered. She strode toward the juncture of the corridors where she could covertly watch the nurses' station. Folding her arms across her chest, she pointedly turned her back to us.

27

"I hope you got some news for me," the padre said, still hovering near the door. "I've been trying that cellphone of yours all day."

"Yeah, about that," I said. "That's the old number."

Father Frank grunted. "Explains a few things. When did you change it?"

"Around the time I lost the old phone in the lake," I replied.

"When you were attacked," he stated flatly. Pity, anger, and recrimination all converged upon his face.

"Look, I'm sorry." I didn't know what else to say. How was I supposed to apologize for a betrayal I couldn't recall?

For a long moment, he just stood in the doorway, intently searching my face. The force of his scrutiny weighed heavy as the wings on my back. I didn't know what he was looking for, but he found something. His chin dipped in a terse nod and he grunted again.

"You need to come to Holy Rosary as soon as you get

the chance." He looked like he wanted to say more, but his gaze flicked warily to where Lil stood watch at the end of the hall. His lips settled into a disapproving line.

Something more significant than prayer spurred the request. Meaning taunted at the edges of memory. As I met his eyes, I almost had it. Then it was gone.

"Padre—it'll have to wait. I've got a ton of shit to do after I see Halley." I craned to look past him into the room. "How's she been?"

Jaw ticking, Father Frank stepped back from the doorway and gestured me in.

"Good, all things considered," he allowed.

Ducking past him, I draped Lil's discarded jacket over a chair. With a final, beetling glance toward where she waited, he pulled the door shut till only a crack of light remained.

There were two beds, but only one was occupied. Halley's room was dark except for the spectral glow of the monitors clustered around her bed. A girl-shaped lump curled in the middle of it, a dark plume of hair trailing from beneath the upper edge of the blanket. Father Frank laid a finger to his lips, cautioning quiet—though from her breathing, I didn't think Halley was actually sleeping.

Still, I kept my voice down.

"You have some history with Lil?" I asked.

"One of us does," he answered. The padre took a long, slow sip of coffee, eyeing me across the lid. "She taking advantage of the fact you don't remember?"

"Knowing her? Yeah, pretty sure."

He grunted, then traced a blunt nail along the seam of the thick paper cup. "Long as you know the kind of person you're dealing with."

I shrugged. "It's the devil you know, right, padre?"

Any response he thought to offer was interrupted by a sudden rustling of sheets. Halley dragged herself into a sitting position, an IV trailing from one thin arm, her pink and green rosary twined around the other. For a moment, she resisted her natural inclination and stared straight at me.

"Wingy!" she breathed, clearly delighted.

I smiled despite myself.

"Don't let Lil catch you calling me that," I said. "I'll never hear the end of it."

"Too late." The voice came from just outside of the door.

The padre shot me a look. "A particularly nosy devil."

She poked her head into the room. "You'll appreciate my vigilance if anything tries sneaking up on us."

Then everything about Lil froze—her stance, her features. She even stopped breathing. Her thundercloud eyes fixed on the slight figure of Halley, crouching on the bed.

"Mother's Tears," she swore. She licked lips gone dry with shock.

Halley didn't return Lil's stare directly. Instead, the girl's dark eyes trailed everywhere around the Lady of Beasts. She raised the hand taped to the IV, tracing patterns in the air with one slender finger.

"Fox," she murmured. "Lion. Weasel. Owl."

As Halley continued reciting the names of various animals, Lil dropped her voice to a furious hiss.

"You didn't tell me you were dealing with one of

those." Her warm, bronze skin paled to a sickly shade. She stared at Halley a moment more, then, without further comment, she slipped back out of sight in the hallway. I could feel her shields slam into place with all the crushing finality of blast doors.

"What's that all about?" Father Frank asked.

Thanks to Terael, I knew—and if Lil could see it at a glance, it was a safe bet others could, too. I didn't answer right away, though.

"Things are a lot more complicated with Halley than we initially suspected." Quietly I pulled the door shut until I heard it click. The whites of Father Frank's eyes stood out in the spectral lights of the monitors.

"She just scared one of the most terrifying women I have ever met," he breathed. "That can't be good." He set aside the coffee and watched me tensely.

"None of the news I have is exactly good," I said.

He grunted, unsurprised.

Suddenly awkward, I hedged. "After everything at the Davis place last night, I guess you know about my crazy life. Still, a lot of this is going to sound strange."

A tightening around his eyes deepened the crows' feet at their edges. It was his only acknowledgement. I swallowed. He wasn't making this easy. I struggled to order my thoughts, but my brain felt scattered.

"All the writing Halley's done," I started. "She hasn't written on herself, has she? Like the cuts we found on the vagrant you clobbered?"

Father Frank's look of horror was answer enough.

Halley shifted position on her bed, worrying the beads of her rosary.

"The ladies went away," she sighed.

That derailed me entirely. I whirled from the priest to the girl.

"What?"

The sharpness in my tone made her cringe. She turned her focus on an apparently random corner of the room, covering her face with her hair. I held my breath, anxious for her answer.

"Red hair. Black hair. Golden hair, gray." She ticked off the colors with a rhythm reminiscent of the old rhyme, "Rich man, poor man, beggar-man, thief." I moved closer.

"Black hair? Dark eyes?" I held a hand up just below my shoulder. "This tall?"

Halley yelped at my sudden motion, retreating back beneath the blankets.

"Zack, you have to go easy with her," Father Frank warned.

"Halley, it's important to me," I said, keeping my voice soft. "Did you see Lailah? Did she tell you her name?" I stopped short of yanking away the covers.

Father Frank grabbed my elbow, his grip like iron through the thick leather of my jacket.

"You won't get anything out of her that way," he said. "Take a few steps back."

He tugged. I resisted. He refused to let go.

"How is this Lailah connected to the Whisper Man?" he asked.

"No. It's nothing like that. I—" My breath snagged on the words.

The lines around the priest's mouth deepened, making his lips look like a parenthetical notation on his face. I finally pulled free of him and paced a tight circuit in the room. With all the layers of shielding I had going, I felt caged.

"I lost someone," I explained. Muscles in my throat strained against the statement. "It's a long story."

He regarded me searchingly. A slight lift to his brows indicated some internal consideration.

"I can walk up and punch most spirits in the face," I said, clenching a fist as demonstration. I swung it futilely at the air, then opened empty fingers. "You'd think I'd notice if she'd been hanging around, but it's been a whole month of nothing. Just dreams."

From where she huddled, Halley started humming to herself. The sound was barely audible through the muffling of the covers, so it took me a few moments to recognize the tune.

"Schism," by Tool.

Stunned, I halted to stare at the girl-shaped lump on bed. The lyrics welled in memory, timed to Halley's whispery refrain.

I know the pieces fit...

The same song had queued up on my iPod outside the art museum, entirely too well timed. It couldn't be coincidence.

"You *can* see her," I said. "How—when all I have are dreams?"

"Zaquiel," Father Frank urged. "Stop, please." This time he reached for my shoulder. Without thinking, I seized his hand to shove it away.

Explosions blossomed in my vision. Wet jungle heat. Cordite—and the cloying stench of old blood. Direct contact with his skin was like a pile driver to the brain.

There was something else—a tether of power binding him to me.

The instant I became aware of it, strength flowed through it. The power caught me in that gnawing hollow just under the ribs, replacing the exhaustion with much-needed warmth. The dull roar of my headache faded, then ceased.

I whipped my hand away like I'd been burned.

"Sorry," I breathed, stumbling away.

Father Frank regarded me with mild confusion.

"I didn't mean for that to happen," I insisted—but I could still feel the connection and the urge to draw on it was almost overwhelming. A guilty part of me wanted to blame my famished grasping on the Eye, but that soul-hunger was all Anakim.

I hid my hands away in the pockets of my jacket. This was a part of my nature I still struggled with, one of the factors that had led me to lock myself away for over a month. Everything I did—every shield, every ward, every journey through the Shadowside—cost me power, and that power was replenished from people.

I hated it.

Father Frank's tone was full of gentle reproach.

"I'd give you a kidney if you needed it, Zack. You know that." He reached for my shoulder again and I was too beside myself to even shrug him away. "You saved my life more times than I can count. This is nothing."

He held out his other hand, palm cupped like he was catching water from the air. Then he exhaled, steady and slow. His eyes fluttered closed. Reflexively, I clenched down on my shields, but that tie between us anchored some place deep. Through the leather, through all my battered layers of defenses, warmth radiated from him to me. Softly glowing in my vision, he exhaled another breath and I felt it filling up the reserves I'd burned through at the museum.

I didn't pull away.

Soaking up the power so selflessly offered, I gained a better sense of the pathway it followed. The connection ran both ways, and if I reached out along it, I could almost taste the memory of when I'd created it.

Then I froze as more images rushed along the current of borrowed life, and in an instant, I knew what I'd made of him back in the jungles of Vietnam. Father Frank was an anchor. *My* anchor. I'd tied him to me, investing him with some of my own power, knowing I would die in that war—and I needed a way home.

"You carried me." It escaped my lips in a breathless whisper. "All the way back to the States. Not my body, but the most important part of me."

I marveled at the face of the man I'd intended— forty-odd years ago—to become my father, wondering what had altered that path in our intertwined lives. My parents still lived in Kenosha. I knew them only as a distant fact. Aside from a card that had arrived on my birthday, we didn't talk.

With the amnesia, I was afraid to reach out.

"I didn't believe what you told me, but I did what you said, and I survived." His breath hitched. "That was the hardest part."

"I can't believe Foul-Mouthed Frankie became a

246

priest." The words spilled from my lips, but they belonged to a wholly different self. Father Frank regarded me with haunted eyes.

"Living wasn't easy when everyone else was dead."

The wretched ache of his desolation hit me along the link, and we both fell silent. Shards of memory prickled behind my eyes, a broken window to another life. I couldn't recapture all of it, but I remembered him—a boisterous kid, barely twenty-two when he enlisted.

He was smart and he was strong—not a crack shot, but he never lost his nerve, no matter how hairy the situation. That counted for a lot.

The words in my head were my voice, yet not. I would have been ecstatic over remembering something, except every stolen moment came laced with the trauma Father Frank still carried in the wounded chambers of his soul.

"You've seen too much death already," I whispered. "I'll make sure we don't lose Halley." The trusting eyes of that raw, earnest kid peered out from the lines of the older man's face.

"I'll hold you to that, Cap."

28

"The first thing I need is to find his token."

We stood apart from Halley, conferring in low voices in the curtained-off side of the room. It was an empty gesture—the curtain did little to muffle sound, and with Halley's preternatural perceptions, I doubted she needed to hear our voices in order to effectively listen in. Still, our only other option was stepping out into the hall, and that meant including Lil.

Neither the padre nor I felt comfortable bringing the Lady of Beasts into our discussion at the moment. We didn't exactly debate that part out loud. We both simply knew, in that way old friends shared opinions without speaking.

Now that I was conscious of the bond between us, I understood my instinctive trust for Father Frank. Even so, I found it challenging to act on that camaraderie. I'd struggled for months with truths about myself, ones that I expected the mortal world to hate and fear. Glossing over details or omitting them entirely came as second nature with everyone. So I covered only the high points of what I'd learned about Terhuziel, hesitantly mentioning that he was one of the Rephaim.

Father Frank knew the term.

"The same ones you went after near Hoi An?" he asked.

"What?" Phantom images flickered in my vision, hovering on the boundaries of conscious perception. The urge to seize the compelling fragments vied with my need to sever Terhuziel's ties with Halley.

Not now.

I squeezed my eyes shut, willing the fragments away.

"Zack?" Father Frank asked.

He gave my arm a tentative shake. I started, my eyes still closed. I couldn't say how long they'd been that way.

"We'll come back to that later," I said. Emotions for which I had little context roiled in the back of my brain. I did my best to quell them. "Has Halley had any more episodes since they brought her to the hospital?"

"No," he answered. "I've been pleasantly surprised."

Mentally, I tallied the distance between the hospital and the Davis house in Little Italy. Then I factored in the Whitethorn address. The Kramer residence was closer to Halley's home by about a mile. Not a huge distance, but then, I could stand ten feet outside of the Cleveland Museum of Art, and Terael couldn't reach me.

"That's good to know," I said. "It means either she's further from his sphere of influence, or she left the token at home." I stopped, then added, "Probably both."

"What's this token look like?" he asked. "Soon as my cell's charged up, I'll text Tammy so she can look for it."

I grimaced. "Uh, about that…"

Father Frank's lips twitched at the corner—his sole tic of displeasure. He was stoic in all other regards.

"You have no idea," he stated evenly.

I scrubbed at my stubbled jaw. There was no accusation in his eyes, but I still couldn't bring myself to meet them.

"It has his Name on it," I offered lamely.

"Zack, she's been writing those same three characters for weeks now. They've been all over her walls."

"I don't exactly understand the distinction myself," I admitted, "but Terael said the token is a crafted thing. I know there's power in the actual shaping of an item." A lot of my recent work with wards had led into that territory. "That's one way relics are made—items that have a solid existence both here and in the Shadowside. It's got to be something like that. He made it sound like a kind of a holy symbol."

Instantly the padre's eyes grew wide, and I saw in them a reflection of my own chagrined revelation. I couldn't tell if I made the connection because of him, or if we both arrived at insight simultaneously.

"Her rosary," he breathed.

I slapped my forehead. "Fuck me running. I'm so dense."

I shoved the curtain aside. The metal fixtures attached to its track in the ceiling screed and clattered against themselves in a flurry.

From her position in the middle of the bed, Halley held the sheet open around her face so that it looked like she peered through a tent flap. As I'd suspected, she'd been listening. The instant I charged forward, she dropped the starched white fabric and gave a little squeak.

"Halley, I need to see your rosary."

"No!" she wailed. "You're going to take it!" She folded in on herself so abruptly, the sheets appeared to implode.

"Let me try," Father Frank said softly. He slipped past my shoulder, moving toward the bed with a patient, measured gait. Settling onto the nearest edge of the mattress, he balanced with most of his weight on his legs so he didn't shift where she crouched.

"Halley," he said, and he made the name a song of gentle supplication. "Would you please show my friend the rosary that you made?"

She burrowed deeper into the mattress, shaking her head so fiercely her hair rustled with a sound like swishing grass. The old priest extended a hand very slowly, not daring to touch her, but simply laying it near an opening in the blankets. He applied enough pressure to the mattress that she would notice.

"Are you certain?"

His words possessed a resonance that went beyond the mellow timbre of his voice, and I realized he was using a power—a power very likely acquired through his bond with me. But where my voice could become a thing of fury and destruction, his held only profound and soothing peace.

"I can't," Halley said miserably. She shook her head again, but it lacked the same vehemence.

"But you've always been so proud of your work," he persisted.

She sobbed enough to shake the bed. "I'll never see Papaw again."

"Halley, your Papaw was very sick. He went on to a better place."

She grew still and very quiet. Tension bunched across her narrow shoulders, which were trembling visibly through the bedclothes. When next she spoke, her voice was so muffled I had to strain to make it out. It sounded like she had her face buried against the mattress.

"Whisper Man has him."

Father Frank and I exchanged worried glances.

"*Is that possible?*" he mouthed.

I shrugged. Judging by all the things I'd witnessed— from shadow-tainted Nephilim to clay vessels enchanted to be soul prisons—I couldn't rule it out.

Still, it didn't sit right.

I stepped closer and said with all the authority I could muster, "He's lying to you, Halley."

She froze. From the arrested tremors in the blankets, she even held her breath. Father Frank's lined features held a look of caution, but he nodded for me to go ahead.

"You know not to trust him," I said. "He's hurt you. He sent people to hurt your mom and your little brother. Why would you do anything for him? He only wants to use you."

"But Papaw…" she murmured disconsolately.

Father Frank shut his eyes against the sharp welling of emotion her piteous tone inspired. I got a tidal backwash of it along our recently refreshed link.

"Did Whisper Man tell you to make that rosary, Halley?" I asked.

Very hesitantly, she nodded. The room had fallen so quiet it was possible to hear the rasp of her forehead against the fitted sheet.

"Have you heard Papaw since you made it?"

Another hesitation, but this time the motion under the blankets was one of slow negation. I crouched down beside the bed, laying my hand not far from Father Frank's. Knowing she could see them, I eased up on the cowl and extended my wings, holding them out to their full span. They tingled unpleasantly where they intersected with the walls of the hospital room. I kept them open anyway.

Urgently, I patted the bed.

"Halley, I know you can see me for what I am. And I know, if you can see me, you can tell if you should trust me. Do you trust me?"

She caught her breath, then swallowed so hard I could hear her throat click. The thin fingers of her hand snaked out from under the blankets. She walked them over to my own fingers, stopping just short of making physical contact.

"I trust you, Wingy," she whispered.

I could see the beads of the rosary where they twined around the prominent bones of her wrist. It took everything I had not to simply rip them away, but that would wreck the trust I'd gained, and I needed every shred of it for what I planned to do once Terhuziel's token was out of the way.

Licking dry lips, I swallowed almost as hard as she had. Cutting him out of my head had sucked. I hoped I understood the technique well enough not to give her a stroke.

"He's lying to you, Halley," I repeated. "He's lying, and he only wants to hurt you. Give me the rosary, and I'll show you how to make him go away for good."

With the xylophone rattle of ceramic beads, she slid the rosary slowly from her wrist. Depositing it on the mattress in front of me, she whipped her hand back under the covers without another word.

Beside me, Father Frank expelled a pent-up breath. Worry stitched deep seams in his face.

"Now what?" he asked.

"Now I cut every tie he's ever made to her."

29

Lying there against the pale expanse of the sheet, the little coil of pink and green beads looked harmless enough, but the minute I touched Halley's rosary, there was no mistaking Terhuziel's token. I could feel his twisted, alien mind pressing against the raw spots where I'd cut his presence out of my head. It stirred unpleasant memories from the incident in the museum.

I slammed down on every shield I had practiced over the past few months, fighting the impulse to hurl the beads across the room.

"Playing on her devotion to her grandfather. That's low," Father Frank growled. "I hope you hurt this bastard good."

I held the gaudy string of thick ceramic beads closer to the soft light of the call button mounted near the bed. Expecting to find the Name scribbled on the back of the plastic crucifix, I saw only a MADE IN CHINA stamp. Then I went decade by decade, inspecting each individual bead.

In the five decades of her rosary, a sequence of ten green beads marked the ten Hail Mary prayers. Carefully tied knots separated each bead. At the end of each decade was a broad, flat bead with the raised pattern of a rose stamped on one side. Shell pink, it sat between two larger knots. That was where the faithful would pray the Our Father before moving onto another set of ten Hail Marys.

The Our Father bead shimmered with an opalescent coating, so the ceramic looked more like mother-of-pearl. As I turned the bead around on its string, a slightly deeper pink caught my eye. Closer to fuchsia and riddled with round specks of glitter, the darker color picked out the first symbol of Terhuziel's Luwian Name in painstakingly delicate strokes.

"Nail polish. Fuck me running," I muttered. "She painted it on with nail polish."

Father Frank leaned over my shoulder, squinting at the prayer beads in my hand.

"First time I'll admit I need bifocals," he grumbled.

Smooth ceramic whispered against my calluses as I advanced to the next decade. Sure enough, the second glyph was painted on the back of the next Our Father bead. I held it up closer to Father Frank, though with the dim lighting in the room, I didn't expect that he would see it.

"As long as she wore this, Terhuziel could reach her, even if she was nowhere near his domain," I explained, "but at some point she had to enter his sphere of influence for him to notice her. Where did she go, around the time her grandfather died?"

I set the prayer beads onto the nightstand, unwilling to handle them any further. Smashing them seemed like the best course of action, but that was going to make a lot of noise—and the ass-ogling night nurse was sure to come running. Maybe Lil had something useful tucked away in that purse-of-holding she toted around.

"The funeral, of course," Father Frank responded. "Before that, she visited him twice at the hospital. They had him at the Cleveland Clinic following a massive stroke."

Under her covers, Halley whimpered, then tentatively extended a hand. She pawed at where the rosary had been.

"I miss Papaw."

Father Frank moved his hand within her orbit. Her fingers fluttered near his briefly, then alighted for a swift, consoling touch. I wondered how much she read from the priest through that contact—and, given his ties to me, how much he was able to sense in return.

"The guy who brought Terhuziel into this country is a doctor," I said. "He was with Doctors Without Borders in Syria, but maybe he also worked at the Clinic. Bobby will know. What about the funeral?"

Father Frank shook his head. "They didn't go through Holy Rosary. That was all her father's side of the family. I can ask Tammy once my cell's back online." He avoided mentioning that he'd worn the battery down with useless calls to me all day. I knew enough to feel a pang of guilt.

"A cemetery's a good possibility. Plenty of statues," I mused, "but not very defensible. The Rephaim are used to temples. I can't see this guy settling for some rinky-dink mausoleum. Not with his ego."

Halley patted Father Frank's hand, and then rolled onto her side under the covers. A moment later, she lifted an edge to reveal part of her face. "I tried to talk to Papaw when they put him in the ground. Are you mad at me, Wingy?"

"Why would I be mad at you?" I asked.

She hid her face against the mattress for a moment, then looked up again, making eye contact briefly through the tangle of her hair.

"Because I let Whisper Man start talking to me."

"I'm mad at him, Halley, not you. I—"

The door swung open and Lil burst in. Her gray eyes flashed fiercely in the dark.

"What the hell is taking so long?" she growled.

Halley squeaked and clapped her hands to her ears. Father Frank shot Lil a sour expression.

"Cool it, Lil," I said. "You're scaring the kid."

"I just had to burn my trust charm to get that nurse off my back. She's not an idiot—she knows it doesn't take this long to sign a damned form."

"Halley's skittish," I answered. "We can't rush this."

"I was saving that charm," Lil snarled. "You owe me, Anakim."

"Put it on my tab," I replied.

She glowered at me, all teeth and fury.

Halley pulled the covers back over her face, scooting away till her back hit the railing of the bed.

"Now look what you did," I grumbled.

"Ten minutes, Anakim," she gritted. "You take any longer than that, and I hit the Whitethorn address by myself."

"You keep talking like that, and it will take another ten minutes just to calm her down again," Father Frank warned.

Lil narrowed her eyes in his direction. I expected a scathing retort, but all she offered was a throaty, "Hrmph."

"If you're bored out there, take this," I said.

Scooping up the rosary beads, I tossed Terhuziel's token at her. It traced an elegant arc of pink and green across the room. Without so much as a glance, Lil snatched it from the air once it neared her. The instant her fingers closed round the thing, she nearly dropped it.

"Warn a girl next time," she growled. She held the offensive item out stiffly, pinching the bottom of the crucifix between the nails of her forefinger and thumb.

"I trust you know how to break it?"

An eager gleam lit her eyes. "I can do that."

"Quietly," I suggested.

"Of course." The smile she flashed carried its own wind chill factor.

"Good. Make with the smashy." I turned back to where Halley cowered on the bed. "I could use one less complication for what I'm about to try."

Lil started pulling the door shut behind her. "Ten minutes," she reminded us before it fully closed. Father Frank scowled at the space she had occupied.

"You seriously trust that woman?" Disapproval was thick in his tone.

"With the kind of enemies I've got, I'm not sure I trust anyone," I sighed, "but for now, she's helping. I'll take it." A muscle in his cheek ticked as he clenched his jaw, but he held his silence.

From the hallway came a dull crunching sound, like glass ground under the heel of a boot. All too readily I could picture Lil dancing a wild Tarantella on the Rephaim token. The sound was accompanied by a backwash of power that battered against my shields. Halley twitched. The room filled with the cloying, sick stink of dead worms after a hard rain.

"You told her to break it," Halley cried accusingly from within the depths of her blanket cocoon.

"I did," I admitted, "but can you hear Whisper Man any more?"

She held her breath, listening.

"He's real quiet now."

"But you can still hear him?" Father Frank asked. He turned a worried frown to me. "I thought he was getting at her through that thing. Why can she still hear him?"

"The token was the easy part," I admitted. A twist of anxiety knotted in my chest, slowly winding its way through my guts.

The old priest worked to hide his concern, but I felt it clearly enough. Halley peeked out from under the covers, watching us from the corner of the lone eye she dared to expose. I had counted on her listening. It was easier than trying to work her up to have the conversation directly.

"He's been weaving ties into her, like fishhooks in her brain," I explained. "I can't say how many exactly, but he's been at it for weeks. Chances are, he's in deep."

Father Frank clenched his fists in his lap and regarded them gravely.

"But you know how to fix it," he said.

Halley had pushed far enough out of her cocoon to

262

expose her whole face. Now she held the blankets tightly at her chin so they wrapped around her hair like a veil. Her gaze darted between the padre and me. I turned my full attention back to Father Frank before she caught me looking.

"That's the thing," I said. "I can't fix it."

The old priest's stiff back slumped just a little.

"That's not to say it can't be fixed," I amended quickly. "But she's the one who has to do it. It can't be me."

"You can help her at least?"

I glanced again at Halley. This time I waited for our eyes to meet. She couldn't hold my gaze for long, but neither did she try to hide her face.

"I can help her, if she lets me."

My own head still felt raw from where I'd slashed away the vicarious tether I'd picked up from Fish-Knife Lady. I had no idea how Halley would fare when it came to cutting his connections to her.

"It's not going to be easy," I added. "I can't do it from out here. She'll have to let me into her head, and even then I don't know exactly how well things will go." I drew a breath, surprised when it didn't shake. "I can tell you, whatever happens when we cut him out, the things he's got planned for her are worse. Much worse."

With slow resignation, the old priest nodded. He slumped forward as far as his taped-up ribs would allow, but gave no heed to the injury. The anxious ache he felt for Halley eclipsed any discomfort in his own battered flesh.

He jumped when Halley touched her hand to his side.

"Don't be sad," she breathed. He reached around

awkwardly and gave her fingers a little squeeze. She allowed it.

I extended my own hand to Halley—my right one, though I tended to favor my left. The hungry power of the Eye would play no part in what I sought to accomplish with the girl.

"I need you to make a place in your mind for me to meet with you," I explained, turning all of my focus her way. I vividly imagined my own process from only hours before at the museum, willing her to understand.

"Memory palace," she murmured. "Like *Sherlock*."

The lift of my brows betrayed my surprise.

"You know what I'm asking you to do?" I pursued.

She nodded, lifting her eyes to meet my gaze. No words passed her lips this time, but I heard her with ringing clarity.

Show me how to cut his ties.

She scooted forward on the bed, pushing some of the covers away. Trailing the IV, she reached her hand to meet mine.

Our fingers clasped and the dimly lit hospital room abruptly faded.

30

I found myself floating in the debris-field of Alderaan. At least, that was the closest thing I could relate to the spreading tangle of chaotic perceptions that confronted me on the outer edges of Halley's mind.

Up, down, right, left—debris floated in every conceivable direction. Reflexively, I spread my wings, struggling to get my bearings. The concentric rings of neural clutter spiraled around a central point—brilliantly intense, like a vast, white spindle. Her memory palace. I knew it instantly, but it was so far away.

Halley's voice rose plaintively from that internal locus. Too faint for words, the tone nevertheless called and encouraged. I struck the air with wings of light, leaving blue-white trails through the inky black as I dodged spinning chunks of memories. The space rang with recollected sound—her father's voice, Tyson's squeal of delight. The rich, resonant rumble of her paternal grandfather's laughter.

Reaching her wasn't going to be easy. This

intermediary space was the jumbled junk drawer I'd previously encountered, multiplied by a power of ten. It took all of my concentration not to get kicked right back into my ordinary awareness, where my body lingered in the hospital room.

I skirted the sharp edges of a scintillating trauma only to run face-first into a cluster of emotional imprints from the psychic landscape of the hospital. The misery of the boy who had occupied the bed before her, chemo from his cancer treatments making his blood turn to poison. Father Frank's adrenaline-drenched flashbacks to a jungle war zone, punctuated by the face of every friend who had died there. Echoes that I recognized as my own thoughts—images of Terael, Lil, and then the heavy, gleaming gold of Neferkariel's Eye. In its central setting, the rough carnelian gemstone wept tears of blood.

With a hoarse shout, I reeled away from the looming icon, reasserting the walls inside my own head. The last thing I needed was to spill into her the way Terael had spilled into me—that would spell doom for the both of us. But the image of the Eye stubbornly lingered. Somehow she'd picked up on it through the barriers of the oath.

I dragged myself away from the uncomfortable reminder of how hard I'd screwed myself last fall, orienting toward the central point once more. A bewildering array of material cluttered the spaces between the more recognizable perceptions, and each time I allowed my attention to be caught by something, it sucked me down as surely as the whirlpool maw of Charybdis.

Memory, sensation, and emotional content all

washed through my mind in an indiscriminate storm. Like a maze without walls, each intense flash of imagery diverted me from my path.

This was maddening—all the colors were too loud, every flash of emotion struck with abrading intensity. If this was Halley's experience of the world, I didn't understand how she managed even the briefest amounts of contact.

Redoubling my efforts to stay on track, I drew upon the lasered focus that engrossed me in research. Shoving my way past a jagged memory of gold-flecked green beads and the grinding crunch of shattered ceramic, I spied a silken thread drifting in the open space. Slow and hypnotic, it rippled as if stirred by a breeze. At first, I assumed the undulating twist of fiber was yet another distraction. Then I tracked its length with my eye, following it all the way to the gleaming nexus.

It was Ariadne's thread—the guideline through the maze. I touched my fingers to the drifting strand, and Halley's voice grew immediately more present. The ringing notes echoed poignantly with loneliness and loss.

Guiding my progress with my wings, I focused exclusively on the spiderweb pathway traced through the debris. At times, I used the strand to merely steer my passage. At others, I clung to it like a lifeline. As I progressed, the fine-spun thread I'd first encountered grew larger and larger, until my fingers were knotted round a twisted rope thicker than my forearm.

After what seemed like a small eternity, I finally reached the core. Before me, the central spindle rose like a great, slitted pupil staring from the heart of a whirling, blinded eye. The gleaming structure was—of all damned things—a huge, ivory tower drawn straight from a fairy story. It had no entrance and no stairs, just a single window near the very top of its fiercely pointed peak.

The ropy guideline trailed down from the window like—

"Fuck me running," I breathed. "Not Ariadne. Rapunzel. Halley likes her Disney Princesses too much."

Hopefully I wouldn't be greeted by a frying pan to the face.

While I understood the potency of the symbol she'd chosen—and I certainly appreciated the help in navigating the maze—there was no way in hell I was climbing to the top of the tower on a strand of her hair. I had better options.

I spread my wings and, with a single downstroke, flew to the solitary window. My engineer boots settled heavily upon the sill. Once I ducked through, the window shifted with the malleable physics of dreams, morphing from a narrow, pointed arch to the curtained picture window from Halley's real-life bedroom. The curtain fluttered shut behind me the moment my feet thudded to the floor.

Halley stood to one side of her bed. She wore a long, sweeping dress of powder-blue silk with pale yellow accents that shimmered as she moved. It was Disney Princess perfect, and reminded me of the winter sun gleaming high against a cloudless vault of sky. Her dark hair—normally a veiled tangle draped across her eyes—was swept back from her face and plaited into two long and heavy braids. They trailed all the way down her back to spill upon the floor, near-endless loops of them curled around the edges of the room.

"Rapunzel, hunh?"

"Let down your long hair," she answered absently as she stepped to her nightstand. With small, neat fingers, she arranged the prescription bottles so they sat in a perfect semicircle around the base of her Tinker Bell lamp.

"You know where we are?" I asked.

"Inside my head." She uttered the words as if such mental meetings were commonplace. "I learned how to make memory palaces from watching *Sherlock*."

I laughed. "That's a hell of a moat you've got out there."

She smiled wanly, offering no more comment than a half-hearted shrug.

"Not that I mind you throwing me a line to get through that mess," I said as she continued to fussily perfect the angles in the room. "But why Rapunzel? You could look like anything in here. What about Tinker Bell? You like wings well enough."

"Rapunzel," she answered firmly. "All alone in her high, high tower." She brushed past me, stepping primly over one of the coils of her hair. "Sometimes, she could invite people up, but she could never climb down on her own."

The desolate ache of her isolation killed my sarcasm dead. I tried to think of something to say, but I was used to relating to Halley in the waking world—which amounted to sending smoke signals across that vast expanse of interposing psychic debris. Here on the inside, she was a different person entirely.

First of all, she looked—well, she looked a hell of a lot older in here. In the flesh-and-blood world, it was easy to forget Halley was a young woman of fourteen. Her words and mannerisms rendered her childlike, and because of her challenges, that was how we treated her, as a vulnerable, fragile thing. But all of those apparently breakable qualities were merely the bricks in the walls of her tower. Inside the solitary prison, she was who she had been born to be.

"Have you come to rescue me?" she asked. The steady focus of her deep black eyes unnerved me, after having her avoid eye contact so much of the time.

"I'm no prince, Halley," I replied, "and you shouldn't have to wait around for one. That's the thing about all the fairy stories. The princess always has to wait for someone to come rescue her, but that's all wrong."

"Why?" As with most communications in this space, the question was layered with nuances of meaning and emotion—longing, curiosity, brittle hope. It fretted upon the air. I met the heavy weight of her gaze and refused to flinch from it.

"A real savior would teach the princess how to rescue herself, don't you think?"

Halley made a thoughtful noise as she pushed the curtain aside. The debris-field was gone, replaced by a vision of the darkened hospital room, only reproduced on a cyclopean scale. I saw my own eye, pale as a lake in January and ringed with a darker band of blue. It took up half the window. Talk about an uncanny valley. I focused on the floor as my perspective swayed.

"I'm not brave like you and Father Frank," she objected.

"That word—I don't think it means what you think it means," I replied.

"But you and Father Frank were soldiers together," she said. "I see it playing in his head, over and over again. You died so he could live. Most days, I can't even bear to leave my room. How can I be brave?"

I ventured a step closer to her, careful not to tread on any of the plaited hair spread across the floor.

"You've been fighting Whisper Man for how many weeks now? And right after losing your favorite grandfather. Don't tell me you're not brave."

She turned to face me and—thankfully—dropped the curtain to the outside world. Her dark eyes glittered with a sheen of tears.

"Whisper Man makes me feel so afraid."

"You can be scared and still be brave, Halley," I answered. "Scared just means you're smart enough to know what you're up against—and that it will take real work to survive."

"I don't know…" She hugged herself, chafing her arms fretfully.

"I think you can get through this," I said. "If you can do what I teach you here."

A single tear spilled over the edge of her lashes, cutting a wet track down her cheek.

"What is he?" she asked in a strangled whisper.

I hesitated—but she deserved an answer. If we got through this, I was going to be explaining a lot to her. Given the legacy that she carried, there wasn't much choice. Out of reflex I tucked my wings tight against my back. At length, I responded.

"He's one of my brothers." I stared doggedly at the floor as I let that revelation sink in.

"He made me think I could see my Papaw again. He lied just so he could get at me!" she wailed. "Are all your brothers such horrible people?" Emotions tumbled from her every word—anger, hurt, betrayal. That last one crashed against the psychic space with such force, it left me weak in the knees.

"I'm not sure most of my brothers even *qualify* as people," I muttered, but she wasn't finished.

"I told him no and no and no, but he said I'd never see Papaw again if I didn't do what he wanted. So I let him inside—and that was terrible, like being locked in a tiny little box, only worse. So I shoved him away, and then he sent people to hurt my family. They hurt Father Frank. They hurt Sanjeet. They hurt you, Wingy." Tears flowed freely. The long ropes of her braided hair twitched and undulated in response to her turmoil. "Why would he do those things? I know what I am—I'm broken and useless. How can I be so important?"

"Broken is not useless."

She squeezed her eyes shut, unwilling to hear it.

"I'm not going to lie and pretend your life could be all puppy dogs and sunshine, if only you believed hard enough. That's bullshit." Her eyes snapped open at the forbidden word.

"Things in your head don't work the way they should. Your body doesn't always cooperate. I know how hard that is, Halley," I insisted. "If you're broken, then I'm broken, too." A shiver ran through me as I admitted it, but I plunged forward anyway. Picking this scab was long past due.

"I barely remember who I am," I told her. I held my arms open at my sides, dropping the layers of shielding I held tight around that painful truth. "I've lived more lives than I could possibly count, and except for bits and pieces, I've forgotten them all. I have powers I can use to save or hurt people, and I can't always tell which is which."

A bitter sting rose at the backs of my eyes as I spoke. Hurriedly, I blinked it away—but not before Halley noticed. Renewed tears welled in her own eyes out of sympathy.

"Wingy!" she objected.

"I'm not done," I said. I resettled my wings against my back, self-conscious as she stared at them. "I'm broken, but I'm here—and I'm going to teach you how to kick this asshole out of your head. Because broken just means you have to work harder to get what you want—it doesn't mean you can't fucking try."

She chewed her lip, considering.

"But what if I'm still not strong enough?" she asked in a small voice.

"I ask myself that every day," I admitted. "When you're broken, it costs you just to get through the little things everyone else takes for granted—and facing the big challenges takes even more effort. You know you're strong, because you've gotten this far."

Hesitantly, she nodded her agreement. The agitated motion of her hair settled as the lines of worry smoothed across her face. She wiped her tears away with the back of one hand.

"You ready to give this a shot? Things in here are going to get real scary if we do," I warned.

Again, she nodded.

"Good," I said. "Let me show you a few of the tricks I didn't forget."

I extended my upturned hand, warning her off when she reached to take it. I gestured instead for her to watch. As I called my power, a wild grin spread across my features. Blue-white flames flickered to life across my fingers, coalescing into the shape of a wickedly curved blade. Halley's eyes echoed my delight.

"It's a lightsaber!" she cried.

Her dad worked at NASA and she was named for a comet—of course she'd seen *Star Wars*. I threw my head back and laughed.

"Don't tell anyone, but I think about them like that, too." I flexed the fingers of my other hand and called the first dagger's twin. The gleaming metal danced with the same bluish light that spread throughout my wings.

"You try," I said.

"How?" She balked.

"Remember when that man was in your room?" I prompted. "He was on the floor, and Whisper Man was trying to come through him. You threw something at him to stop it. Call that up again."

"But that's different from a lightsaber," she objected.

"No, it's just energy. It's all in how you shape it." I eased my own lightshow down a notch. Even in this shared mental space, maintaining the blades took a lot of power, and I'd need my reserves if this didn't play out the way I hoped.

After a couple of deep breaths, Halley extended her hands exactly the way she'd seen me do. Screwing her eyes shut, she strained to call her power. The long plaits of hair winding through the room shifted restlessly with her effort. Her lips moved as she concentrated, murmuring some private rhyme. After a few tense moments, her features collapsed in a pout.

"I can't!" she cried. "He's going to win. I can't do it!"

A sound like distant thunder shuddered through the floor.

"Halley, don't panic," I said. "You did it before. It's just a matter of focus—"

The thunder came again, underscored by that same dead-worm scent I'd caught in the hospital room.

"Wingy?" She gulped.

"Get behind me." I spread my wings and raised my blades.

The whole floor tilted in the next instant, and the space around us shivered with a shriek like tortured metal. Symbols started bleeding through the walls—the three glyphs of Terhuziel's Name. They repeated over and over again, spreading like ink spilled upon porous paper.

"I thought breaking my rosary meant he couldn't get to me," she quailed. She clung to my side under the cover of one protective wing, her breath coming in huge, hiccuping gulps. The ropes of her braids flailed madly with her panic, like Princess Leia's hair had gotten gene-spliced with a tentacle monster.

"He still has ties. Focusing on him brings them out. That's why they need to be cut away."

With a sound like ripping canvas, all the iterations of Terhuziel's Name tore open on the walls. The ragged edges of the glyphs worked like obscene lips. Beginning with a whisper, they murmured his rhyme, climbing in volume until the whole room shook with the rhythmic roar.

Hands to take and eyes to see. A mouth to speak—

"Don't listen to that," I warned Halley. "Sing something. Recite 'Mary Had a Little Lamb'—or anything else. I don't care. Just don't focus on that."

"I'm trying!"

I shook out the gathered power that shaped the blade in my right hand. Blue-white fire still limned my fingers.

"Take my hand," I said.

Her little fingers were dwarfed by my own, but she squeezed with desperate ferocity. I squeezed back with all the reassurance I had to offer. Beneath our feet, the floor canted at an awkward angle. The curtains billowed and the plastic fairies dangling from her lampshade swung in a frenzy.

Gripping the spirit-blade in my left hand, I defiantly bellowed the syllables of my Name. The blue-white fire leapt from me to Halley, licking halfway up her skinny arm. She stared at it, captivated, and as her attention shifted away from the threat of Terhuziel, the invading wind lost some of its bluster.

"Is that coming from me?" she marveled. She reached tentative fingers toward the dancing spirit-light.

In between tongues of my diamond-bright flame, another energy softly flickered. Amorphous and subtle, it glimmered with a pale lavender sheen. It held neither the intensity nor brilliance of my own power, but it was undeniably there.

"See?" I said triumphantly. "You're not some helpless princess locked up in a tower. You've got an arsenal of your own."

Halley gazed raptly at the proof of her power. Slowly, she straightened beside me. Her little chin lifted in a gesture of defiance, and her eyes glittered—not with tears, but with determination.

"Now I hurt you back," she snarled.

Still clutching my fingers, she darted forward, her right hand bearing a sliver of lavender light. It glittered like an icicle, shaped less like a blade and more like a wand. She stabbed it into the nearest set of Luwian symbols. The Whisper Man rhyme halted abruptly, and all the impossible mouths shrieked with rage.

Symbol by symbol, Halley cut them from her space, until only the first grouping remained. These last three leered from above her toy chest, pressing inward so forcefully, they visibly distended the wall. As she approached, they gaped wide and disgorged a voice I knew all too well.

SHE WILL BE MINE, ANAKIM. YOU CANNOT DELAY MY REBIRTH.

Her wand still aloft, the lavender light sputtered uncertainly.

"Last one, Halley, and he knows it. He'll say anything to get you to stop." I squeezed the little fingers that had never relinquished my own, holding my blade at the ready. Its light burned steadily.

The symbols gnashed upon the wall, then spilled forth another voice—deep, with a bit of a rasp. I recognized it immediately from the memories I'd encountered of Halley's favored grandfather.

"*Halley, child. You have to help me. This monster's going to swallow my soul.*"

"Papaw!"

The walls of her memory palace started to crumble.

The symbols of Terhuziel's Name split like a maniacal grin, and the wallpaper around the central strokes peeled back to reveal a pitchy darkness beneath. A vision flickered in those stygian depths—a high stone tower, its battlements stained black. A ring of looming gargoyles. A tall, peaked roof against a backdrop of forking lightning.

The perfect abode of a fairy-tale villain.

"That's the heart of his tie to you, Halley," I said. "Cut it away, and you're done!"

CUT ME OUT, ANAKIM, AND I SHALL ONLY RETURN. I AM EVERYWHERE. YOU ARE BUT ONE.

Halley's spirit-light winked out almost entirely. Her grasp on her power was too fresh, and the loss of her grandfather too raw.

"You're lying, Whisper Man." Her voice was thick with emotion. "That's not my Papaw." But the words held little force.

She was going to lose the fight.

I released her hand and stepped past her. The distorted symbols of Terhuziel's Name quivered inches from my face. A fetid stink poured from them into the room—it figured a dead god would have bad breath. Through the gaping holes torn by the sigils, I could sense his final tether, and I knew in that instant that I couldn't break it by myself.

But I could replace it.

The knowledge welled up in me, perhaps spurred by my earlier exchange with Father Frank. I could make the girl an anchor. She'd let Terhuziel in, but she'd welcomed me, as well, and right now, I was closer. He had only a pipeline. I stood right inside her fucking head.

It was the simplest solution.

Gleaming whorls of blue and silver fire sprang to life before my eyes, tracing the outlines of my ancient Name. All I had to do was carve those symbols into the wall with my blade.

And I almost did it.

Halley drew up beside me. I folded her close with one wing. I could feel the untapped potential inside of her—diluted, but a treasure all the same.

Terhuziel didn't deserve to drink such precious fire.

"Wingy?"

Her voice was so small compared to the thunder inside of my head. Timorously, she tugged at my hand. The connection did it—the trust inherent in that small gesture. She didn't deserve to be bound. Not by me. Not by anyone. I seized her by the wrist, bellowing my power to raise her own.

"*Get out of her head*!" I shouted.

Dragging Halley along, I lunged forward. She emitted a startled squeak—but quickly recovered. Her yelp turned into a cry of defiance. Lifting our voices together, I twined my power to hers and guided her in a final sally to drive Terhuziel from her mind.

In the silence that came after, the enormity of what I'd almost done jettisoned me from the projection.

I jerked upright, nearly tumbling from the edge of Halley's narrow bed in the hospital. My eyes were stubborn to focus. The ghostly outlines of those potent, ancient letters swallowed everything else.

31

With a rough shout, I staggered back from the bed. Father Frank caught me. Flailing, I whacked him in the ribs for his trouble. All the air rushed from him, but he took the blow without complaint.

"Halley?" he gasped.

All the worry from before sat heavily on his features.

"She's fine—she's fine," I said quickly, striving to believe it. I struggled to catch my own breath.

Halley stretched against the covers, fluttering her eyes as if rousing from a dream. She smiled as she looked up at me—then bashfully ducked her face against the pillows. A tangled skein of dark hair flopped over her features.

"Sleepy," she murmured.

The taut anxiety in the padre's grip slackened.

"You did it, then," he breathed. "The way you twitched, I was afraid something had gone horribly wrong. She's really free of him?"

My hands still buzzed from the power I'd called, and I could feel every inch of my extended wings. I settled them tight against my back in a gesture I realized was the equivalent of nervously clasping my arms. I still felt sick from what I'd nearly done to Halley.

I took a halting step back toward the bed. Shoving my hands into my pockets, I clenched them into hard, tight fists. I didn't dare put my hands on her, not after that.

"Halley, listen to me," I said. "You've got to put all your walls back up. All of them. Even to me, you understand? Make a fortress in your head. Don't let anyone in. Not *anyone*."

Stifling a yawn, she nodded.

"It's OK, Wingy," she assured.

"No, it's not," I responded flatly.

Against the pillows, her voice was muffled. "You're nicer in my head than Whisper Man."

That was even worse.

"Zack, what's the matter?" Father Frank caught me by the shoulder.

I couldn't bring myself to answer.

A sound like thunder rumbled outside. It was answered by a series of booming knocks as Lil pounded on the door. She didn't wait for anyone to answer, just slammed the thing open with enough force to squeal the hinges.

"What the fuck was that?" she demanded. Backlit on the threshold, she loomed like a fury incarnate.

The padre stepped fluidly to put himself between Lil and the girl.

Outside, the rumbling started again, working up to a peal of thunder that boomed with such ferocity it rattled the windows. The answering lightning summoned echoing flashes in Lil's ferocious eyes.

"Is that you?" I demanded, jerking a thumb toward the window to indicate the gathering storm. "That better not be you."

Lil scowled as the place shook with another monstrous peal.

"No, you idiot," she snarled. "What did you expect to happen when you piss off a storm god? Now, explain yourself, Zaquiel." She went to push her way past the padre, but Father Frank held his ground. Lil turned those hurricane eyes on him, glaring over the rims of the spectacles—which diminished the effect somewhat.

"Look, priest, I'm not angry at you," she growled, "but you know better than to stand in my way."

"Zack?" Father Frank said.

I went to the window, concern about this new development eclipsing some of my inner turmoil about Halley.

"Let her in," I answered with a weary sigh. "I'm done." Huge, fat flakes of snow swirled madly in the lights outside of the hospital, so dense it was impossible to see the lot below. Another rumbling complaint echoed through the heavens, and this time, I counted—a rhythmic, breathless chant.

"One, one thousand, two, one thousand, three, one thousand, four, one thousand, five, one thousand, six—"

Lightning split the night.

"Within a mile," I whispered. "If he's at the heart of it, he's set his domain within a mile of here."

Lil marched over to the window and smacked my arm.

"Forget the storm. What were you up to in here, Anakim? That felt more like building ties than severing them." Her red hair had worked its way loose from its bun, and long strands of it tumbled wildly around her face.

"I didn't go through with it," I said with quiet fervor.

Father Frank looked up from checking on Halley. Despite the storm and our raised voices, she appeared to have drifted off to a peaceful sleep.

"What are you two arguing about now?" he demanded.

I squirmed beneath his earnest gaze.

"Halley's brain is prime real estate," I explained haltingly. "I didn't think that would be a temptation for me—and I was wrong."

Lil went to smack me again, and I whipped my hand up as an afterthought, catching the blow on my forearm.

"You were going to *bind* her to you?" she demanded. "A girl like *that*? Have you taken leave of your senses, Anakim?"

I whirled away from her, muttering, "I'm no better than any of my brothers. I've just forgotten half the things that make me a monster."

"Zack!" the priest objected.

I rounded on him, an echo of the storm's fury resounding in my voice.

"When I did it, padre, did I ask you?"

"Yes," he answered in a voice that did not waver.

"But did you really understand it?" I persisted. "Did I explain enough to let you truly have a choice about the world of grief you were signing on for?"

Stricken, he met my eyes—and looked away.

"Didn't think so," I murmured. Outside, the wind

gusted, singing through the wires. Another massive peal of thunder shook the skies. In the following cascade of lightning, something at the far end of the lot erupted in a shower of sparks. The streetlamps in the parking lot flickered and went out. One of Halley's monitors emitted an unhappy whine, but the power in the hospital held without fail.

Sharply, the padre cleared his throat. "I wouldn't have understood it if you had," he said. There was an edge to his voice that made me look up. "And I wouldn't have believed you—just like I didn't believe you about what would happen when you got yourself killed."

Beside me, Lil clucked her tongue, derisive and dismissive all at once. Father Frank shot her a look forged of gunpowder and steel.

"None of that matters anyway, because if I had it to do over again, the answer would still be yes." With swift, sharp movements, he crossed the short distance between us, hands fisted at his sides. Some of his power infused his words, increasing their resonance above volume alone.

"Maybe I didn't know what I was signing on for with you, but I knew what I was signing on for when I joined the Corps." He held himself rigidly at his full height. We stood nose to nose and eye to eye. "*Semper Fidelis* covers a lot of things—none more so than the men you promised to fight and die alongside. Or—" His voice cracked here, just a little. "—in my case, fight and *live* for."

The weight of that final sentence bore down upon his features. He drew a breath, slightly arrested by the tape around his ribs. When next he spoke, his tone was softer, but no less intense for it. He leaned close enough that I could feel the punctuation of every consonant.

"I understand that you lost a lot last fall. I know a little about loss myself. What I don't understand is regret. You don't regret the choices you make to protect the people you care about. You do what you have to, and you carry on, even when those choices are hard. And you know who taught me that?" he demanded, jabbing me hard in the chest. "*You* did. So suck it up. If you seriously intend on fixing the shit-storm going on outside that window, you'd best stop wallowing in self-doubt. *Sir*."

At this last, his right arm twitched with the urge to end on a salute. Instead, he squared off his shoulders and pinned me with the heavy burden of those worn copper eyes. He never blinked. After a moment, he turned smartly on one heel and went back to tend to Halley.

I gaped after him, speechless.

"You're both missing the point," Lil growled. "That girl—whatever else she might be—has obvious mental deficiencies. Getting her permission is not the biggest issue here. How on earth do you trust someone like *that* to be responsible with power?" She stabbed a painted nail in Halley's direction.

"*That's* your problem?" I choked. "I thought you were busting my balls about consent. It's what's eating me."

She scoffed. "Consent requires equal measures of capitulation and understanding. We're immortals, Zack. How do you expect the average person to understand all of what we are—let alone someone who's mentally deficient?"

"Halley is not deficient," Father Frank declared, biting off the end of each word. He stood protectively over the girl as she shifted languidly under her covers.

Lil darted forward and snatched the chart from the rails of the hospital bed. She slipped the glasses down her nose.

"Autism. Sensory Processing Disorder with a note to keep the lights low. Epilepsy—grand mal seizures. Hypoglycemic. A litany of allergies from penicillin to oranges, and on top of all of that, she's lactose intolerant and has celiac disease?" With a baffled air of disgust, she returned the chart. "If there's a mind in there that can think and reason, that's so much worse. She's trapped! How does prolonging her life strike either of you as a good idea?" She snorted. "Kill her now and let her start over. It would be kinder."

"Get out!" Father Frank roared.

"Yep. You're definitely one of Zack's." Lil tucked her hair back in its bun, gratuitously rolling her eyes. "You're infected with his stupid." At that she stomped to the half-open door, the heels of her boots sharp against the tiles. Another volley of thunder shook the building, followed by lightning so intense the ozone prickled on my tongue.

Lil paused at the entrance to the darkened room, sparing a glance over her shoulder. "You two keep tilting at windmills. I'll be in the hall intercepting the night nurse again when she inevitably comes to investigate all the noise."

Father Frank stood vigil at Halley's side, glaring at Lil till she slipped from the room. With my hands fisted in my pockets, I moved to stand beside the padre.

"I'm still not going to do it," I murmured. A muscle in his jaw twitched and he drew breath to speak. Before he could voice his objection, I said, "Not for any of the reasons Lil gave, and not because I'm some kind of self-doubting coward. You made your point on that."

"It could give her a fighting chance," he urged.

"Maybe," I allowed, "or it could paint an even bigger target on her head. Think about it. How many enemies do I have?"

His silence was eloquent.

"Because of the amnesia, I don't even remember what this anchor shit does. I didn't know I could do it until our exchange in this room." I shot him a look. "And it's permanent, isn't it?"

"As far as I can tell," he acknowledged, "but it's a gift, Zack. Don't you doubt that for a second. It's saved my life a hundred times over. I'm sixty-nine. I'll be seventy this August. I have been shot up, blown up, and gassed. I run marathons for charity—and I rank near the top. I teach girls like Sanjeet at the dojo, and I can take more punishment than black belts half my age. The way I see it, you didn't ask because who the hell would believe you were serious with an offer like that?"

I wanted to agree with him, but the queasy fluttering in my gut never subsided. The blind fervor in his voice didn't help. All I could think of was Roarke and all the other no-necks like him, kowtowing to their Nephilim masters. All the padre had done was drink a different flavor of Kool-Aid.

"There are no down sides," he insisted.

Mutely, I shook my head. "I'm not sure you'd be able to see them, even if there were."

His frown stamped stark lines between his steely brows.

"Just trust me on this," I said. "I didn't like where the impulse was coming from. If I were to even consider it, it would be for Halley. When I tried to do it inside her mindscape, it wasn't about saving her. The impulse was something uglier than that—something selfish."

"Selfish is denying her because you're having a crisis of faith."

"I've got enough guilt without your help, Mazetti," I snapped. Leaning on the rails of the bed, I gazed down at the girl in question. Halley murmured in her sleep, eyes tracking rapidly beneath waxen lids. The way her dark hair pooled around her on the pillows, the fairy-tale comparisons were almost unavoidable—Snow White, Sleeping Beauty, never mind her favorite of Rapunzel in her tower. I felt the same protective ferocity that clearly drove the padre—but it was time to shift the narrative.

I bent and murmured close to her ear.

"Hey, Rapunzel—I know you can hear me, even through that crazy minefield you got leading up to your high tower." The ceaseless motion beneath her lids halted and I felt the subtle brush of her mind as it sought my own. "You keep working on those walls like I told you," I continued. "And use that crazy moat to your advantage. It keeps you in, but it can keep everyone else out. Make it your strength in this. We cut the ties, but believe me—he *will* try to get at you again."

"Zaquiel..." Father Frank began. His broad, high

brow creased with worry, and contrition.

"Let it go," I cautioned. I straightened, rolling my shoulders. The leather of my jacket creaked, jarringly loud in the relative hush of the room. The thunder now raged outside, unabated, a dramatic reminder that we'd blackened Terhuziel's eye. There would be a reprisal— the storm was just the first act of the show. I laid a hand on the padre's shoulder, felt the watchful, weary tension he carried in his old bones.

"She's got the tools she needs for now, and I'm going to go out there and do everything I can to get the bastard before he gets his claws in her again. Then we won't have to worry about things like anchors."

Silently, he nodded. He remained standing over Halley as I strode to the door.

Outside, the Lady of Beasts fumed at the end of the hall.

"Come on, Lil, we have a crime scene to break into," I said before she could start. "I want to figure out where Ter-hoo-ha's hiding, and put this nightmare to bed."

32

I fell into step behind Lil as we turned the corner to the nurses' station, making a token effort at upholding our initial ruse.

I needn't have bothered.

A tall and honey-voiced gentleman leaned jauntily on the counter overlooking the station. He wore nondescript scrubs and a white lab coat, but somehow managed to make them look suave and dapper. He could have passed for Denzel Washington's younger clone, and he flashed the nurse a smile that unironically oozed charisma. There was no mistaking what was on his mind.

The older woman swooned like a tween at a Bieber concert, giggling as he joked.

Lil could have saved that trust charm—the night nurse was well and truly distracted.

Lil and I strode right past the station, making for the elevators. The night nurse wiggled her fingers pleasantly as we went by, shooting Lil a suggestive wink. The Lady of Beasts smiled back, subtly gesturing toward the doctor, whose back was to us. She gave the woman the thumbs up as the elevator swallowed us.

"Looks like someone's getting lucky tonight," she mused, stabbing the button with the butt-end of her pen. "He's cute."

I leaned against the back wall of the elevator, staring at her reflection in the ceiling.

"All you think about is sex."

Her lips curled in a sphinx-like smile. "That's not fair. I also think about murder."

I snorted. "Remind me again why I hang out with you?"

"Because you like murder, too." Her smile widened till it became a feral baring of teeth. The air around her reeked of spice and vanilla, and the scent stirred some atavistic part of my brain that held little differentiation between sex and violence. My traitor pulse sped up, sending a rush of blood to points south of my beltline. I squirmed under Lil's knowing gaze, but offered no denial. Her laughter rang full and throaty in the tight compartment as we moved toward the lobby.

"You never get tired of tormenting me, do you?"

"You haven't disappointed yet." She grinned.

We picked up another two passengers at the third floor, and Lil fell quiet till we made it the rest of the way down. I pressed my back against the wall and tried to ignore how tight my jeans had become.

Stupid body. Damned thing had no idea how to prioritize.

The lobby was mostly empty, save for a few stragglers.

Most stood at the big bank of glass doors gawking at the blizzard outside. A few held their car keys, clearly reluctant to go out. Thunder growled and the answering lightning flashed against an unrelenting sheet of white. It was as if the world beyond the hospital had stopped three feet out, everything lost to a snowy void.

"This is going to suck," Lil grumbled. She tugged the scrunchies out of her hair, shaking loose all her long curls. "You left my jacket upstairs."

"I thought you were as immune to the cold as me," I ventured.

She made a face as the wind gusted. "Two words. Snow, and cleavage." A swirling wall of white surged against the doors. "Even if I were the ice queen, that would still suck."

She plucked off her glasses and slipped them back into her purse. The clipboard had already disappeared. I didn't remember seeing her put it down, and for all I knew, that had been swallowed by her TARDIS-like handbag as well. I didn't think the thing had a bottom.

Lil pressed close to one of the doors, scowling ferociously at the raging sea of white. Not bothering to hide my smirk, I leaned above her, reaching to press my hand against the frigid glass of the door.

The wind fought me—I didn't have leverage for shit at this angle—but I managed to push it partly open. I was rewarded with a gale-force gust that drove a column of snow through the crack, hitting Lil full-force in the face. She glared up at me, white flecks speckling her lashes, her hair, and—most importantly—the perfect stretch of flesh exposed by her plunging V-neck.

"Asshole," she spat.

"Payback's a bitch," I said, stepping around her to plunge headlong into the storm.

The lights were still out in the parking lot. Not that it mattered—the snow was so thick, lights wouldn't have helped anyway. I couldn't see any of the cars till I was right on top of them. I kept my head down and aimed in the general direction of the garage. Lil was right behind me—I could hear her cursing even over the thunder.

"I've felt that thing you do with heat lightning when you get really pissed off." I yelled to make myself heard. Even so, the wind tried to steal my words. "Don't you have some control over the weather?"

"A little," she called back, "but to counter something like this, you'd need my sister, the Lady of Storms." Her hair whipped across her face and, spitting, she shoved it back. I bet she was regretting taking out the scrunchies.

"How many sisters have you got?" I asked.

"Alive, or dead?" she countered.

"Does it matter?"

I didn't hear her response, assuming she offered one. Lil could be maddeningly dodgy about who and what she was. Last fall, Sal had let slip the sobriquet "Daughter of Lilith," so I had a few ideas—but they were vague at best. The only thing I knew for certain was that Lil was immortal, though exactly how her immortality worked remained a mystery.

Among my siblings, each tribe differed in the way they clung to the flesh-and-blood world. My tribe, the Anakim, were the most prosaic. We got born the old-fashioned way, and when we died, we sought out a new set of parents to do the whole thing over again.

Last time around, I'd intended for Frank Mazetti to be one of those parents. That was one of the purposes of an anchor. I'd gotten that much in the flash of memory up in the hospital room. I wondered again about the circumstances that had altered the path so that instead, he became a priest.

I'd have time to ask him.

Later.

The unforgiving press of the wind subsided somewhat as we finally made it to the parking garage. The exterior lot wasn't that big, but it felt like we'd crossed the Antarctic. I stood on the lee-side of a concrete pillar, shaking clumps of ice from inside the collar of my jacket. The interior of the parking garage yawned cavernous in front of us. The power was still out, and not even emergency lighting had kicked in.

"Fuck," I muttered.

Lil caught up to me, her bronze features fixed in a perma-scowl. Snow was matted in her hair, weighing the russet curls down till they hung practically to her waist. She reached down the front of her blouse, grabbed the slush that had collected there, and lobbed it at me.

"Happy?" she snarled.

I swiped the icy meltwater from where she'd pelted it at my cheek and grinned.

"Yeah, actually."

She muttered a blistering curse in a long-dead tongue.

"Come on, Lil," I chided. "That wouldn't be fair to the sheep."

"Fuck you," she replied. "Where did we park?"

"Three-E," I said automatically.

"Well, let's start walking." She shook clinging crystals of ice from the ends of her hair.

I moved in the opposite direction. "Elevator's this way."

"No power, no elevator, Einstein," she spat. "I think the stairs are over here."

"Don't they have back-up generators?" I asked.

Broadly, she gestured. "Do you see any lights?"

Muttering my displeasure, I trudged glumly along. The concrete cavern of the parking garage was bad enough with no power, but the sheeting snow cut off any ambient light from outside. I put one boot carefully in front of the other, fighting the urge to reach my hands out so I could feel my way through the shadows.

Ahead of me, Lil moved quickly, swift and sure as a cat. She walked on the balls of her feet, rolling her arches forward so the heels of her expensive boots never touched the cement of the floor. Once she realized how far I'd lagged behind, she halted. I could barely make out the look of irritation that creased her features.

"Yeah, yeah, spare me the insults," I muttered. "I'm just not as cool as you when it comes to creeping around in the dark."

Lil's full lips twisted into a smug grin as she started to respond. Then, all of a sudden, she froze. Canting her head, she listened intently, then sniffed the air. I fell silent, straining my own senses. All I heard was the thunder and the wind.

The next instant, she dashed off, crouching below the line of the cars. Certain now that the storm had been some sort of cover, I angled my back to a wall, whispering my power. Subtle light danced around my fingertips, ready to explode into deadly brilliance once the enemy closed.

To my left came the sound of a scuffle. The shadows swallowed any sign of who or what it was. I heard Lil hiss a rapid string of curses, followed by a meaty thump, like she'd dropped a body to the ground.

That body complained immediately in accented tones.

"Really," it said. "You don't have to pull a knife on me."

"Remiel!" she snarled. "I could have killed you."

My brother barked a dry, ironic laugh. "Hardly."

Fussing with the lapels of a smartly tailored woolen coat, the Nephilim stepped into my line of vision and moved toward me. His sleek fall of black hair was swept away from his face and plaited into a tight braid that ended at the small of his back. He had porcelain-pale skin that seemed almost luminescent in the gloom of the concrete parking structure. Model-perfect features boasted cheekbones that could incite some Hollywood actors to envious acts of murder. Angled above his brow was a jaunty fedora. He'd worn the damned things so long, they'd come back into fashion.

Lil emerged behind him, tucking a folding knife back into her purse.

"You should know better than to sneak up on me like that," she grumbled sourly.

He arched a delicate brow at her. "I wasn't exactly sneaking."

Lil frowned, pushing an unruly tangle of curls back behind her ear. She took several swift steps to catch up to him and then—incredibly—leaned in and sniffed his elbow. Going up on tiptoes, she trailed her nose all the way up his arm, ending close to his collar. Remy regarded her with mild confusion throughout this curious display, which was weird even for Lil.

She stepped away, wrinkling her nose.

"I don't recognize this cologne," she complained.

"Cologne?" He blinked azure eyes that glimmered faintly in the gloom.

"Why do you think I jumped you?" she demanded, slapping his chest with the back of her hand. "You don't smell like you."

I shook the lingering power from my fingers, willing myself to relax now that the threat had proven to be nothing more than my soft-spoken brother. Maybe Terhuziel had run out of minions to throw at me, and the storm was his best attempt at an attack. That would be a nice change of pace. My life could use fewer complications.

Delicately, my brother sniffed at the edge of one sleeve. "Oh," he murmured. "You're probably smelling Jimmy. I was with him before I came here."

"Who's Jimmy?" Lil asked. She managed somehow to package curiosity, suspicion, and a subtle promise of reprisal into just two words.

Lil and Remy had been married once upon a time. It had ended poorly, which should have been a shock to no one. Since I'd become reacquainted with the both of them, Lil waxed hot and cold with my brother—and, for some reason, Remy put up with it. I didn't ask. Mostly, I tried to steer clear of their endless squabbles. Not tonight.

"Jimmy Roarke," I ventured. "Remy's pet police officer. Am I right?"

Remy nodded, adjusting the brim of his fedora.

"Who is, I might add, rather irate at you."

"I don't like cops," I grumbled.

"Well, your behavior last night didn't exactly endear you to Roarke—and he wasn't exactly your chum to begin with."

"Why are you here?" I asked.

Lil continued scenting the air around Remy, a little more subtly this time. Her features creased in a pensive expression, like she was contemplating how much trouble it might be to hunt the officer down later. Remy pointedly ignored her behavior.

"I had Jimmy drop me off so I could talk to the girl," he explained, "but I saw you and Lil making your way through the parking lot, so I decided I'd just ask you instead."

"Ask me what?"

"The meaning of those letters cut into the attacker's chest. *Attackers'*, plural," he corrected. "They found similar carvings on a frozen corpse just outside of Lake View," he added, perking a brow pointedly as he fixed his azure eyes on mine. "There have been a number of corpses turning up of late."

I made a noise in the back of my throat that wasn't any kind of answer, and started walking in what was probably the direction of my car.

"This is serious, Zaquiel," Remy called after me.

"Yeah," I agreed, "and I've got places to go." I kept walking. The Nephilim hesitated, then jogged to catch up to me. He reached for my elbow. I jerked it away. Lil hung back, most likely enjoying the show.

MICHELLE BELANGER

"There are altars being set up all around the city," he said. "They bear those self-same glyphs. There have been murders and other activity that appear to be sacrifices." His words came out swift and urgent. He grabbed for my elbow again. "You have to know what that portends."

Stopping suddenly, I whirled on him. "You knew about this, and you didn't let me know?" My voice echoed through the cavernous structure. "This is my city!"

"*Your* city," Lil scoffed.

I glowered at her in the gloom, then turned the same unhappy glare on Remy.

"This shit's been ramping up for the better part of a month," I growled. "Why didn't you tell me?" Remy met my eyes without blinking.

"Perhaps someone should more regularly check his phone," he said witheringly.

The messages.

I refused to concede his point.

"You know where I live."

"Ha!" he barked. "I know better than to violate your sanctum sanctorum when you are in one of your moods, brother. But I'm glad to see that you're taking an interest now. *Finally*," he added. "Old alliances with the Idol-Riders may prevent Sal and myself from becoming directly involved."

"Is that who sent you?" I demanded. "Saliriel?"

Remy loosed a sigh of frustration. "Really, sibling. You're impossible when you let your judgments rule you."

"That's different from normal how?" Lil asked.

I snarled at her. "Hey, whose side are you on anyway?"

"Mine." She smiled with all the self-assured hauteur of a Madame du Pompadour. I prepared myself for another salvo of vitriol when I thought I heard the scuff of a shoe against the concrete floor.

Remy's head whipped in that direction, and the subtle light in his unnaturally blue eyes sharpened to a full-on glow. He dropped his mellifluous voice to a whisper.

"We are not alone."

33

They crept up on us while we argued, using our raised voices to cover the sound of their advance. Terhuziel had stepped up his game—probably because he now knew he was dealing with me, as well as the padre.

I spotted three of them right off, and heard a fourth moving behind the pylons to my right. One of them stepped out from behind a black SUV, hands locked in a familiar stance.

"Gun," Lil breathed.

The bullet ricocheted off the wall behind me as soon as her warning left her lips. The report was shatteringly loud, and my hearing dulled to a low buzz in its wake.

Remy moved with that blurring speed that only the Nephilim could muster. I could move fast when I needed to, but would never match that sight-tricking alacrity. One instant, he was behind me. The next, I heard the wet snap of bone as he disarmed the gunman—almost literally.

The attacker collapsed, screaming, against the SUV.

His weapon dropped to clatter beneath a nearby car. Lil dove to retrieve it.

With the first one wounded, the others scattered, but these were Rephaim anchors, and the gunman proved it in the next instant, levering himself up despite the injury. As Remy turned to track one of the others, he launched himself at my brother. Shrieking unintelligibly, the man clung to the Nephilim's shoulders, broken wrist and all.

The primly dressed vampire blurred again and, in the next heartbeat, he had the attacker's head between his hands. He twisted, whipping the man onto the ground, then stomped on the fellow's lower back, grinding down with the heel of his sleek Italian shoe. At the same time, he twined his long fingers beneath the man's jaw and yanked upward sharply, bending him the wrong way in half.

The ratcheting crackle of the man's severed spine was almost as loud as the next volley of gunfire.

"Take cover, you idiot!" Lil snapped. That was meant for me. The Nephilim healed so fast, bullets were merely a nuisance. Remy was probably more worried about getting holes in his trim-waisted wool coat.

As if to prove his superiority, Remy stepped disdainfully over the corpse and oriented himself in the direction of the next shooter. Three muzzle flashes erupted in the depths of the lightless parking garage. Remy moved toward the gunfire, slow and unhurried, drawing attention away from Lil and me.

The shooter was half a floor up, aiming down from between stanchions. I had no idea how the person could see—though, if their aim was any indication, they couldn't, not really. The first two bullets flew wide of their mark. The third caught Remy's fedora, knocking it off of his head. His hand snapped up to catch it, but he was a nanosecond too late.

His placid features twisted into a mask of perfect fury. "That was one of my favorites!" he snarled, theatrically baring his fangs—then he launched himself in the direction of the muzzle-flares, blurring again.

I dropped to all fours and skittered none too gracefully for cover between the nearest two vehicles. Squatting low, my back against a large pickup, I was all elbows and knees. Pulling the SIG out, I held it up, but wasn't about to fire blindly into the dark. Not being able to see was really pissing me off, and the way sounds rebounded within the depths of the parking garage, there was no hope of relying on my ears.

So I ground my teeth, feeling the next best thing to useless.

"Dammit, why'd you have to leave my coat behind?" Lil hissed.

I peered under the car between us. "Why the hell do you need your coat? Aren't your weapons all in that little purse?"

She ducked down to glare at me. "My best amulet's in the coat pocket," she snarled.

"Well, boo-hoo," I said. It wasn't like Lil needed the help. She fought like a fucking ninja.

A cry erupted in the direction of the second shooter. Abruptly, it cut off. Remy made not a sound. Normally all fuss and etiquette, the Nephilim could be terrifying when he wanted to be.

"Two down," Lil noted.

"I think there were only four," I whispered.

"I counted five with that second shooter."

"Don't you two know to stay quiet when people are hunting you?" Remy called. His lightly accented voice carried throughout the structure. *He* wasn't worried about quiet.

I heard Lil rummaging around in her clutch purse. A couple of items clattered to the floor—a tube of lipstick, a ball-bearing, and three green beads that looked like they'd come from Halley's rosary.

"Hey," I hissed. "Didn't you smash that thing?"

Lil ignored me. Still digging in the handbag, she made a little sound of triumph.

"This'll do."

The next instant, she vanished. I peered under the sedan just to be certain. Above the stink of motor oil and gasoline, I caught a faint whiff of ozone. I also caught sight of one of Lil's ghost ferrets. The blonde-furred creature chattered at me, haunches wriggling.

"Great," I sighed. "Did she leave you behind to babysit?"

The thing twitched its whiskers, fairly grinning. It snaked behind a wheel well, then tumbled playfully against my ankle. It wasn't a flesh-and-blood creature, but I could still feel its impact, like an intimation of weight.

I wondered where Lailah's soot-gray screech owl might be. Lil was attended by a host of spectral animals, and each held some enigmatic tie to her sisters. I still hadn't worked out whether the animal spirits *represented* her sisters, or somehow *were* the sisters in totemic form.

A sharp tug on my ankle garnered my attention. I didn't react much at first because I thought it was the ferret again. Then I felt the distinct grip of fingers digging for purchase against the leather shaft of my engineer boot. A streaked and dirty hand extended from beneath the vehicle at my back.

Like a tattered version of Rambo, the guy had belly-crawled all the way across the parking level, a knife clenched between his teeth.

I should have been more vigilant—the truck behind me had oversized tires, so it stood higher off the ground. The undercarriage provided the attacker ample space to maneuver.

"You had one job, ferret," I snarled. The little critter sneezed its objection. I jerked my ankle, trying to break free of the floor-troll's grip. The emaciated hand clung with a desperate strength, and its owner dragged himself closer by inches. With his other hand, he went for the knife.

The instant I saw the glint of the steel, power leapt to my fingertips. It was instinct—but my hands were on the grip of the gun. It was a good thing I wasn't dumb enough to ride the trigger, or I'd have squeezed off at least one accidental round—and probably shot my damned toes off.

I used the burst of power to fuel my speed, angling forward and bracing a shoulder against the floor. With the guy still scrabbling to hamstring me, I fired off two quick rounds at point-blank range.

They got him in the forehead and in the cheek. This close, the bullets didn't tear things up too much going in, but the back of his head erupted in a mess. For a frozen instant he stared at me with wide, startled eyes. They were hazel, shot through with striations of a pale yellow-green. Some elusive quality fled the depths of those glassy orbs and his head tottered forward, blood streaming from his distorted mouth.

The grip on my ankle went slack. He dropped the knife, though I couldn't hear its clatter through the ringing in my ears.

The scent of hot metal mixed with the tidal-pool stench of his blood. I crouched there staring mutely as the dark fluid spread closer to me by inches. It washed over the knife, one of my brass casings, and I still didn't move.

I'd meant to kill him, but did I have to?

The guy looked to be in his mid-forties, his features weather-roughened, his hair prematurely grayed. The jagged white line of a scar ran across his scalp from his temple. The knuckles on his outstretched hand were battered with old, puckered wounds, as well. This guy had seen a rough life. The way he'd snuck up on me suggested a military background.

The Rephaim didn't care if these people wanted to be his soldiers. He forced his influence on them—like I'd almost done to Halley. It helped if they were battered by drugs, biology, or trauma.

Could this guy have been saved?

"What the *hell* are you laying there for?" Lil squawked. She seized the collar of my leather jacket and yanked. I was a hundred and eighty pounds of wiry dead weight, but she had my upper torso a couple feet off the ground before I could twist away.

"Quit it," I objected. I flicked the safety back on.

"Dead people. Parking garage," she snapped. "Major hospital one lot away," she added. "Get your ass in gear, Anakim."

"They're all dead?" I levered myself up, tucking the gun back in its holster. Then I worked my jaw, trying to get my ears to pop. Everything still sounded tinny in the wake of the gunfire.

Remy sauntered over, retrieving his fedora. Frowning, he stuck a gloved finger through the hole near the top. A matching hole, crisped around the edges, went out the other side.

"I doubt I'll be able to salvage this," he sighed. He tucked the perforated hat reluctantly beneath one arm. "I can stay and make certain Roarke is the one who gets to the scene," he offered. A spatter of crimson arced across one cheekbone, fresh enough that it was still gleaming. He seemed unaware of it until Lil pointed. Self-consciously, he swiped a finger across his cheek, looking back to Lil. She nodded.

"You have a handkerchief or something in your purse?" I asked, scrubbing at the faint speckling of blood on my knuckles. I probably had it on my face, too, considering I'd shot the guy at such close range. I couldn't feel it, but my nose was still thick with the wet copper tang.

"A bandana work?" She shoved her hand into the purse and yanked out a square of patterned blue cloth.

Without answering I took it and bent to scoop up the two spent casings from my gun. They'd gelled into the blood already, sticking a little and leaving a negative space where I plucked them from the floor. Lil made a disgusted noise.

"You didn't say you wanted it for that," she grumbled.

I ignored her, wrapping the casings till I was sure none of the wet would seep through to my pocket.

"I would have taken care of that," Remy offered.

"I don't want to get into the habit of leaving shit like this behind." I pocketed the wad of bandana and fished out my keys. "Let's go, Lil."

"Zaquiel," Remy called after me.

"What?" I stopped, but I didn't turn around. Lil kept walking.

"You never answered my question," he huffed.

"Which question?" I asked wearily.

"The glyphs," he said. The words came out harsh and clipped, and loud enough that he didn't seem to care if we were overheard. "Which one are we dealing with?" he demanded.

I debated briefly the consequences of invoking the Name.

"Terhuziel," I said.

I heard my brother draw a sharp breath.

"Oh," he murmured. "Oh, my."

34

Twenty paces from the Hellcat, I clicked the button on my key fob, then muttered an inchoate curse, fighting the urge to smash the useless bit of plastic to pieces.

Lil, who was ten paces closer to the car than I was, walked through the pitchy shadows of the parking garage like she was out for a lazy Sunday stroll. On hearing my bellyaching, she turned and shot me a bemused look.

"Problems?"

"Fucking batteries," I snarled.

She snorted. "Be glad the mortals haven't figured out how to power their guns with that lithium-ion stuff. You'd be screwed."

That just reminded me of the man I'd shot in the face. Two people had died by my hand in as many days—maybe unavoidably, maybe not.

One floor below us, I could hear Remy moving things around—and by "things," I meant bodies. Under the scheming auspices of his Decimus, Saliriel, Remy had been manipulating criminal investigations in the city since the days of the Mayfield Road Gang. I shouldn't have resented the Nephilim's influence over the local police—it enabled me to fight some of the nastier things that ran amok in the city, and not end up with a jail sentence.

A necessary evil.

Didn't mean I had to like it.

I ground my teeth, and moved faster to get the fuck out of this lightless vault of death and cars.

Dropping into the bucket seat behind the wheel, I unlocked all the doors from the controls on the armrest. The engine turned over with a comforting rumble, and I felt grateful for one aspect of the parking garage—the cover it provided. If I'd parked in the open lot, I'd have spent the next ten minutes scraping snow and ice off the car.

The iPod skipped from Nick Cave to Jim Morrison crooning "Riders on the Storm." I didn't even remember that being on the playlist.

Lil squinted, then threw her head back and laughed.

"A personal soundtrack with a side of irony?"

I had an inkling now it was Lailah, exerting some kind of control over the sound system. Just then, it was a tease more than a comfort, and the frustration at my continued inability to perceive her reached critical mass. I yanked out the wires and chucked the device behind me without looking to see where it landed.

"That temper, Zack," Lil chided.

"Stuff it," I growled.

She clucked her tongue disapprovingly. If she had any sense of her sister, she wasn't sharing, which pissed me off more. I white-knuckled the steering wheel while I fumed, adrenaline from the fight still jolting through all my limbs. Lil grew bored, redirecting her attention to her phone. Squinting at my hastily scrawled sticky note, she entered the Kramer address into her mapping function.

"Under five miles," she announced. "Major roads till we get to Whitethorn. Shouldn't be too bad, even with this snow." She tilted the screen so I could see it.

"I know the way to that part of town," I growled.

"So get a move on," she urged.

I put the car into gear, but kept my foot on the brake.

"We need to check on Halley."

Lil gave a choking cough. "I can count six reasons that say we're getting the hell out of here before Remy's police friends arrive," she snapped.

"There were six?"

"Counting the one you put down, yes," she replied. "Now drive before we have bigger problems than a hit squad."

"The last time the hit squad was a distraction," I said. "He's not after us. He's after the girl."

"The hospital has security," she replied. "How far do you think they'd get?"

"We got pretty far," I answered.

She smacked the dash. "At least move this damned thing while we argue."

Conceding that much, I pulled out and started threading my way down to the exit.

"We just need to make sure she's safe," I insisted.

"Mother's Tears," Lil hissed. Radiating impatience, she dug around in her purse, and produced a loop of

313

string with half a dozen green beads still attached—and a single flat pink one.

"For fuck's sake, Lil," I snarled—and nearly ran over one of the sprawled attackers as I took the turn to the lower level. Not that hitting him would do anything but make a mess. He was dead already. Reaching out with one hand, I tried to nab what was left of the rosary from Lil.

She jerked it swiftly away.

"You were supposed to destroy that!"

"I did… mostly," she allowed, dropping it back into her handbag. "But it's this they're tracking. Since you're so hell-bent on keeping that girl alive, I thought it would be useful to draw them away."

"That's—that's brilliant, Lil."

She opened her mouth, then blinked in stupefaction.

"Did someone drop you on your head, flyboy?"

"I thought you wanted the girl dead," I responded.

She sighed. "I like to be prepared—and I know what kind of bleeding heart you've become." She tossed her curls back from her face, her expression cold as the wintry night beyond the car. "I still think killing her would solve a host of problems, but I know to pick my fights."

That didn't exactly leave me thrilled, but I didn't push her on the subject. We drew up to the kiosk a moment later. The bar was down, and it was automated. Useless as fuck with the power still out.

"Just drive through," Lil said.

I shook my head, putting the car into park. "Paint transfer," I explained. "I don't want any chance they can trace my car to the mess back there."

All it took was a solid kick from my size thirteens to crack the bar from its mooring. I toed it aside, then got back into the Hellcat.

"Admit it, flyboy," Lil chuckled. "You didn't want to ding your shiny new toy."

"I hate this car," I responded, pulling out of the parking structure.

"Sure. Keep telling yourself that."

35

It should have taken ten minutes, tops, from University Hospital to the address on Whitethorn. With the road conditions, it took closer to twenty. According to the radio, nearly eight inches had fallen in under an hour, and the city's transportation department was caught unprepared.

Ice and slush smeared the windshield. No snowplows were visible anywhere on the roads. Even Euclid Avenue—a main artery through downtown—was an uninterrupted ribbon of white. If any cars had passed through the storm before mine, the wind had scoured their trace.

I missed my old Buick. The Dodge was a slick and gorgeous machine, but it simply couldn't match the Buick's traction. I crawled along, fighting not to fishtail every time I had to make a turn, while Lil grew progressively more restless beside me. Her irritation grated like fingernails on the inside of my skull.

"Unless you want us to end up in a ditch, I'm not going any faster," I said, heading her off.

"You drive like somebody's grandpa," she complained.

"Not everyone treats residential driving like it's NASCAR."

"And yet I still get to where I'm going twice as fast, and without so much as a scratch on my bumper." She gave a dismissive toss to her flame-kissed curls.

"Yeah, you're the epitome of a safe driver," I replied. "So long as you don't count the accidents you cause for the poor bastards who scramble to get out of your way."

"Their fault," she sniped.

Arguing with Lil was a Sisyphean exercise, so I dropped it. We were almost to the Kramer house anyway. I took a left onto Whitethorn—or at least where I thought the street was. Curb and pavement alike were blanketed by a foot-tall drift of snow.

"How far does the little GPS doohickey say the house is down this street?" I asked as I nosed the Hellcat through the drift. If the snow got any higher, the car was going to stall out. I could already feel the heavy powder dragging along the undercarriage.

She pressed a button and the screen of her smartphone cast eerie light on her face.

"Not quite to the cul-de-sac."

I peered unhappily through the slush. Even with the heater on full blast, the wipers kept freezing up. The headlamps revealed a landscape more suited for the Winter Olympics than for driving anything short of a tank.

"Fuck it," I said. "I'm backing out and parking at the cross-street. At least the snow there wasn't up to my grill. We can walk."

Lil didn't object. I threw the car into reverse, backed

carefully through the tracks I'd already cut on my way in, then pulled off to one side. Killing the engine, I opened the door. The bottom carved a neat arc through the snow piled up on the road.

"Terael said this guy was still building his power," I observed, slamming the door shut. "If that's the case, I'd hate to see what he can do on one of his good days."

Lil barked a dry laugh. "You know the Flood story, right?"

I shot her an incredulous look.

"Temper tantrum in Mesopotamia," she explained, and she smirked. I couldn't tell if she was joking.

Shoving my fists into my pockets, I slogged through the drifts toward the entrance to Whitethorn, aiming in the general vicinity of the sidewalk. The city lay quiet beneath the thick shroud of snow, and only the blaring sirens of emergency vehicles cut through the chill night air. Lightning still fretted between the bellies of the clouds, but the wild peals of thunder had subsided to token grumbles. A stark and solitary beauty limned the blackened branches of all the laden trees.

Still smirking, Lil followed a few steps behind, placing her feet neatly in the prints left by my boots.

The Kramer house looked deceptively serene against this frigid landscape, draped as it was in a veil of pristine white. It was easy to miss the yellow gloss of police tape sealing the front door on the other side of the ice-encrusted screen. At the top of the driveway, I held my keys out to Lil.

"You don't need to stand around while I search the house," I offered. "You can wait inside the car."

"Are you kidding me?" She shot me a look that rivaled the weather's wintry fury. "I didn't trudge through all this snow for shits and grins," she snapped. "I'm going in there with you."

"No," I said, shaking my head. "I want to do this clean and quick. I'll pop in through the Shadowside, look for any sign of where the doc took Terhuziel, and then get right back out."

"I'm going in," she said flatly. She shoved my keys away, hard enough that I nearly lost them in a drift.

"It's an active police investigation, Lil," I protested. "If we both go in, we double the chance of leaving some kind of evidence behind."

"If you're that concerned with evidence," she said, "then you must have brought gloves, right?"

I hadn't, and she knew it.

"Well, look here..." She withdrew a pair of blue nitrile gloves from her handbag and dangled them in front of me. "Imagine that. It's like I know a thing or two about breaking and entering."

I resisted the urge to grab them from her hand. She'd only pull them away at the last instant, and I refused to be Charlie Brown to her Lucy.

"You do your shadow-walk routine," she continued. "I'll wait for you to unlock the back door once you're inside. That way, I won't have to do anything so obvious as picking a lock."

I could see where this was going.

"No point arguing with you, is there?"

"Have you won one yet?" She smiled sweetly, showing all her teeth.

Sharks had more comforting grins.

"Then we do this quick," I said.

She just scowled and shoved me in the direction of the house, tossing the gloves after me.

"It'll be quicker if you shut up and get on with it."

I caught the gloves.

"Careful when you put them on," she warned. "They're sized for my hands."

I frowned, flexing my fingers. The gloves came down approximately to my second knuckle.

"No kidding."

"Oh, and take these." Plastic crinkled as she drew out two tightly folded grocery bags.

"I'm not planning on taking anything out of the house," I objected.

"No, Einstein. They're for your feet. Your boots are covered with snow. You'll track it all over." She shook the bags out, gesturing. "Tear the handles at the seam and use them to tie the bags off at your ankles."

I stared, a little nonplussed.

"Can't a girl have hobbies?" she demurred.

I wadded the bags back up and stuffed them both into one of my pockets. Then I held out my keys. "Here."

"I'm not going back to the car," she said sharply.

"No. I already gave up on that. You'll do what you want the minute my back's turned anyway," I replied. "But I don't want to wreck the electronics any more than I already have. Hang onto them for me."

She pushed the keys aside, quipping, "It's dead, Jim."

I blinked, not sure I'd heard her correctly. "Did you just make a *Star Trek* reference—and in context?"

"I hang out with you too much." She looked past me at the Kramer house. "Is there a reason why you're stalling?"

The stately old Tudor rose in the gloom about twenty feet away.

"I've seen some of the photos from the crime scene," I muttered.

Impatience flickered across her features, but then something changed. Maybe she caught the weary look in my own eyes. I couldn't say. In the next instant, her face didn't soften exactly, but she tucked the caustic expression away and traded it for something merely ironic.

"You didn't see enough in those photos, or we wouldn't be here," she stated evenly. "Do you want to help that girl, or not?"

She certainly knew how to motivate me.

I turned and headed toward the house. The trails my boots cut in the snow were so obvious, our concerns about stealth seemed foolish, but skirling flakes were still coming down. With luck, the storm would obliterate any signs of our passage.

The cloying energy of the Crossing plucked at my cowl as soon as I mounted the front steps. It made the shadows deeper and all the lines go wrong. Someone had died very close to the front door—probably just on the other side of the threshold. If I relaxed my eyes and opened the part of my vision that peered across to the Shadowside, I could see faint echoes of the struggle.

They drew me in, and I had to make an active effort to cross on my own terms. The stain of death was fresh, and I'd yet to encounter anything quite so intense since my unwilling rebirth in the dark waters of Erie.

"This is going to suck," I told myself—then I took a deep breath and crossed to the other side of reality.

The door melted before me. The barriers that guarded the entrance and exit points of all our buildings had little substance on the Shadowside. The paths that people cut through their daily comings and goings guaranteed that the energy there always wanted to move. The pull was less in a residential building, as compared to the irresistible undertow that swirled at the entrance of a public location. Even so, the current was noticeable.

I relaxed and let it sweep me into the home.

36

I face-planted right into the replay of a death. Actually, it was a pair of deaths layered one on top of the other, so intertwined, they were difficult at first to distinguish. Two figures—and then three, and then four—strove with one another just inside the front entrance to the house. They flickered like old-time filmstrips, their colors drained to gray.

Sometimes spirits lingered on the Shadowside, but these weren't ghosts. They were impressions—echoes of trauma imprinted on the space. The collision of imagery made it hard to pick apart the exact sequence of events. It was like two projectors had been aimed at one screen and left to play dimly on top of each other. Even then, the action wasn't linear. It stuttered and skipped around, as only the most intense moments of conflict were captured with any clarity.

I moved to the furthest edge of the imprint, trying to make sense of what I could perceive, tying on Lil's ridiculous makeshift booties as I did. I only had to wait for the action to blink back to the beginning, since echoes like this played on infinite loop and would repeat their grim recording until the emotional residue that had created them finally wore away. That could take decades—centuries, even. I watched, tasting the stultifying play of emotions that surged within the imprint—pain and rage and a single-minded flavor of hate.

One figure was that of a woman—not short, exactly, but certainly smaller than the others flickering through the replay. Her features were painted in shadow, blurred and indistinct. The darkness was thick, saturated with all the horror that had transpired between these walls. The woman became clearer the more I focused on her, so I narrowed my attention, carefully tracking her movements as they unspooled from the front hallway to the door.

The woman—almost certainly Dr. Kramer's wife—approached the door as if to answer it for someone. I saw her reach cautiously toward the knob, her other hand poised behind her as if hiding something from view. The item itself didn't leave enough of an imprint to show what it was, though from her position, I suspected it might have been a knife.

The action stuttered, and suddenly she twisted in vicious combat, the imagery confusing because sometimes she struggled with one attacker, other times it appeared to be two. The second one burned like an afterimage in the tracks of the first. I had no idea what to make of that.

The second attacker faded in and out like the ghost of a ghost. Judging from their builds, both attackers were male, and both outweighed the woman by quite a bit. In fact, the second one was immense. Taller than me—taller possibly than my sibling Saliriel who easily stood six foot six. His shoulders appeared impossibly broad, and every movement left trails in the air behind him, lingering like curls of dense smoke.

It took me a moment to process what I was seeing.

Wings.

Wings that spread behind him like a ship's sails blown to tatters upon the mast.

Fuck.

Instantly my attention narrowed to that wavering figure. Details unwound. Smoke and shadow roiled around him, shot through with guttering streaks of red. Normally there was little color on the Shadowside, as everything dulled to black and gray. That red gleamed low and angry, like embers kindled in the heart of a forge. The color crackled startlingly between the winged figure and the slightly smaller echo of the man, wedding the two so they moved as if one grew out of the shoulders of the other.

Was this the Rephaim, then, riding a mortal vessel?

That didn't parse—nothing about the echo of the woman implied that she knew the man who'd showed up at her door. I was certain she was Mrs. Kramer, and I'd have bet good money that her husband was Terhuziel's primary anchor.

No, this had to be the mysterious fifth man—Booker, the black ops guy who'd gone AWOL and turned up dead. Was he one of the first foot soldiers Terhuziel had claimed? Then why the hell was he attacking the doctor's wife?

Little wonder Bobby and Garrett were pounding their heads against this case. Maybe I had it all wrong, and Dr. Kramer hadn't been the one to smuggle the idol into the country. But then why would a possessed Marine randomly show up at the Kramer house?

The doctor was the one with a penchant for less-than-legal souvenirs, and if he'd smuggled the idol into the country, he was the likeliest vessel for Terhuziel to have conquered. It wouldn't have been a quick takeover—the doc didn't strike me as soft in the head—but depending on when Kramer got his hands on the artifact, the Rephaim could have taken his time. Smarter minds needed to be coerced with more finesse.

If the doc was the main guy—Terhuziel's high priest, as it were—then what the hell was up with Booker?

Shoving aside all my assumptions, I stepped directly into the replay so I could experience it from the closest possible perspective. Phantom forms ghosted through me as they repeated their endless cycle of conflict and death, waves of imprinted emotions crashing against my wings. I tried focusing again on the woman, but my senses were overwhelmed by the chaos.

A second winged figure stuttered into view.

This one appeared vastly different from the first, rising like a broken colossus of metal and stone. Shattered wings cut an abbreviated arc in the air behind it, and all the limbs hung in sections, their jagged edges grinding against themselves. Whole portions of his body winked in and out of existence. The stone giant swung a massive fist to swat the figure of smoke and flame like an irksome bug. It raised the other arm as if to swing it, but that limb disappeared in the next instant, leaving him with a useless stump.

The punishment.

Terhuziel was literally in pieces. Suddenly his cries to rebuild himself made all the sense in the world.

Battered and broken, and that asshole still managed to wreak havoc on my town. What kind of nightmare would he become if he actually succeeded in seizing Halley to buttress his power?

Fuck. Fuck. Fuck.

I redoubled my efforts to sort through the entangled layers of imprinted data so I could understand what had gone down in this misery-stained house. At an impatient wave of my hand, the impressions focused around the wife scattered like mist. The second sequence of imprints grew clearer. Baffled, I stared briefly at my hand. I hadn't actually expected the gesture to work. That was a useful trick.

I filed it away for later. My heart was already laboring as the inescapable pressure of the Shadowside bore down on me. My time on this side was limited. I had to make it count.

The second layer of events flickered across the psychic landscape. The woman was dead, and the stain of her trauma left cloying streaks of dark upon the space. There was no way to tell how much time had passed since she'd lost the struggle against her unexpected visitor—maybe minutes, maybe hours.

Two human figures clashed furiously inside the threshold, little more than person-shaped silhouettes dwarfed by the winged hitchhikers rising from their backs. It was an epic battle—stone and metal versus shadow and flame.

The scene stuttered again, seeming to rewind, and I saw the man who had attacked the wife gliding toward the door along a path that eerily echoed her own. He was inside the house, and he was alone save for the winged being that shadowed his every step. He... it... *they* crept to the door as if preparing an ambush. The conjoined pair slipped to one side, crouching down in the space that would be shielded once the door swung open.

The imprint flickered back to the struggle. Power arced between the riders and the mortal forms as they grappled. The image flickered again, and the mortal who played host to Shadow-and-Flame suddenly held a blade. It was fucking massive.

The mortal attached to Terhuziel—it had to be Dr. Kramer—dodged but stumbled to one side. His next few motions listed to the left as if burdened by something that was heavy enough to throw off his balance. A messenger bag? He swung it to the ground and the projection of Terhuziel went with it.

The idol. Terhuziel hadn't been riding the doctor— Kramer had entered the house carrying the idol in some kind of shoulder bag. That was startling. Terael's statue back at the museum stood close to four feet tall. Carved of solid basalt, it weighed as much as some cars. Terhuziel's idol fit in a fucking messenger bag.

Whatever was left of it.

Two-handed, the other guy lifted his sword, and it was just plain ridiculous. He had to be compensating for something. Wreathed with the same swirling shadowfire that eddied through the rider's tattered wings, the weapon cut a vicious arc through the air—aimed not for Kramer, but for the Rephaim. Power crackled as the blade connected, and the concussion of its impact sent up a rain of blinding sparks. Even as an imprinted memory, that blast packed a hell of a punch, and I staggered back, blinking.

The replay shuddered forward. Shadow-and-Flame jerked suddenly. The body he rode collapsed to its knees. The blow came from Kramer, not Terhuziel. Shadow-and-Flame had gotten so focused on the Rephaim, he all but forgot about the doctor. That mistake had cost him. The mortal body pitched forward. He wasn't quite dead, but it was coming soon.

Terhuziel had won.

The mortal vessel's death-throes spread their stain upon the space, twining with the dark veins of agony previously imprinted by the wife. In a last-ditch motion, the dying man's arm snaked out, striving for the idol in the messenger bag. A glimmering object tucked against his palm. With the desperation of the dying, he flailed to get it to his goal. He never made it. His whole body spasmed and the object tumbled to the floor.

A white disk. Spinning rings of arcane runes pulsed within its center. Like a tiny star, it blazed in the twilight of the Shadowside.

Without hesitation, I knew it for what it was—one of those seals from Terael's fevered memories, used to lock the shattered Rephaim into their stones.

Just like the one Bobby's partner had flipped so carelessly across his knuckles outside the station.

Dr. Kramer recognized the item as well. Viciously, he crushed it beneath his heel. In a backwash of power, the entire scene whited out.

There was little chance Booker's seal had survived.

When I could see again, both Kramer and Terhuziel were gone, but echoes of Shadow-and-Flame lingered on the air, fretting with rage and frustration. With Booker dead, he didn't seem to have anywhere to go. I couldn't place his tribe, so I had no way to guess how he might handle the loss of his vessel. He wasn't Nephilim—that was the only thing I knew for sure. From this perspective, they looked like walking circulatory systems.

Another flash-forward, and only the rank stain of the two mortal deaths remained in the foyer. Shadow-and-Flame was gone. An uneasy awareness crawled across my scalp—I had a feeling I knew what'd happened.

Steeling myself against the persistent drain of the Shadowside, I re-watched the events in the foyer from start to finish, just to be sure. Shadows flickered as everything rewound. The wife, knife behind her, approached the door. Clearly, she didn't want visitors. Booker had to be the man who she let in—and he killed her for her trouble. Time passed. Booker was elsewhere in the house doing... something.

He heard someone at the door, so he came back to it, cautiously. That was the doctor, with Terhuziel's idol in a bag. They fought. The thing riding Booker was going to beat Terhuziel, but the doctor did something unexpected.

Maybe he brought a gun to a knife fight, I thought.

That parsed. Shadow-and-Flame raged. Booker, with his dying strength, tried to slap the soul-lock in place.

He failed. Kramer destroyed it, then fled with Terhuziel's idol. That left Shadow-and-Flame trapped where Booker had died, chewing the air in futile rage until...

Until Bobby and his partner received the call.

Again, that shiver of revelation. At some point after his vessel had died, Shadow-and-Flame found a way out. What if he'd hitched a ride?

Bobby had said his partner started acting strangely once they investigated these murders. From the man's behavior at the station, "strange" was the understatement of the century. A change that extreme didn't happen overnight, no matter how stressful the job.

What if David Garrett had one of my brothers tagging along in his head?

That explained the seal in his possession, even if it didn't tell me where he'd gotten his hands on one. Those things had to be pretty rare.

It could have been Bobby.

That thought punched me right in the gut. Good to know some part of me remembered our friendship—and didn't like the idea of losing it.

But why Garrett, and not Bobby? Maybe it was just a matter of who stepped first through the door. Whatever the reason, Bobby dodged the bullet, but his partner wasn't who he thought he was, and I had no clear prediction of Shadow-and-Flame's endgame. He'd faced off with Terhuziel, but if the enemy of my enemy was my friend, the guy had a lousy way of showing it.

I needed more information.

So get a move on, I chided myself.

With little desire to witness Dr. Kramer butchering

his three little girls, I plunged reluctantly into the rest of the house. Imprints replayed with the speed of thought, so I'd only been on this side for a handful of minutes, but I didn't have all night.

The place was huge, and its Shadowside echo shifted subtly between various incarnations of the home. One version had a wholly different arrangement to the walls. Fortunately, that was an old and worn echo, shimmering faintly through the building's modern design.

I picked my way along carefully regardless. I didn't particularly like the idea of getting stuck inside a wall.

The front hallway banked left, leading past what I took to be a living room or parlor. Only a few pieces of furniture were visible, and even those were amorphous at best. Sharper imagery came from the emotions imprinted upon the walls. The dark pall of disaster had settled over everything, but brighter moments sometimes broke through the cloud—happy family memories, incandescent moments of joy. They glinted with the desperate, tragic beauty of a cormorant struggling in the eddies of an oil spill.

I walked past a yawning chasm that had to be a door to the basement. It felt more like an entrance to the abyss. Faint cries echoed up from the depths—a girl's voice, full of aching desolation.

"Daddy, no! Daddy, why?"

On this side, sounds were muffled when they could be heard at all. As with colors, the entropic atmosphere ground them swiftly away. That I could hear her at all suggested that she was more than an imprint.

This daughter might just be a ghost.

"Hello?" I said. "Leah? Alana?" She sounded too old to be Kaylee.

The cries came again, repeating the exact same words.

Darkness swirled beyond the threshold, cloying and thick. I pressed against it, only to discover that the echo to that level had no stairs. In their place were jagged timbers, jutting from the pit like broken teeth. I caught myself before I pitched forward, reflexively spreading my wings. Bracing them against the walls, I leaned over the edge.

"Hey! I can hear you," I called. My voice rang flat against the darkness.

"*Daddy, no! Daddy, why?*" The words were identical in pitch and timbre, drenched with emotion, but lacking awareness. An imprint after all. I considered flying down into the darkened cellar, just to be sure, but then something brushed past me on its way up. A memory of motion. Shadow-and-Flame.

But this imprint wasn't connected with any kind of trauma. All I felt was a trace of his power, and a profound, simmering rage. I wondered if I left such an obvious trail, carving echoes of light and blue fire in the wake of my wings.

In the shadowed depths of the cellar, the imprint of a slaughtered girl repeated her plaintive question.

"*Daddy, why?*"

If I wanted answers, I wouldn't find them with her.

I stepped back from the chasm and followed Shadow-and-Flame.

37

I lost him for a bit, but caught a hint again at the end of the hall. Stairs led up to the next level, and these had solid substance. I followed in the swirls of soot and embers trailing from his wings. Up the stairs, down the hall, into a room on the left. I wondered why his passage was so obvious—then it dawned on me.

He wasn't cowled—wasn't even trying to mask his presence. Had he been *inviting* discovery?

The dark tendrils of another psychic stain drew my attention to the room. My unnamed sibling's presence flickered in my vision, overwhelmed by the echo of yet another death. This one had been swift, but misery etched the walls. She had lain here, weeping, disconsolate. The impression of despair outweighed even the imprint of her passing.

He had killed her in her bed. His motions suggested a blade—though it was nothing compared to the bastard sword of blackened fire he'd wielded in the foyer. Judging by the girl's size, this was the middle daughter.

She lay listless as he approached.

She didn't even fight.

I backed out of the room as the ripples of her snuffed life washed over me like a bubble popping. The girl seemed strangely relieved to die. That bittersweet emotion drove daggers into my gut. What had been done to her that death provided such sweet escape?

"I fucking hate this," I murmured to myself, but I had one more to find—Kaylee, the youngest daughter, whose blood had painted the walls.

This would be the worst.

My sibling, riding upon the back of a Marine, swept past me. His steps tracked a memory of fury and doom into the fabric of the house. He halted near the end of the hall, raised one booted foot and, from the looks of it, kicked down a door.

Slipping after him, I tried to steel myself for what I would find, but it was more than the stifling atmosphere that made my breath catch in my throat. All the bright emotions that danced upon the walls in the littlest girl's room had run to black and gray. The haunting echo of a child's pure laugh lingered just beneath the memory of her cries, fractured like an artifact in a recording that had been saved over too many times.

Shadow-and-Flame dragged her from the room, painting the halls with her terror. His actions were slow and deliberate, and there was no mistaking his goal. Pure torture. I wanted to look away, but that grinning face from the photo deserved someone who could bear witness and understand.

She struggled in his arms, mouth gaping wide in a

pleading wail. The Shadowside mercifully swallowed all remnants of the sound. He only gripped her tighter.

I followed the echo of atrocity down the hall to another set of stairs. A turn at the landing, and then a room familiar from Bobby's crime scene photos. The trendy color of the paint on the walls didn't translate. I only saw the red.

My sibling scrawled his message in the little girl's screams. Threads of power wove through the letters scribed upon the wall with the angry glow of molten lava. Magic pulsed in the glyphs, fueled by little Kaylee's death. I still couldn't read the Luwian, apart from Terhuziel's Name, but meaning nevertheless teased at the edges of consciousness. Dreading the contact, but curious to learn more, I stepped through the blackened pool of tears and horror left behind by Kaylee's gruesome execution.

I pressed my hand to the wall.

The murderer's voice boomed in my head, carried on the power he'd poured through his words.

I have slaughtered your woman. I have slaughtered your food. I will come for you and cast you back into the prison you have earned with your crimes.

Face me, coward.

The words were a tripwire, and their meaning shrapneled into my brain. Something else triggered when I touched them, but I couldn't parse the spell. It blew past with such strength, it thrust me forcibly back into the flesh-and-blood world. I landed with an inarticulate cry, dropping to my hands and knees as my legs crumpled. I gulped air, and everything tasted like ash.

Those bloodstained letters blistered in my mind, eclipsing all else.

Blinking in the wake of that red haze, I found myself staring at pointy-toed boots, covered ridiculously in white plastic bags sporting a Wal-Mart logo. The stench of soot and brimstone was chased from my nostrils by an aggressively orange scent rising from the carpet beneath those boots.

I rocked back on my haunches, gaping at Lil.

"Found a sliding glass door on the patio," she chirped, tucking something that might have been a nail file back into her purse. "Couldn't resist." She canted her head as she looked down at me. "You OK, flyboy?"

"Need a minute," I choked.

"You know, you'll negate that whole 'leave no evidence' thing if you toss your cookies on the rug."

"Fuck you, Lil," I spat. Shakily, I stood. She held out a hand, but I didn't take it.

"How about we get to work?" she suggested, letting the hand fall back to her side.

I glowered at her. "I *am* working."

"Oh, yeah? So what you got?"

"Terhuziel wasn't the only one of the brethren in this house."

"Really?" she asked. Lil's eyes gleamed with a cold gray light in the thickness of the shadows. She leaned closer, all her muscles going taut as if preparing to pounce.

"Flame and shadow, tattered wings," I murmured, calling his image to memory. It wasn't hard. I was probably going to see him in my nightmares, hunched over the little girl.

"Really big sword?" Lil asked.

"Yeah," I responded. "How'd you know?"

The weak light spilling through a distant window painted her features in stark angles and planes. "Gibburim," she spat. The word sizzled on the air.

"Not a fan," I ventured. "Are there any of our tribes you *don't* hate?"

"The Malakim aren't so bad," she allowed. "The rest of you—assholes and boneheads in equal measure. But a Gibburim hunting Tarhunda might work to our advantage. Save us a whole lot of effort, at any rate."

"Terhuziel," I corrected automatically.

Lil rolled her eyes, refusing comment.

"That hunting part might be a problem," I said, gesturing to the wall behind me. "He left a message, taunting the Rephaim, but I'm not sure he expected to get an answer so soon. Ter-hoo-ha handed him his ass just inside the front door."

Lil peered past me, squinting at the wall.

"What message?" she asked.

I turned to follow her gaze, wondering how in the hell she could miss it—only to discover that on this side, the wall had been cleaned. Come to think of it, *everything* had been cleaned. That was the source of the nasty orange scent hanging on the air. Industrial disinfectant.

"Fuck me running," I grumbled.

Lil piqued a brow. "I always wonder where you picked that phrase up, and then I realize—it's probably some obscure movie I don't give a shit about."

Ignoring her, I scanned the darkened interior as best I could, since my eyes tipped more toward mortal. We stood in what might have been a study, with a desk and a few bookshelves arranged along the walls. All the furniture was sleek and heavy and looked to be hand carved from exotic wood. Everything was clean and neat as a realtor's model home.

I'd encountered nothing but death on the Shadowside—no tethers, no images of a hideout. No clues as to Terhuziel's whereabouts.

The now-blank wall jigged to the left, leading to a little alcove. From what I could recall, that was where Kramer had kept his displays of smuggled antiquities. Maybe that still held something. I stepped around the corner, only to find that the shelves had been cleared of every single item.

Collected as evidence. Hell—the things were probably going to end up on my desk at the art museum. Way too late for them to be of any use to me, though.

"Fuck, fuck, *fuck*," I spat with exceptional feeling.

Lil regarded me. "We going to search this place or just stand around all night?"

"Half of what I need is probably in an evidence locker," I growled.

"Mother's Tears, why didn't you think of that before?" she said through gritted teeth. Then, a little less caustically, she said, "Fine. We'll work with it. The police never get everything anyhow. I'll start by going through the desk. You take this."

She drew a small, gray item from her purse. Vaguely mouse-shaped, it was wide at the bottom and had an intimation of ears near the tip. It dangled from the end of a key chain. I stared at it in confusion.

"What's that?"

She cupped a hand around the tip of the item, pressing one of two buttons atop what should have been its head. A weak beam of light cut through the shadows. "I decided to take pity on you," she explained.

"You had this the whole time?" I said. "Back in the parking garage?"

She rolled a shoulder. "Hold it low and point it toward the floor." She moved her own hand close to her body in demonstration. "And avoid the fucking windows."

Immediately, I pressed the wrong button. A little red dot shone on the floor.

"I knew it," I said. "This is a cat toy." I laughed tightly. "Why the hell are you carrying a cat toy around in your Purse of Many Things? Don't tell me Lulu the Lioness likes playing with it."

Lil just marched over to the desk. "What the hell am I looking for, Anakim?"

I aimed the laser pointer toward her feet, still chuckling over the image of her massive spirit-lion chasing the little red dot. Lil shot me a look so scathing, it should have scoured away a full layer of skin. I stopped fucking around.

"Secondary properties," I said. "Any kind of paperwork indicating places where the doc might run, now that he can't return here. If the storm's an accurate marker, he's close to University Hospital—within a mile or so."

"That's not much to go on," she grumbled.

"Halley picked up Terhuziel either at the Cleveland Clinic or at her grandfather's funeral. I'm betting the funeral. Worse comes to worst, I should be able to sense the edge of his domain, as long as I'm right up on it. I just don't want to have to search a square mile of University Circle on foot," I sighed, and ran my knuckles wearily across my jaw.

Leaving Lil to search the study, I headed deeper into the house. The temptation to find the kitchen—and a coffee maker—ran high, but I kept my head down, focused on the weak pool of light aimed at my feet.

The next room off the study was a recreation room with a huge fifty-two-inch flat-screen mounted to one wall. Floating shelves held a few exotic-looking trinkets, but on closer inspection, most of them were standard décor—the kind of stuff cranked out in Indonesian sweatshops.

I strode carefully through the rec room to what could only be classed as a man-cave, then down a hallway that opened on one side in a double-wide archway leading to an elaborate dining room emptied of table and chairs. Blood darkened the polished teak of the floor—even the cleaning crew hadn't cleared all the stains. The plastic bags tied round my boots crinkled with every step.

That sound must have covered his movement, because I had no sense that anyone was behind me until I felt the cold barrel of a pistol pressed against the base of my skull.

I froze.

Basso laughter dragged prickling shards along my spine.

"I could have killed you ten times over," he boasted, his tone chillingly flat. "You have gotten soft, Zaquiel."

38

"Garrett?" I even managed to sound flippant about it, as opposed to pants-shitting scared. I didn't turn around to confirm my suspicion—the cold stamp of that barrel was a great deterrent against any kind of sudden motion.

"You do not need to keep up your ignorant act," he answered. "You can acknowledge your old ally by Name."

Old ally. I closed my eyes, exhaling very slowly as my mind raced around its many vexing holes. What kind of ally would hold a gun to my head? I fucking hated my brothers. At least I knew I was right about Shadow-and-Flame.

"Didn't want to discuss business in front of your partner," I lied. I curled my fist around Lil's flashlight, calculating just how quickly I could dive through to the Shadowside.

Not quick enough to avoid a bullet.

"He is annoying," Garrett acknowledged in his curiously flat tone. "And persistent. I did not realize that you were acquainted."

"You know me," I said, laughing tightly. "Always making friends."

Behind me, Garrett snorted. He didn't remove the gun.

"You been following me all night or just since I got here?" I asked.

"I do not wish to repeat what happened in Damascus," he said flatly. "I announced my business with the seal. You could have showed sense and backed off." He ground the barrel a little deeper. "The decimus is my responsibility. You will leave him to me."

"I don't feel particularly cooperative when someone holds a gun to my head," I snapped. "Besides—it's not like a bullet will get rid of me."

"Long enough for me to hunt down my quarry," Garrett scoffed. "I will have twenty years, perhaps thirty, to prepare myself for when you retaliate."

"Sounds like you got it all figured out," I said.

"I learned from our last disagreement," he growled.

So much for bluffing.

Every muscle screamed for me to whirl around, grab the gun, and smash it into his face repeatedly while I shouted the names of each of the girls who had died in this house—starting with little Kaylee. There was something soul-killing in knowing how he had robbed the world of the youngest girl's smile. Her gutting terror still echoed, only one room away.

My power ratcheted up for that inhuman burst of speed, but I couldn't risk it. He might match me and pull the trigger. I ground my teeth in futile rage.

"Well, I guess you have no honor, then," I said, uncertain why I chose that particular word. From the subtle shift of the gun, I must have hit a nerve. I ran with it. "If you're going to shoot me in the back of the head like some honorless cur, get on with it." "Cur" was probably pushing it. I held my breath. Shockingly, Garrett eased up on the pistol.

"I could lecture you on honor," he spat. "You, who abandoned our crusade—all for the sake of a woman. Do the cries of her pleasure salve your conscience at night?"

I gaped, and he probably took it for shock. Was he talking about Lailah? I wanted to pin him to the wall and demand explanations, but I couldn't risk playing my hand. For the moment, he didn't know about my amnesia.

"I don't tolerate people gossiping about my sisters like that."

Lil stood at the end of the hallway, one shoulder casually braced against the wall. Lightning threatened in the gray wells of her eyes. I wondered how long she'd been standing there, waiting for him to take the gun away.

Giving in to the urge to move, I put some distance between me and Garrett—and whoever was riding around in his head. I ended with my back against a wall. If I was going to take a bullet, at least I'd see the muzzle-flash.

"I have no desire to trade words with you, hellcat," he said.

"Gibburim," she spat. "Which one are you? You all look alike." Garrett—or the Gibburim, rather—ignored her entirely, turning to me.

"You stink of Nephilim, and consort with the Daughters of Lilith." He pointed the pistol toward the floor, lifting his finger from the trigger. "I do not even know you."

That makes two of us, I thought. With my out-loud voice, I asked, "Nephilim have a stink?" Pointedly, I sniffed the arm of my leather jacket. "I guess you're right, Lil. Remy really needs to do something about that cologne."

She choked on a laugh. "That mouth is going to get you shot, Zaquiel." The steely glint of her fury returned the instant she lasered her attention back to Garrett. "There's two of us and one of you. Why don't you find somewhere else to be?"

Shadows boiled in the air around him, shot through with gleaming flashes of red that would have been at home in the cracks of Mount Doom. He spoke with a voice ghosted through with a second, deeper tone.

"You are interfering with my hunt."

A form appeared, riding on his back, complete with two sets of eyes shot through with angry flames. All four eyes were riveted on me. I focused on a point to the left of his flesh-and-blood mouth. That was safer for my sanity.

"What are you even doing here?" I asked.

The edges of that wide, flat mouth dragged down. "That is a question I will ask of you. You are the one who tripped my wards to this place, and you ruined hours of work, defacing the message meant for Terhuziel."

"Hours of work?" I bellowed. "Is that what you call torturing an innocent little girl?" I couldn't stop myself.

"Nothing touched by a Rephaim is innocent any more," he replied.

Fuck his gun.

Power leapt to my fingers. Hissing the syllables of my

Name, I let my rage stoke the blue-white fire till all my muscles sang.

"She was *four*!" I shouted. Kicking off the wall behind me, I lowered my shoulder and launched myself at him. My hands went for his gun.

"Zack—" Lil called.

I crashed heavily into his sternum. He coughed a startled breath and rocked back beneath my weight, but I might as well have shoulder-checked a tank for all it budged him. His gun hand jerked up, and I scrambled to seize it before he could point it anywhere useful.

Digging the fingers of one hand into his wrist, I aimed for a pressure point while I closed the other hand over the ass-end of the pistol. Glocks were notoriously sensitive, and I was happy his finger wasn't on the trigger as I twisted to break his hold on the grip. Power still crackled through my hands, and I used it to my advantage, jamming more than my fingers into the soft hollow between tendon and bone.

The extra jolt did the trick—his hand jerked and I pried the firearm from his control. With his other hand, he cuffed the side of my head. Detective David Garrett might have been flesh and blood, but the thing that rode him made his fist feel like it had been carved from granite. The blow sent me reeling.

I didn't care—I had the gun.

Thanks to the stupid makeshift booties, I skidded on the rug, barely managing to keep my feet. Righting myself, I dropped into a wider stance to compensate for my tricky footing. Gibburim Garrett maneuvered back a few steps. Before he could strike again, I brought the

Glock up, sighting for the space between his thick brows.

Those twin sets of smoldering eyes narrowed at me from above Garrett's startled human face, and he froze—then he threw his head back and emitted a belly laugh that boomed against the walls.

"Yes!" the Gibburim cried, teeth bared in a grin both exuberant and ferocious. "Shoot this police officer in reprisal for the deed committed in another warrior's skin. That will be irony, if not justice."

I kept my finger poised, but my grip grew uncertain.

"The hell with justice, just shoot him already," Lil urged.

"Will you be executioner as well as judge?" Shadow-and-Flame demanded through David Garrett's mouth. Around his human eyes, I saw the smallest twitch of fear. "No thought, no hesitation, only fury and death. Is this not the very certainty you condemn in me?"

Holding it stiffly to hide the tremor I felt, I pulled my forefinger well away from the trigger and lowered the gun. Garrett's features briefly flashed relief, swiftly eclipsed by the Gibburim's scorn.

"I had hoped for better from you, brother," he intoned. "There was a time when your rage was not so swiftly quenched."

"Get out," I said, gesturing toward the door.

Again that booming laugh pounded against my ears. Garrett's voice dropped several registers, the second set of tones overwhelming the first. That other voice was so deep, it rumbled like bass at a metal concert.

"Leave?" he responded. "*Fah!* To honor our past association, I will let you walk out without arresting you for the crimes committed in this tainted home." At my look of incredulity, he sneered, "It would be easy enough. Does a lifetime in mortal prison appeal to your sense of martyrdom?"

"Don't give me a reason to hurt you, Gibburim," Lil warned. "Carly would be disappointed if I wrecked these nails clawing that arrogant smirk off your face." The threatening growl of an angry lioness punctuated her words.

Garrett and his rider didn't even spare her a glance—which was seriously stupid of them. Despite her joke about the manicure, Lil's threat of violence was deadly serious.

"Don't even think about hanging this on me," I snarled. "You murdered a four-year-old girl just to paint a message on the damned wall, and then got your ass kicked by the guy anyway."

Streaking flames leapt from the twin set of inhuman eyes.

I'd struck a nerve.

"You know the cost of such magics," he replied.

"Oh, sure," I scoffed. "Cutting a little girl to ribbons while she begs you to stop—totally justified. And now you're riding around inside a cop. I'm sure *he's* as willing as she was."

"There is always a choice," Shadow-and-Flame rumbled—but Garrett's eyes didn't look so certain. The thing riding him asserted control, and those scared, mortal eyes narrowed to match the inhuman ones. "This vessel cast his lot with me. But if you harbor doubts about my actions with the girl, then cease insulting me with empty words and call a trial. Or have you grown too soft in your retirement to even dare?"

I almost agreed, right then and there, but stopped myself. Did we even have tribunals? A few moments before, he was goading me to be judge and executioner, so I had no clue. Neither Sal nor Remy had ever said anything of the sort, but would the Nephilim even bother? Likely not.

That decided it.

"I want to smash your face in for what I saw you do to that little girl," I said, "but I'll settle for a trial. Kaylee deserves at least that much."

"Dammit, Zack, don't let him bait you into this," Lil hissed.

"If I am guilty," he stated, "I will make reparations. If not, you will join me in hunting Terhuziel. Once I have locked him down with the new seal, we shall work together to purge everything from this city that bears his taint."

"You're guilty," I stated flatly.

"Then we are agreed?"

"Sure."

A hard, flat crack echoed through the hall. Lil's palm, impacting her forehead.

"Mother's Tears, Zaquiel," she cried. "You need a killswitch for that mouth."

We both ignored her. The Gibburim Garret grinned.

"Then let us begin."

With a hissing exhalation, he called the power of his Name. The syllables washed over me like a blast of heat from an industrial oven, evoking sparks all the way down to the tips of my wings.

Mal phãel.

The acrid stink of sulfur filled my nose, and in the next instant, a blade leapt forth in Garrett's hand—three and a half feet of blackened steel edged in blood-red flames. It was a hacking weapon, built like a falchion, but on a much larger scale. Falchions were typically one-handed weapons. This blade required two. It had a single sharp edge and a flat end that angled backward to a point. A wavering corona of heat spilled around it, chewing the air.

"Shall we dance, my brother?" he asked. Gripping its over-long hilt in both of his big-knuckled mitts, Garrett held the flaming weapon angled protectively across his body. That maniac grin never slipped from his face.

"Hang on just a minute," I said quickly. "I thought we had an agreement."

"We do," he replied. "Trial by combat. Honor must be served."

Fuck me running.

"Zack, screw the honor-bound shit for once," Lil snarled. "Just cut the vessel out from under him so we can get out of here."

Even as she said it, something tugged deep in my chest. Backing out now didn't feel like an option. With growing trepidation, I kept my eyes locked on Malphael while I caught the edge of one plastic bag with my heel. I tugged till I tore my boot free, then did the same with the other one. No need for handicaps.

Malphael took it for stalling.

"Have you grown so weak you would concede my point without so much as raising your blades to meet mine?" the Gibburim taunted. He rose onto the balls of his feet, already swaying with the urge to strike.

"I'm not going to help you purge this city when you think the murder of children is an acceptable action," I replied. With a roar, I invoked the syllables of my own Name. Twin blades flashed to life in my hands, their wicked curves dancing with blue-white fire. I held the spirit-daggers out to either side, already planning where I'd plant them first.

"Mother's Tears, Zaquiel," Lil groaned.

"I shall take pity on you," Malphael intoned. "The winner is he who lands a *second* strike after his first." His eyes flicked toward Lil. "No interference from the hellcat."

My blades thrummed with a familiar weight against my palms. Slowly, I nodded.

"Now bring it, asshole."

Lil made an exasperated noise, and I heard her smack her fist into the wall.

"Fuck it," she huffed. "You're on your own. When you two are done with the dick-waving, let me know." She turned on her heel and stomped off down the hallway, plastic bags crunching.

All other words were lost to a blaze of light and fury.

39

We fought with a formality as familiar as my blades. For the first pass I lunged, swift and low, testing his reactions. Garrett was a big man, Malphael even bigger. While the Gibburim didn't have to worry too much about physical barriers like the ceiling and walls, Garrett did. I drove him back past the archway that opened on the dining room, hoping to limit his mobility. There wasn't a whole lot of room to maneuver in the hall.

He dodged with unhurried grace, taking a step back but working it into a swift turn so he retained a clear angle on the opening. All the while he kept that cleaving length of blackened steel angled across his body, warding off any easy strikes.

He had to expose himself to swing the blade, but the thing had such a massive reach, my head and shoulders would be wide open even if I tried ducking to get under his attack. We made a few more passes, each studying the other, neither fully committing to any strike.

I fell back, keeping my body low, and readjusted my grip on my blades. The power singing through them thrummed all the way up my arms, focused by the endless repetition of three potent syllables in the substrata of my mind.

Zaquiel.

My magic, my station, my Name.

It took both concentration and energy to maintain the weapons in such a physical form—but I'd had practice keeping them going in long fights with cacodaimons. The shape of my blades wasn't a conscious decision, but it held a fortunate practicality. The less mass I had to focus, the less juice it took to maintain the things. Malphael's blade—that was like a Humvee to my Corvette. A huge energy sink. Endurance was going to be a factor in this fight. If I drew things out, I could turn that to my advantage.

Even better if I had my daggers.

The thought came unbidden, complete with a vivid recollection of two very real steel daggers forged in the image of my spirit-blades. The memory—as well as the sharp pang of longing that accompanied it—was foreign to me. I'd never seen those daggers before.

Had I?

The intensity of the associations shattered my focus on the fight. Malphael made a pass and nearly got me square on the shoulder. At the last instant, I danced away, shoving the distracting thoughts to the back of my mind.

Later.

We circled again, and while I studied him, it occurred to me that his weapon had seemed even bigger in the

Shadowside imprint of his battle with Terhuziel—comically big. Maybe that had merely been a distortion of the imprint, but it might indicate wear and tear on his part. Malphael had gotten his ass handed to him at the end of that fight, and he'd been running around in a new body since. That had to take a toll.

The Gibburim could tell when I was thinking too hard, and before I could finish the next thought, he came at me, bringing his weapon down like an axe. I was half a heartbeat too slow to dodge, so I brought my twin daggers up, catching his sword where they crossed. Red flames met blue in a shower of angry sparks.

He bore down, trying to break my defense with brute force. I held my ground, but all I could see was the wicked edge of the blood-rimmed steel a few bare inches from my nose. I struggled to get a foot into play, balancing precariously as I aimed for his gut. It connected. With a shout, I hurled him backward.

Before he could fully recover, I feinted forward, making a half-hearted stab in the region of his stomach. That got the reaction I desired—he angled his body away, dodging the dagger, then brought his great sword down in an arcing swing.

I ducked the blow with the intent of rolling behind him. As quick as I was with my blades, I would catch him in the small of the back while the momentum of his strike was still carrying him forward. Although I successfully avoided his blow with my physical body, he clipped me on the wing. I staggered, roaring with pain and fury, then pivoted near his unprotected back, too shocked by the bite of his steel to land a jab of my own.

"You left yourself open," he taunted.

"Won't. Happen. Again."

I crouched at the entrance to the dining room. Pain from my wing radiated all the way down to the tips of my fingers on my right side. That hand tingled sharply as I shifted my grip.

Right. So we were playing with more than just our physical bodies. That changed the game. I hoped he understood the kind of shit-storm he just invited. Then again, it worked in my favor if he never saw it coming.

Cocky now, he shifted briefly to a one-handed grip, rolling his wrist to cut a circle in the air with the massive falchion.

"You want Terhuziel, right?" I asked.

"I will not be distracted by your talking."

We sketched slow circles around each other, neither letting his guard drop.

"Not distracting," I continued. "A little extra wager on the outcome of this fight. Don't you want something else if you win?"

Ignoring the question, he drove me back with another powerful blow. I sidestepped in time, darting forward to catch his leg with one of my blades. Arcing jolts of power flickered against the walls as he swung his weapon around in time to block.

"I want you gone," I said. "Along with Terhuziel." He feinted, and I danced away, falling further back into the dining room. He followed, and I grimaced to cover my smile. "Far as I can tell, you chased him here, and your little feud's brought nothing but death and chaos to my city."

"Little feud?" he countered. Echoes of Malphael's flames danced in the depths of Garrett's eyes. "Have you strayed so far from your station in the House of Righteousness that you would demean our sacred duty?"

No clue what he was talking about, but it sure sounded important. I dashed forward, rolling onto my good shoulder—careful this time to tuck my wings. I almost managed to hamstring him, but he was just a touch swifter, blocking with his sword again. Soot and brimstone stung my nose as I deflected his counterattack.

Then he was in position, all the bits that were Malphael spreading wide to the vaulted ceiling of the dining room. I'd herded him effectively. Nothing behind him for about three feet, no walls pinning him on either side.

"So what else do you want if you win?" I prompted.

"You are losing." He laughed. "Yet you would bargain?"

"You know me. I'm cocky like that."

The molten cores of Malphael's strangely twinned eyes danced with more amusement than fury.

"Yes. I remember. You have always fought with the heart of a Gibburim."

Wasn't sure that qualified as a compliment, but I kept that opinion to myself. He needed to agree before I launched this gambit.

"So, if I win, you get the hell out and take Terhuziel with you. I don't want to see your ugly face again."

"Only till the end of this flesh," Malphael suggested. "Garrett, and Westland."

I chewed my cheeks to hold back my grin. Not long now. He made another sally. I responded with a flurry of blows, my blades arcing so swiftly they left blue-white trails burning on the air behind them. He defended by dodging or catching them on the edge of his sword each time—just barely.

"I can agree to that," I said. "What's your price?"

A smile split his face—both the Garrett-face and the visage of shadow and flame hovering above it. It was a look born of blood, ferocity, and a naked lust for warfare. Tatters of memory stirred, and my mind welled with the roar of fire and the endless clashing of blades.

I clung to my memory of his atrocity, because *dammit*, a part of me *missed* that wild music of battle.

"You will come back with me," he replied. The basso notes of Malphael's voice thrummed beneath Garrett's. "Pledge this flesh once more to our crusade."

"We don't fight the Blood Wars any more," I choked.

"One must fight to keep the peace. You have turned your face away, but you know we remain our brothers' keepers."

He is not the good guy, I reminded myself, but fuck, it was hard to argue with his sentiment. I had four of our brothers tucked away in my desk at home, and I sure as hell didn't trust them enough to let them go.

I fucking hated my family.

"Fine," I said evenly. "I'll go with you if you win."

But I won't let you win, you child-killing asshole.

"Done."

The instant he agreed, I charged—phasing out halfway through. The Kramer house was one big Crossing thanks largely to Malphael's unspeakable crusade. The brief transit through the Shadowside stole my breath and pressed like a low front against my ears.

I popped back into reality immediately behind him, digging the tip of one of my daggers into the soft flesh over his kidney. It wasn't a physical wound, but that didn't mean it was painless.

"Tag," I hissed against his ear, then spun away as he turned to chop viciously across my arm.

"That is a cheat," he bellowed.

My blades blurred again, neatly keeping his big-ass sword away from all of my tender parts. I noticed with grim satisfaction that the swirling aura of heat and flame was starting to fade. Effort gnawed a hole under my own ribs, but I was used to fighting on empty. I was happy to win this last point through a war of attrition.

"Didn't say I couldn't," I replied.

"Then I will stop holding back as well." Rage made curling drifts of smoke and embers rise from his words. I would've felt better about that if I knew what to expect.

Too late to worry about it now.

Malphael poured on the speed, moving faster and more nimbly than anyone his size had a right to. Suddenly I found myself on the defensive, hard-pressed to keep up with the scything arcs of his oversized blade. He got my back to the windows before I had time to think about which direction I'd planned to lure him into next.

He drew a breath, and *roared* at me.

Blood and smoke, fury and flame all reverberated in that inhuman sound, underscored by the deep, throbbing notes of his Name. My brain raced, but the mortal part of me froze like food before a predator. Adrenaline made my pulse pound so hard, lights chewed at the edges of my vision.

My body yelled, *Run!* but the sound scrambled something in my nervous system so all I could do was gape. With a taunting grin, he prepared for a final, punishing strike.

He roared again as he raised his sword, and my legs buckled, all my strength run to water. I was down on one knee, trying to get my blades up to protect my head. Intoning my own Name, I shook off enough of the paralytic effect to move, but it was going to be too late.

Malphael's flame-kissed steel loomed like the judgment of Armageddon, and then my left hand flickered forward, Nephilim-quick. My dagger on that side dispersed, and I caught him by the wrist. My elbow locked, holding back his strike. As he strained against me, I sought out the burning thread of power that forged his blade and I *ate* it. His weapon faded in a swirl of smoke and ash.

I was conscious enough of the action—and what I tapped into to accomplish it—so I stole only the energy he expended to sustain the blade in that moment, not the knowledge or essence of the blade itself. That would've revealed the cheat.

All six eyes stared at me in shock and horror. Still holding his wrist, I swept my other hand up toward his belly, cutting a wide slash with my remaining blade. The weapon didn't touch the cloth or the skin. No matter how solid the energy, it couldn't make a physical cut, but Garrett still cried out, and behind him, Malphael reared back, bellowing in pain.

I shoved him away, finally relinquishing my hold on his wrist. I curled my left hand against me, not entirely trusting it—the scar on my palm felt like it was chewing its way out of my skin. I shook out the power of my remaining blade while Malphael staggered back, gaping. He might not be able to prove what I'd just done, but he suspected.

I looked up from where I crouched on the floor, blowing the hair back from my eyes.

"I play to win."

40

Malphael lurked at the other end of the dining room, glowering at his hand as if the meaty digits had risen up in a profoundly personal betrayal.

"You're guilty," I said. "You're going to get the hell out of my city, and take that bastard Terhuziel with you."

"You consumed my power," he growled. "What treachery have you learned?"

"Consumed it?" I laughed. "I just waited until you ran out."

It wasn't true, but I sold it like my life depended on it—because it probably did. Malphael struck me as a sore loser, and tapping the Nephilim icon was a hell of a cheat. I wasn't exactly thrilled with myself for using it again, but there'd been no other way to win.

Maybe that was an easy excuse to feed my conscience.

I rose slowly to my feet, wincing as I jostled the wounded wing. I stretched, testing it, and there didn't seem to be any permanent damage, but it stung like a sonofabitch. I probably should have felt winded from that fight, but aside from the twinge along my wing, I felt great. There were definitely upsides to devouring the power of the enemy.

I swore not to get used to it.

The Gibburim eyed me warily, absently rubbing his wrist. I eyed him right back.

"I don't know if you've noticed, but you've spun yourself pretty thin," I observed. "You just misjudged your strength in that last assault."

"I did not misjudge my strength," he objected sullenly.

"Yeah?" I chided. "Is that what you told yourself when you lost to Terhuziel? I saw that fight in the front hallway—you left imprints all over this house." At that, Malphael snarled something that wasn't exactly English. It sounded wrong coming out of Garrett's mouth.

"My vessel failed to notice that the physician carried a firearm," he countered.

"You have a funny way of saying you fucked up."

"The error was the vessel's," the Gibburim insisted, "and then he let weakness claim him before we could get the old seal back in place."

"Saw that, too," I said. "If, by 'weakness,' you mean death. Good thing ol' Garrett came along when he did, otherwise you'd still be gnashing your teeth uselessly in the front room."

"He is convenient, but irritating." Malphael scowled, and it took Garrett's features half a second to follow suit. "He bucks like a spirited horse and complains that this is not what he signed up for."

That was interesting.

"Does he get a vote?" I pursued.

"Why should he?" Malphael replied. "He made his choice." As he said it, though, his voice and Garrett's lips were jarringly out of sync. The detective's human eyes sought my own, pleading and full of fear. Malphael's double set of burning orbs narrowed to slits, and I could feel the Gibburim reasserting his dominance in an acrid wave of heat.

Garrett fell away from his own face like a drowning man.

Sickened fury rose bitter in the back of my throat. Malphael saw my expression and simply laughed.

"I felt his rage when he entered this space," the Gibburim mused, and the mortal and immortal aspects aligned smoothly once again. "This David Garrett is a righteous soul, and the futile war of justice ate holes in his warrior's heart. I promised that we would hunt the beast that destroyed this family. He leapt at the offer of power he knew he lacked."

Garrett's hand clenched into a fist at his side, and it was unclear which one of them was using the meat-suit for the gesture.

"You didn't bother to tell him that you were the one who killed two of the girls, though, did you?" The words tore low and ragged from my throat.

Malphael only glowered in response.

"I hate to interrupt your charming family reunion," Lil chimed in, "but we need to leave." She stood at the mouth of the hallway, holding aloft the battered remains of Halley's ceramic rosary.

"What is that?" Malphael demanded—though from his expression, it looked like he had a clue. He took a step toward her, ready to pluck it from her hand. Nimbly, Lil kept it out of his reach. Her gray eyes danced with wicked delight.

Lucy Van-fucking-Pelt.

"Oh, it's a token scribed in the Name of Terhuziel." For once, she gave the Name its proper pronunciation. "I broke it, but I guess they can track it anyway."

"Dammit, Lil," I hissed. I didn't know what she was playing at, but it might end with Halley getting killed. If anything alerted Malphael to the girl's existence, he would hunt her down and "cleanse" her, just as he had the Kramer children.

If he so much as dared, I'd do a lot more than "best" him.

"Who has tracked the token?" he demanded, taking another step toward the Lady of Beasts. She dodged again, making no effort at all to hide her grin.

"I counted two creeping up in the bushes out in the yard, but I'm sure there's more," she replied.

"Fuck," I complained. "Does this asshole ever run out of minions?"

"He licks the crap from the bottom of the barrel," Lil said. "There's plenty of that to go around."

"You will give me that," Malphael commanded. He looked back and forth between us, his expression darkening by degrees.

"I don't take orders from *anyone*," she replied in a voice like velvet draped over the cold edge of a scalpel. "Especially not assholes like you."

Malphael lunged. With a defiant lift to her chin, Lil flicked the rosary beads in an arc behind her. They clattered somewhere in the shadowed depths of the Kramers' rec room.

"Bitch," Malphael spat.

He dove after the token. Lil neatly sidestepped as he charged past her down the hall. She stuck out one foot, tangling his ankles. Malphael stumbled, but recovered, spewing long-dead curses in his subsonic, rumbling tone. He didn't let his fury distract him, however.

With a nasty laugh, Lil dashed toward me and snagged my wrist.

"Front door," she hissed in the lowest of whispers.

"If he's got people out back, there has to be—"

She didn't let me argue, just yanked me down the hall.

Malphael had already cut the police tape and left the door unlocked. We burst into the chill morning and pelted through the drifts toward the car. The way she'd been talking, I expected to encounter lurching ranks of the hobo army, but the street was empty. Ours and Garrett's were the only tracks anywhere to be seen.

"Mind telling me why you handed the fucking token over like that?" I demanded.

"Just get to the car," she hissed, breath pluming. "You'll thank me."

We slogged through drifts of snow, skidding as we ran. Lil managed to make it look graceful. I was just happy not to land on my ass. The street still hadn't been plowed, and probably another two inches had come down while we searched the house.

The thunder was silent now, but the wind angrily scoured the landscape, dragging sheets of snow from the existing drifts.

"There aren't any minions out here," I said.

"Your powers of observation astound me," she called. Her hair streamed in a red tangle behind her as she pulled farther ahead.

My foot found a canted chunk of sidewalk and I nearly launched myself onto my face. I tried to compensate with my wings. Stupid reflex—and it hurt like hell.

"What's the rush?" I demanded, venting all my anger in the words.

Lil didn't stop. We were almost to the Hellcat. At least the cross-street had been plowed.

"I found a picture of Kramer," she said.

"And we're running," I panted. "Why are we running?"

Lil skidded to a stop by the driver's side of the car. Her eyes caught the weak light of the streetlamps. "We've seen him before."

"*What?*"

"The guy chatting up the woman at the nurses' station," she said.

"Fuck, fuck, *fuck*!" I roared.

"Quit yelling." She opened the driver's-side door, the bottom scraping noisily against the built-up snow. "I want to be gone before your meat-head of a brother thinks to follow us."

"The token was a distraction."

"No shit, Sherlock," she hissed.

I tried to get past her into the car. "You're on the wrong side. It's my fucking car."

She shoved me so hard, I skidded back in the snow.

"You gave me the keys. I drive."

41

Lil taught me what it felt like to run the Olympic slalom strapped into three thousand pounds of streamlined fiberglass and steel.

I had no idea it was possible to use a car like a snowboard, but she managed it, urging the souped-up Dodge again and again into controlled slides, then harnessing the momentum to skate us through the icy streets at record speeds.

She skidded into the parking lot of University Hospital, sliding the car sideways into an open space—a maneuver made ten times ballsier by the fact that the lot was crawling with police. Most of them were on the far end near the parking garage—surprise, surprise.

One lone straggler—a lean, sour-faced fellow—was pacing and smoking while he talked on a cellphone, away from the rest. He watched Lil's grand entrance, nearly dropping his cigarette in a grip gone slack with shock. When she and I poured from the car, he took one look at our forbidding expressions and decided the overtime wasn't worth it.

We raced into the lobby. Despite the hour—it was somewhere in the neighborhood of three in the morning— people were clustered against the front windows, gawking at the fleet of black-and-whites out in the lot. Towering near the back of the crowd was the steely-haired figure of Father Frank. I elbowed my way through till I made it to him.

"Is Halley all right?" I asked.

"She was a little bit ago," he answered. "The night doc came through and gave her a sedative to help her sleep. Woke her up to do it, too. You know how stupid they can be about that."

"And you left her?" I demanded.

Anxiety deepened the furrows exhaustion had already etched into his brow. With practiced discretion, he steered our conversation to a more isolated corner.

"They didn't give me much choice in the matter," he said. "Ordered me out to get some sleep of my own. I've been cooling my heels till I can sneak back up there." His dark eyes flickered toward the front windows. Blue and red lights stuttered against the glass. "What's wrong? Does it have something to do with what happened out there?"

"We have to get to Halley," I said, dragging him toward the elevators. He was too stunned to resist. The carriage was stopped half a dozen floors up. I stabbed the call button repeatedly, snarling, "Hurry up, hurry up, hurry up."

"I'll cover the stairs," Lil said. She took off down the hall at a jog.

Father Frank looked searchingly between us. "Tell me what's going on."

The elevator dinged and I shoved my fingers between the doors the instant they slid apart, trying to drag them open faster through sheer force. Inside, the orderly waiting with a gurney stared at me like he was mentally calculating the measurements of an appropriately fitted straitjacket.

I shouldered past him.

"What floor was she on?" I asked the padre.

Father Frank stumbled in after me, pressing the button. His patrician features wavered between bewildered and annoyed. The orderly vacated as quickly as he could.

"I wouldn't have left if I thought something would happen to her. That doctor—"

"Tall guy, kind of looked like Denzel Washington?"

"Well, now that you mention it," he allowed. I jammed my thumb against the CLOSE DOORS button.

"Works for the bad guy," I snarled.

Father Frank's eyes flew wide. "But, Zack, he was lucid. He was joking—"

"I *know*," I shouted, smashing my fist into the burnished metal wall of the elevator, pulling the punch at the last instant. "I couldn't tell either."

"I thought he only went after weakened minds," the priest objected hollowly.

"Those are the easiest for him, but Terhuziel's been working Kramer over since the guy was in Syria. I don't know how long." I curled my fingers into a tighter fist and thought about hitting the wall again. I focused instead on the sharp bite of my nails against my palm.

The elevator crawled through a slow succession of floors.

"I'm supposed to be able to see this shit, padre, and I had no fucking clue!"

"You'll make it right, Zaquiel," he insisted.

I turned away from the pain in his expression—and the hope.

42

I swept from the elevator as soon as I could shoulder my way through the door. The rubber heels of my engineer boots thudded against the tiles as I pelted down the hall. The night nurse from before looked up sharply, yelling the instant she caught sight of me.

"Hey! Where you going? You can't run like that in here." She was a big woman, boxy in her scrubs. She slammed her hand on the counter, ready to leap over and wrestle me to the ground if necessary. She had an appropriately intimidating presence, but I just didn't care. I'd faced off with vampires and cacodaimons. One angry desk attendant wasn't going to convince me to stop.

I whipped past her station, heedless of her objections.

"I'll call security!" she threatened, jumping to her feet.

"Call them," I yelled over my shoulder. "Probably going to need them." I hit the turn at the end of the hallway, boots squealing against the flooring. Halley's

375

room was the last one on the left. The door was open—and both beds were unoccupied.

"Fuck!"

I paced futilely outside the empty room, muttering the same word over again in a percussive expression of frustration. The night nurse came charging around the corner, her face like perdition itself.

"There are kids on this ward," she hissed, not in the least intimidated by either my appearance or my height. "They don't need to hear garbage like that." Tipping her head back to glare into my eyes, she said in a low and heated voice, "You need to turn your skinny butt around and get off of my floor this instant."

Lil burst from the door at the end of the hall, red hair wild from racing up all those flights of steps.

"He didn't go that way," she said. She wasn't even out of breath.

"You, too, now?" the nurse demanded. She planted her hands on her ample hips, angling her head so she could glare at the padre. He stood quietly at the bend in the hall. "Father Mazetti, do you mind telling me what's going on?"

Father Frank looked to me.

I shook my head. "She's not here."

The nurse shifted her gaze from Father Frank to me, then to Lil. "Well, *some*body better start talking, *fast*," she huffed.

The padre stepped forward, laying a hand on the nurse's shoulder. "Halley Davis," he said, meeting her belligerence with a look of practiced patience. "What happened to the girl? I haven't been gone ten minutes, and now she's not in her room."

The night nurse—her name tag declared her as "Hildy"—relaxed a little, though she still side-eyed me.

"You folks are getting yourselves worked up over nothing," she declared. "The doctor was worried about some of her levels. He just took her downstairs to run a couple of tests."

Father Frank and I exchanged worried glances.

"Is this the same doctor you were flirting with earlier?" I asked.

"Only the good father here is a registered care-giver for the Davis girl," she muttered, pressing her full mouth into a frown. "You shouldn't even be on this floor, lover-boy." Behind me, Lil made a choking sound.

I just ignored her—it wasn't the time.

Father Frank tightened his hand on the nurse's shoulder, gently but insistently capturing her attention.

"This is important," he said. He met her eyes, pouring all his commanding charisma into his voice. "Have you ever seen that doctor here before? Halley was in here because people broke into her house. They were trying to kidnap her. Can you understand why we're worried?"

"They switch guys out nightly, Father," she objected, but it lacked her previously strident conviction.

"Did he give you a name? Could you maybe check to see if he's working?" he persisted. Power threaded through his voice, exerting subtle but inexorable pressure.

"We know who took her," Lil muttered angrily to herself. "We know why. No point waiting around for security and more delays." So saying, she pushed her way past me into Halley's room. I was confused for a minute—but then she marched right back out with her jacket gripped in one hand. "You were going to forget it again," she said, shooting me a look. Then she strode back to the end of the hall, the heels of her boots sharp against the tiles.

She hit the door to the stairwell with enough force that it banged echoingly against the inside wall.

"Hey!" Hildy called after her.

Father Frank never took his hand from the woman's shoulder. "Would you please check?"

"Fine," she said. The obdurate tension across the nurse's back sagged toward exhaustion. "If it will get you all to settle down." Pointing at me with the air of an overworked kindergarten teacher, she added, "And don't think I don't remember you from before. Both you and your girlfriend. You're coming back to the desk with me so I can keep an eye on you, Mister."

Two uniformed members of the hospital's security staff stepped from the elevator as we walked back to the nurses' station. The older of the two—a bald guy built like a beer keg with legs—gave me a once-over, his bushy brows beetling over his glasses. He chewed the edges of a walrus mustache that looked inspired by Wilford Brimley.

Shooting a questioning glance toward the nurse, he touched a can of mace clipped to his belt. His partner was a tall, gangly kid who hadn't yet outgrown his pimples. His oversized hands were big enough to palm a basketball and then some. The kid ambled up to me with an affable grin on his face.

"That's a nice jacket, sir," he said. "Can I ask you to take it off?"

378

"Not yet, Rodney." Hildy held up a hand. "I'm checking something."

Rodney—who looked like a strong wind might topple him regardless of his height—backed off a step.

Nurse Hildy sorted through the papers on her desk, making a small sound of triumph when she located a pad emblazoned with the logo of a drug company. A phone number and name were scrawled across the top sheet in bold strokes of blue ink. She bent to her computer, typing with quiet rapidity. Rodney and his partner kept their eyes on me and Father Frank, angling themselves between us and the elevators.

Hildy paused, then her typing grew a little more frenetic. She added something further, hitting the enter key hard enough that her keyboard shifted. Her dark eyes flicked to the security guards, and she motioned Beer Keg over, speaking with him in hushed tones. Father Frank wearily rubbed his face, wincing when his fingers snagged the tape above his brow.

"Didn't find him, did you?" I asked. I thought dismally of Lil's trust charm—the damned thing had worked too well.

Nurse Hildy lifted her scowl my way, then turned her back, practically in a huddle with Beer Keg. Rodney started to look worried. The walkie on his belt crackled and a woman's voice—brisk and authoritative—snapped off something about officers and the parking garage. I almost felt bad for the kid and his stumpy friend. It was a tough night to work security at this hospital.

"Hey, Rodney," I said. "Is Officer Roarke on site?" From Remy, I knew he had to be—though asking for him was a gamble on my part. I'd left Roarke pretty pissed off the other night. Rodney ogled me like he expected Roarke to turn out to be my parole officer.

"You're going to want to get him up here," I said. "He's been working this case." At the kid's stupefied look, I said, "Don't act so shocked. Not all the good guys wear white hats. Just humor me and call for him on that walkie, OK? Tell him Westland's asking for him."

Rodney shifted his gaze toward Captain Beer Keg, clearly hoping for direction, but he and Hildy were still hunched together, exchanging rapid whispers.

"Come on, kid," I urged. "You're in for a long shift, either way."

Father Frank moved to brace his shoulders against the nearest wall, letting his head tip back as he rested his eyes. I wondered what kind of toll the voice trick took on him. I didn't think he'd slept since yesterday.

Long shifts all around tonight.

Rodney's lips twitched and I could practically see the numbers scrolling above his head as he calculated the odds of getting chewed out if he made a decision and it turned out to be the wrong one. He tried catching Beer Keg's attention one last time, then, with a hangdog look, walked to the far side of the elevators and murmured into his radio.

"Roarke, really?" the padre murmured without opening his eyes. "You two didn't seem all that friendly back at Tammy's house."

I rubbed the back of my neck, trying to lip-read Rodney, but the angle was all wrong.

"Yeah," I sighed. "That was a... misunderstanding.

We have a mutual acquaintance. Hopefully he'll forgive me if I apologize."

Father Frank snorted, eyeing me from under one lid. "In other words, you really pissed him off." His eye slid shut again, and he exhaled a long, slow breath. "Shouldn't you be asking for that other guy?" He batted the air fretfully with one hand as he searched for a name. "You know the one I'm talking about—the Korean kid."

"Bobby Park," I supplied.

The priest's chin dipped severely downward in a nod, then he rolled his head back against the wall. I worried that he might fall asleep right there. Anchored to my power or not, his body had seen nearly seventy years of wear and tear, and the news of Halley's abduction had settled over him like a crushing weight.

"That's a problem right now, padre," I said, scrubbing a hand along my jaw. "Bobby's partner has one of the Gibburim riding around in his head, and if that guy learns about Halley—"

"Gibburim?" His head snapped up. "When did they get involved?"

A starkness settled across his face, hardening all the lines. In the sallow lights glimmering from the ceiling of the children's ward, his skin looked more like weathered wood than living flesh. The cuts and bruises he'd sustained in the fight to protect Halley stood out in livid relief.

"You know about them?" I asked. .

His lips twisted downward. His answer was one curt word. "Vietnam." A rush of questions leapt to my lips, all vying to tumble out first—but the padre caught my eye, jerking his chin in the direction of the elevators.

Rodney strode back in our direction, a completely different expression settling over his long features—not respect, exactly, but at least not outright suspicion.

"They say he'll be right up."

I nodded, then gestured to Father Frank. "I don't imagine you'd let my friend here go scare up a cup of coffee or something? He's been keeping watch at the girl's bedside most of the night." The old priest had settled back against the wall, ostensibly resting his eyes again—though tension now ratcheted through his arms from shoulder to tightly clenched fist.

"Hawkins," Beer Keg called from the other side of the nurses' station.

"Yes, sir." Rodney straightened like the guy was a drill sergeant. Hildy hovered over her computer, checking and re-checking the screen. She looked sick.

"I need you to run down to HQ and take care of a few things for me," Beer Keg said. His unibrow bristled over his glasses, and he frowned so deeply his mouth disappeared under his Wilford Brimley mustache.

"Yes, sir," Rodney repeated. His eyes cut back to the padre and me. He ducked his head apologetically, saying, "Uh, sir, can I let the priest here get some coffee?"

Beer Keg dipped his head in a brusque gesture. "Don't leave the building," he said to the padre.

Eager to carry out his orders, the kid rushed to the elevator—somewhat uselessly, as the car was still all the way down in the lobby. Father Frank pushed off the wall.

"Zack, did you want coffee—or something else?"

I angled away from the security guard. "If you see Lil down there, she has my car keys," I said. "And see if she wants anything."

"I'm not buying her coffee, too," he replied.

"She always takes care of herself," I reminded him. "Just check in with her, OK?" The padre didn't look thrilled about it, but he nodded anyway. I hoped to hell he knew we weren't actually talking about coffee.

He strode to the elevators, Rodney shifting awkwardly beside him. The right carriage dinged a moment later, disgorging Officer Roarke. The thick-necked ginger didn't look like he'd gotten much sleep in the past forty-eight hours, any more than the padre had—but, considering Remy's off-hand comment in the parking garage, maybe the young officer's washed-out pallor resulted from something more than exhaustion.

Halley's insight about blood crawled from my hindbrain, and as soon as I cracked open the door to that line of thinking, I slammed it right the hell shut. What Remy did on his own time with his people wasn't worth contemplating—at least, not if I planned on looking either Roarke or Remy in the eye without feeling seriously weird.

"Westland," Roarke sighed. The name on his lips was both accusation and curse.

"Good to see you, too, Jimmy," I said with all the fake cheer I could muster. "I get the feeling it's a busy night, so I won't take up much of your time."

He chuffed unhappily through his nose. Stepping some distance away from Nurse Hildy and Captain Beer Keg, I gestured for Roarke to come closer. From the way he scowled at me, you'd have thought I'd just asked Officer McMountain to retrieve a donut from a bear trap.

But Remy must have had words with him, because, despite the veins standing out against his temples, he lumbered over my way.

"What do you want?" he grunted.

I met his glare evenly. "Look, I know we got off to a bad start," I said in low tones. "I was an asshole. I'm sorry."

He blinked lucid green eyes that seemed a little too small in his big, square face, working his mouth around words that would not come. If I had pulled an Acme Anvil out of thin air and dropped it on his head, he couldn't have looked more stunned. After staring for a little while, he settled back into a scowl, clenching his jaw till I heard something pop.

"Just tell me what you want."

"Dr. Alan Kramer came into this hospital and abducted Halley Davis," I said in low and rapid tones. The words hit McMountain like another anvil. "And yeah, I mean *that* Dr. Alan Kramer—the one from Bobby and Garrett's investigation. Do you have any idea where he might have taken her?"

His scowl deepened.

"What's he want with that kid?"

"It'll take more time than we've got to explain it," I answered. "Do you know where he'd take her? Even a guess is more than I have at this point."

He shook his head, and I could almost hear the grinding of his internal gears as he debated pressing me for more answers. He kept his voice low, half the words a mere rumble in his chest.

"The guy's a ghost. We got his face plastered all over. Lots of reports, no results. Park could tell you that. Why don't you bother him?"

"I can't. If Garrett learns Kramer has an interest in the girl, he'll hunt Halley down and kill her."

"Just a damned minute…" Roarke replied, huffing. His voice carried. Nervously, I glanced over to the nurses' station. Beer Keg was on his walkie. Hildy was on the phone. Both were far too intent on their own conversations to pay any attention to ours. Even so, I lowered my own voice to barely a hiss.

"It isn't only Garrett running around in that head."

Roarke's lips flattened into a pale line. We leaned our heads together as we spoke, close enough that I got a noseful of his cologne. I'd smelled it before—on Remy. I almost checked his throat for teeth marks. Instead, I focused on his shoes.

Remy's business, I told myself. *Don't need to know. Don't want to.*

"That's a hell of an accusation," he muttered.

"It is," I allowed, "but he hasn't been acting right lately, has he?"

Roarke huffed again, less a sound of anger than one of resignation. "Park's outside right now, tearing his hair because his partner didn't show for this call. Garrett's not answering his phone, either. A month ago, he'd be first on the scene, no matter what else he had going on. So, yeah."

"Dammit," I breathed.

The big officer straightened, stepping away from our impromptu conference. He still didn't look thrilled with me, but I'd started to think Roarke had the male equivalent of "resting bitch face"—although it came across more as "resting Hulk-smash face." He rolled his neck, stretching, and the Kevlar of his vest creaked beneath the stiff polyester of his uniform.

"I want to say you're wrong," he grumbled, "but it explains a lot."

"How so?" I asked.

Roarke's eyes cut to Captain Beer Keg, who was off his walkie now and looking expectantly our way. He took the eye contact as approval, and started heading over. Roarke lifted a giant-sized mitt and gestured him off.

"I got this," he assured the guy. Turning back to me, he said, "Elevator."

We got in. I took one back corner, Roarke took the other. He hooked his blunt thumbs into his service belt, planting his feet wide.

"I still don't like you," the officer said.

"And here I was afraid we might hug."

He shot me a glare through short lashes the color of rusty straw. I should have kept my damned mouth shut—we didn't have much private time in this makeshift office. I was about to choke out another apology, when Roarke started back up.

"We've been investigating these weird incidents—animal sacrifice, ritual stuff," he explained.

"I saw some reports on the news sites," I answered. "Wasn't sure how much was exaggerated."

"Resting Hulk-smash face" got smashier, though for once, his ire didn't seem directed at me. The no-neck officer wasn't even looking in my direction. He grunted through his nose as the elevator whispered between floors.

"It's worse." I waited, but he clammed up as the

elevator came to a stop at one of the floors. We both watched the doors expectantly as they slid open. No one stood in the hall beyond.

McMountain and I both reached for the CLOSE DOORS button at the same time—he with his right hand, I with my left. We brushed shoulders, jerking back as if we'd bumped against an electric fence. While we were still scowling awkwardly, the doors closed on their own.

Roarke cleared his throat, settling back to his side of the elevator. "Another thing we been keeping out of the news—every time we track down the perpetrators, someone gets to them first."

"And by 'gets to them,' you mean kills them, don't you?" I pressed. One of Remy's statements back in the parking garage made more sense now. He'd mentioned the dead woman outside of Lake View, and I'd been so fixated on that being my fault, I'd glossed over his mention of *bodies*—plural. She hadn't been the only one found out there, and I'd let her buddy get away.

"So far, all indigents and vagrants," Roarke answered. For a moment, I marveled that McMountain even knew what an indigent was. If he caught my incredulous look, he ignored it, continuing, "I found something at one of the scenes that made me think it was a cop, gone all Batman or something. I mentioned my theory to Garrett. Next day, the evidence disappeared from the lock-up."

Big words, and now a Batman reference. Maybe McMountain had more than a slab of beef between his ears. I still didn't see us trading stories over a beer any time soon.

"You knew it was Garrett?" I asked.

A shrug rolled like a seismic event. "Didn't make sense," he said. "He's a stand-up officer. Too good. He's not the kind who breaks the rules."

As opposed to Roarke, who regularly bent them for his Nephilim master.

Or Bobby, for that matter, I thought disconcertedly.

"So you didn't confront him," I ventured.

He shook his head.

The terrible sights imprinted on the Kramer home replayed across my mental movie screen with excruciating clarity. That hadn't been Garrett, exactly, but he had the same asshole riding shotgun in his head. Malphael could rant all he wanted about justice, but he wasn't one of the good guys.

"Probably for the best," I murmured.

With a faint rattle of machinery, the elevator settled at the end of its run.

"I know it's asking a lot," I said urgently, "but, seriously, try to keep as much as you can about the abduction under wraps, and for fuck's sake don't tell—"

The chime sounded, and the doors slid open. Bobby Park, his glossy black hair sticking up from the wind, caught sight of me and stopped mid-sentence with Lydia Potts.

"Bobby!" I cried, turning the name I'd been about to say into a greeting. I even managed to smile.

Beside me, Roarke stood silent as a gargoyle.

43

Bobby blinked once as he processed my uncharacteristic exuberance. Lydia flicked wintry blue eyes between her partner and me. Long strands of her bright blonde hair had worked loose from her ponytail, making her look like some windswept Valkyrie. Whatever she picked up on in our body language, it didn't make her happy.

She crimped her lips, biting back some comment.

Roarke hunched his shoulders like a kid caught spray-painting the neighbor's poodle. He sidestepped our little greeting party as he slipped from the elevator. Potts huffed through her nose and gave immediate pursuit, leaving just Bobby and me.

"Zack. What are you doing here?" he asked.

"Uh, a friend called me to pick him up," I lied.

"Hell of a night to play Good Samaritan," he said. I stepped the rest of the way out of the elevator just as the doors started closing again.

"Yeah," I answered. "What's going on? It looks like the whole station is here tonight."

Keeping his back to the chaos in the lobby, Bobby restlessly dashed fingers through his mussed hair. He grimaced as he flicked off styling-gel-laced meltwater. It landed on the tiles.

"A real mess," he sighed. "I've got six in the parking garage and a partner who didn't show for the call."

"Six?" I echoed, scanning the crowd over his head for any sign of Father Frank or Lil. There were cops and security personnel everywhere.

"No survivors, no IDs, and no witnesses," he said sourly. Following my gaze, he frowned as an orderly began shouting with one of the uniforms near the hospital's front doors. Park hovered on the edge of striding over to break it up, but they quieted. Turning back to me, he continued, "Jimmy thinks it's drug related. Lyds disagrees. With what I've seen, I'm siding with Lyds. It's not your standard shoot-out."

"Oh?" I asked, not daring to offer anything further.

"If all we had were gunshot victims, Roarke might have a point. The hospital's right here, and we found oxy on one of them. But the violence done to these bodies…" A shadow of revulsion twisted his features, and he rubbed his eyes as if the gesture could somehow erase the memory. "We found guns and some casings, but bullets didn't kill these people. One guy's head was twisted all the way around on his neck, and his back looked like someone had folded him in half."

I winced, recalling the sound.

"All the cameras out there were down during the power outage and lightning blew out a transformer, so not even the back-up power kicked on. Now we've got squat to go on, and I heard on the radio some kid's gone missing from the children's ward. I was just heading up there," he explained, stepping past me to hit the call button on the elevator. With a plaintive note, he added, "I hope it's a mix-up. I can't handle any more dead kids this week, Zack. I really can't."

That makes two of us, I thought.

"Hey, flyboy—what are you standing around for?" The distinctive sound of Lil's heels crescendoed in swift approach. I whirled in time to ward off her hand as she slapped at my shoulder.

She'd lost the harried nurse outfit, trading the lab coat for her recently reclaimed brown leather jacket, zipped snug. Her hair hung loose again, spilling wildly across her shoulders. Bobby's eyes cut from me to the Lady of Beasts, taking in the whole of her appearance.

"This your friend?" he asked uncertainly.

Her lips pursed for some sharp-tongued answer— then his suit jacket shifted to reveal his badge. She switched personas so fast, it gave me whiplash.

"I'm so sorry for snapping," she said in a meek voice that belonged on somebody else. Drawing back a step, she tipped her face to the floor so all her hair swung forward. It was a perfect imitation of Remy at his most obsequious. The russet tresses obscured her features, further muffling her voice so I had to strain as she muttered, "You know how I can be when I'm worried."

If her swift change puzzled Bobby, he buried it under polite professionalism.

"I'm sorry, Miss, but we have to keep everyone a little while longer for questioning."

"Zack, tell him," she whined. "The poor man's nearly seventy. He needs to be home, where he can sleep. He's been through so much already."

"Who's she talking about, Zack?" Bobby asked.

I almost didn't tell him—Father Frank's connection to Halley was too direct. We needed to divert Bobby and get the hell out so we could start tracking the girl. Under her lashes, Lil shot me a look. The hand nearest to me twitched, the nail of her middle finger jerking once in a direction back and to my left. I flicked my gaze that way.

Father Frank was already walking toward us, his knotted fingers firmly gripped around a steaming cup of vending machine coffee.

"Father Frank," I said, both in answer and salutation. Bobby tilted his head as he studied the rangy old Marine.

"Hey, I know you," he said. "You were the guy who broke up that scuffle during the Feast of the Assumption parade, last August. You say mass sometimes at Holy Rosary, right?"

"Not if I don't get some sleep real soon," the padre responded, flashing a smile that was equal measures apology and chagrin. He hefted the coffee cup like a talisman. "Been a long night of praying by the bedsides."

Without a word, Lil shifted to stand beside the taller man. She slipped one hand through the crook of his elbow, clinging like a frightened toddler. Father Frank stared at his arm as if it had suddenly sprouted a grotesque tumor.

Lil didn't budge, ducking her chin so any portion of her features not hidden by hair was angled away from Bobby behind the priest's shoulder. She strained toward the main doors, tugging hard enough that the padre had to struggle not to spill his coffee.

I took the hint.

"We really need to go," I said.

Bobby scrubbed his palm against the back of his head, looking miserable. At his hip, fragments of harried voices crackled from his two-way. His name stood out in the jumble. He ignored it for the moment, staring pensively at the call buttons for the elevator.

"I don't suppose you can help much in this chaos," he sighed.

"We showed up after the cops did, Bobby," I said. "What could I possibly offer?"

Dark eyes sought my own and lingered, beseeching. I knew what he was hoping for—though he was careful not to say it in front of either Lil or the padre. I shook my head once, firmly. Bobby's shoulders sagged further and I looked away, sickened by the way I misdirected the earnest young investigator.

Halley's safety made it necessary.

I'd just keep telling myself that.

Park unclipped his walkie. "I'll tell the guys at the door you're clear. No point in everyone having a shitty night." When he realized he'd sworn in front of the padre, Bobby actually caught his breath.

"Sorry for the language," he muttered.

Father Frank offered the tightly wound detective a rueful half-grin.

"Son, in your shoes, I'd be swearing, too."

"I've had better nights," Park admitted. As he arranged things over the walkie, we started heading for the doors. Relinquishing her death-grip on the padre's arm, Lil pulled ahead, the keys to my car already jingling in her hand.

"We could have been out and tracking him by now," she grumbled.

I jogged to catch up. "You have a lead?"

She pushed past the two uniforms standing at the main bank of doors. The orderly who'd been yelling earlier started up again the minute he realized they were letting us free ahead of him. I dodged that train wreck, leaving the whole mess for Bobby and his co-workers to sort out.

Once we stood on the sidewalk out front, I asked the question again. Lil shook her head irritably.

"Not Kramer," she said. "Malphael."

"Malphael?" Father Frank echoed.

"The Gibburim," I supplied. Lil rolled her eyes at the two of us, then made a beeline for the car. I grabbed her by the elbow and turned her back toward me. "Malphael's no good. By the time he gets to Halley, she'll already be—"

"Don't say it," Father Frank interrupted. "Please. I can't bear to imagine a world where that's true."

"Sorry, padre." To Lil, I demanded, "And how exactly are you tracking Malphael? You didn't get within five paces of the guy back at the house."

"You don't think I gave up that rosary for nothing, do you?" With a grin of triumph, she held up a single bead of green ceramic.

"He told you to destroy that," Father Frank spat. He lunged, and I stepped between them before things got out of hand. Most of the police were in the lobby, but there were officers visible out here, too. Roarke and Potts stood within earshot, the blonde Amazon clearly dressing down her hill-giant of a partner.

"Is that how this monster found his way to Halley?" Father Frank strained against me, cords standing out along his neck. "I told you, you couldn't trust this woman, Zack."

"Cool your cassock, priest," she responded. "I broke everything that was important." She dropped the gleaming bead into the depths of her bottomless handbag. "No way I was running around with a direct pipeline to one of the Rephaim. That's just asking for trouble."

Father Frank ground his teeth in aggravation. I wasn't exactly thrilled with Lil myself.

"You were going to tell me about this *when*?" I asked. The wind teased the hair back from her face, revealing her Mona Lisa grin.

"Whenever I decided it was time."

The padre hissed a curse beneath his breath and tore away from me, pacing a length of sidewalk while he shook aggression from his hands. Lil shot him a contemptuous look.

"While you two dicked around in the girl's hospital room, I worked up a spell to trace it back to its source," she explained. "I didn't have time to finish but I've got enough to—" Abruptly, she stopped, nostrils flaring wide. "Do you smell that?"

"Smell what?"

"Calvin Klein Eternity." She pronounced it with all the gravitas of a sentencing judge. Her gray eyes settled onto Roarke like a lightning stroke. It took McMountain several heartbeats to realize she was staring at him. He glanced up from his tête-à-tête with Potts.

"Can I help you, ma'am?"

Ignoring the "ma'am," she marched right over to him and stabbed a shamrocked fingernail in his chest. I tried to be invisible.

"You're wearing Calvin Klein Eternity," she accused.

His pale brows furrowed. "So?"

Potts just stared at the smaller woman.

Lil tipped her head back, minutely studying McMountain's rough-hewn features. Her lips twisted with distaste.

"It won't last."

With that, she whirled on her heel, leaving both Roarke and his partner staring after her.

"Of course he's a redhead," she growled as she stomped past me toward my car. Taking advantage of her distraction, I plucked the keys from her hand. She punched me in the arm as an afterthought.

"Did you know?" she demanded.

"We're going now," I reminded her.

"How *long* did you know?" she pursued.

I slipped the keys in the lock, opening her door without really thinking about it.

"Didn't you divorce my brother?"

"I died," she snapped. "There's a difference."

Father Frank observed this exchange with an air of baffled exasperation.

"We need to head back to Holy Rosary," he said, pulling up his coat collar against the stinging cold. "Then you should drop me at Tammy's place."

"We're going after Malphael," Lil insisted.

"Kramer, you mean," I corrected. "We find him, we find the girl."

"I don't have a tracking spell active on Kramer, you idiot," she argued. "Mal will find the girl for us. We focus on him."

"And I'm telling you, if we focus on Malphael, we run the risk of losing Halley. You heard him back at the house."

Father Frank strode up and closed his hand around my keys. A tingle of power arced through the contact, followed by a wash of frustration, anxiety, and steely-edged will.

"We are going to my church," he said, "and then you are driving me to the Davis home. No arguments." There was power in his words.

"Praying's not going to help anything," Lil spat back, "and you'll waste precious time at the girl's house. Neither Kramer nor Mal are going to head back there. There's nothing there they want."

Father Frank rounded on her, condemnation whittling his features.

"A deranged child-killer just kidnapped her daughter. I need to tell Tammy in person. That's not something a mother should hear on the news."

44

Lil refused to get in the car.

"Quit fucking around," I snarled. "Every delay costs us."

"Which is why I'm going after Garrett."

She folded her arms across her chest, chin jutting stubbornly. The lights in the parking lot picked out a scattering of perfect snowflakes trapped in the waves of her hair.

"Leave her behind," Father Frank growled. He ducked past me and slid into the passenger seat, slamming the door after him. I marched over to the driver's side, glaring at Lil across the roof of the car.

"You pick the worst possible times to be a brat."

"You think that's what this is about?" she shot back. "You don't even know where Tarhunda is located, and if he pulls things off with that girl, we are all completely screwed."

"Rub it in a little more," I said.

"You're chasing ghosts, Anakim. I'm going after the

sure thing." She turned smartly on her heel and started across the lot.

"At least let me drop you off at your car," I called after her.

"The way you drive?" she replied. "I'll get there faster if I walk."

Roarke tracked her progress from where he stood beside his partner. Shifting his attention my way, he shot me a quizzical look. I held my hands up in a gesture of frustration. If he wanted insight into the mysteries of Lil's behavior, he was looking at the wrong guy.

"Come on, Zack." The driver's-side door bumped against my stomach as Father Frank pushed it open from the inside. "It's better if she doesn't tag along. There are some things at Holy Rosary you need to see."

"What are you even talking about?" I asked.

"Get in." He nudged me with the door again, every line of his face telegraphing his urgency. "You'll understand once we get there."

Lil was already at the far end of the main lot. No one stopped her, though Roarke continued to stare at her retreating form—probably committing her details to memory. I wondered if he would ask Remy about her later.

That would be an awkward conversation.

I hesitated another moment, squinting as a gust of wind scoured my face with ice crystals. Then, muttering unhappy things about the tactics of splitting the party, I ducked into the Hellcat.

The hospital's lot had been plowed and salted since the storm, no doubt a fringe benefit of an early morning visit from a battalion of cops. Snow was still coming down in swirling flurries of white, though it was nothing like the flash-freezing blizzard that had pummeled the city earlier. I hit the ignition, cranked up the defroster to clear the scrim of ice forming on the windshield, and headed for Euclid.

It was a short drive to Holy Rosary, but I found myself glaring at the clock every thirty seconds. Time sped faster than I could urge the Hellcat on these roads. The plows had been busy clearing snow and spreading salt, but the pavement was slick with melt and little patches were already freezing over. We practically crawled up Mayfield, and I resisted the urge to pummel the steering wheel every time the tires struggled for grip.

"Ease up on yourself, Zack," the padre said. "You'll find her in time."

I loosed a string of curses as the light ahead of us went from green to yellow in record time. Father Frank didn't even twitch. When I hit the brakes, the Dodge started to fishtail, so I laid on the horn and just coasted through. The horn was more reflex than necessity. No one was going to broadside us—they weren't stupid enough to be on the roads at this hour.

"I wasn't swearing at you," I said by way of apology. "Lil's right, though," I continued, shoving the hair back from my eyes. "I have no idea where Kramer's taken her. I don't even know where to start."

The old priest stared out the window at the passing buildings, their eaves and every lintel lined with fine traceries of snow.

"That's why we're going to Holy Rosary before anything

else," he responded. "You need access to your supplies."

"I've got supplies stashed at the church?" I asked. "Why didn't you say something earlier?"

"I did, back at the hospital," he said. "At least I tried to. Didn't want to say too much in front of Ms. Gibson."

It took me a moment to realize he meant Lil.

"Before that, I left a bunch of messages on your cell—lot of good it did me." He fixed me with a look of reproach that felt distinctly paternal. "You still haven't given me the new number, by the way."

Unlocking the screen one-handed, I held my current phone out to him.

"Text yourself or something. With everything going on, I'll forget again."

He snorted. "Same old Zack."

The road dipped to go under the train tracks, both lanes narrowly girded by stout pylons of concrete. Both hands went on the wheel—it felt like I was threading a needle. Even without the road conditions, it wouldn't have been fun squeezing the Hellcat through the abbreviated lane.

As we emerged on the other side, the retaining walls blossomed with a vibrant mural celebrating the history of Cleveland's Little Italy. The domed spire of Holy Rosary rose in the distance above the slumbering neighborhood, the arms of its cross bearing a rounded mantle of white.

"What kind of things are we talking—weapons?" I asked hopefully. "A Rephaim-sized bazooka would be great about now. Or a magical tracking device. I really could use one of those."

Underneath the jokes, my mind raced through possibilities. Tools and weapons for the current crisis would be handy, but what I longed for—and truly needed—was knowledge to fill some of the holes in my existence. The journals in my apartment were crammed with tons of general information on wards and energy and theories about the tribes, but they were frustratingly sparse when it came to personal details.

Impressions too vague to be classed as memories suggested that I didn't trust the apartment to be safe enough to leave truly transparent notes about myself. But this stash was in a church with Father Frank—my anchor—to look after it. If that wasn't safe enough…

A brittle, yearning hope welled up, sharp enough it stole my breath.

Those blades I imagined would really, really be nice.

It was as close to praying as I got. Father Frank's voice interrupted the moment.

"Hey. Slow down. You'll pass the entrance." His arm jerked toward what might have been an empty lot, laden with drifts. Belatedly, I realized it was parking for the church.

I tapped the brakes, but 4,500 pounds of top-of-the-line Detroit engineering wasn't going to stop in time for that turn.

"Fuck me running," I grumbled.

"Never mind." He gestured to a crosswalk just past the church. "Go up to the Montessori school. There's a side street you can use."

The thin stretch of concrete qualified as more of a sidewalk than a proper street, but I nosed the Hellcat

403

over a mound of snow at the curb, and cut the engine right next to the stairs leading to the side entrance of the stonework cathedral. Rime-covered saints looked down on us from their vigilant posts across the pediment.

Father Frank unfolded himself from the passenger side, digging a substantial set of keys from the depths of his coat pocket. He gripped the metal railing in one gloved hand as he navigated the snow-covered stairs to the door at the top. Grabbing my phone from where he'd left it on the seat, I trailed after him.

"You never answered my question," I said.

"You were too busy gathering wool to hear me."

The padre bent over the lock, sorting through his collection for the right key. The thick suede fingers of his heavy gloves made it a painstaking process. He didn't say anything for a while. Impatient, I smacked my hand against the railing. Fragments of ice shivered off, dropping into the drifts below. I stared at their jigsaw imprints, wondering if we'd killed Halley by taking this side trip.

"Hard to be specific anyway. Over the years, I've seen you bring all kinds of little packages in and out. Last time you came through was around All Souls' Day." Cursing, he banged ice from the lock, then tried the key again without success. "It was my turn to say mass, so I only caught you in passing," he explained. "I'll be kicking myself about that for a while."

"All Souls' Day." I did some mental math. "That was right before—"

"Your 'incident?' Yeah." He kept his back to me, shoulders stiffening beneath his coat. "Like I said, kicking myself. You came in with some weapons I've seen you carry everywhere. I should have known you were in trouble when you left them both behind."

His displeasure at being lied to, or at least misled, prickled palpably through the frigid air. And I felt bad—I really did. But all my guilt failed to stand before the rush of hope his words inspired. Twined through that rush was a quieter sense—nothing so certain as a memory, but a comfort all the same.

Beyond this door lay tools that would help me win the fight for Halley.

As much as we were pressed for time, Father Frank had made the right call in bringing me here.

The padre finally got the key to work, ice grinding audibly in the lock as he turned the haft. He had to yank on the side door to drag its bottom across the buildup of snow outside. I reached out to give him a hand.

Once inside, we stood in a narrow antechamber with a clutter of snow shovels angling against one corner, together with a squat bucket of salt. He gestured for quiet.

"I've got to take us the long way," he said in a hush. "Father Cerilli is probably already up and getting ready for six o'clock Mass. Easier not to interrupt him—he'll talk our ears raw."

Tapping slush from his boots, he led me down a narrow flight of stairs deep into the bowels of the church. We passed through a storage area with ranks of folding chairs—the old metal kind that made it impossible to get comfortable, no matter how you sat.

Shadows crouched in the furthest corners, together with drifts of cobwebs and dust. We passed a boiler room, then more storage, only to emerge into the church hall. Father Frank strode across the vacant space, his damp boots making soft squeaking sounds on the highly polished tile.

Through the double doors at the far end of the hall, we followed a long, narrow corridor to its end. The padre used another key to open the door, reaching in to flick on a single light inside.

Exposed masonry lent a vault-like feeling to the roughly fifteen by twenty space. Wooden rafters stretched dusty and bare over a water-stained cement floor with a worn tan rug positioned roughly in the middle. Old copper pipes ran the length of the left-hand wall, hugging the ceiling to disappear deeper into the building.

Holy Rosary was an old structure, and it showed in the foundation—hand-quarried stone, it was held together with a sandy-colored mortar. Flecks of silica caught the light. An interior section of cinderblock running half the length of the room stood out as a more recent construction, dull and gray by contrast.

Attempts had been made to turn the underground space homey, with framed images of nature photography arranged on three of the walls. In the far corner, a heavy bag hung from the rafters, with a treadmill and a rack of free weights nearby. The treadmill angled so it sectioned off the gym space. A patched green couch that sagged in the middle made up the other divider for that side of the room with a battered old Army trunk squatting in front of it in lieu of a coffee table.

Nestled in the nook created by the cinderblock addition was a spartan desk of pitted wood. Neatly arranged on the desk were some file trays, a tower computer with an ancient CRT monitor, and a triptych of photos in a hinged wooden frame. An old brass crucifix overlooked the desk from the narrowest cinderblock wall, probably hung with masonry screws.

"Be it ever so humble," Father Frank murmured, gesturing me to precede him into the room. My eyes were drawn immediately to the crucifix before my brain consciously registered the reason. A play of light seemed to glimmer deep within the tarnished brass. Curious, I teased open my vision.

The cross blazed like a beacon.

"Is that a relic?" I asked. I didn't mean it in the Catholic sense, and from his face, Father Frank knew it.

"You've called it that," he responded. "I know it's got something to do with your disappearing act."

I strode past him to investigate. The cross fairly thrummed as I approached it, layers of emotion and purpose spilling from the worn brass image. On the Shadowside, most objects in the physical world showed up as echoes, if they showed up at all. Relics were items that possessed weight and substance on both sides of reality. Like a Crossing, they were often associated with mortal trauma or death.

More than that, they could function like portable Crossings—although they took a hell of a lot more effort to use. It was the difference between stepping through a neatly opened door and squeezing through a partially collapsed tunnel.

"I think I get it," I murmured, looking past the crucifix to the cinderblock wall. Wards glimmered in the spaces between each gray block, scribed minutely into the cement with what might have been a felt-tip pen. Blue and faded, the scrolling spellwork was nearly invisible unless you peered at it from inches away. When I trailed my hand along a line of mortar, power prickled against my skin.

I recognized it immediately as my own.

"You did good, Mazetti," I said, not bothering to look up.

"I knew even without your memory, you'd figure that part out," he responded.

Pressing my fingers against the wards again, I tasted their purpose and resistance. No doubt about it. The two sections of cinderblock had been added to enclose a hidden space large enough to be a walk-in closet— except there was no door. I'd put the Anakim equivalent of a bank vault in the basement of the padre's church.

Slipping to the desk, I emptied out my pockets of cellphone and keys, dropping them in a heap by the three-way picture frame. Father Frank shrugged out of his coat as he watched me, mild interest vying with exhaustion in the lines of his face.

"You always do that," he said. He gestured to the pile of electronics. "You never say why."

"Wrecks the phone when I cross sides," I explained. "Something about the energy."

Thoughtfully, he grunted, then settled on the couch. I leaned over the side of the desk to reach the crucifix, lifting it away from its masonry screw. The old, charged metal buzzed against my palm.

I opened myself to it.

A host of visions unspooled within my mind—an elderly soldier praying on his death bed. Another voice prayed along with him, the whole scene guttering with golden candleshine.

The prayers faded and another sickroom took form. An elderly woman curled beneath a massive heap of blankets, gnarled fingers twined through the threads of a crocheted woolen comforter. A gift from her daughter. Handmade. She breathed her last, still gripping her treasure.

Next was a child, body broken and half her face a slushy mess. Her single eye fixed upon the ceiling, blessedly ignorant of her circumstance. Again the prayers and candles—and in her case, a silent plea for justice.

Death upon death upon death unfolded from the cross, each linked by the ritual of final absolution. A deeper imprint threaded between the rest—the death of the owner. Broad frame wasted to nothing. Mottled hands. Wisps of hair worn white by time, and the tabbed collar that he proudly wore as a priest of the Catholic faith. He clutched the precious crucifix to his breast as he lay dying, remembering a lifetime of last rites.

Seizing the steady, solemn weight of his emotion, I dragged myself across.

45

The transition stole my breath. Still gripping the crucifix, I waited for the world to stop reeling.

The century-old church rose as a palpable presence above me, the stone walls of its foundation standing as solid on this side as they had in the flesh-and-blood world. The age of the building, combined with its significance for a whole population of mortals, guaranteed that it stood sturdy and unassailable. The newer cinderblock addition, tucked away where very few people could see it and thus reinforce its existence, shouldn't have held the same impenetrable weight.

But the wards changed all that.

Floor to ceiling, power wove through them, glimmering a deep, electric blue. In the approximate center of the main wall, finely written symbols picked out the lines of a doorway. A thick mesh of warding sealed the portal. I'd relearned enough in the past few months to recognize some seriously aggressive defenses. Whatever I'd stored in that room, I'd wanted it well protected.

Promising.

Pressing my palm flat against a central point of resistance, I struggled to recall what I needed to make it open. The lines of power leapt at my touch and I felt the magic recognize me. A familiar rush spread through my wings—the same sensation that flooded me when I called my blades through the intonation of my Name.

"It can't be that simple, can it?" I murmured. But our Names were our magic, our station, our identity. There was nothing simple in that immutable truth.

Certain that I had the answer, I drew a breath and intoned the syllables of my Name. As the sound vibrated from my core, the sigils scribed around the threshold erupted in a play of silver fire. Threads of it leapt from the dense strata of warding, cascading across my face, chest, and wings. Testing me.

There was that recognition again, more profoundly this time. An instant later, the mesh of power flickered, and the door stood open.

"The soul equivalent of a retina-scan," I muttered. Tucking the relic crucifix into the inner pocket of my jacket, I stepped through. The warded door snapped shut as soon as I crossed the threshold.

In the crowded space beyond, the boundaries of the secret room stood thick and inviolable. Ceiling, floor, and walls all were reinforced with glimmering rows of wards. Another series of sigils—larger and paler than the ward-signs—picked out a small circle on the ground, arranged in the middle of the hidden space. I instinctively understood what it was for.

Stepping inside the circle, I shifted back over to the

flesh-and-blood world. The guiding lines of the circle guaranteed that I reappeared away from everything crowded together in the lightless space.

I emerged into utter darkness, stale air heavy with dust. A tiny pinprick of light filtered through a crack in the floor above me, serving only to reinforce the choking blackness of the interior space. Through touch, I got vague impressions of crowded shelves rising above a narrow stretch of unfinished wood. I fumbled at the rough counter in front of me, my hand brushing something that clattered to the floor. It struck the bare concrete with a fatal shattering of plastic.

"Shit."

I stood very still, unwilling to crush more of whatever I'd broken under my boots. I felt all shoulders and elbows in the tiny space. With the walls so solid on both sides of reality, my wings were as cramped as the rest of me, heightening the overall feel of claustrophobia.

Light would make it better. At least I'd stop knocking things over.

A tattery memory of a candle and a box of strike-anywhere matches drifted from the depths of my mind, with no conscious sense of where in the room I might find these things. I screwed my eyes shut—not that it made much difference—and blindly struck out in the direction that seemed right. The edge of my hand impacted what felt like a brass candlestick. Jerking with surprise at my success, I heard it tip. Without thought and without being able to see it, I seized the candlestick before it tumbled to the ground.

"Why couldn't you manifest the ninja skills five

minutes ago?" I chided myself, still wondering what I'd broken in my initial foray. Plastic parts rattled as I gingerly shifted my feet.

I found the matches by setting the candlestick on top of them. Fighting not to rush and spill them everywhere, I grabbed the box and slid it open. I shook a couple matches into my hand, striking the first one on the wall next to me. The sudden eruption of light left me blinking.

Shelves everywhere—pigeonholes, really—crammed with a baffling assortment of stuff. Rolls of paper, little boxes, yellowed envelopes sealed with tape. I put the match to the wick of the candle, making sure the flame transferred before I shook it out. The candle sputtered once, then the flame burned straight and bright. The scent of molten beeswax mellowed the lingering sulfur from the match.

All too conscious of Halley's dwindling time, I lofted the candle and dug frantically through the contents of the pigeonholes, searching for the weapons Father Frank had mentioned—tracking spells, scrying mirrors—anything that might be useful in the current situation. I dragged down stacks of silver certificates, thick rolls of more conventional cash, and checkbooks for accounts in a variety of names.

One newer-looking envelope disgorged a slew of fake ID cards, all of them bearing my face. Boxes of ammunition—9mm, .38, .45—were hidden behind tightly rolled papers that turned out to be pages cut from medieval texts.

"Fuck me running," I snarled. "Where's the stuff I actually need?" Seizing a promisingly paper-wrapped parcel, I discovered only a stack of assorted passports, several left over from the Vietnam version of me. Temper frayed, I slammed the heel of my free hand against the unfinished wood of the shelves. No blades. All my instincts clamored they should be here.

If they're anything but a pipe dream.

The whole rack of pigeonholes jumped at the impact—nothing anchored it to the back wall. Packages and little boxes tumbled out in a riot of dust.

With faster-than-human speed, I tried catching one before it hit the plywood counter. I overshot, and my hand struck the box in mid-air. Its aged cardboard lid flew open, disgorging a swatch of black silk. This arced to the right, weighted with something inside. It came to rest on a sleek wooden chest angled at the far end of the counter.

The candlelight glittered off of gold and gems.

A ring rested in the folds of silk. I peeled back the rich scrap of fabric, sensation prickling my fingers— the cloth was delicately warded, tiny sigils stitched with blue thread around the seam. The ring itself shone in my vision, four mismatched gems gleaming with a depth far beyond their simple oval faceting.

Another relic. I knew even before I touched it.

Flickers of information danced across my brain as my fingers grazed the object—a child for each of the birthstones, even little Joey who didn't see more than two days in the world. The dead son's name hit with a wrenching sense of loss as brutal as a train wreck.

Hastily, I scooped the ring back into its protective swatch of silk, pocketing them both. A portable Crossing was never a bad thing to keep around.

A woman's name—Mary Reilly—and a date—1956—were both scribed on the underside of the little box that had held the ring. It was my handwriting, faded with time. My distinctive scrawl was visible across a larger piece of paper resting where the ring box had fallen. An envelope. I nudged the container aside to investigate.

From Zaquiel, to Zaquiel, I thought wryly.

Then an unreasonable feeling of dread seized me.

Despite this, I snatched up the envelope from where it lay diagonally across the wooden case. With numb fingers, I tore the seal. I had to set the candle down before extracting the letter within—my hands were shaking too much to safely manage both.

The single sheet of folded paper was covered in my angled cursive, both front and back. The letters were spidery with haste. A vertiginous feeling of unreality washed over me as I read the date at the top of the letter. November 3.

I'd written this the day before I woke on the shores of Lake Erie.

I took in the first paragraph in a glance.

Zaquiel—
If we're reading this, then things went badly out on the lake—but we're not stuck in some jar, so I hope we got the Stylus like we'd planned. If you're not Zachary Aaron Westland any more, then all we did was get ourselves killed. That's actually good news. The alternative is

uglier, because if you don't remember being me, that means Dorimiel got his hands on Neferkariel's icon, and that's a whole level of fucked I'd hoped to avoid.

"I wasn't saving Lailah. I went to get the Stylus," I breathed. "It was a suicide run."

For a moment, my entire world seemed to come unhinged. I couldn't bring myself to read the rest. Folding the letter up, I stuffed it hastily back into the envelope. I could deal with it, and all its gutting revelations later.

Assuming I have a later, once I go toe-to-toe with another decimus, I thought bleakly.

I shoved the envelope into my jacket, but got it hung up on the crucifix. The instant I shifted to reach for the candle, the letter fluttered to the floor.

"Fuck," I hissed, crouching so I could grope around under the counter. Mostly I found bits of broken plastic, then a palm-sized hunk of circuitry.

My goddam missing phone.

It looked like a cheap burner. With little hope that it was anything but junk after knocking it from the counter, I shoved what was left of the little flip-phone into my pocket. Maybe some data had survived.

Fat chance.

I found the envelope and stood, surveying the collected detritus of a life I no longer knew. I'd left the letter. I'd left the phone—all in hopes of what? That I'd remember enough to find this place? That I'd be able to piece it all back together once I did? I couldn't have expected Father Frank to still be around, not at his age.

If Malphael was right, death and rebirth took conservatively fifteen years for me to get my head screwed on enough to remember who I was. Maybe I'd been counting on Remy to guide me. He'd done it before.

Did he know about this place?

Why hadn't he told me before now?

Too many questions—and they all led down a rabbit warren of uncertainties. I didn't have the fucking time. I reached for the crucifix so I could cross back out of the stifling hidden closet. There wasn't anything in here I could use for the present crisis. I'd just have to wing it, so to speak.

Maybe Lil was having better luck.

As I gulped a breath in preparation for the crossing, something halted me. Too nebulous to be a hunch. More like one of those dream-flashes that feel shatteringly profound in the moment but scatter like smoke when examined.

Why was the letter on that particular wooden case?

The phone had been over there, as had the matches and the candlestick. Examining the patterns in the dust, I confirmed it. Everything on that corner of the narrow counter had been carefully arranged to create a tableau, with the chest at the very center. There had to be a reason for it—all the other junk in here was haphazardly scattered or stuffed artlessly into brimming pigeonholes.

As I pondered the intentions of a self I no longer knew, the broad case of polished wood called to me. It was a literal sensation of music, like a chime striking inside my head.

Wards crackled against my fingers the instant I

reached to lift the smooth lid. Swift on the heels of their sting rushed a heady sense of triumph. I knew what rested inside this case, waiting to be recovered—knew it with galvanizing certainty.

The blades. They were real.

A simple brass latch secured the front of the case with what at first appeared to be a tiny padlock. On closer inspection, the lock turned out to be a magical seal crafted from wire and paper. Interwoven characters formed a sigil-phrase on the reverse of the "lock."

Even as I turned it toward the candle for closer inspection, the words of the sigil-phrase rose unbidden to my throat—their knowledge stored so deep, it hooked more to muscle-memory than to thought.

The paper of the lock ignited in a burst of magnesium-white flame. In an instant, the whole thing sizzled away, leaving neither embers nor ash. A little twist of wire remained threaded through the brass latch. Despite the sudden light show, the metal wire wasn't hot.

I untwined the scorched filament, then reverently lifted the lid. Glinting curves of metal danced with the candle's yellow light.

Twin blades—by all appearances, hand-forged—rested against a lining of gray foam cut to their precise shape, one fixed to the bottom, one strapped to the inside of the lid. The blades were about six inches in length, the full weapon stretching just shy of a foot. Each appeared to be crafted from a single piece of steel, running uninterrupted from pommel to tapering tip. Smooth strips of supple leather twined together to cover the hilts.

Meticulously scribed sigils shimmered along the

leather of the grips. The blades themselves were unadorned save for a single symbol etched just above the cross-guard. There, gleaming with subtle threads of blue-white power, shone the first syllable of my Name, scribed in that alternately sinuous and angular script I'd seen referenced in my journals as the First Tongue.

These weapons were the physical doubles of the spirit-blades I could summon—or at least, their closest feasible equivalents in the flesh-and-blood world. They were the daggers I'd remembered in that brief flash during the duel with Malphael, and as they lay gleaming in their polished case, I wondered how any power had stolen away their memory.

I held my free hand poised above the bottommost blade, caught in a delicious moment of anticipation. With measured reverence, I closed my hand around the hilt. The contact sent an exhilarating electricity all the way to the tips of my wings. A faint corona of flame erupted along the blade, and the sigil above the hilt burst forth with blue-white brilliance. In the backwash of power, the flame of the single candle wavered, then winked out.

Didn't matter. With the flame-kissed blade, I had ample light by which to see.

Thrilling with excitement, I grabbed the lovingly crafted twin of the weapon. Wrapping my fingers around the hilt felt like the completion of a circuit. I held the blades crossed in front of me, my face uplit in their ghostly blue glow. The wind of power blew the hair back from my brow.

Had any mortal witnessed my grin in that moment, they rightly would have trembled and fled.

46

I stepped out of the sealed storeroom with the knife case clutched to my chest, that maniac grin still creasing my features. If my expression—or sudden materialization—startled Father Frank, he didn't show it. The priest stood alone in his basement sanctuary, his back rigid with patient determination. He held his coat draped over one arm, ready to throw it on at any moment. A Desert Eagle rested in a shoulder holster set for a right-hand draw.

There was something deeply surreal in seeing the lines of the holster strapped over the priest's black garb.

"You look like a cat who found a whole cage full of canaries," he said.

"Way better than that."

Returning the crucifix to its peg, I laid the knife case near the pile of electronics on the desk and drew out the blades. The padre's brows lifted as I brandished the glittering weapons with a triumphant flourish.

His chin dipped in a swift nod of approval. "Now you look like you."

"You don't happen to have sheaths that might fit these things, do you?" I ventured.

"Weren't they in there?"

"In that mess?" My laugh came out bitter. "I almost overlooked the blades. Did you know I have silver certificates in there? Do banks even take those any more?"

Father Frank made a pensive sound. Tossing his coat across the back of his desk chair, he bee-lined for his footlocker. A mug, a stack of papers, and some other personal clutter rested on its surface. With quick, efficient movements, he transferred these to the floor. As he worked to get the lid open, the rattle of its latches stirred green-drenched echoes in a distant corner of my mind.

"I think I've got enough to MacGyver something," he said. Dragging the footlocker closer to the couch, he bent almost bodily into the depths of the thing, rummaging through its contents.

"Take your time," I sighed. "I still have no clue where to look for Halley."

"No tracking charms in there, then?" He withdrew a tattered sheath of woven nylon cloth, olive green and stained along one side. Holding it up, he eyeballed it against the length of the blades. With a downward quirk of his mouth, he cast it aside.

I grimaced. "Nothing I recognized as such."

He bent back to the trunk, sorting through a baffling array of old military gear—including, if I trusted my eyes, a moth-eaten old ghillie suit. A few more sheaths made it to a growing pile by his feet, none of them quite the proper length or width for the daggers.

Waiting was never my strong suit, and I paced a

restless circuit of the room, hands still fisted round the blades. The sigil-inscribed leather wrapped along the grips thrummed against my palms with a familiar tingle of power.

"It's probably good Lil struck out on her own," I said, struggling to convince myself of the fact. "We'll cover more ground."

Father Frank scoffed. "You think she's still working on this? I bet she got in her car and drove straight out of town. She's not much of a team player, Zack."

I thought back to Lil's cool efficiency on board the *Scylla*. She'd taken down most of Dorimiel's blood-powered goons all by her lonesome.

"It's best to count Lil as her own team," I responded. "Army of one."

"Sure. She's efficient when it suits her," he allowed. "Doesn't mean you can trust her to see a job through to the end." He chucked a battered sheath of water-stained leather in my direction. "Try this."

It wasn't wide enough by half and the loop at the top was cracked through the middle. Even if it had fit either of the knives, there was no way I could fix it to my belt. I tossed it back.

"No dice?" he asked.

"Nope."

"It's the damned curve on those things," he said.

I tried sticking one of the daggers into the inner pocket of my jacket to see if I could make that work. The second time I jabbed myself in the ribs, I gave it up as a bad plan. Chewing my cheeks, I debated putting the blades back in their case and just leaving. Even if I had to fly around the Shadowside and do an aerial search for Terhuziel, it would accomplish more than just waiting around.

"I think I got it," he announced.

Gathering his collection of scavenged supplies, he brought the pile over and dumped it onto the desk. From a drawer, he produced a roll of electrical tape. I eyed it skeptically.

"What are you going to do with that?" I demanded.

"Trust me for once," he said.

Boiling over with impotent fury that had nowhere else to go, I glowered at him, knuckles whitening as I gripped the daggers. He glared back and didn't flinch— not even when faint shimmers of blue-white fire licked along the blades.

"Put those things down for a minute, take off your jacket, and calm the hell down," he said tightly. "Rage may get you through a fight, but it rarely helps you plan it."

Maybe he used his voice trick on me, because some of the singing fury in my veins abated. Huffily, I put the daggers on the desk next to their polished wooden case. Calm returned by slow degrees. Shrugging out of my jacket, I draped it over Father Frank's coat on the back of the chair.

"You're right," I admitted.

As soon as I extended my forearm, he started building the sheath along the underside, layering cardboard and nylon and wrapping it all in place with lengths of electrical tape. I held the weapon steady while he tested the fit, making little adjustments along the way.

"Now, think." He kept his voice low as he continued

working, the rhythm of the process finding its way into his words. "About Halley. About this rogue Rephaim. About his plans for her." He finished on one wrist and started up on the next. The heft of the dagger strapped to my forearm dredged up a potent kinesthetic memory. It felt *right*. Father Frank kept up his soothing patter. "You've probably picked up on something already and you're just too frustrated to see it."

"Maybe," I allowed. I flexed my fingers and rolled my wrist, adjusting to the bands of tape hugging up and down my arm. "I don't know. I've forgotten how half my brain works any more."

He gestured for me to hold the dagger on the other arm. He was almost out of electrical tape. "If not your brain, what about Halley's?"

"Hunh?" I stood with my right arm extended, the left clasping the blade along its length while Father Frank dug around in his desk for another roll of electrical tape. The one he found was halfway gone. I hoped it would be enough.

"You were in her head, Zack," he reminded me. With a blunt nail, he picked at the leading edge of the tape, holding the roll nearly at arm's length as he tried to see the little line of black against black. "While you were in there, what did you see?"

I shrugged, casting my thoughts back to the experience.

"It's all fairy tales and Disney Princesses," I said.

Father Frank gave up squinting at the electrical tape to turn a disapproving frown at me. "You're telling me this bastard spent weeks insinuating himself into her psyche and he left behind not a single footprint you could track?"

I shook my head. "The only thing weird in there, aside from me, was this classic villain's castle that belonged on the cover of *Better Homes and Dungeons*. It showed up when the Rephaim attacked."

"Castle?" he pursued. "Describe it to me exactly as you saw it."

"It was just a symbol," I objected. "Believe me, it was too over-the-top to be anything else."

"People pack a lot of information into symbols, Zack." He hitched his jaw in the direction of the cross. "You should know that better than anyone." He finally got the tape to cooperate and was back to anchoring the second makeshift sheath to my forearm.

"All right," I conceded. "It's not like we've got anything better to go on."

Stilling my breathing, I focused on my memory of the girl's psychic space, building each element as vividly as I could. My eyes slid shut in concentration and the persistent tug of tape along my forearm as the padre continued to work faded into the distant background. Like a movie advanced in slow motion, I rolled each frame of the encounter forward in my mind until I came to that final confrontation. When I spoke, my voice had dropped to a soft rumble, the words coming slow and sleep-thick.

"A castle. Black stone. Round, peaked roof. Gargoyles. Maybe trees in the background. Definitely lightning."

With sudden urgency, Father Frank grabbed my hand, guiding it to a bit of tape.

"Tamp that down and we're done. I need to find something." Puzzled, but too focused on my internal landscape to argue, I pressed along the edge of the tape and secured the final loop.

The sound of drawers being upended made me crack open one eyelid. Father Frank rooted through his desk with frenetic purpose, scattering files and small office items across the floor at our feet. With a bark of success, he yanked a little booklet from the very bottom of a stack of fat manila folders crammed in the lowest drawer of the desk. It was a brightly colored tri-fold brochure—the kind they often gave out in tourism offices. He waved it at me like a talisman.

"Like this?" He stabbed a finger at a picture on the back of the brochure.

It wasn't a castle, but a tower. Dark stone. Round, peaked roof. The image was almost too small, but I could pick out the figures of gargoyles ringing the top.

"Kind of," I allowed, "if it was blacker, and I was looking down from about ten feet above the roof. Where is this?" I turned the booklet over curiously.

It was a brochure for plots at Lake View Cemetery.

"Fuck me running," I hissed. "That damned place."

"The building you saw is the Garfield Monument," Father Frank said. He snatched the brochure from my hand, hurriedly flipping to the inside. "There's a massive statue of the former President."

"*Fuck, fuck, fuck!*" I snarled. "He's been right up the hill this entire time!"

As I railed, my phone on the desk went off like a joy buzzer. The sound was so unexpected, I nearly yelped.

It was a call coming through, not a text, so the cycling vibrations made the device skitter sideways across the pitted wood. I caught it before it shook itself right off the edge.

Only three people who mattered a damn in my life had this new number, aside from the padre—Bobby, Remiel, and Lil.

I didn't recognize the number.

"You going to answer that?" Father Frank asked.

The phone kept buzzing. I almost hit "ignore."

Curiosity won out. I tapped the button for the call.

"About fucking time," Lil snarled from the other end.

47

"Hello to you, too," I said.

"Shut up and listen. I don't have a lot of time." I could barely hear her over the blare of music and a constant, rhythmic thrum.

"Are you driving?"

"Again those wonderful powers of observation," she snapped. "I found Mal with my tracking charm. I'm tailing him right now. He had the same idea, though—he's using pieces from the rosary to home in on Tarhunda—but I think I know where he's headed."

My eyes settled on the tower looming darkly on the back of the brochure.

"Let me guess," I said. "Lake View."

"Ahead of me for once. Color me impressed," she allowed. "But that cemetery covers acres of land. The Rephaim could be holed up in any of the mausoleums."

"It's the Garfield Monument," I replied. For once, I allowed myself to gloat. It wasn't often I was more clued-in than Lil. "I've got a picture in front of me.

Enclosed structure, easily fortified, big-ass statue that's pretentious as fuck—exactly the sort of thing a former godling would want for his evil lair."

"Hrm," she said. I could hear the ratcheting of her fingernails even above the noise of the car.

"What about Halley?" I demanded. "Any sign that Mal's learned about the girl?"

Beside me, Father Frank grabbed both of our coats from the chair. Tucking his into the crook of his arm, he held out my jacket, making sure the sleeves didn't catch on the daggers as I put it on. The tips snagged a little at the elbows if I bent my arms too severely, but otherwise, the improvised sheaths held.

Father Frank slipped into his own coat, nodding once toward the door. I nodded back. With the phone clamped to my ear, I hit the hallway at a jog.

"Forget the girl," Lil said. "You need to let Mal get there first. He's got the telluric seal. He slaps that thing on Tarhunda, it'll lock him in his body. A poor man's binding. It shuts down all his power."

"I can't let Malphael get to Halley," I said, charging through the empty church hall. "He'll kill her just like he's killed everyone else the Rephaim's touched."

"Mother's Tears, Zaquiel, we're dealing with a decimus here. Accept the sacrifice and let the Gibburim handle it. He's got more protections against the Idol-Riders anyway."

"He's also a child-killing maniac," I growled.

The breath from Lil's exasperated sigh crackled across the line. "I know you're all buddy-buddy with Terael, but Tarhunda's a different story. You rush in before Malphael hits him with that seal, you might as well be committing suicide."

"Wouldn't be the first time," I muttered darkly.

I hit the stairs leading out of the basement with Father Frank close behind, and honestly didn't know how he did it at his age. His boots thudded on the risers as we raced to the top. At the side entrance, I shouldered the door with such force, it rebounded on the stopper. I caught it jarringly on my elbow so it didn't hit the priest. The impact shuddered through my fingers and I nearly lost the phone.

"Spare me the melodramatics, flyboy," Lil said. "Just be smart for once and—oh, fuck. Hold on." In the background, tires squealed. The Sebring's engine cycled higher. The Lady of Beasts spat a string of profanities accusing the Gibburim of sex acts Caligula would have spurned.

Outside, thick clouds hung pendulously over the city, backlit by the gray and watery light of impending dawn. I didn't want to think about what time it was, and how long that left Halley in the hands of Kramer and his bat-shit crazy master. Unlocking my door, I folded myself into the Hellcat, reaching across the seats to open the passenger side. Lil's music poured from the phone—some kind of Middle Eastern hip-hop, about as unexpected as the Dixie Chicks.

"Lil—talk to me. What's going on?"

"I said hold on," she muttered. More screeching tire sounds. A horn blared and Dopplered. The thrum of the Sebring changed as she downshifted. "He's on to me. I've got to go."

The roar of another vehicle vied with the sounds coming from her car.

"Lil?"

Father Frank latched his seatbelt and gestured toward the road. His brows shot up as a howl of animal fury rose deafeningly from my phone.

"*You sonofabitch!*" Lil bellowed.

A crash—equally deafening—made me jerk the receiver from my ear. When I put it back again, the line was dead.

Numbly, I blinked at the screen.

CALL ENDED

48

We sat in the Hellcat, the only sound the impact of ice pellets dragged from the drifts by rising gusts of wind.

Father Frank broke the silence first.

"If I know anything about that woman, it's how well she can take care of herself, Zack. She'll be fine."

"Yeah," I responded. I still felt stunned.

Another gale scoured the street, casting swirling patterns across the windshield.

"Storm's starting back up," he observed.

"Nothing to do about it." Whether I meant the unnatural storm, or Lil's uncertain fate, even I wasn't sure.

Hitting the locks, I keyed the ignition and threw the car into reverse. The tires spun a little on the powder, then finally gripped. I backed us over the curb, the wrist-sheaths of the daggers tugging the lining of my jacket as I worked the wheel. The solid weight along my forearms offered subtle reassurance. I was going to hurt these guys when I found them—Malphael and Terhuziel both.

It was only a few blocks to the Davis home. I wasted no time getting us there. Parking as close to the house as the drifts would allow, I got out of the car and handed the priest my phone and keys.

"What are you doing?" he asked.

"Walking."

"In this?"

"The Mayfield Gate is just up the hill. Pretty sure I'll find a Crossing there—someone died outside that gate the other night. Lots of trauma." I didn't bother explaining how I knew—and if I was wrong about the Crossing, there was always the relic ring I'd claimed from my stash.

Father Frank pocketed the keys, but he didn't look happy about it.

"What about the phone?"

"Shadowside. It'll kill it," I reminded him. "Also, Bobby's number is in there. You don't see me in about an hour, give him a call. Tell him Kramer's holed up in the Garfield Monument—and let him know he'll need a SWAT team to take down what they find in there."

If he has any hope of taking it at all.

That part, I chose not to share.

He scowled at the mobile device, then lifted his eyes to peer speculatively up the hill. The clouds grew darker up that way, and I caught a flash of greenish lightning in their roiling depths.

"I don't like this," he said.

"I don't either, but it's what I'm doing. Can you ballpark the location of the monument in the cemetery?" Tapping the side of my head, I explained. "I should probably know it, but there are these inconvenient holes in my memory."

"From Mayfield?" He closed his eyes, consulting some internal map. Papery lids fluttered as he sketched a hand through the air. "Toward Euclid. Bank left. Maybe a thousand feet from the entrance. It's on a hill overlooking the skyline. Damned thing's big. Hard to miss."

"I'll count on that."

Thrusting my hands into my pockets, I hurried toward the main road. Father Frank looked glumly at Tammy's house, mustering the courage to give her the news.

"Hey, Zack," he called after me. I paused on the corner. The priest's earnest brown eyes sought mine through the flurry of flakes already starting to fall.

"Yeah?" I called back.

"Bring her home."

49

Dark clouds boiled in the sky above Lake View, deepening as I closed on the gates of the cemetery. A swirling vortex spun slowly outward, swallowing the early morning light with ever-expanding arms of shadow. Ugly cascades of lightning—all the colors wrong—flickered near the heart, punctuated by basso rumbles almost too deep to process consciously.

"Thunderer of the Northern Hills," I mused. "Not even bothering to hide any more." I tilted my head back. The actual source of the disturbance was lost behind trees as tall as my apartment building. My gut told me the ominous lightshow was connected to Terhuziel's ritual to overtake Halley.

I listened to my gut and hurried.

Running the final twenty feet despite treacherous patches of black ice, I approached the oily stain of trauma where I expected to find the Crossing. Waves of vertigo seized me the instant I hit the leading edge. There was something here, all right, but it didn't quite feel like a death. Teasing my sight open to see precisely what I was dealing with before I blindly plunged through, I halted, numb with shock.

Déjà vu didn't begin to cover it.

This whole time, I'd expected Fish-Knife Lady's death to form the crux of the Crossing, the terror and panic of her final moments imprinting the replay that sundered the boundaries between the realms.

I'd been wrong.

Fish-Knife Lady and her male counterpart sketched the barest of silhouettes in the fabric of the imprint. My figure, on the other hand, blazed like Industrial Light and Magic had been hired to paint a Jedi phantom on the sidewalk—except, with wings.

Pain and terror had stamped this Crossing, but it wasn't from the woman whose life I'd drained. *I'd* made the Crossing—my desperate struggle to survive burned into the very fabric of the Shadowside.

With queasy fascination, I watched the echo of me get stabbed, over and over again. The shadow-Zack stumbled backward, mortally wounded. The imprint flickered, and I was dragging myself to my feet, face distorted with fury. Again the action stuttered, and I had Fish-Knife Lady by the throat. My eyes—blue even in the washed-out palette of the Shadowside—blazed with ferocious light.

The color spilled suddenly to a vibrant green—like copper sulfate poured upon a flame. The hue hung startling and ugly against all the hazy grays and then— swift as a heartbeat—a shadow rose behind me. It trembled quick as a fever-dream. I could half-believe I'd imagined it.

Red mist. Winged.

In that quick flash, the figure of the Nephilim overshadowed the image of me just as Malphael's form had overshadowed David Garrett.

"No," I breathed.

My pulse thundered—half with the backwash of emotion raging from the fresh Crossing—but the other half was stark and very personal terror. This was the path I'd set myself on the instant I'd paid the blood price to the Nephilim icon.

I didn't want it.

That didn't change a fucking thing.

Gulping a swift breath, I threw myself into the morass of pain and horror imprinted outside the cemetery gates. The air splintered as I bulled my way from one side of reality to the other.

In the midst of the transition, all I could taste was the cloying power of Nefer-Ka.

50

Fierce winds tore at me the instant I stepped through. The storm raged on this side, as well, though the ice and snow were conspicuously absent. I pulled my wings tight around my body, creating a living shield. It was that, or get blown halfway down the darkened echo of Mayfield like a runaway kite.

Flying in this wasn't going to be easy.

Working to get my bearings after the ominous revelation of the Crossing, I put as much distance as possible between myself and the replay of my fight with Fish-Knife Lady. The cemetery gates sketched weird figures of stone and iron against the boiling sky, half again as tall on this side as they stood in the flesh-and-blood world. The enervating atmosphere already bore down on me, made weightier by the nearby presence of the Rephaim decimus. I needed to find the Garfield Monument and cross back over quickly, if I wanted any strength left. So I took a few steps back, made a running leap, and launched myself headlong against the punishing storm.

Staying airborne took real work, and I pounded the currents with my wings. The swirling blasts yanked me this way and that. Each time I corrected, I arrowed higher in an effort to get above the turbulence.

The warped and shifting echo of Lake View spread out beneath me—no snow on this side, but the washed-out hues of the faded grass conveyed a similar effect. Flickering echoes of half-forgotten tombs danced like shadows against the landscape, while memorials imbued with greater significance squatted substantially among the acres of rolling hills.

The taste of ozone hung sharp in the air, with lurid flashes igniting deep in the churning black eye of the storm. I aimed for that swirling heart and soon caught sight of the huge Gothic tower.

As promised, the Garfield Monument perched on a hill overlooking the Cleveland skyline. The lightning crackling near its peak made it seem more like the lair of Dr. Frankenstein than the mausoleum of the twentieth President. I flew straight toward the tower, hoping Terhuziel's domain was as limited as Terael's. If the wounded godling had managed to spill out beyond the walls of the building, I wouldn't see the boundary until I'd crossed within his sphere.

The instant that happened, I'd have a decimus thundering angrily in my head. So I worked to shore up my ranks of mental barriers.

Muscles across my shoulders and back burned from the effort of fighting the wind. Catching a current, I circled higher, peering down at the tower to plan my attack. From a dizzying vantage point, I spied a way in from the air.

The leering gargoyles ringing the peaked roof of Garfield's tower overlooked an observation deck, open to the elements. I could drop from the sky and gain access that way, rather than fight my way up from the ground. It was exactly what I'd been hoping for.

Human-shaped smudges, bleary and indistinct, traced a restless pattern on the observation deck—lookouts. I couldn't tell how many. Four? Five, maybe. From this perspective, living beings cast uncertain shadows, shifting like flotsam on some great tide that ceaselessly carried them near to focus, then dragged them right back out again.

However many there were, I needed to get the drop on them.

On my second pass, I spotted a defensible corner that put my back near two walls. Perfect. I tucked my wings and started to dive, dodging flashes of lightning. The distance closed rapidly and I was already lining up for my landing when I crashed shatteringly through the edge of the domain. It extended invisibly about a hundred feet beyond the tower.

No warning.

No convenient gleam of a force field.

I hit it like a bug against a windshield.

The damned thing was *solid*.

My controlled dive spun into a free fall. About halfway down, I recovered, beating the currents with desperate strokes. I managed finally to pull out of my tailspin and regain a little height, exploring the leading edge of the domain with more caution. The lip of the tower stood maybe eighty feet away, but the vast, invisible wall kept it out of my reach.

Still hoping for a stealthy approach, I sought any weak point along the outer boundary. It didn't take long. The edges shifted dramatically, pressing hard against me one instant, contracting feebly the next. Terhuziel's power was still in flux, and that was a good thing for me.

I waited for the invisible obstruction to waver again, all the while fighting the wind to remain aloft. The instant I felt a variation, I darted forward. The narrow aperture closed around me, nearly catching the tip of one wing.

But I was through.

I expected to be assaulted by the Rephaim the instant I passed within the boundary. Terhuziel's power saturated the air, making my wings feel like lead, but his attention wasn't focused on me. At least not yet.

I sped toward the open deck.

Fifty feet.

I tried slapping up a cowl, hoping to at least obscure my presence, but it was next to useless. Every stroke of my wings shredded the fragile shroud of energy.

Thirty feet.

Thunder boomed right on top of me, so loud, it rattled my eyeballs. Half a heartbeat later, another peal erupted inside my head.

THE LAST TIME IT TOOK AN ARMY.

Terhuziel's "voice" struck with such stultifying force, my field of vision bled to searing white. For one terrifying instant, all I could see were his bitter memories of war—a broad, high temple, stairs rising toward its top. An Eye-of-Sauron view of the fields stretching beyond its walls. The clash and stench of battle, dust of the plain churned thick to rusty mud. Every soldier fallen was another offering to his god.

Mercifully, the vision faded, but I couldn't keep him out for long.

"Contact goes both ways, asshole," I muttered.

I called up images of his miserable hobo army—ragged vagrants so damaged they'd had no hope to resist his influence—and launched a mental assault of my own. Pulling up the pain from Fish-Knife Lady's memories, I shoved until I felt him choke. His fury nearly blinded me again—but while we tangled inside my head, my body flew.

Less than twenty feet.

"Broken minds and broken soldiers for a vicious, broken god," I spat.

I WILL GRASP THE LIVES WITHIN THIS CITY AND CLAIM THEM FOR MY OWN.

"You sure you have enough hands for that?" I stropped the barb with a clear image of Terhuziel, futilely trying to swat Malphael with his jagged stump. Taunting the angry godling as he bellowed in my mind wasn't exactly a good idea, but it got the desired result.

The Rephaim flew into a frothing rant, the word-sense of his thoughts degrading into little more than a red haze tinged with rage.

Ten feet.

Five… and no angry bolts of lightning fried my wings before I could land. He was too distracted. I didn't flatter myself—I knew it wasn't just my witty repartee. I only had a small shred of his attention. The bulk of his power was focused elsewhere.

That spelled bad news for Halley.

Time sped by too fast.

I hit the observation deck hard, skidding straight into a wall. I caught the impact on my forearms, unsurprised when the stones squished a little beneath me. On the Shadowside even solid objects lacked rigidity. Time and mortal perception had bequeathed substance, but it was still just an echo.

I started to step through to the flesh-and-blood world, but the division pushed back with unexpected resistance.

Taunting laughter filled my head.

YOU STAND IN MY DOMAIN. IT ALL BENDS TO MY WILL.

I shoved again, calling power to my hands as I sought to shred the barrier.

I couldn't tear through.

Heart laboring, I fought a rising sense of panic. I'd been on the Shadowside long enough that I was really feeling the burn. Much longer, and I wouldn't be good to anyone.

CURL UP AND DIE, ANARCH. YOU ARE TOO LATE. THE CHILD OF YOUR TRIBE WILL BECOME MY VESSEL.

I WILL BE REBORN AND I WILL HOLD YOUR SOUL HERE AS YOUR FLESH WITHERS TO DUST.

Terhuziel assaulted me with another wave of harrowing images—only these were from the present, not the past.

That made them even worse.

Halley, shivering in nothing but her hospital gown— how she wasn't hypothermic already, I couldn't guess.

She thrashed on marble tiles in a vaulted chamber. The severed head of a statue—all that remained of Terhuziel's ancient idol—lay pressed against her thin chest. Another statue loomed over her, so painted with blood that I barely recognized the visage of James A. Garfield.

Corpses spread at the feet of the statue in an untidy ring—birds, cats, a dismembered toddler. The doctor held a knife. He and another man fought to hold Halley down in the midst of all that half-frozen gore. The knife poised above her, ready to make the fatal cut—but the doctor held back.

A manic surge of relief helped me drive Terhuziel from my mind.

Halley was still fighting. Her mind hadn't yet fallen.

There's time—there's still a little time.

It was both prayer and revelation.

"You can't break her!" I shouted defiantly into the air. "And you can't break me!" I drew the twin daggers from their makeshift sheaths, bellowing my Name to kindle my power. It was so much easier than calling the weapons from pure spirit. Light blazed forth, licking up and down the curved blades.

I threw my head back, laughing hysterically as I slashed my way from the Shadowside. I spilled into the flesh-and-blood world in a torrent of fire and steel. My point of entry put me directly behind one of Terhuziel's goons, leaning over the wall, firing inexpertly at someone on the steps below.

He paused to reload his rifle. It was a single-shot. Break action.

Bad luck for him.

I didn't look to see who he was trying to shoot. I just lunged forward and let the blades do their work. Their power sang upon the air, a ringing counterpoint to Terhuziel's cries of frustration.

51

The first guy went down in a welter of blood and gore. He was dead before he could even scream, but more of Terhuziel's mind-fucked hit squad still guarded the platform. I counted three.

Blades trailing blue fire, I moved with swift muscle-memory. With sure and practiced motions I slit the throat of a woman who carried a cheap hunting rifle like the kind sold at Wal-Mart. It discharged over the ramparts and clattered to the frozen ground below. She died while still blinking away the arterial spray from the guy next to her.

The woman got out a gurgling cry before jerking out of my grasp to dramatically pitch over the edge of the platform. Her fatal swan dive seemed incredibly slow, blood jetting from her severed carotid to stream like a scarlet banner in the frigid air alongside her.

Time snapped back to its regular pacing when the woman's body folded around a metal railing set into the stairs far below. The impact tore the structure from its moorings. Her blood painted the snow.

I've done this before.

It wasn't a memory—it was a sick realization, and the moment I stopped the slaughter long enough to consider it, I lost some of my easy momentum.

Terhuziel's mind surged into mine.

YOU WILL DIE, ANAKIM!!!

The remaining two minions jumped at the call of their master. The first was a rangy guy with bushy rust-colored hair and a beard to match. In his black-and-red checked flannel, he looked like a lumberjack—or a hairy checkerboard. His companion was shorter but half again as broad, with powerful shoulders and a deep chest. He was dressed like he'd been plucked from some arctic expedition, complete with parka and ski mask.

Checkerboard fired wildly with his rifle, clearly unused to its kick. His single shot arced into the sky, well over my head. He fumbled to reload the thing, patting down his pockets frantically before breaking it open to get at the chamber. He dropped the slug. While he scrambled, Ski Mask aimed more carefully. He had a shotgun—single barrel, still cheap as fuck, but definitely not something I wanted pointed at my head.

No time, and no cover—I was just lucky these guys had been set up for range.

Arcing forks of lightning reflected in my blades as I streaked forward in a crouch. Ski Mask struggled to get a bead on me as I zigged left, then right, faster-than-human quick. Each time he readjusted, he hesitated half a second too long. That was no good for me—I needed him to waste the shot. With the weapon empty, I'd be on top of him before he could even break it open to reload.

For a breathless second, I froze. It left me wide open—and that was the plan. The world narrowed to the surge of my pulse and the matte-black barrel of the gun. Ski Mask's mouth split into a rictus grin, finally sure he had me. Finger twitched on trigger. Before the motion was completed, I threw myself to the ground, hitting the icy stones hard with one shoulder as I tucked and rolled.

A hail of pellets sang over me, tearing stone chips from the far wall. The blast of the shotgun punctuated the desperate fury of Terhuziel's storm.

Before Ski Mask could even dig for his ammo, I slammed into him, knocking the gun to the ground. With a sweep of my boot, I sent it skittering in the direction of the pellet-scarred stones. Ski Mask stumbled backwards, narrowly avoiding my blades. Beside us, Checkerboard bellowed unintelligibly. He'd never managed to reload. I couldn't vouch for the state of his brain before Terhuziel sank his hooks in it, but the man had all the reasoning powers of someone lobotomized with a rusty screwdriver. Wildly, he swung his useless rifle at me and I smacked it from his hands.

One problem down.

Unless Terhuziel could magically reload their guns while the two dodged my blades, the weapons were useful only as clubs.

Roaring like a wounded bull, Checkerboard struck out wildly with a haymaker, while the stumpy one tried to get my legs out from under me. I dodged the first but ran afoul of the second, spinning a little as I fought to shove him away and remain standing.

Terhuziel stepped up his game, wrapping power around his soldiers till the speed of their reflexes was a match for my own. Their eyes blazed with borrowed light, and an answering flicker began building around their hands. I lashed out, laying open Checkerboard's forearm to the bone, but he just kept fighting. Blood speckled the snow, so dark, it looked black. The man's slack features registered no pain.

Ski Mask still had a few synapses firing, but not many. He danced back from my assault, diving for Checkerboard's abandoned rifle. He let Checkerboard take a few more hits, tracking my motions with eyes half obscured behind the cold-weather mask.

As he dug through his pockets for ammo, I closed on him again. None of his shotgun shells fit. Wielding the rifle like a truncated staff, he deflected my flurry of blades.

"You think I'm going to give you time to shoot me?"

In answer, Ski Mask lunged forward, swinging the butt of the rifle in an arc toward my head. I caught the blow on the top of my forearm, pivoting my wrist so the bunched muscles took the brunt of the force. Jabbing forward with my left-hand blade, I went for his belly, but he pulled his torso back just far enough so all I tagged was the parka. Down feathers fluttered on the air, drifting slowly to mingle with the snow.

Too late I realized Ski Mask was herding me toward Checkerboard. The storm above us intensified, peals of thunder punctuating the desperation of our fight. The lumberjack wannabe flanked me, a nimbus of electric power crackling around his outstretched hand.

He sought to wrap that hand around me, little jolts dancing painfully between us. Whatever juice Terhuziel was pouring through them required an element of physical contact. Every instinct clamored for me to avoid it at all costs.

Checkerboard's sparking fingers brushed the leather of my jacket. My whole arm jerked like he'd tased me, and I almost lost my grip on the dagger.

Not good.

He threw all his weight into a grapple, slamming forward to wrap his arms around me. I sidestepped his first pass, but he pivoted immediately at my back. Ski Mask came at me again with the rifle and in deflecting that blow, I spun straight into the other guy.

Checkerboard seized me from behind, closing his arms in an odious bear hug. The initial contact released a stunning jolt of electricity, and he lofted me a foot off the ground. My legs and arms twitched spastically. Both wrists were pinned at my sides, which made my blades next to useless. I thrashed against him, kicking for any purchase. None of my muscles wanted to work right. Ozone prickled the back of my throat.

Ski Mask danced a manic jig.

"Rumble, heavens," he cried. "Split the sky. Call the power, make him die!" He spewed ugly laughter as I struggled, revealing a mouth bereft of all but three blackened teeth. Raising the rifle like a triumphant standard, he stumbled back from his buddy. The tang of the ozone intensified until I could taste nothing else.

Too close to my ear, Checkerboard grunted his own

supplications to the storm god, spittle and beard hair slick against my cheek. The clouds above us contracted, cascades of lightning whipping through their depths.

With desperate strength, I bucked in Checkerboard's grip, twisting my whole body until I smashed the back of my head into his face. He staggered with the impact and I kicked away just as a bolt of lightning hammered down from the heavens. It lanced straight through the top of Checkerboard's head. Shrilling like a teakettle through his teeth, he somehow managed to direct it.

Heavenly fire leapt in a deadly arc, seeking me.

The bearded man jigged and twitched as the Thunderer's rough blessing flowed through him. Triumph and terror both filled his eyes. I didn't even know if I could block something like that, just brought my blades up with a startled shout.

Fire and electricity clashed in a blinding display.

All that raw power drove against my crossed weapons like a freight train, arcs of electricity snapping angrily from hilt to tip. Ski Mask held his rifle-club poised but didn't go after me—even lobotomized by Terhuziel's power, he was too smart to make contact while I wrestled a fucking lightning bolt.

My feet slid by inches as the assault poured forth. Static crackled in waves across my skin. I couldn't hold this wild power, wasn't meant to. Even as I thought it, resonant syllables erupted from my throat. With a defiant shout, I managed to turn the electricity from my daggers, hurling the power back to its living lightning rod.

The punishing bolt rebounded, blinding in its intensity. Snapping arcs looped between the deflected stream and the pillar still lancing from the heavens. The human conduit overloaded with the feedback. Smoke erupted from the top of Checkerboard's head and he was flung back. He landed to flop like a sock monkey against the far wall. Twin scorch marks marred the stones where he had stood.

Thunder god. Right.

I needed to get the hell off the exposed observation deck. Anticipating that reaction, Ski Mask rushed to bodily block the nearest door leading into the tower. He held the rifle across his squat torso, eyes shining like beads of tar through the slits in his mask.

He was shoved to his knees in the next instant as Dr. Kramer erupted from below. He ran encumbered, curling around the weight of Terhuziel's battered stone head like a running back with a massive football. Malphael's dual-voiced bellow resounded from the bottom of the stairwell.

"You will not escape me, physician! All the Thunderer's servants die this day."

The Gibburim's footfalls pounded upward in swift pursuit.

Kramer dodged to the side of the doorway, throwing his back against the wall. Adjusting his grip on the Rephaim's idol, he scanned the platform, brows knitting as if he expected to find something—and it wasn't me.

A moment later, Halley came through the other door on the far side of the tower. Shivering in the bloody tatters of her hospital gown, she clapped her hands to her ears, screaming over and over again.

"I'm *me!* You can't be me! *I'm me!*"

Terhuziel's presence lashed the air.

YIELD AND MAKE ME WHOLE AGAIN. Crashing peals of thunder punctuated the Rephaim's demand.

Kramer and I both charged toward the girl, as Ski Mask scrambled in the snow for the slug dropped by Checkerboard. He couldn't find it in time and instead darted to block me. Swinging wildly with the rifle butt, he landed a lucky shot across my jaw. Fireworks dazzled my vision and I staggered under the ringing blow. He raised the weapon for another strike.

Recovering, I feinted with my right. His lunge carried him past me. I lashed out with my left-hand blade. With an arcing twist, I laid his belly open. The rifle clattered from his grip as his guts spilled out, clotted with down from his parka. He sank to his knees, blood staining his fingers as he sought to catch the steaming coils of gray intestines spilling forth.

Halley ran straight for the edge of the platform, heedless of the snow clinging to her feet. Kramer rushed after her, his handsome features distorted with rage.

"There's nowhere to run," he barked.

The girl didn't hesitate as he grabbed for her—just climbed out onto one of the gargoyles and balanced with her bare feet on its icy stone head. The city spread out before her as she teetered precariously over the drop.

"Halley, no!" I called.

Her head whipped up at the sound of my voice. The gusting wind blew her hair from her face, freezing tears to her lashes. She held my gaze for a poignant instant.

"Wingy," she said.

I thought she was going to drop right then. Kramer

froze as he realized what she threatened to do.

YOU ARE MY CHOSEN. YOU MUST YIELD.

Halley shook her head.

"Die first."

"Smart girl," Malphael crowed. He stood framed by the door at the top of the stairs, one hand loosely cupped around the palm-sized seal. His nose was bloody, maybe broken. A host of little cuts speckled his forehead and cheeks, each seeping red. The friction burn of a seatbelt stood out lividly on his neck.

None of it slowed him down.

Halley wobbled when she spotted him, her eyes locked to the form rising behind David Garrett's head.

"Halley, get back before you fall," I called.

"No," Malphael said. Fire kindled in his human eyes as he whispered, "Jump."

"You fucking leave her alone!"

Kramer lunged forward reflexively, then abruptly drew up short. He couldn't grab Halley without dropping the stone head, and he was clearly loath to do that. Seizing this moment of hesitation, Malphael leapt in a sudden blur. The Gibburim hit Kramer with a flying tackle, connecting with such force I feared shocks of the impact would knock Halley from her perch. The two thrashed across the stones of the observation deck, Kramer curled protectively around Terhuziel's head as Malphael sought to press the seal home.

A subtle depression above the statue's chipped brows suggested where the confining device belonged. Kramer twisted and bit, forcing Malphael to pry him bodily from the Rephaim's broken idol. Tiring quickly of this, the

Gibburim took a great lungful of breath and bellowed inches from Dr. Kramer's face. Incomprehensible words crashed upon the air with a fury to rival Terhuziel's thunder.

The man convulsed in the face of that power, keening with stark and mindless terror. His fingers slipped from the idol, and the battered piece of statue rolled ponderously toward one corner. It fetched up against one of Checkerboard's singed boots, blind eyes angled heavenward.

Malphael snapped the helpless doctor's neck and dove for the severed stone head.

NO! NO! NO!

Terhuziel's panic surged in waves across the platform.

I rushed for Halley.

Something caught my ankle. I pitched forward mid-charge, dropping both daggers as my hands went out instinctively to break my fall. The steel clattered ringingly across the stones. Spitting curses, I crashed after them, twisting to free my leg.

Ski Mask clung to the hem of my jeans with blood-caked fingers. He lay tangled in his own intestines, eyes wild with hatred and pain. I kicked furiously at him, planting my steel toe in the center of his face. The cartilage of his nose gave a satisfying crunch.

"Fucking die already."

I kicked again, and his grip slackened. Picking myself up, I rushed to reclaim my blades. I wiped the daggers on the thighs of my jeans as I went, hastily resheathing them so I could grab Halley.

"I'm me. He can't be me," she breathed in rhythmic repetition. "I'm me. He can't be me."

Malphael knelt directly in my path to Halley. One-handed, he palmed Terhuziel's head like it was some grisly basketball. Above his mortal shell, the Gibburim clashed in heated battle with the broken Rephaim. Their shouts and imprecations echoed through the Shadowside.

In the physical world, thunder raged and a hail of lightning dropped from the sky. I danced back with a warning to Halley. The girl yelped and nearly overbalanced. Malphael didn't even flinch.

Smoldering scorch marks dotted the stones around Garrett in a neat and perfect ring. Nothing aimed for me or Halley. When the rain of fire ended, I edged closer to the girl. A few more feet and I would reach her.

I willed for her to hang on.

"Such a desperate waste of power," Malphael growled. "You're wide open to me now." On the other side of reality, Terhuziel shrieked as the Gibburim pinned him with his massive spirit-blade.

Smoke rising from his lips, Malphael intoned the fallen god's Name. Rings of roughly scribed sigils leapt with answering fire within the seal. They filled the air with acrid power. The Rephaim decimus loosed a thought-numbing wail.

BY ALL OUR VOWS, KILL ME THIS TIME, MY BROTHER.

"I owe you no mercy," Malphael boomed. "Sentence was passed. You are confined once more to your vessel." He slammed the seal against Terhuziel's brow even as the Rephaim shrieked and pleaded. The rings of sigils spun like tumblers in a lock and the clay disk fused to the stone.

Terhuziel's voice cut out abruptly. The next instant, the storm ceased.

I dove for the girl.

"Halley. Now. Take my hand."

Her eyes sought mine, fleetingly. Shivers wracked her thin body, threatening to steal her balance. One foot slipped on the gargoyle's head.

I pressed myself against the waist-high wall, stretching out to reach her.

"Come on," I urged.

Behind me, Malphael growled in that eerie, two-toned voice.

"Everything touched by the Rephaim is tainted."

I turned just in time to see him puff his chest with a gulping breath. Glowering at Halley, he loosed his fury in a roar.

52

Halley cringed before his onslaught of raw, paralytic power. That motion alone was enough to carry her over the edge.

She didn't scream—just loosed a tiny startled sigh as she slipped from the head of the gargoyle. For an awful, breathless moment, she seemed to hover on the air, her wide, dark eyes locked to my own.

I reacted before my brain could tell me it was a bad idea.

With faster-than-human movements, I leapt and spread my wings. They were useless on this side of reality, but that didn't register. I vaulted over the gargoyle, slamming into Halley before she'd dropped below its open jaws.

I caught her in my arms and she clung to me—but now we were both going over, and there was nothing but concrete and death stretching ninety feet below.

Behind me, Malphael made a derisive sound—maybe it was words, maybe not. I lost the meaning to my racing thoughts.

There was only one place where I could fly, but nothing like a Crossing hung upon the air. Even if I could shadow-walk, that wouldn't help Halley. I'd save my own hide, leaving her to die.

Two thoughts occurred to me in the milliseconds that passed as my feet traded stone for empty air.

I had a relic in my pocket.

Terhuziel had called Halley the child of my tribe.

That made sense—so much sense. From the start she'd done things that I did. Channeled languages. Peered through the Shadowside. Plucked thoughts and emotions from others with just a touch. Even her reactions to the cold—she shivered, but she shouldn't have been able to function this long in such ill-suited clothes. But I was so used to my own reactions, it had failed to register as unusual.

Anakim blood beat in her veins—diluted perhaps, but still potent. We were the only tribe who could bodily make the transition. So what of our descendants? I thought at her in a rush, thrusting layers of complicated concepts through all the words. The message flashed in the space between one heartbeat and the next. I knew from my own experiences with Terael how bad that felt, but there was no time to be delicate.

The wings you can see aren't here where your body is. There's another direction. Follow me.

Her panic hammered against both of us.

I kept one arm around her, digging with the other in my pocket. Time raced and the ground rushed up. The warded silk tingled against my fingers, but the ring was lost in its folds. Halley clung to my neck, burying her head against my chest. Her hair lashed my face.

Don't die with me, Wingy.

Visions of her tower, Rapunzel, a cat I hadn't even seen at her house, her little brother—treasured things, laughter, regrets, all cascaded through her head. Books and stories and lost goodbyes, all so fragile.

I won't let you die, I promised.

I tore at the silk. Finally my fingers brushed the ring, and the power of the relic hummed beneath my touch. I closed my hand around it, and there wasn't even time to gulp a breath.

Here we go.

I held my mind open to hers as I reached through the relic's connection to the other side of reality. My body stuttered on the verge of transition, and I experienced the mechanics of crossing in excruciating detail—the sense of the veil, pushing to rip it, fighting to drag all that I was from one side to the next.

I felt every iota of what I attempted to pull across—my jacket, the deadly blades strapped to my wrists, the heavy steel-toed boots.

And the girl.

Frail as she was, she hung like an anchor wound around my neck. I struggled against that resistance, while the tower streaked past.

It wasn't going to work.

I need your help, I thought.

My wings beat uselessly against the pummeling air.

Like a curtain. Rip.

Everything flew by, faster than thought. Too fast.

I shoved against the veil again, thundering directions

at Halley with an urgency that defied words. The bent railing, the woman's broken body—all of it was terribly, fatally near. I could see where the fallen rifle had cut its shape through a nearby drift of snow.

Zaquiel!

With unexpected power, she intoned my Name—the same way that I did, each syllable a spell. Light and meaning surged within me, and together we rode that rush. The relic burned against my hand, little shards of precious gems embedding themselves into my fingers as the stones shattered with the effort of dragging us both across.

Together, we broke through.

The ground flickered, snow replaced by a memory of grass, leached of all color. I shouted my exultation, though I barely had breath for it. Halley twined around my torso and I dropped the shards of the spent relic to cradle her with both arms. My wings caught the wind of our free fall and I guided us into an arc.

"Wow," she breathed. I felt more than saw her head tilt up, tracking the motion behind my shoulders.

"Pretty fucking cool, right?"

She nodded, shivering against me. I shifted my grip on her, climbing higher to avoid the naked branches of twisted Shadowside trees. I aimed us toward the Mayfield Gate, far beyond Malphael's reach.

"Way quicker than walking, hunh?"

That time, I couldn't feel her nod, though I heard the chatter of her teeth even over the rhythmic sound of my wings. She was such a frail thing—she weighed next to nothing. Even so, I felt the strain the longer I kept her aloft—I wasn't exactly built for passengers. The ground sped by beneath us, exhilarating now that the worst threat was past.

As I closed upon the cemetery gate, her hands went limp and slid from my neck.

"Halley?"

I shook her. She sagged in my grip. Her head lolled back.

From the tail of my vision, I could see her eyes, half-lidded. Only white peered through the fringe of dark lash.

"Halley!" I cried. I moved to support her head, one arm under her shoulders, the other under the small of her back. Her legs dangled, dragging the air.

"Fuck, fuck, fuck," I hissed, angling toward a clearing.

Dead weight now, she made it hard to maneuver. As I tried to land, her legs tangled in my own. I hit, hard and awkward, curling my body around hers as I rolled into the fall. I tucked one wing in time, wrenching the other nearly out of joint as I skidded across the ground, taking the brunt of the impact on that wing and shoulder. I bit my tongue as the top of Halley's head banged against my chin.

I tore back to the flesh-and-blood world with a cry that was anger and panic and frustration all thrust together in one excruciating sound. Halley lay limp on the snow beneath me.

She wasn't breathing.

53

I heard Bobby Park before ever seeing him.

"Where did you even come from?" he gasped. The young detective's words barely registered. He stood maybe twenty feet away, his service pistol drawn in gloved hands. His grip wavered as he aimed in our direction. Shock grayed his features.

"Zack?" he called. "That's you, right?"

I crouched over Halley in an open stretch of undisturbed snow.

"No... Halley," I cried. "No!"

Her lips were already turning blue.

"There aren't even footprints," Park muttered. He pointed the muzzle of his weapon toward the ground as he approached.

"Bobby!" I yelled. "Do you know CPR?"

His eyes grew wide, only now taking in the prone form of the girl. He holstered his weapon and rushed over.

"Sorry. I didn't see her." He ducked his head as he breathed the apology. "Yeah, I do."

Struggling out of my leather, I lifted Halley's shoulders to slide the jacket beneath her. Bobby peeled out of his own coat, shuddering as he shoved it my way. I wrapped the girl's legs as he bent an ear to her mouth.

Frowning, he flicked his eyes to mine.

Without saying anything, he cleared her airways, tilting her head back and lifting her chin.

"Hold her like this," he said. "Forehead back, chin up." He spoke rapidly as he matched word to gesture. "Pinch her nose. Close your mouth around her mouth and breathe. Two full breaths, not too deep. I'll do the chest. That's the tricky part."

"We have to get her out of the cold," I said.

"We have to get her breathing first," he insisted. "*Now*."

While I bent over and breathed for Halley, Bobby picked off his gloves and moved his fingers around the base of her ribs, searching for the place to begin compressions. He found it.

Two breaths from me, and then Bobby shoved hard against her sternum. Ribs crackled, but he didn't even blink, just pushed the heels of his hands about halfway into her thin torso, repeating the gesture with swift and steady speed as he kept a whispered count.

I bent to breathe for her again, but he shook his head sharply.

"I reach thirty, then two more," he said. "Next round, grab my cell off my belt and call 911."

"I thought you *were* 911. Where are the others?"

Evasion darkened his features. "I came alone."

"What the hell?" I demanded.

"Breathe—*now*," he hissed.

Two more breaths. Bobby started back up with his thirty-count, muscles on his neck cording.

"You were supposed to be the cavalry," I said. "Didn't Father Frank tell you to bring backup?"

He didn't look up from Halley this time.

"Garrett's involved in this, isn't he?"

My silence was all the answer he needed.

"He's a good man, Zack. You know that."

I didn't bother with the tired refrain. Between us, Halley lay pale and unresponsive. The blue tint around her lips had lessened somewhat. That was something, at least.

"Shit went wrong the minute we walked into that house," Bobby continued. His voice vibrated a little with each compression. CPR took real work. Despite the chill, beads of sweat stood out on his brow. "I can't explain it, but it's not him doing these things. I know it. I had to give him a chance to make it right, before calling it in."

I held my silence, bending once more to breathe. Mentally, I reached for Halley, seeking any sense of her locked within her body or drifting as a spirit nearby.

Rapunzel, Rapunzel, let down your long hair.

The faintest contact brushed my mind in response, clinging like strands of spider silk.

This time, Snow White, she corrected.

With that uncomfortable symbolism at the front of my thoughts, I locked my mouth around hers and filled her lungs with breath.

Halley's body jerked with a spasm. Bobby stopped

469

MICHELLE BELANGER

the compressions. She sucked air on her own, then sputtered, choking.

"Turn her head, turn her head," Park instructed. He drew back from his work, swiping a hand across his brow.

I rolled her onto her side, and just in time. She vomited into the snow.

"That happens," he said. "It's normal."

All our focus was on Halley when Lil's voice rang through the air.

"You wrecked my car, you bastard!" she yelled.

Both our heads snapped up. The Lady of Beasts stood about ten yards away, legs spread in a firing stance. Her wild curls blew back from her brow, revealing a purpling bruise at her hairline. The wound was shocking—I'd never seen Lil with so much as a paper cut. She straddled the path to the front gate, holding not her Derringer, but a much larger pistol. It looked a lot like Bobby's gun.

"What the hell?" Park demanded.

From the opposite direction, a familiar voice boomed, deep and flat.

"A fair price for your interference, bitch."

Malphael strode toward us, wearing Garrett's body, a blood-smeared messenger bag slung across his chest. With each step, it bounced heavily against his thigh. There was little doubt what it contained.

"Zaquiel," he called. "I am holding to our bargain. You will give me the girl, and then I will leave."

"That's close enough," Lil called. The gun never wavered.

"Zack, what's going on?" Bobby hissed.

Mutely, I hunched over Halley. She curled around

470

herself, still spitting weakly into the snow.

"Call off your woman, Anakim," Malphael boomed.

"*His* woman?" Lil barked. "I will feed you your balls." She sighted the pistol a little lower.

"Drop the gun, lady," Park called. He grabbed his own weapon again, and held it at the ready.

"She's on our side," I hissed.

I mostly believed it.

"He's unarmed," Bobby insisted.

"Hardly," I replied. To Malphael, I called, "You got what you came for. Now get the hell out of my city."

Bobby's grip on his pistol wavered. He looked pleadingly toward his partner. "What's he talking about, Dave?"

Malphael didn't even spare him a glance. His smoldering eyes remained fixed solely on me. "I will take her by force."

"Like hell you will."

I leapt to my feet, the daggers drawn before I even thought about it. Blue-white fire danced on honed curves of steel.

"Holy shit!" Bobby choked, nearly losing his gun.

Malphael beckoned me closer, his cruel smile spreading wide through David Garrett's battered features. The scent of sulfur grew thick upon the air as he brought his hands together to call his own flame-kissed blade.

"Oh, for fuck's sake," Lil spat. "Not this again."

She shot him.

54

The bullet crashed into Garrett's shoulder, right at the joint. Blood flecked with fragments of bone speckled the drifts at his feet. He staggered back, bellowing in pain, arm dangling uselessly. The coalescing energies of his two-handed blade dispersed like smoke on the morning air.

"Jesus, no!" Bobby cried.

The basso notes of Malphael's unearthly voice drowned out Garrett's as he howled with wordless rage.

"Aw, did I break your meat-sack?" Lil taunted.

Halley shrilled in the wake of the gunfire, arms curled round her head.

"Bobby, get her out of here," I said.

"Your friend shot my partner!" he yelled.

"You gotta know that's not Dave any more."

Bobby faltered a moment, avoiding my gaze. Shuddering with more than the bitter temperature, he holstered his pistol and bent for Halley. He cradled her awkwardly, struggling to keep her wrapped in both of our coats. She was nearly as tall as he was.

Lil chambered another round.

"His vessel's a cop, Lil!" I warned.

"I haven't killed him yet, flyboy," she snapped. She kept the gun trained on Malphael, stepping sideways in a wide arc until she had a clear line of fire well away from the rest of us.

Bobby paused in an ankle-deep drift halfway to the main path. Halley clung weakly to his neck.

"You can't let her kill him," he pleaded. "There's a good man in there. You don't remember, but—"

"Get the kid to a hospital. I'll handle this."

Still, he hesitated.

"Go on, Bobby," I urged. "You've got to trust me on this. It's not safe for either of you while he's still here."

With a doleful glance toward Garrett, he turned with his burden, hurrying toward the cruiser parked further up the hill.

Beyond us, Malphael fumed as the body he'd overtaken teetered awkwardly. Blood sluiced freely down the wounded arm. His good hand twitched to put pressure on the wound, but in the next instant it jerked away. His features warred with themselves.

Lil drew ever closer.

"I will see you bound in the desert for your interference," he spat.

"Shut up and bleed on the snow," she replied.

Malphael tried moving the injured arm as he called his power again. I held my blades at the ready. Garrett's face went a doughy gray as Malphael struggled.

"Joints are such a bitch," she taunted. "Don't you need two hands for your favorite toy?"

The Gibburim raised an infuriated cry. His vessel's knees buckled. Sputtering curses, he sank heavily to the ground. The figure of smoke and flame that overshadowed Bobby's partner reared back, hatred spilling from his twinned sets of eyes.

"Can't get it up?" He didn't respond, and Lil kept the gun trained on him, circling in an ever-tightening spiral. "Stretched yourself too thin. Even left your pistol behind after you tried to off me. Sloppy."

Malphael muttered scathing imprecations. Closing now, Lil jammed the muzzle of the weapon against the back of his head. At the contact, one of them—the Gibburim or Garrett—twitched.

"Better jump ship now," she said breathily against his ear, "unless you want the full experience of a bullet through the brain. If the vessel dies with you still in it, don't you get stuck here till some new sucker comes along? How long you think that'll be?"

"Just knock him out, Lil," I said. "We can deal with Malphael later." I moved to put action to words. As I leaned closer, a spasm rolled through the muscles of the fallen man's face. His whole body seized and for one brief moment, Detective David Garrett looked up at me with eyes that were wholly his own.

"Kill me," he choked.

"You don't have to ask me twice." Lil slid her finger over the trigger. "Zack, move out of the way."

"No—there's got to be a way to save him." I fumbled for something to tie off the bleeding arm. Abruptly the body went rigid as Malphael struggled to reassert his control.

"You are the honorless cur, and I refuse to count you as my brother," he snarled, lips and words now jarringly out of sync. "This isn't over. I will come back for what is mine."

A terrible cry ripped from his throat, and he vomited a gout of black, sulfurous smoke. Lil danced to the side as the man's spine bowed, his head practically kissing his heels.

The shadow of the Gibburim rose up, spreading tattered wings. He launched himself heavenward, his shape more like a dragon than a man. His bottom half spooled out from the body like thread being yanked from a badly stitched seam.

As the last bit unwound, the fiery shadow tore free, and Garrett crumpled empty at my feet.

EPILOGUE

David Garrett lived. He wished he hadn't.

When he woke up from surgery, he started screaming about all the people he had murdered. No one in recovery paid attention at first because for some patients, waking up from anesthesia is like tripping balls—they say all kinds of wild things that they never remember. After a while it becomes white noise for the nurses.

Then Garrett ripped out his IV and tried killing himself by jamming the needle repeatedly into his throat. He knew to go for the carotid artery, not the jugular, so hospital staff had a real mess on their hands before they got him sedated.

They moved him into a psych ward after that.

Nothing was going to go to trial until he started giving up the dump locations for the bodies of no less than thirteen vagrants. He described their murders in explicit detail. His buddies on the force still didn't want to believe it, but DNA evidence linked him decisively to the mutilated corpses.

His lawyer had no trouble submitting a plea of insanity.

* * *

I got the ongoing details of the trial secondhand from Bobby Park. He'd been working behind the scenes to keep my name out of the mess.

We walked along Ford to Euclid, heading for Brewster's Coffee next to Ninja City. Across the street, the black polyhedron of the MOCA building caught lights from the evening traffic in countless angled windows. Students from Case and the Cleveland Institute of Art took advantage of the balmy spring night, hanging out in the concrete park that sprawled around the Uptown museum. They lounged with books at picnic tables or chatted beneath slender birches, sleeves rolled up and jackets tied around their waists.

Snippets of their conversations carried intermittently over the sounds of horns and motors, full of youthful speculation on the nature of life, debates on world politics, and one rhapsodic monologue praising the elegance of physics.

"They can't find records of that friend of yours anywhere," Bobby said. "The prints on the gun belong to a dead woman. The wrecked Sebring is registered to a lady in her eighties who has Alzheimer's so bad, she doesn't remember her name, let alone whether she bought a car in the past ten years. Officially Lil's a ghost."

"This is my shocked face," I replied, pointing to my deadpan expression.

"Is she like you?" Bobby pursued. "What was the word? Anakim."

The term still felt strange rolling from his tongue, and

I fought an irrational urge to shush him. Still, I'd been the one to open that door—after everything he'd witnessed at Lake View, Bobby had earned some insight into my world, so I'd offered. He'd jumped at the opportunity, meeting every revelation not with terror or incredulity, but with open curiosity.

I hadn't told him everything, though. Just enough.

"Not exactly," I hedged. "She's something else."

Bobby pulled ahead to be the first through the door to the coffee house, short legs pumping. Inside, the place was packed, the line threading halfway to the door. The scent of dark roast and flavored syrups hung heavily on the air.

We took our places in the queue.

"She's immortal," I allowed. "As to the rest of it, I honestly don't know—and she likes it that way. I wouldn't dig if I were you."

"I'm not the one doing the digging," Bobby insisted. "I've been running interference, like you asked, but I get a lot of questions. Garrett is—*was* my partner." At the slip, his mouth took a downward turn, and he restlessly scrubbed a hand across the buzzed part of his scalp.

"Not your fault," I reminded him. "Not any of it."

"You could have told me sooner, you know."

"This again?"

The wounded look in his eyes made me immediately regret how sharply the words came out.

"Look, Bobby," I said, trying to copy Father Frank's trick for weaving positive emotions through my tone. All I managed to do was speak so quietly, he had to lean forward to hear. "I've told you a hundred times now, nothing you could have tried would have changed anything. And the minute Malphael knew you suspected him, he'd have killed you."

"You can't know that for sure."

He said it too quickly.

"You saw everything else he did. Death is the only solution he understands."

The guy in line ahead of us edged a little closer to the young couple in front of him, doing his absolute best to ignore whatever snippets he caught of our conversation. He side-eyed me, decided he *really* didn't want to know, then slipped a phone from his pocket and resolutely focused on its glowing screen.

I resettled my cowl—more reflex than necessity.

"You could have let me make the decision for myself," Bobby said with quiet fervor. He turned his gaze to the window. The shadows that marched across his features weren't reflections from the street. His hand strayed to the badge he wore clipped to his belt, fingers tracing the lines of the shield. "It's my life to save or risk for my partner—that's part of what I signed up for when they swore me in. But you kept me in the dark, Zack—you didn't even give me the option."

Helplessly, I shrugged.

"It's the decision I made at the time," I said. "Can't change it now."

New lines on his face deepened, and I could tell he was reliving those breathless, awful moments in the cemetery. We both were.

"No, you can't," he finally sighed. He turned his earnest eyes back to me and some of the shadows remained. "Has he turned up since?"

"Not yet," I responded, honestly mystified. "The first couple weeks, I stayed vigilant—given his posturing at Lake View, I was certain he'd come after Halley the minute he found another host. But, so far? *Nada*." I thrust my hands in my pockets, hunching my shoulders.

"How's she holding up?" he asked. "She really scared me at the hospital when she started seizing."

I closed my eyes, not trusting myself immediately to answer. The guy in line behind me bumped my elbow and I was so wound up, I almost punched him out of reflex. My hands remained fisted in my pockets—just barely.

"Zack?" Bobby prodded.

"She's good," I said too quickly. "At least, better. The grand mal seizure she had a week after her rescue was a setback, but she's rallying. Just... she hadn't had one that bad in a while."

Despite Halley's own assurances that such seizures were normal for her, I blamed myself for their increased frequency—that trip through the Shadowside had cost her.

Better than the alternative, I reminded myself.

It didn't help.

"Father Frank and I are taking turns looking after her. Tammy's grateful for the extra hands," I said. "I've warded the fuck out of their house—it's one of the only things I know how to do to protect the kid," I admitted.

The line crawled forward. We shuffled after it.

"And in the meantime, you wait." He didn't sound thrilled about it.

"Believe me," I said. "I'd hunt Malphael down if I had the first clue how to look for him. I don't."

Bobby rubbed the back of his head again as coffee-house chatter surged around us. It cycled in rhythms, intensely loud one moment, dropping to a murmured hum the next. I wondered idly if any of the mortals had a conscious sense of the shifting tides of their collective emotions.

"Any chance he just forgot?"

I snorted unhappily. "Not likely."

The enormity of Malphael's promised return settled palpably around us. I tried to shrug it off—worrying wasn't going to solve the problem, and I'd already done everything I could. Terhuziel's sealed idol was hidden in my stash, locked down with even more protections. Halley's secret heritage was as cowled as I could make it. And Father Frank had my back. If Malphael—or anyone— came for Halley, we would do our best to fend them off.

Our best would have to be enough.

A third barista emerged from the back and the pace of the line picked up. Awkward Phone Guy ordered his double-shot soy latté and got the hell out of Dodge, casting a final, nervous glance my way. My height or the leather jacket spooked him. Probably the combination of the two. He didn't look smart enough to be afraid for better reasons.

I was still scowling after him when the tattooed kid behind the counter asked me for my order. He had to repeat himself to get my attention. Peering up at a menu board crowded with a bewildering variety of steamed, frothed, and flavored drinks, I experienced a sudden, poignant longing for the black and bitter coffee of an old-school diner.

For a moment, my whole field of vision narrowed to that vivid scrap of memory. There'd been a waitress who'd always looked after me. Hazel eyes. Cute uniform. I *almost* remembered her name.

Annoyed now, the barista asked a third time, raising his voice in case I was deaf, as well as stupid. Moving briskly, Bobby stepped in and rescued me. He flashed his badge as he rattled off the details of his drink, then nudged me in the ribs once he was finished.

"Zack, did you want anything?"

"Uh… coffee," I answered. "Just coffee."

The barista's eyebrow twitched.

"Light, dark, or blonde roast?" he asked, nipping the ends of the words.

"Dark—black. Whatever," I said.

"Name?"

"Westland."

He scrawled it on a cup and whirled away.

Our drinks came up, and we headed over to a remote table at the back. It wasn't exactly quiet, but it was one of the few spaces still open. Cleveland's Uptown was hopping—probably the weather.

Bobby pulled out his chair, carefully setting down a wide-brimmed mug filled with some caffeinated confection that was more whipped cream than coffee. I plunked down my to-go cup, just then noticing that the barista had written "Wasteland" on it.

"Cute."

I turned the cup around so Bobby could read it, too. He snorted.

"Making friends wherever you go," he observed dryly.

"It's a gift," I answered.

Dragging out the chair across from Bobby, I swung it around to sit on it the wrong way. As I leaned my arms across the back, the new wrist-sheaths of my twin daggers pressed into my forearms, not exactly comfortable, but too familiar to annoy.

Silently Bobby etched swirling patterns with a plastic stirrer through his drink's crown of whipped cream. I took an experimental sip from my own cup. With a grimace, I put it right back down.

"Pretty sure that kid gave me decaf," I grumbled.

"I should arrest him," Bobby joked." Coffee is serious business."

"Protect and serve—but never decaf?" I chuckled. "Don't sweat it. I didn't come for the coffee, anyway."

Reaching inside my jacket, I fumbled around for the sheet of notes I'd stuck next to the letter that hadn't left the interior pocket since I'd found it at Holy Rosary. Unfolding the page, I angled it toward my friend.

"I've got a favor to ask," I said.

He leaned forward, squinting at my crabbed handwriting. Taking a sip of his coffee, he somehow managed not to wear half the whipped cream across his upper lip.

"You need me to track these people down?" he inquired.

"Right now, I just need more information than what I've got," I explained. "I don't have last names, descriptions, or dates of birth. I know they're mother and daughter. There's a connection to Parma and to a safe deposit box."

"Not much to go on," Bobby murmured.

"Tell me about it," I said sourly. "I've done all the digging I can, but I've hit a wall. I need access to better records than the crap I can search on the Internet."

With one nail, he tapped the paper. "Why are these ladies important?"

"They're keeping something of mine." Anticipating his next question, I said, "I don't know what."

"Dangerous?"

"Probably."

On impulse, I pulled out the letter itself. It had been folded and refolded over the past couple months, dog-eared and crinkled from riding around in my pocket. With hands that threatened to tremble, I spread it on the table.

There were things in there I hadn't told anyone—things I was reluctant to accept even for myself. Every instinct I possessed clamored against letting him read it. *This is stupid,* a voice said. *There's no way this will end well.* I closed my eyes and told my instincts to shut the hell up.

"This is—here are those names in context," I said. My tongue fell over itself.

Bobby's brows knitted as he glanced at the date. He caught and held his breath, digesting its implications.

"Isn't this from when you went missing?" he asked.

Wordlessly, I nodded. Sal's oath about the Eye prickled in the back of my head, limiting what I could say—but not what Bobby could read. Still, I had to flatten my hand against the table to keep myself from snatching the letter back on reflex.

Bobby's features darkened as he scanned the first few

lines. "Are you sure this is something I should be reading?"

"No," I answered bluntly. "You can stop if you want to. Fold it up, shove it back at me, walk away." I swallowed against a sudden dryness in my throat. "I wouldn't blame you if you did."

He pushed back thoughtfully from the table. From the tension fighting through his shoulders and neck, he seriously considered it.

"It's more than just Malphael and your friend Lil," he said. It wasn't a question.

Again, I nodded. "When I told you the incident on the *Scylla* was tied up with the weirder parts of my life, I didn't tell you *how* tied up it was." Puffing my cheeks, I relinquished my grip on the letter. It sat on the table between us—a door or a barrier, depending how this went. "The rabbit hole goes deep, Bobby. Real deep. You may not like the ride."

His eyes flicked from me to the paper and back again.

"Thank you," he blurted.

"Hunh?" I asked, totally thrown. "Why?"

"For letting me make the decision myself this time."

Setting aside his coffee, he pulled the letter closer and started reading.

Upside down, I made myself read along with him, all the way to the end.

Zaquiel—
    If we're reading this, then things went badly out on the lake—but we're not stuck in some jar, so I hope we got the Stylus like we'd planned. If you're not

Zachary Aaron Westland any more, then all we did was get ourselves killed. That's actually good news. The alternative is uglier, because if you don't remember being me, that means Dorimiel got his hands on Neferkariel's icon, and that is a whole level of fucked I'd hoped to avoid.

If I'm dead, hopefully I'm drowned, with the icon or icons at the bottom of the lake. That's the priority. Those things need to be buried deep where no one can use them any more. All the silt at the bottom of Erie will make them a bitch to recover, even if Dorimiel figures it out. Lailah knows the plan. Problem is, she's the only one who knows how deep this rabbit hole goes, and I can't hear her any more. Not even a whisper. That's not a good sign.

Check the Gandhi statue in the Cultural Gardens for the jars. We couldn't break the seals in time. Some idiot at the museum leaked the find to the press. I know that's why Dorimiel showed. Must have made him crazy when the looters hit that stash.

I have to include Sal on this last part—I can't get close to Dorimiel otherwise. He's a paranoid fuck. Don't breathe a word to her about the Stylus. She doesn't know. The Eye's my bargaining

chip—even the chance that it's there.
She saw what it did to Remiel during the
Wars. She wants it buried again as much
as we do.

On that note, keep Remy the hell away
from that thing. It nearly ate him once.

On the topic of Remy, he's the
executor for Westland's will and for
Damien Walsh both. Find him. He'll get
you keys to the properties he knows
about. And if he's been good, he'll have
boxed everything in the main residences
once we're officially dead. Most of the
codes for the stashes and other things
are hidden in the manuscript pages.

Remy doesn't know about that part.

I've left this same letter in five of our
stashes. I figure you'll sort out how to
get to at least one of them. I hope you're
standing in the basement of Holy Rosary
right now, because the blades were a gift,
and there's only one other set left. Those
are in Chicago. Lailah will know.

If Frankie's still kicking, make sure
you thank him for leading you here. He's
been good to us.

None of our eggs are in one basket.
Try the place on Euclid Heights first,
then the one in Tremont. Lots of
redundancy, so don't worry if something
gets destroyed. That's just how this

game works. Marjory has the key to the second safe deposit box. She's in Parma, as of this letter. She knows to leave it to her kid, Tabitha. Phone's in Holy Rosary. Number's in the phone. You'll crack the codes no problem.

Best-case scenario, Dorimiel's in a jar, dropped down along with the icons. Doubt that will happen, but I can wish. But you have to remember—he's only a pawn. They've puffed him up to think he's a major player, but this conspiracy runs deep. It's not just his tribe. There are others. Now that they know we're onto them, they will be coming.

Ending this with "good luck" seems pretty self-serving. But we need it.

Good luck.

Bobby pushed back from the table again, skin taking on a greenish cast as he blanched. He took a long swallow of coffee, staring at a point beyond my ear. The sound and feel of all the people swelled suddenly, pressing like some rough beast against my cowl.

A sigh escaped him. A portion of the young detective's innocence seemed to flee with the sound.

"The human monsters are bad enough," he murmured.

"What happened to Garrett wasn't usual. Things like that…" I trailed off, acutely aware that my next word could be a lie.

The time for lies was over.

Bobby studied me for a long moment, then his gaze strayed to the people gathered in the coffee house. He lingered on each in turn, keen eyes taking in details of their stance, their dress—all the little stories each telegraphed unconsciously about their lives. He turned solemn eyes back to me, all but pleading.

"Can we protect them?" he asked. "Is there even a chance?"

The inside of the coffee shop grew cavernous, like I might lose myself if I relinquished my grip on the back of the chair. Fiercely, I dug my fingers into the metal.

"I'm going to try," I said. "I swear it."

ACKNOWLEDGMENTS

Many thanks to Lucienne Diver at the Knight Agency for continued help in navigating the daunting territory of contract negotiations and industry jargon. More than that—I value you also for your willingness to listen as a friend. Steve Saffel—you're in the same boat. In your role of Dark Editorial Overlord, your uncanny talent for crawling into Zack's head has vastly improved me as a writer, but it's your candid insight that makes the whole process enriching on a personal level.

To all the people at Titan whose hard work ferried *Harsh Gods* from manuscript to mass market—Miranda Jewess, Cat Camacho, Vivian Cheung, Nick Landau, Laura Price, Paul Gill, Lydia Gittins—rarely do your names get attached to all the work you help bring into the world, but without your tireless effort and support, the Shadowside series would still be living on my hard drive. Among the Titan crew, special thanks go out to Chris Young, whose email responses are as speedy as the Internet realm which he oversees, and also to Julia Lloyd

491

for transforming my sketchy notes into amazing covers. I can't believe you found a jambiya!

Finally, to my devoted Elyria, bringer of tea, wrangler of emails, and distractor of cats—you are the reason I can keep doing this no matter what else is raining down on me from life. Thank you for reminding me to get out from under the keyboard once in a while.

ABOUT THE AUTHOR

Michelle Belanger is most widely recognized for appearances on television's *Paranormal State*. A leading authority on psychic and supernatural topics, her non-fiction research in books like *The Dictionary of Demons* and *The Psychic Vampire Codex* has been sourced in television shows, university courses, and numerous publications around the world. She has worked as a media liaison for fringe communities, performed with gothic and metal bands, lectured on vampires at colleges across North America, and designed immersive live action RPGs for companies such as Wizards of the Coast. Her research on the Watcher Angels has led to both a Tarot Deck as well as the album, "Blood of Angels." Michelle resides near Cleveland, Ohio in a house with two cats, a few friendly spirits, and a library of over four thousand books. More information can be found at

www.michellebelanger.com.

A TASTE OF BLOOD WINE

Freda Warrington

A tale of passion, betrayal... and blood...

On a First World War battlefield vampire Karl von
Wultendorf struggles to free himself from his domineering
maker, Kristian. The Neville sisters flourish in decadent,
hedonistic London society in 1923: champagne, parties
and the latest illegal substances. All except Charlotte, the
middle of the three sisters who hides in a corner wishing
she were back in Cambridge helping her professor father
with his scientific experiments.

When Charlotte meets her father's new research assistant
Karl, it is the beginning of a deadly obsession that divides
her from her sisters, her father and even her dearest friend.
What price are they willing to pay to stay together?

For more fantastic fiction, author events,
competitions, limited editions and more

VISIT OUR WEBSITE
titanbooks.com

LIKE US ON FACEBOOK
facebook.com/titanbooks

FOLLOW US ON TWITTER
@TitanBooks

EMAIL US
readerfeedback@titanemail.com